THE DEEP BLUE ALIBI

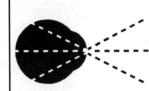

This Large Print Book carries the
Seal of Approval of N.A.V.H.

A SOLOMON VS. LORD NOVEL

THE DEEP BLUE ALIBI

PAUL LEVINE

WHEELER PUBLISHING
An imprint of Thomson Gale, a part of The Thomson Corporation

Detroit • New York • San Francisco • New Haven, Conn. • Waterville, Maine • London

LIBRARY OF CONGRESS CATALOGING-IN-PUBLICATION DATA

Levine, Paul (Paul J.)
 The deep blue alibi : a Solomon vs. Lord novel / by Paul Levine.
  p. cm. — (Wheeler Publishing large print softcover)
 ISBN-13: 978-1-59722-552-6 (softcover : alk. paper)
 ISBN-10: 1-59722-552-5 (softcover : alk. paper)
 1. Trials (Murder) — Fiction. 2. Florida — Fiction. 3. Large type books.
4. Large type books. I. Title.
PS3562.E8995D44 2007
813'.54—dc22   2007012106

Published in 2007 by arrangement with The Bantam Dell Publishing Group, a division of Random House, Inc.

Printed in the United States of America on permanent paper
10 9 8 7 6 5 4 3 2 1

To a funny and loving lady, Sally Levine.
My mother.

ACKNOWLEDGMENTS

Many people have been generous with their time and expertise. My thanks to:

Roy and Jackie Cronacher, owners of the *Force Majeure* and experts on the Caribbean. Boater, record-holding angler, and *bon vivant.*

Cory Hexter, boat captain, spear fisherman, and scuba diver.

Angel Castillo, who has been teaching me (unsuccessfully) to speak Spanish for the last twenty years.

Jim Jimirro, who has an encyclopedic knowledge of the Great American Songbook.

Joe Klock, Sr., real estate maven and master wordsmith.

Dr. John McManus, expert on coral reefs and professor of marine biology, Rosenstiel School of Marine and Atmospheric Science at the University of Miami.

Edward and Maria Shohat, lawyers who

comport themselves with the highest standards of ethics and dignity.

Special thanks to my friend Randy Anderson and my wife, Renée Braeunig, who tirelessly dispense advice and criticism, long after I cease requesting it. Another nod to my agent, dapper Al Zuckerman; my editor, the sagacious Kate Miciak; and my publicist, the astute Sharon Propson. While we're at it, give my regards to Broadway — 1745 Broadway, that is — home of Bantam Books and the savvy band of publishing professionals: Irwyn Applebaum, Nita Taublib, Barb Burg, Cynthia Lasky, Betsy Hulsebosch, Susan Corcoran, Carolyn Schwartz, and Kelly Chian, among others. And thanks to Carol Fitzgerald and Sunil Kumar, gurus behind www.paul-levine.com.

ONE:
WORLD'S RICHEST LOBSTERS

"Forget it, Steve. I'm not having sex in the ocean."

"C'mon," he pleaded. "Be adventurous."

"It's undignified and unsanitary. Maybe even illegal."

"It's the Keys, Vic. Nothing's illegal."

Steve Solomon and Victoria Lord waded in the shallow water just off Sunset Key. At the horizon, the sun sizzled just above the Gulf.

"In this light, you're really magnificent," he said.

"Nice try, hotshot, but the bikini stays on."

Still, she had to admit that there was something erotic about the warm water, the salty breeze, the glow of the setting sun. And Steve looked totally hot, his complexion tinged reddish bronze, his dark hair slick and lustrous.

If only I didn't have to drop a bombshell on him tonight.

"It'll be great." He slipped his arms around her waist. "A saltwater hump-a-rama."

Dear God. Did the man I think I love really say "hump-a-rama"?

"We can't. There are people around."

Twenty yards away, a young couple with that honeymoon look — satiated and clue-less — peddled by on a water bike. On the beach, hotel guests carried drinks in plastic cups along the shoreline. Music floated across the water from the hotel's tiki-hut bar, André Toussaint singing "Island Woman."

Why couldn't Steve see she wasn't in the mood? How can someone so good at pick-ing a jury be so oblivious to the ebb and flow of his lover's emotions?

She pried his hands off her hips. "There's seaweed. And sea lice. And sea urchins." She'd run out of *sea things.* "We can do it later in the room."

"Bor-ing."

"So you find our sex life a big yawn?"

"I didn't say that."

She sharpened her voice into cross-exam mode. "Isn't it true that after a few months, all your girlfriends start to bore you?"

"Not the ones who dumped me."

"Do you realize you have relationship attention disorder?"

"Whatever that is, I deny it." He pulled her close, and she could feel the bulge in his swim trunks. "I love our sex life. And the room's fine. Clean sheets. A/C. Nice view. Why don't we go in now and get started?"

Get started? Makes it sound like cleaning the kitchen.

"You go. Start without me."

"C'mon. We can catch the sunset from the balcony."

She looked toward the horizon, where thin ribbons of clouds were streaked the color of a bruised plum. "We won't make it in time."

No way she was going to miss the orange fireball dip into the sea. She loved the eternal rhythm of day into night, the sun rising from the Atlantic, setting in the Gulf. Day after day, year after year. What dependability. She doubted Steve understood that. If he had his way, the sun would zigzag across the peninsula, stopping for a beer in Islamorada.

She had another reason to postpone the lovemaking.

The bombshell.

She'd been thinking about it all the way to Key West. A pesky mosquito of a thought, buzzing in her brain. She hated to ruin the

11

evening, but she had to tell him, and soon.

"Okay, I give up," Steve said. "*Coitus post-ponus.* What time do we meet your uncle?"

She brought her legs up and floated on her back. Looking toward the horizon upside down, the sun floated at the water-line, connected to its reflection by a fiery rope. "Nine o'clock. And I told you — he's not really my uncle."

"I know. Good old Hal Griffin. Your father's partner, the guy who bought you fancy presents when you were a spoiled brat."

"*Privileged,* not spoiled. Uncle Grif's the one who named my mother 'The Queen.' "

"And you 'The Princess.' "

So Steve had been listening after all, she thought. "You think the name fits?"

"Like your Manolo Blahniks."

She started swimming, heading out to sea, toward the setting sun. Smooth strokes knif-ing through the water, now glazed a boiling orange. Steve swam alongside, struggling to keep up. "What I don't get is why Hal Grif-fin called you after all these years."

The same question had been puzzling Vic-toria. She hadn't seen Uncle Grif since her father's funeral when she was twelve. Now, without warning, a phone call. "All I know, he has some legal work for me."

12

"You mean for *us*."

"He didn't know about you."

"But you told him, right? Solomon and Lord."

"Of course."

Is this how it begins? A little white lie, followed by bigger, darker ones.

God, she hated this. She had to tell Steve the truth. But how?

He was flailing away, kicking up a storm, trying to catch her. Except for swimming — all splash, no speed — Steve was an accomplished athlete. He'd run track in high school and played baseball at the University of Miami, where he was a mediocre hitter but a terrific base runner.

"Solomon takes off . . . and steals second!"

A good primer for lawyering, Victoria figured. Conning the pitcher, pilfering the catcher's signs, then *stealing* a base. Even the word would appeal to Steve. He had been particularly adept at spiking opposing fielders and kicking the ball out of their gloves. But like a lot of athletes, he didn't know his limitations. He thought he was good at everything. Poker. Auto repair. Sex. Okay, he was good in bed, very good once she taught him to slow down and stop trying to score from first on a single.

A hundred yards offshore, she started

treading water, waiting for him to catch up.

"So where are we eating?" he asked, breathing hard.

So very Steve. He would plan dinner while still eating lunch. "Uncle Grif made reservations at Louie's Backyard."

He made an appreciative *hmm* sound. "Love their cracked conch. Maybe go with the black grouper for an entree, mango mousse for dessert."

Sex and food, she thought. Did he ever think about anything else?

"And we'll be back in the room in time for *Sports Center*," he continued.

Yes, of course he did.

Was it his imagination, or was something bothering Victoria? Steve couldn't tell. She'd been quiet on the drive down the Overseas Highway, occasionally glancing toward the Gulf, where red coral heads peeked through the shallow turquoise water. He'd asked how her cases were going — they divided up the workload as *his, hers,* and *theirs* — but she didn't want to talk shop. He'd sung some old Jimmy Buffett songs. But she didn't join his search for a lost shaker of salt.

Now he told himself that nothing was wrong. After all, he was holding Victoria in his arms as they treaded water. In the glow of the twilight, she was stunning, her skin blushed, her butterscotch hair pulled back in a ponytail, highlighting her cheekbones. Small breasts, long legs, a firm, trim body. He felt a pleasurable stirring inside his trunks. The air was rich with salt and coconut oil, and he was with the woman he loved, a woman who, for reasons inexplicable, seemed to love him, too.

By his calculations, they still had time to hit the room, make love, and meet Griffin at Louie's. Maybe do it in the shower as they cleaned up for dinner, the Solomon method of multitasking. He just wished the sun would hurry the hell up and call it a day.

Nearby, two windsurfers caught a final ride. Overhead, seabirds dipped and cawed. From the beach, he heard the sound of salsa coming from the bar's speakers, Celia Cruz singing "Vida Es un Carnaval."

Damn straight. Steve felt his life was a carnival, a sun-filled, beach-breezed, beer commercial of a life. This was better than knocking off a mega-insurance company for a seven-figure verdict. Not that he ever had, but he could imagine. Better, too, than stealing home in a college baseball game. That he'd done, against Florida State. Of course, his team lost. But still, a helluva moment.

"Steve, we need to talk," Victoria said.

"Absolutely." He watched a pink sash of clouds at the horizon turn to gray. A slice of the sun nestled into the water. On the beach, the tourists yelped and cheered, as if they had something to do with this nightly miracle. "What do we need to talk about?"

"Us."

Uh-oh.

In Steve's experience, when a woman wanted to talk about *us,* life's carnival was about to fold its tent. He quickly ran through his possible misdemeanors. He hadn't been rude to her mother, even though Her Highness loathed him. He hadn't left the toilet seat up for two weeks, at least. He hadn't flirted with other women, not even the exotic dancer he was representing in a prickly lewd and lascivious trial.

"So what'd I do now?" Sounding defensive.

Victoria put her hands around his neck, twining her fingers, as they treaded water in unison. "You treat me like a law clerk."

Oh, that. At least it wasn't something that would toss him out of bed.

"No I don't. But I am the senior partner."

"That's what I mean. You don't treat me

16

as an equal."

"Cut me a break, Vic. Before you came along, it was my firm."

"What firm? Solomon and *Associates* was false advertising. Solomon and *Lord* is a firm."

"Okay, okay. I'll be more sensitive to . . ." What? He'd picked up the phrase from Dr. Phil, or Oprah, or one of the women's magazines at his dentist's office.

"I'll be more sensitive to . . ."

You toss around the words when your girlfriend is upset. But it's best to know what the hell you're talking about. "Your *needs*," he finished triumphantly. "I'll be more sensitive to your needs."

"I'll never grow as an attorney until I have autonomy."

"What are you talking about?"

"Don't get all crazy. It's not going to affect our relationship, but I want to go out on my own."

"Your own what?"

"I want to open my own shop."

"Break up the firm?" Stunned, he stopped bicycling and slipped under the water. She grabbed him by his hair and pulled him up. "But we're great partners," he sputtered, spewing water like a cherub on a fountain.

He couldn't believe it. Why would she

want to trash a winning team?

"We're so different. I do things by the book. You burn the book."

"That's our strength, Vic. Our synergy. You kiss 'em on the cheek, I kick 'em in the nuts." Peddling to stay afloat, he took her by the shoulders and eased her closer. "If you want, I'll change my style."

"You can't change who you are. As long as it's Solomon and Lord, I'll always be second chair. I need to make a name for myself."

He almost said it then: *"How about the name Mrs. Victoria Solomon?"*

But he would have sounded desperate. Besides, neither one of them was ready for that kind of commitment.

"I'm not going to beg you to stay," he said instead, brusquely. "If it makes you happy, go fly solo."

"Are you mad?"

"No, I'm giving you space." Another phrase he'd picked up somewhere. "I'm giving you respect and . . ."

A rumbling, grumbling growl in the distance.

What the hell's that noise?

Jet Skis? They ought to ban the damn things. But even as he turned to face the open sea, he realized this sound was different. The roar of giant diesels.

A powerboat roared toward the beach. And unless it turned, straight toward them.

From the waterline, it was impossible to judge the size of the boat or its speed. But from the sound — the rolling thunder of an avalanche — Steve knew it was huge and fast. A bruiser of a boat, good for chasing marlin or sailfish in the deep blue sea. Not for cruising toward a beach of swimmers and paddlers and waders.

Steve told himself to stay calm. The jerk would turn away at the piling with the *No Wake* sign. The boat would whip a four-foot mini-tsunami toward the beach, everyone on board having a big laugh and a bigger drink.

Okay, so turn now.

"Steve . . ."

"Don't worry. Just some cowboy showing off."

But the boat didn't turn and it didn't slow down. Instead, it muscled toward them, its bowsprit angled toward the sky like a thin patrician nose.

Now Steve was worried.

Five hundred yards away. The boat leapt the small chop, splatted down, leapt again. He could see white water cascading high along the hull, streaming over the deck. The roar grew louder, a throaty baritone, like a dozen Ferraris racing their engines. The son-of-a-bitch must be doing forty knots.

Still it came, its bow seemingly aimed straight at them. In twenty seconds, it would be on them. Windsurfers scattered. Swimmers shrieked and splashed toward shore. On the beach, people in chaise lounges leapt to their feet and backpedaled. A lifeguard tooted his whistle, drowned out by the bellow of the diesels.

Squinting into the glare of the sinking sun, Steve could see there was no one on the fly bridge. A boat without a driver.

"C'mon!" Victoria cried out, starting to swim parallel to the beach.

Steve grabbed her by an ankle and yanked her back. They didn't have the speed or maneuverability. What they had were five seconds.

"Dive!" he ordered.

Wide-eyed, Victoria took a breath.

They dived straight down, kicking hard.

Underwater, Steve heard the props, a high-pitched whine that drowned out the diesel roar. Then, a bizarre sensation, a banging in his chest. Like someone smashing his sternum with a ballpeen hammer. A split-second later, he heard the *click-click-click* of a bottlenose dolphin, but he knew it was the boat's sonar, bombarding him with invisible waves. Suddenly, the wash of the props tore at him, dragging him up then shoving him down. He tumbled head-over-ass, smacked the sandy bottom with a shoulder, and felt his neck twist at a painful angle. Eyes open, he swung around, desperately looking for Victoria, seeing only the murky swirl of bottom sand. Then a glimpse of her feet headed for the surface. He kicked off the bottom and followed her.

They both broke through the water just as the boat ramped off the sandy incline, going airborne, props churning. Steve heard screams from the beach, saw people scattering as the boat flew over the first row of beach chairs, slashed the palm-frond roof of the tiki-hut bar, and crashed through a canvas-topped cabana. The wooden hull split amidships with the sound of a thousand baseball bats splintering, its two halves separating as tidily as a cleanly cracked walnut.

"Vic! You okay?"

But she was already swimming toward shore.

Victoria ignored Steve's shouts to wait. No, the *senior partner* would have to catch up on his own. She had seen the lettering on the stern as the big boat lifted out of the water: *FORCE MAJEURE IV.* She instantly recognized the name, remembered the first *Force Majeure,* even after all these years.

How could it be?

In a place where most boats were christened with prosaic puns — *Queasy Rider, Wet Dream* — this craft could be owned by only one man. In the law, a *force majeure* was something that couldn't be controlled. A superior, irresistible force. Like a powerful yacht . . . or its powerful owner.

Steve was still yelling to wait up as she scrambled onto the sand and ran toward the broken boat. The bridge was lying on its side in the sand, the chrome wheel pretzled out of shape. Shards of glass, torn cushions, twisted grab rails, were scattered everywhere. The fighting chair, separated from its base, sat upright in the sand, as if waiting for a missing fisherman.

Half-a-dozen Florida lobsters crawled across the sand, a shattered plastic fish box nearby. Something was impaled on one lobster's antenna. It took a second for the bizarre sight to register.

A hundred-dollar bill. The lobster's spiny antenna was sticking right through Ben Franklin's nose.

Then she saw the other bills. A flutter of

greenbacks, blowing across the beach, like seabirds in a squall.

"This one's breathing, but he's messed up bad."

It was the hotel lifeguard, bent over a thin man in cargo shorts and polo shirt. He lay on his side, motionless, his limbs splayed at grotesque angles, a broken doll. The lifeguard turned the man gently onto his back, then gasped. A metal spear protruded from the man's chest.

"Jesus!"

Victoria got a look at the man's face.

Thank God. It's not him.

"Another one! Over here!" A woman's voice.

Victoria navigated around a thicket of splintered teak decking. A female bartender was crouched in the sand over a thick-bodied man in a white guayabera. Rivulets of blood ran down the man's face from a gash on his forehead. "Don't move," the bartender ordered. "We're gonna get you to the hospital."

The man grunted. He appeared to be in his sixties, with a thick neck and thinning gray hair. His eyes were closed, either from pain or the blood running into his eyes.

Victoria edged closer.

Could it possibly be him?

"You should put a compress over the wound," she said.

The man opened his eyes, and Victoria recognized him at once. "Uncle Grif!"

"Hello, Princess." Grimacing through the pain, Hal Griffin pushed the bartender aside. "Leave me alone, dammit. I need to talk to my lawyer."

■ ■ ■ ■

Solomon's Laws

■ ■ ■ ■

1. If the facts don't fit the law . . . bend the facts.

Two:
The Irresistible Force

Lower Keys Medical Center wasn't far away, but the streets were jammed. Locals on bicycles, teenagers in flip-flops, cruise-ship passengers scorched from the Caribbean sun. With Victoria sitting shotgun, Steve was at the wheel, stuck in traffic, bogged down behind a Key West taxi, pink as Pepto-Bismol. Steve banged the horn, but the taxi didn't pick up speed. Of course not; its bumper sticker read: *"What's Your Hurry? This Ain't the Mainland."*

They had taken the ferry from Sunset Key and picked up Steve's rusty orange 1976 Eldorado from its parking spot off Mallory Square. The old Caddy, whose throaty rumble had once sounded dark and velvety, like a pot of brewing coffee, now hacked and belched like a geezer at the Sand & Surf Retirement Home.

"So who's the other guy on the boat?" Steve asked.

"All I know, Uncle Grif was bringing someone to dinner. He didn't say who."

Steve honked at a bearded jaywalker with tattooed snakes crawling up his bare back. "And just now, on the beach, he didn't tell you?"

"It didn't seem to be the time for introductions." Trying to shut him up. She knew Steve well enough to read his mind. He was already thinking there was profitable legal business scattered in that boat wreckage.

Sure, Steve, but it's gonna be my business, not yours.

"And how the hell did that guy get a spear in his chest?" Not letting up. He was like a fifty-ton Mud Cat dredging the harbor, a *force majeure* in his own right.

"I don't know any more than you do, Steve."

"Three possibilities," he persisted. "One: accident. Griffin's showing the guy the speargun and it fires. Then we've got a civil case to defend."

"We," she thought, her heart sinking. God, hadn't he been listening?

"Two: They fought over something. The guy clobbers Griffin, who shoots him with the spear. Then, we've got aggravated battery, maybe murder if the guy dies. Self-

28

defense a possibility if Griffin feared for his life."

Try poaching Uncle Grif's legal work, you'll be in fear for your *life, sweetheart.*

"Three: a boat malfunction. The steering goes out, we sue the manufacturer or repair yard or parts supplier for damages. That doesn't explain the spear, but —"

"Let's just see how Uncle Grif is doing," she interrupted icily, "and not worry about business."

"Sure thing, but we could be looking at big bucks here."

"We" again. When you're already upset with your boyfriend, his everyday aggravating habits seem even worse. There's a multiplier effect, like the bank compounding interest. Here he was, once again not listening to her, once again not picking up the nuances of her voice, the rhythms of her mood.

Dammit, Solomon. You can read the flutter of a witness' eyelashes. Why can't you hear me unless I scream?

They passed the marina at Garrison Bight, ancient houseboats slouched cockeyed in the water, unrehabilitated hippies sprawled on front porches, drinking the night away. Two tourists on motor scooters hogged the middle of the road, and Steve banged the horn again. He hung a left at College Road onto Stock Island, headed past the pungent garbage dump and landfill, and pulled between two rows of royal palms into the hospital parking lot. A helicopter descended noisily, heading for the concrete pad near the Emergency Room entrance. But if there was any emergency, it was journalistic, not medical. The chopper was from Channel 4 in Miami.

Great. Just great. Steve never met a camera he didn't love.

A Monroe County sheriff's car sat angled at the hospital's front entrance. Perched on the hood of the car, like a long-legged ornament, was a white ibis. If she were superstitious, Victoria would have considered it a bad omen. The bird watched them walk into the lobby, Victoria's mind swirling with memories.

Why *had* Uncle Grif called her after all these years? And why had he *not* called all these years?

The Lords and the Griffins.

When she was a child and Lord-Griffin Construction Company was booming, the two families were inseparable. Nelson and Irene Lord, Harold and Phyllis Griffin. Dinners, bridge games, vacations. For Victoria, before her world collapsed, it was a time of

30

nannies and cruises, tennis camps and Shetland ponies. Her favorite playmate was Hal, Jr. They'd played doctor when she was four and Junior was six, kissed for real when she was twelve and he was fourteen. Such innocence. Such promise. Until her father leapt off the roof of one of the Lord-Griffin condos. Then came the lawsuits, bankruptcies, Grand Jury investigations. Something about bribery and extortion in the building trades. Hal Griffin took his family to Costa Rica and laid low for several years.

Victoria and her mother lost track of them, but then Uncle Grif turned up in Singapore and Indonesia, building hotels and accumulating a fortune. Over the years, he worked his way back home, developing resorts in the Caribbean. Then, a year ago, there'd been a story in the *Miami Herald* when he bought Paradise Key, a small, private island in Shark Channel, just off the Gulf side of Islamorada. There was speculation in the business pages about a new Griffin project in Florida, but nothing official. Then, last week, Uncle Grif finally called. He apologized for having been out of her life all these years. Then said he'd been keeping tabs on her.

Keeping tabs. That had sounded mysterious. But it must have been true. Uncle Grif knew all about her honors at Princeton and Yale Law. He knew about her brief stint in the State Attorney's Office, and he'd heard she was in private practice. Now he had some legal work that might interest her.

Her.

Not the senior partner at some deep-carpet firm. Not Alan Dershowitz. Not Steve Solomon. But her.

Victoria Lord, attorney-at-law. Sole practitioner.

Dammit! How could she get Steve to accept that?

Now, there's a guy who really fills a hospital bed, Steve thought, getting a glimpse of Harold Griffin. Burly chest, wide shoulders, thick neck, a white bandage on his forehead, and his right arm in a sling. A still handsome, still rugged man in his mid-sixties, Griffin had pale blue eyes and bushy, sun-bleached eyebrows.

"My God, you're all grown up, Princess," Griffin said as Victoria walked to his bedside.

"How are you feeling, Uncle Grif?"

"Nothing but a separated shoulder, a couple cuts, and a monster headache." He looked toward Steve. "You must be the young man Victoria mentioned."

"Steve Solomon." Wondering just what Victoria had said. "Young man" made him sound like a boyfriend, which he was. But this was business, right? Hadn't Victoria told him about the firm? "I'm Victoria's partner."

"Partner," Griffin repeated. "Used to be, when you said you were someone's partner, everybody knew what you meant. Like Victoria's father and me. Borrowed money together, built condos together, covered each other's ass. These days, it might mean a couple of interior decorators playing house." He barked a laugh and said, "Come to think of it, they're covering each other's ass, too."

"What happened out there, Mr. Griffin?" Steve asked.

"Call me Grif. I was bringing Stubbs down from Paradise Key to discuss the new project. Ben Stubbs from Washington. Environmental Protection Agency. Poor sucker's in the ICU right now. Never saw so much blood in my life, and I was in 'Nam."

"What's the EPA have to do with your project?" Victoria asked.

Griffin motioned her to move closer. "Cop still in the hall?"

"Right outside the door."

"Did he happen to say if he was protecting me or confining me?"

33

"Didn't say anything, Uncle Grif."

True, Steve thought. The deputy, a gum-chewing, jug-eared, close-shaved kid, had been too busy gaping at Victoria's tanned legs.

"Can't talk to you about Stubbs until we sweep for bugs," Griffin whispered. "I once bid on a shopping center in Singapore. Figured my hotel room might be bugged, so I made all my calls from the bathroom after turning on the shower. But every move I made, a competitor beat me to the punch. Turned out, there was a bug in the toilet-roll dispenser."

In Key West, Steve thought, the only bugs in hotel bathrooms were likely to have eight legs. He couldn't envision Willis Rask, the sheriff, illegally eavesdropping in a hospital room. Same for State Attorney Richard Waddle, even if his nickname was "Dickwad."

"Can you just tell us what happened on the boat?" Victoria asked.

Griffin used his good arm to wave them even closer. Victoria scooted along one side of the bed, Steve the other. It was starting to look like a sleepover at Neverland Ranch. Griffin continued so softly, it was nearly impossible to hear him. "I don't know how the hell Stubbs got that spear in his chest.

34

And that's the truth."

"You make any stops? Refuel, that sort of thing?" Steve asked. Thinking they needed a third party coming aboard. A mermaid with a speargun would do.

Griffin looked around, as if someone might be listening. When he didn't find anyone, he whispered: "One quick stop. A couple miles west of Black Turtle Key, one of those no-name islands. I keep my lobster pots offshore there. Pulled up a few critters for our dinner."

"I thought we were going to Louie's Backyard," Victoria said.

"You ever have their lobster jambalaya, Princess?"

"Never saw it on the menu."

" 'Course not. They make it just for me. I bring the lobster, they do the rest, from the andouille sausage to the spices."

Speaking louder now, apparently not concerned if eavesdroppers stole his recipe.

"I think I saw our dinner crawling across the beach," Victoria said.

"Lobsters are out of season," Steve reminded them.

"So sue me," Griffin shot back.

What do you make of a guy who brings his own food to the best restaurant in Key West? Probably the same thing you'd say about someone who names his boat *Force Majeure*. This guy lives large, fills a conference room the way he fills a hospital bed. A man used to getting his own way. So what does he do if things don't go his way?

"All those hundred-dollar bills blowing across the beach," Steve said. "What was that about?"

"Louie's is expensive," Griffin said. "I was gonna pick up the check."

"Uh-huh."

"Seriously, I just keep a lot of cash around."

"How much? On the boat today."

"Maybe a hundred thousand. More or less."

All that cash. One man with a spear in his chest. Another with a bump on his noggin. And a mess of out-of-season lobsters. Where do you look in the law books for this one?

"See anybody on that little island where you stopped?" Steve asked.

Griffin shook his head.

"You head straight from there to Sunset Key?"

Again, Griffin lowered his voice to a parched whisper. "At thirty-five knots. I'm up on the fly bridge, wind blowing my hair, or what's left of it. I asked Stubbs to keep me company up there, but the lazy bastard stays in the cockpit, getting a tan, drinking a Bud. Few minutes later, I look down, and he's not there. I figure maybe he's inside, sacking out or taking a leak. Little while later, I still don't see him, so I get on the intercom, but there's no answer. I get worried, think maybe he fell overboard. He'd been drinking pretty good and he's clumsy on his feet, especially on a wet deck. So I put her on auto and went down the ladder."

He paused and gnawed his lower lip. Steve didn't have to try a hundred cases to know that what was coming next was either a careful lie or the painful truth. The trick — the damned near impossible trick — was to distinguish the two.

"Soon as I open the door to the salon, I see Stubbs," Griffin said. "On the floor, slumped up against a bulkhead, bleeding like a stuck pig, that spear in his chest. I run out of there, climb back up the ladder. I was gonna call the Coast Guard, head for Marathon."

"Fishermen's Hospital."

"Exactly. But then, *boom.* The lights go out."

"Meaning what?"

"I don't know. My next memory is being down on the deck, my head split open, drifting in and out. Maybe someone up on the fly bridge whacked me across the skull as I came up the ladder."

Oh, shit. The phantom strikes. Twice. First in the salon, then on the bridge.

"Next thing I know, I'm on the beach with a stomping headache, and here comes the Princess, looking just like her mother all those years ago." He turned toward Victoria. "How is The Queen, anyway?"

"Before you two catch up on old times," Steve interrupted, "did you tell that story to the police?"

"What do you mean by 'story,' Solomon?"

"Nothing. Just asking if you gave a statement."

"Don't bullshit me, kid. Spit it out."

Steve took a breath, fired away. "What you just told us, it's the worst story I ever heard. Worse than Scott Peterson's phone calls to Amber Frey."

"Steve," Victoria said. Her warning tone. "You're not talking to some thug in the lockup."

He ignored her, cut to the heart of it. "There are only two of you on the boat in the middle of the Gulf, right?"

"Yeah."

"So who speared Stubbs?"

Griffin's eyes narrowed. "When Stubbs comes to, ask him."

"And if he doesn't come to?"

That stopped Griffin a moment. Then he said: "My theory is, someone stowed away below before we left my dock."

"Like in that book by Joseph Conrad," Victoria said.

"What book?" Steve asked. *Just what's Miss Princeton summa cum laude talking about now?* In college, Steve had read the Cliffs Notes of *Heart of Darkness,* but he didn't remember any stowaway.

"The Secret Sharer," Victoria continued. "A ship captain hides a stowaway who's accused of killing another seaman. The captain sails close to shore and lets the stowaway swim to safety."

"And when the boat crashed on Sunset Key," Steve said, "what happened to this secret sharer fellow?"

"I don't know," Victoria said. "It's just an idea."

"I don't know either," Griffin said. "And I didn't give a statement to the police. You think I'm a damn fool, Solomon?"

"No. I pity the man who takes you for one. Or who crosses you."

"Steve, please." A command, not a request. "Uncle Grif, I'm sorry. Steve can be abrasive sometimes."

"No problem, Princess. I like this punk."

"You do?" She sounded stunned.

"Most lawyers stick their tongues so far up my butt, it tickles my nose. Sorry, Princess. Your mother used to say I was uncouth. Not like your father. All polished fingernails and luncheon clubs. Of course, if Nelson had begun life spreading hot tar on roofs, his hands might not have been so clean." Griffin turned back to Steve and showed a crooked smile. "I told the cops my head hurt, and I'd talk to them later. I do good, Counselor?"

"Real good. Not a word to the cops until we hear what Stubbs has to say. Then we'll draft a statement for you. Assuming you want us to represent you."

"We'll see. Give me a game plan."

"We have to prepare for the worst. Stubbs comes to and says the two of you argued, and you speared him like an olive with a toothpick. We get a doctor who'll say that after losing all that blood, Stubbs is hallucinating."

Griffin winked at Victoria. "I like the way this punk thinks."

"So who knocked Uncle Grif unconscious?" Victoria said.

"The same guy who shot Stubbs," Steve answered.

"And that would be . . . ?"

"Jeez, we've been here ten minutes. Give me a chance to come up with our one-armed man."

"Steve, you can't just spin stories out of thin air," Victoria said.

"Sure I can. It's one of Solomon's Laws."

"What laws are those?"

"Steve makes them up as he goes along." Victoria pursed her lips, showing her displeasure. " 'If the law doesn't work, work the law.' That sort of thing."

" 'If the facts don't fit the law,' " Steve said cheerfully, " 'bend the facts.' That's another one."

"I like what I'm hearing." Griffin seemed to be enjoying himself, despite his injuries. "What else, Solomon?"

"I want to be there when the cops question Stubbs. Or better yet, question him first."

"It'll never happen," Victoria said. "The police won't let you near him."

"There are ways," Steve said.

"Don't even think about it."

"What's going on?" Griffin asked.

"Steve likes to crash parties. Once, he faked a heart attack to get into an ER."

"It wasn't a big deal," Steve said, "until I got the bill for my angiogram."

Griffin coughed up a laugh. "You're an

asshole, Solomon."

"Yeah?"

"But my kind of asshole." He turned to Victoria. "Princess, you did real good hooking up with this guy. You're hired. Both of you."

Three:
Intensive Care

How could this be happening?

Steve taking over as if they were still partners and he was *numero uno*.

How did I let this happen again?

Victoria had intended to split up the firm, and here was Steve poaching *her* client. Winning over Uncle Grif with all that macho crap.

Steve excused himself, saying he'd give the two of them a little time together, then catch up with Victoria in the hospital lobby.

Victoria waited until the door closed behind him, making certain the deputy in the corridor couldn't hear her. Maybe there was still a way to push Steve out, or at least into the second chair. "Uncle Grif, what's the legal work you called me about? Does it have anything to do with Stubbs?"

"My son will give you all the answers. You remember Junior, don't you, Princess?"

"You don't forget the first boy who kissed you."

Griffin nodded. "Junior's done nothing but talk about you since I told him we were getting together. Your father always said our lives always would be intertwined, our families connected. Nelson even thought you and Junior might end up together." His eyes seemed to focus on a distant memory. "It's a damn strange world, Princess, but the older I get, the more I believe in destiny. Like some things are just meant to be."

The man in the white lab coat with the stethoscope draped around his neck hurried through the swinging door of the ICU, nodded to an attendant at the nurses' station, and kept moving at a brisk pace.

Always keep moving. Act confident. Look like you belong.

Steve's rules for trespassing. He'd once confessed to a fictional crime to get access to a police station holding cell. Another time, he'd crashed corporate offices in an exterminator's uniform and sprayed the baseboards with insecticide. He'd even picked up a personal injury client by pretending to be a paramedic.

Paramedic to doctor. One small step for a man. One giant leap for a lawyer.

With wide-open physicians' locker rooms, hospitals were among the easiest venues to crack. Scrubs, lab coats, stethoscopes. Samples of the newest amphetamines, if you're into that sort of thing.

At the moment, Steve wore rubber-soled white shoes, scrub pants, and a lab coat with a name tag reading, *"G. Koenigsberg, MD."*

Spotting a cop standing outside a closed door, Steve headed that way. "Officer, how's our patient doing?"

"Damned if I know," the deputy answered. Another young one with hair shaved close enough to show scalp through the buzz cut. "Your people won't let us in."

"I'll check and see if he's up to talking."

Steve entered the room, closing the door behind him. An oxygen clip in his nose, Ben Stubbs lay on his back. A snarl of tubes and wires sprouted from him. He was a small man with a narrow face and sunken cheeks, his skin the unhealthy gray of an amberjack. His chest was thick with white bandages, and a bedside machine beeped in sync with his heartbeat.

"And how are we feeling today, Mr. Stubbs?"

Stubbs' eyes were open but unfocused. He seemed to be in a twilight state of semi-consciousness.

"We'll have you waterskiing in no time. Unless you never skied before. Then it might take a little longer."

Still no reaction.

Steve moved closer to the bed. "Mr. Stubbs, can you remember what happened?"

The man's pale eyes blinked and he moved his head slightly.

"Who did this to you?"

Stubbs' lips moved. No words came out. Slowly, he raised his right hand a few inches above the bedsheets. Shakily, he held up two fingers, like a scalper selling a pair of Dolphins' tickets. A very weak scalper.

"Two? What are you saying? *Two* men did this to you?"

Stubbs' hand fell back to the bed, and the door flew open. A middle-aged man in a suit and tie stormed into the room, two uniformed deputies at his heels. "Just who the hell are you?" the man demanded.

"You first," Steve shot back.

"Dr. Gary Koenigsberg. Head of trauma."

"Marcus Welby. Internal Security. Florida Department of Medicine. As a matter of professional courtesy, I'll just write up a warning today."

"Warning? What the hell are you talking about?"

46

Steve unclipped the name tag and tossed it to the doctor. "You've got some real security problems here, Koenigsberg."

■ ■ ■ ■

Solomon's Laws

■ ■ ■ ■

2. Always assume your client is guilty. It
   saves time.

Four:
Presumption of Guilt

"You're impossible," Victoria fumed. "What would you have done if a patient really needed a doctor?"

"Surgery," Steve suggested.

"I leave you alone five minutes, and you get arrested."

"I wasn't arrested. More like escorted out."

"It's humiliating being your partner. Can you see why I need to be on my own?"

"Loosen up, Vic. I got some information from Stubbs."

"He talked?"

"Not exactly. But I think two guys might have attacked him."

Steve told her about Stubbs raising two fingers, but she seemed unimpressed with his sleuthing. "It could mean anything," Victoria said. "Or nothing."

It was just after nine on a muggy night, and they were back in the old Caddy headed north on U.S. 1. Well, the sign said, *North*. Steve knew they were on a portion of Useless 1 that ran due east. The Keys were a scimitar-shaped archipelago running northeast to southwest, from Miami to Key West. Though Key West was a coastal city, if you drew a line due north from Sloppy Joe's Bar on Duval Street, you'd actually end up west of Cleveland. The curving coastline created the geographic oddity, like Reno, Nevada, being farther west than Los Angeles.

Victoria was silent a few moments. Always an ominous sign.

Preferring to take his whipping in one dose, Steve asked: "You're not still pissed about the hospital, are you?"

"I didn't care for the way you spoke to Uncle Grif."

"C'mon, he loved it."

"It's like you assume he's guilty."

"I always assume clients are guilty. Most of them are, so it saves time."

"Uncle Grif would never kill anyone."

"How would you know? You haven't seen the guy since you were a teenybopper, making out with what's-his-name at the country club."

"Junior. And you're right. He taught me to French kiss."

"Remind me to thank him. My point is,

our perceptions of people are skewed by our own circumstances."

"No kidding? Look who took Psych 101."

"You remember Griffin as someone who gave you great birthday presents. I see him as one tough customer."

"Maybe he's a little rough around the edges, but underneath, he's a sweetheart."

"All of us are capable of murder. Even you, Princess."

"Don't call me 'Princess.' "

"Why not? Sweet old Uncle Grif does."

"He doesn't make it sound like an accusation."

Traffic was light as they crossed the bridge at Boca Chica. Overhead, two jet fighters banked in formation, practicing night landings at the Naval Air Station. Steve hit the gas and passed a Winnebago, giving the tourists a look at the Eldo's license plate, I-OBJECT. The car's top was down, the air rich with the salty aroma from the tidal pools. In a few minutes they would be at Herbert Solomon's houseboat, where they would spend the night. Steve was already tensing up at the prospect of seeing his father, and here's Victoria busting his chops.

He looked over at her. "I do something wrong?"

"I hate it when you lecture me."

"All I said —"

"The self-anointed *senior* partner dispensing wisdom. 'All of us are capable of murder.' Of all the fatuous clichés . . ."

"Sorry. Only original thoughts from now on."

"I really care for you, Steve. You know that?"

"Why do I think there's a 'but' coming?"

"But you're overbearing and arrogant and egotistical. . . ."

He decided to wait it out.

"And your T-shirt is ridiculous."

"I don't think this is about my shirt." He'd bought the black cotton tee at Fast Buck Freddy's on Duval Street. The shirt had a drawing of a man on a bar stool with the inscription: *"Rehab Is for Quitters."* "So what's really going on here, Vic?"

"You stole my client."

"*Our* client."

"Weren't you listening? I'm going out on my own."

"C'mon, we have a big new case. Uncle Grif wants me on this."

"Don't call him that. He's not your uncle."

"As much as he's yours."

"Infuriating. I left that one out. You're overbearing, arrogant, egotistical, *and* infuriating."

"And you hate my shirt. But we're co-counsel on Grif's case. It's what he wants."

She knew Steve was right, which only made her angrier. "All right. But it's our *last* case. It's the only way I can grow as a lawyer. And the only way to preserve our personal relationship. I want to be with you, but not in the courtroom."

"You're sure about it? You really want to break up our firm?"

"Most of the time, I love being with you. You can be warm and funny and caring. But at work, you drive me crazy."

"Really, really sure?"

"Yes, dammit!"

"Okay, then. Our last case. Win, lose, or mistrial."

"And I sit first chair."

"What?"

"You heard me, Steve."

"Okay. Okay."

"You really accept it?" Sounding suspicious.

" 'Course I do. You're the boss. This is our swan song. After this, you fly solo. Get that autonomy you're talking about."

"You respect my feelings on this?" Still not quite buying it.

" 'Course I do. I can lay down a bunt for the team."

But that wasn't what Steve was thinking. He was thinking that he'd square around to bunt, then pull back and smack the ball past the third baseman. Sure, he'd give Victoria more authority. At first. Then, when she got in trouble, he'd be right there to rescue her. She'd see how foolish she'd been to even think about splitting up the firm.

"I can trust you on this?" Victoria Lord asked. "You'll respect my wishes?"

"Would I lie to you?" Steve Solomon said.

FIVE:
RECOVERING LAWYER

When they reached Sugarloaf Key, Steve hung a right onto Old State Road, and after another two miles, he brought the Eldo to a stop under a gumbo-limbo tree. The past few minutes, he'd been thinking of something other than his relationship with the brainy and leggy woman in the passenger seat.

"When are you going to tell your father about the Bar petition?" Victoria asked, getting out of the car.

Jeez, reading my mind.

He'd filed a lawsuit to get back his father's license to practice law but neglected to mention it to his old man. "Not till I have some good news to report."

They walked on a path of crushed shells toward the waterline at Pirates Cove. Victoria's leather-soled slides were, well, *sliding* on the moist shells, and she shortened her stride. "I wonder if that's the right way to do it. Keeping it secret, I mean."

Her roundabout, feminine way, Steve knew, of saying, *"You're really messing up here."*

"Trust me, Vic. I know how to handle my old man."

Steve knew his father desperately missed being a lawyer. Not just any lawyer, but Herbert T. Solomon, Esq., a Southern-born, silver-tongued, spellbinding stem-winder of a lawyer. And then a respected Miami judge. Before his fall.

Now Herbert spent his days fishing, usually alone. But today he'd been taking care of his grandson. On the trip down the Overseas Highway the day before, Steve and Victoria had dropped off twelve-year-old Bobby Solomon. Bobby lived with Steve instead of his own mother, Steve's drug-addled and larcenous sister, Janice, who recently claimed to be growing organic vegetables in the North Carolina mountains. Steve made a mental note to check if the government's food pyramid listed marijuana under vegetables.

As they approached the houseboat, Steve could hear the wind chimes — beer cans dangling on fishing line — on the rear deck. The old wreck — the boat, not his father — was tied to a splintered wooden dock by corded lines thickened with green seaweed. Herbert Solomon owned five acres of scrubby property off Old State Road, but docking the boat there was still illegal, even under the Keys' notoriously lax zoning. Even in the dark, the boat clearly listed to starboard. From inside came the sounds of calypso, Harry Belafonte singing, "Man Smart (Woman Smarter)."

"I'm wondering if you should be the one to handle your father's case," Victoria volunteered.

"Who'd be better?"

"Someone who can be objective."

"I don't plan to be objective. I'm a warrior, a gladiator."

"You know what I mean. You have to separate the truth from fiction. When your father was disbarred —"

"He resigned. There's a difference."

Christmas lights were strung on the overhang of the houseboat, even though it was May, and even though the Solomons were descended from the tribes of Israel. Splotches of green paint haphazardly covered divots of wood rot in the stern deck.

Steve could see movement on the rear porch, his father getting up from a wooden rocker, a drink in his hand. Herbert's shimmering white hair was swept straight back and flipped up at his shoulders. His skin, remarkably unlined for a man of sixty-six, was sunbaked, and his dark eyes were bright and combative.

"Hey, Dad," Steve said.

"Don't 'Hey, Dad' me, you sneaky son-of-a-bitch."

"What'd I do now?" Steve stepped aboard, thinking he'd been asking that question a lot lately.

"Victoria," Herbert said. "How do you put up with this gallynipper?"

"Sometimes, I wonder," she replied.

"You could do a helluva lot better than him."

"Maybe I'll go check on Bobby," Victoria said, "let you boys play."

"He's asleep," Herbert said. "Tuckered out from poling the skiff all day."

"I'll go inside, just the same," she said.

"Coward," Steve told her as she headed through a door into the rear cabin.

"There's rum on the counter, soda in the fridge," Herbert called after her, gesturing with his glass, sprigs of mint peeking over the rim. Deep into his evening mojitos. He turned back to Steve and scowled. "You best cut your own weeds, son, and stay out of mah tater patch."

Even when reaming him out, the old

man's voice maintained the mellifluous flow of molasses oozing over ice cream. Savannah born and raised, Herbert still spoke the honeyed patois of his youth.

As a boy hanging out in the courthouse, Steve heard his father call a witness "So gosh-darned crooked, he could stand in the shadow of a corkscrew and nevuh see the sun. So slippery, gittin' ahold of him is like grabbing an eel in an oil slick. So low a critter, ah had to drain the swamp just to find him."

Herbert could, as they used to say, talk a cat out of a tree. Even though four years at the University of Virginia followed by law school at Duke had polished his diction, Herbert had quickly figured out that playing the Southern gentleman with a tart tongue had its advantages in court. All these years later, whatever regional expressions Herbert still employed came not so much from his youth but from impersonating characters straight out of Mark Twain.

Now, standing on the rear deck of his sagging and splintered houseboat, Herbert T. Solomon, recovering lawyer — *rekoven loyyuh* — was giving his son a piece of his mind.

"Who told you to petition the Bar on mah behalf?"

61

"How'd you know?"

"You think ah'm a senile old Cracker?" *Ole Cracka.*

"Jews can't be Crackers, Dad. Unless they're *matzohs.*"

"Now, ah was just a jackleg country lawyer, but ah know when ah'm being pole-axed."

"Maybe jurors fell for that muskrat-in-a-tub-of-lard shtick, but I don't. So cut the crap, or I'll tell everyone about your Phi Beta Kappa key."

"Don't change the subject. Ah got friends in Tallahassee who say you been poking around in mah business."

"All right, so I filed papers to get your license back."

"Don't want it back."

"We could practice law together."

"Got a good life here."

"You know what the headline on your obituary will be? 'Disgraced Ex-Judge Kicks Bucket.' "

"So what? Ah'm not gonna be around to read it."

"Well, I will."

"So ah should do this for *you?* Why don't you just practice law with your beautiful lady and lemme alone?"

"Vic wants to split up, go solo."

Dammit. Steve hadn't planned on revealing that. But now that he had, maybe he could get some sympathy.

"She'll do better without you," Herbert fired back. "If you're not careful, she'll kick you out of bed, too."

"If the *Herald* interviews me for that obit, I'm gonna say how supportive you always were."

"Aw, don't be such a pussy. Ah remember when those Cuban kids kicked the living piss out of you in the ninth grade."

"Do you remember my coming back with a baseball bat? Breaking some ribs?"

Herbert drained his mojito. "I recollect going to see Rocky Pomerance at the police station, bailing you out. And you say I didn't support you?"

His father's support, Steve recalled, was equally divided between lackadaisical indifference and caustic criticism. Still, as a child, he had idolized the headline-grabbing lawyer, the respected judge. Part of his own psychology, Steve knew, was the childhood fear that he could never measure up to the standards Herbert T. Solomon had set. Then, when his father was implicated by a dirty lawyer in a zoning scandal, everything fell apart. Now Steve couldn't understand why his father wouldn't let him paste it all back together.

"I'm not dropping the case, so you might as well hear me out. I've got a great plan of attack."

"Ah ain't listening."

"You resigned from the bench and the Bar but were never impeached or disbarred."

"So what?"

"You can still pass the 'moral character' test."

"Let it be, son."

"I can win this, Dad."

"Sleeping dogs, son. Let 'em lay."

"What are you saying? Did you take bribes to rezone property?"

"Screw you! You know better than that."

"Then you should have fought back. Hired counsel. Jeez, Dad, if you were innocent —"

"Innocent until proven broke. Ah walked away. That's mah right."

"I'm gonna subpoena Pinky Luber, force him to recant his allegations."

"Son, you ain't got enough butt in your britches to take on Pinky."

"That little old man? He's . . . He's . . ."

Steve tried to come up with a down-home expression to keep pace with his father. Just how did you describe Pinky Luber, ex-lawyer and ex-con, the sleazeball who fingered his father?

Softer than a pat of butter?

Greasier than a deep-fried donut?

All vine and no taters?

Skipping dinner seemed to make all his metaphors turn on food. Steve settled on: "Pinky's nothing. Nothing at all."

"Don't be fooled by appearances. Pinky always had scary friends, even when he was a prosecutor. Dirty cops, thugs, P.I.'s. And he probably made a few more acquaintances in prison."

"Is that what you're afraid of, Dad? Pinky coming after you?"

"One thing you never learned, son. You start turning over rocks, you best be expecting snakes, not flowers."

Six:
A Dream Called
Oceania

It was just after eight a.m., but the humidity already hung in the air like damp sheets on a clothesline. Overhead, the clouds were fleecy white with just enough gray to warn of afternoon rain. Victoria, Steve, and Bobby walked along a scrubby beach at Pirates Cove, waiting for Hal Griffin's seaplane to pick them up and take them to Paradise Key, where Junior would be waiting.

A turtle as big as a garbage-can lid slid from the sand into the water and paddled away. Victoria wished they'd had time for a morning swim. Preferably without Steve's plea for an underwater hump-a-rama. And preferably without crashing boats and cash-carrying lobsters.

Bobby and Steve were skipping stones across the shallow water, betting who could get the most skips, the loser having to peel mangoes for their afternoon smoothies.

Despite his numerous flaws, both personal and professional, Steve was a terrific surrogate father. If Victoria kept a scorecard of her boyfriend's pluses and minuses — and what woman doesn't? — Steve's care for Bobby would be his finest attribute. Once, while sipping a glass of Chardonnay, she had scribbled notes on a legal pad, grading Steve's potential as a life mate:

1. Great parenting skills
2. Makes me laugh
3. Makes me come

The negatives took up two pages, but still, those three positives carried a lot of weight.

Her cell phone rang, the readout showing the hospital. "Morning, Uncle Grif. How do you feel?"

"Lousy, Princess. Those fifty-dollar sleeping pills don't work."

"What about your headache?"

"Like a drill bit going through bedrock."

"How's that guy Stubbs doing?"

"I ask but they don't tell. Listen, Princess — lying awake last night, it all came clear to me. Someone's trying to sink Oceania."

"Oceania?"

"A dream of mine that's almost a reality. It's what I was coming to talk to you about. Junior

will tell you everything."

"So who's trying to sink Oceania?"

"Whoever shot Stubbs. That's your case. Someone wanted me out of the picture. No more Hal Griffin, no more Oceania."

Whatever that is. Victoria swatted at her neck, where a mosquito had settled for breakfast.

"What I'm saying," Griffin continued, *"if Stubbs doesn't make it and I'm charged with killing him, you can't just poke holes in the prosecution's case."*

"That's the way we defend most circumstantial cases. Show reasonable doubt."

"Not enough here. You gotta find the guy who did this."

Oh, is that all? she thought. "Let's pray that Stubbs lives. He'll clear you, right?"

"I hope so."

She had hoped for a confident *"Damn right."* Not a wishy-washy *"I hope so."* Griffin's ambiguous answer raised more questions, but you don't ask a client on the phone whether he shot somebody. Instead, she urged him to get some rest, and they clicked off.

She caught up with Steve and Bobby — the Solomon Boys — kneeling, faces close to the sand, as if searching for a lost contact lens. Competing to see who most resembled

68

the white egrets wading in the shallows, pecking their snouts into the water.

Steve stood and spit out a tiny shell, leaving a mustache of wet sand on his upper lip. Looking altogether too innocent for the crafty trial lawyer he was. "So what's our client say?" he asked Victoria.

"That he's been framed."

"Gee. Never heard that one before."

Bobby scrambled to his feet and wiped off his bare knees. He wore cutoffs and a University of Miami football jersey. He was short and skinny, and even Steve's ham-and-cheese paninis and fruit smoothies hadn't put much meat on his bones. "Where's the plane? I'm bored."

"Seaplanes make a helluva racket taking off," Steve said, knowing that loud noises could rattle the boy. "I don't want you to get scared."

The boy snorted a laugh. "I'm not a sis."

"Not saying you are."

"I'm not scared. The Grumman Mallard has a great safety record."

"You researched it?" Victoria asked.

"On the Net. It took, like, thirty seconds. Anything you want to know about flying boats, just ask. Then I checked with NOAA. No storms, winds steady from the southeast." A born mimic, the boy lowered his voice into weatherman mode: "A grand day for flying, fishing, or just relaxing in the sun. More at eleven."

Victoria hoped for a smooth flight. Her stomach was queasy from the mess of sharpies Herbert had fried with cornmeal for breakfast. If catfish at dawn were not enough, he'd also cooked grits with chorizo sausage and cheddar cheese, all washed down with sugar-laced rocket fuel *café Cubano.*

"If you ever need any research, come to me," Bobby instructed. "I'm ten times better than Uncle Steve on the computer."

She tousled his already messy hair. "You're the smartest boy I know."

Victoria adored Bobby and marveled at the progress he'd made. Less than two years earlier, Steve had rescued him from a religious cult, where the boy's mother had abused and neglected him. At first, diagnosed with unnamed central nervous system damage — some characteristics of Asperger's syndrome, some autistic tendencies — the ten-year-old was uncommunicative and afraid, his body wracked with tremors. Doctors could find no organic brain damage, and under Steve's care he rapidly became more socialized. He also began to demonstrate what doctors called paradoxical

functional facilitation, a fancy term for sa-
vantlike abilities of memorization and
echolalia, the ability to repeat verbatim
anything he heard or read. Bobby was still
nervous around strangers but had warmed
up quickly to Victoria. She had become his
mother figure and worried what might happen to Bobby if she and Steve ever broke
up. Lately, she'd worried about it even more.

Steve, apparently chastised by her criticism of yesterday's T-shirt, had changed into
one with a different logo: *"The Only Mark
I've Made in Life Is in My Underwear."* Did he
honestly think that was an improvement, or
was he just taunting her? Well, it would
surely make an impression on Junior Griffin, Mr. Preppy from her past.

Victoria wore a white tank top and a
short, crochet ruffle skirt in aquamarine,
the same color as the ocean. Her Manolo
Blahnik sandals picked up the hue of the
skirt. Two sexy side straps ran up to her
ankles, drawing attention to her calves. Well,
that was the idea, wasn't it? The sandals had
been a gift from Steve. Sort of. He'd represented a truck driver at the Port of Miami
who had a habit of delivering cargo containers to his own U-Store-It warehouse instead
of the proper recipients. Steve lost the case
and the truck driver was broke and headed

for prison. But a cargo container brimming with expensive Italian shoes had conveniently fallen off his truck before the man's conviction, and Steve was paid in leather, instead of greenbacks. If business didn't pick up, Victoria might go hungry, but never barefoot.

Before leaving Herbert's houseboat, she'd carefully applied eye shadow, a color called "Cognac," which seemed to go well with the Tropical Sunset lipstick. Sexy, sure, but not trampy. Her blond hair was casually messed. What Steve had called her "Meg Ryan look," though the last time Victoria had seen her in a movie, Meg's hair was neither blond nor messed.

Now, on this sticky morning, waiting for the ride to Uncle Grif's private island, Victoria wondered just why she'd taken such care dressing. And what's the pleasurable buzz she was feeling? Was the *café Cubano* even stronger than usual?

Okay, let's be honest here. I'm going to see Junior, all grown up, after all these years.

She shot a look at Steve, who did not seem to share the same electrical buzz. He'd eaten two platefuls of the fried fish and had a sour look of aggravation combined with indigestion.

"How come you slept onshore last night,

Uncle Steve?" Crouched at the water's edge, Bobby scooped up crabs no larger than a fingernail.

"The boat makes me seasick."

Bobby laughed. "It doesn't even move."

"I like the hammock."

"I thought it made your back hurt."

Steve grunted something unintelligible.

Bobby looked up at him. "Usually you and Victoria rack out together. But last night —"

"Who are you — Dr. Phil?" Steve interrupted, expelling a burp of fried sharpies.

"Are you two fighting?" Bobby asked.

"Absolutely not."

Bobby stood up, cocked his head at an angle, and studied his uncle through thick eyeglasses. "Why do grown-ups always lie?"

Victoria didn't want Bobby to get upset. He was always asking when the two of them were getting married. So far, she hadn't told Bobby about splitting up the law firm. Last night, he had probably overheard them quarreling about who would take the lead today. Steve had insisted she would go too easy questioning Junior. One day in, and he was already taking over, violating their agreement. They squabbled a while, and Steve — not getting his way — had stomped off the boat in his Jockeys and dived into the rope hammock strung between two sabal palms. This morning, he was scratching at mosquito bites and barely speaking to her. Did he really think Bobby wouldn't pick up on their squabbling?

"I'm not lying," Steve told the boy.

"You're a lawyer," Bobby said. "You don't even know when you're lying." The boy lowered his voice into an eerie impression of his uncle. "The relationship between the truth and Mr. Solomon is like the relationship between the color blue and the number three. Occasionally, you'll see the number three written in blue, but you don't expect it. Same thing with Mr. Solomon. If he tells the truth, it's just a coincidence."

"Excellent, Bobby," Victoria said. "You're amazing."

"Yeah, great," Steve said, without enthusiasm. "Verbatim from my closing argument in Robbins versus Colodney."

"Except I changed Robbins' name to yours."

"What I don't get," Steve said, "is how somebody who remembers everything he hears forgets to take out the trash."

"Steve, we have to settle this about Junior." Victoria decided to turn the conversation away from Steve's distant relationship with the truth. "Are we on the same page?"

"I hate that expression," Steve said. "I'll bet you learned it in the DA's office. 'Same page. Team player. Push the envelope.' Crock of bureaucratic clichés."

"Excuse me if we're not all rebels like Steve-the-Slasher Solomon."

"I knew you two were fighting," Bobby said.

"We're resolving some professional differences," Victoria told the boy.

"So why couldn't Uncle Steve just say that?"

"Because your uncle thinks the shortest distance between two points is a winding road." Victoria turned to Steve. "I'm taking the lead when we interview Junior. Is that clear?"

"Who's Junior?" Bobby asked.

"Some guy Vic used to French kiss when they both wore braces."

"Sometimes, Stephen, you are really spiteful," she said. Using his full name, trying to clue him in as to just how angry she was. "And for the record, I didn't wear braces." Giving him an exaggerated, toothy smile.

"Junior's a spoiled rich kid," Steve said. "La Gorce Country Club. Daddy's platinum American Express card. Boarding school."

Victoria spoke to Bobby, pretending Steve wasn't even there. "Junior Griffin was the hottest boy at Pinecrest."

"I went to high school with the *Marielitos.*"

Mr. Macho, as if he'd served with the Magnificent Bastards battalion of the Marines.

"Miami Beach High," she reminded him. "Not exactly Baghdad."

"I had to fight for my lunch money."

"When Junior laughed, he had dimples and the cutest little cleft in his chin," Victoria said with a wicked smile.

"They do that with surgery," Steve said.

She turned toward Bobby but aimed her words like spears at his uncle. "Junior was captain of the swim team and king of the junior prom. My mother called him 'Dreamboat.' "

Steve made a guttural sound, like a man choking.

"He had this kind of Brad Pitt look," she persisted, "blond and rugged."

"Brad Pitt's real name is William Bradley Pitt," Bobby said. He squeezed his eyes shut, and Victoria knew he was unscrambling an anagram from the actor's name. After a moment, he grinned and said, loudly: "PARTLY LIABLE DIMWIT."

She still didn't know how Bobby did it. When she had asked him, all he said was that he saw letters floating above his head and he pulled them out of the air.

"Those high school studs like Junior," Steve said, "twenty years later, they're bald, fat losers."

"You still haven't answered me. Are you going to butt in with Junior like you did with Uncle Grif?"

"You win. Take the lead, Vic. Have a ball."

"Good. We need to be in perfect sync. If there's a criminal case —"

"Oh, there's a criminal case."

"How do you know?"

"Because Willis Rask didn't come here to wish us bon voyage." Steve gestured toward the two-lane blacktop fifty yards from the shoreline. A Monroe County police car pulled to a stop, and Sheriff Willis Rask climbed out and hitched up his belt.

■ ■ ■ ■

SOLOMON'S LAWS

■ ■ ■ ■

3. Beware of a sheriff who forgets to load his gun but remembers the words to "Margaritaville."

SEVEN:
COLUMBO OF THE
KEYS

The sheriff waved and headed their way.

"Let me handle him," Steve said.

Victoria bristled. "There you go again."

"Trust me, Vic. I've known Rask a long time. Hey, Willis, how's the speed-trap business?"

"Hey, Stevie!" Rask shouted back. "Still chasing ambulances?"

If it hadn't been for his uniform, Steve thought, Willis Rask could be mistaken for another forty-five-year-old Conch who spent too much time in the sun with too many chilled beverages. He was overweight and had a brush mustache and long sideburns. He wore his graying hair tied back in a ponytail. His shirttail flopped out of his pants, and his Oakley sunglasses, on a chain of tiny seashells, were surely nonregulation. In one buttoned shirt pocket, the round shape of a metal container was visible under the fabric. Unless he'd switched to Altoids,

Rask still indulged in chewing tobacco. His sunburned face was usually fixed in a quizzical half smile. The sheriff did not give the overall impression of a spit-and-polish lawman. Spit, maybe. But not polish.

Steve knew the sheriff's story better than most. As a young man, Rask ran a charter fishing boat, back when the main catch in the Keys was "square grouper," large bales of marijuana. Rask off-loaded from mother ships, and got busted on his third run. His lawyer was that silver-tongued windyspinner, Herbert T. Solomon, Esq., who provided free counsel on the condition that Rask would go to college and stay straight. Herbert did that a lot in the old days. He taught young Steve that a lawyer owed a debt to all of society, not just to paying clients. Steve followed his father's lead, which might explain why he drove a thirty-year-old car and had an office in a second-rate modeling agency with a window overlooking a Dumpster.

Though he couldn't have been older than ten at the time, Steve could still remember his father's closing argument in Rask's trial. Wearing a seersucker suit with suspenders, Herbert glided around the courtroom like a ballroom dancer, smooth-talking the jury, earnestly declaring that his client had performed a public service, not a criminal act. Young, naive Willis Rask had fished that soggy pot out of the Florida Straits to protect the birds and the boats.

"Those bales of devil weed were a hazard to navigation," Herbert proclaimed with a straight face. *"Thankfully, Willis was drawn to the area by a flock of terns that hovered overhead, feasting on the seeds. Willis saved untold boats from being sunk and birds from becoming ill. Without this young hero's quick thinking, there'd have been no tern left un-stoned."*

That made the jurors smile, and they came back in twenty minutes with a not guilty verdict. Willis danced down the stairs, kissed the kapok tree on the courthouse lawn, then hugged his lawyer. He kept his promise, finishing college at Rollins, upstate in Winter Park, then law school at Stetson over in DeLand.

A dozen years later, Rask came up with a novel platform when he ran for sheriff of what locals called the "Conch Republic." He'd clear drunk drivers off the narrow roads and jail husbands who beat their wives. But he wouldn't arrest anyone for possession of small amounts of marijuana. The limited resources available to law enforcement were too precious to waste on

victimless crimes. In the permissive Keys —
where Jimmy Buffet's "Why Don't We Get
Drunk and Screw" was an unofficial anthem
— it was a brilliant tactic. Rask won in a
landslide. Some voters lit up a joint on the
way out of the voting booth.

"Glad I caught you." Rask met them at
the shoreline. "Yo, Bobby."

"Safety's off on your Glock," Bobby said.

Rask pulled the gun from his holster and
checked the lever. "Jeez, you're right. How'd
you see that?"

"Bobby notices stuff," Steve said.

"And there's no clip in it," Bobby added.

"No wonder it's so light today." Rask
hefted the gun, then turned to Victoria.
"And you must be Stevie's partner."

"Victoria Lord," she said.

"My deputies told me Stevie had hooked
up with a real looker." Rask winked at her.
"And they weren't lying."

"Red light, Sheriff," Victoria said. "That's
inappropriate."

Her tone reminded Steve of his fourth-
grade teacher, a woman who'd slap his
knuckles with a ruler whenever he acted up.

"Whoa, sorry," Rask said. "Got your
hands full with this one, huh, Stevie?"

"She keeps her safety off, too, Willis."

"They're fighting, Sheriff," Bobby added.

"Quiet," Steve said, then turned to Rask. "Thought I might see you yesterday at the hospital."

"Just got back into town," Rask said. "Jimmy had a concert in Orlando."

"I'm jealous, you old parrothead."

Rask grinned and sang a few lines of "A Pirate Looks at Forty," all about making money smuggling grass but pissing it away just as fast.

Steve laughed. "You *are* a pirate, Willis, but if you're looking at forty, it's in the rearview mirror."

"Are you here on official business, Sheriff?" Victoria's tone erased both men's smiles and cut off the notion of singing any more tunes.

"You don't like Jimmy Buffett?" Rask made it sound like a crime.

"She likes Freddy Chopin," Bobby said.

The sheriff let out a low whistle. "Can you drink to his stuff?"

"I recommend it," Steve advised.

"Go ahead, Steve. Make fun," she said. "I'm sure you think those slacker songs are better than a piano étude."

"Ooh," the sheriff said, "sounds like somebody needs a 'License to Chill.' "

Steve gave Rask the thumbs-up, extra points for working a parrothead song title into his repartee. "So, Willis, when's the last time you and Jimmy went fishing?"

"Couple weeks. Chased some wild-ass tarpon off Key Largo."

"You know Jimmy Buffett?" Victoria asked. Her skeptical schoolmarm tone again.

Both men chuckled, and Steve said: "That song, 'A Pirate Looks at Forty.' It's all about Willis."

"Really?" She smiled so sweetly, Steve knew she didn't believe a word of it.

"Steve knows Jimmy, too," the sheriff said.

Victoria cocked her head. "Funny he never mentioned it."

"Not a big deal. We fish a little, drink a little. Why? You never met Chopin?"

In the distance, they heard the whine of turboprop engines. Four hundred feet above the water, the flying boat shone silver in the morning sun.

"Sheriff, we have to be going," Victoria said briskly. "So if you have any business . . ."

"Couple of questions, is all."

"Careful, Vic," Steve said. "You're dealing with Columbo of the Keys."

"I'll bet," she said.

"One of Solomon's Laws: Beware of a sheriff who forgets to load his gun but

86

remembers the words to 'Margaritaville.' "

"Willis Rask," Bobby said, biting his lip and concentrating while he dug up an anagram. "IS RAW SKILL."

"Got that right, Bobby," the sheriff said. "Stevie, we been looking into that fellow who got stuck with the spear. Ben Stubbs."

"You're doing actual police work?" Steve said. "Tarpon must not be running."

"Stubbs was staying at the Pier House." Rask pulled a battered notebook from a shirt pocket, flipped a page. "He bought three charts — all of the eastern Gulf — at Charlie Simmons' store two days ago. Stopped at the Oceanographic Institution, used his federal ID to get access, spent some time in their library and computer files. Pulled up some topographic maps of the ocean floor a few miles west of Boca Chica. Two nights in a row, he ate dinner at Cienfuegos. Snapper with a mango salsa." Rask looked up from his notebook. "You two know any of this?"

"No," Victoria said.

"All of it," Steve said. "Except the mango salsa."

"Uncle Steve's lying," Bobby said.

"I know," Rask said. "Your uncle lies, even when the truth's a better story." He flipped another page in his notebook. "After dinner, Stubbs had two beers at the Hog's Breath, then spent a couple hours at Fat Mary's over on Whitehead."

"Fat Mary's?" Victoria said.

"Strip joint," Steve said. He added hastily, "Or so I'm told."

Rask returned the notebook to his pocket. "That reminds me, Stevie. Fat Mary says howdy. Anyway, I was just wondering what Stubbs was doing on your client's boat."

"Fishing," Steve said.

"Research," Victoria said.

"They don't know," Bobby said.

"I see," Rask said. "Will Mr. Griffin give us a statement?"

"No," Victoria said.

"Yes," Steve said. "Later."

"How 'bout a polygraph?" Rask asked.

"Under the right conditions," Steve said.

"Under no condition," Victoria said.

Rask scratched at a sideburn. "You two do this on purpose to throw off honest constables such as my own self?"

"Yes," Steve said.

"No," Victoria said.

The whine of the Grumman's props grew louder. The plane was about to splash down offshore, its nose pointed toward the beach.

"Anything else, Sheriff?" Victoria asked.

Rask made a show of removing his Oakleys, breathing on the lenses, and wiping them on his shirttail. "Now that you mention it, I did forget something."

"I knew it," Steve said.

They waited a moment as Rask slipped the sunglasses back on. Offshore, the seaplane hit the water with a *splat* and continued toward the beach. On the fuselage was a blue logo of cascading waves and the name *"Oceania."*

"Stubbs left his luggage in his room at the Pier House. Had a briefcase with the usual. Laptop, government papers, antacid pills. Plus forty thousand dollars in hundred-dollar bills. Now, what do you suppose a civil servant was doing with all that money?"

"Tipping big at Fat Mary's?" Steve suggested.

The seaplane rolled onto the beach, the pilot waving at them through an open side window of the cockpit.

"We gotta go, Willis," Steve said, above the noise.

"Ah, almost forgot. One more thing. My dang memory . . ."

"C'mon, Willis," Steve said. "Give it up."

Rask shook his head, sadly, milking the moment. "That Stubbs fellow died this morning."

"Oh, shit."

"Yeah, Stevie. I figured you'd be broken up about it. And your guy Griffin? He's facing a murder charge."

EIGHT:
DEAD AHEAD

The world was all blues and greens. The deep cerulean blue of the sky, the ever-changing turquoise of the water, the viridescent greens of the endless string of wooded islands, fanning out like a string of emeralds in a balmy sea.

Only Bobby seemed to be enjoying the view through the seaplane's tinted windows. Steve was scribbling numbers on a pad, trying to figure how much they could charge for a murder trial, and Victoria was back on the cell phone with Hal Griffin.

"Forty thousand in cash?" Griffin said. *"Where'd Stubbs get that kind of money, Princess?"*

"I was hoping you'd know."

"Stubbs dying is bad. The money only makes it worse. Someone's gonna say I was bribing the bastard."

"To do what?" Thinking Uncle Grif's sympathy seemed to be reserved for himself.

"Not that Stubbs didn't hint around. Sees my house, says something about how he got into the wrong racket. Gets on the boat, same thing. 'You builders got more money than Croesus.' Jesus, Princess, this is just like with Nelson and me."

The mention of her father's name startled her. "What do you mean?"

"Those condo towers on the beach up in Broward. Some snitch claimed we were bribing zoning officers, but we weren't. A competitor of ours paid the son-of-a-bitch to make it up. It's one of the things that drove Nelson over the edge."

"What were the others, Uncle Grif?"

"Aw, jeez, Princess. I'm not a shrink, and it was a long time ago."

She heard a voice in the background on the line, then Griffin told her a doctor needed to examine him.

After the phone clicked off, Steve said: "Let me guess. Uncle Grif's conscience cried out and he confessed."

"Do me a favor, Steve. When we meet Junior, drop the sarcasm."

"Why? Won't he get it?"

The Grumman swooped low over the crystalline water, the engines a peaceful drone. No one had spoken for thirty minutes —

meaning it had been half an hour since Victoria reminded Steve she was sitting first chair — when Bobby shouted: "Dolphins!"

They looked out the windows. Below them, two bottlenose dolphins leapt skyward, knifed back into the water, then leapt again. All in perfect unison.

"Yeah, your buddies," Steve enthused. Wondering if the dolphins were mates. Wondering, too, if the female complained, "*Next time,* I'll *say when we jump.*" And was the male confused when she said she was tired of being treated like one of his groupers?

"They're beautiful," Victoria said.

"*Tursiops truncatus,*" Bobby said.

The kid knew his dolphins. He'd studied them, telling Steve that fifty million years ago otters returned to the sea, where they developed into the silvery creatures who can swim at thirty knots and can be trained by the Navy to clear harbors of mines. For nearly a year, Bobby had been a regular at a dolphin sanctuary on Key Largo. That first day, he was afraid of the animals. Of course, then he feared people, too. The kid had all the symptoms of the abused child: nightmares, tantrums, eating disorders. But once he was in the water, the dolphins seemed to calm him, taking to him immediately, *ping-*

ing him with their sonarlike sound waves, which Bobby said tickled him all over, then letting him hitch rides, or nudging him through the water with their snouts.

A marine biologist at the facility told Steve that dolphins somehow sense when children are ill. Something to do with their echolocation abilities. Dolphins emit ultrasound frequencies, like an MRI scan in a medical facility, he said. If you put four healthy children in the water and one suffering from Down's syndrome or leukemia or autism or cerebral palsy, a dolphin will approach the ill child.

Hanging out with Bobby alongside the penned-off canal in Key Largo, listening to the dolphins *chirp* and *creak,* Steve learned all the stories about their strange powers. There was JoJo, the docile female dolphin who one day inexplicably butted a girl in the rib cage. The bruise was so severe, the girl was treated at the hospital, where an X-ray revealed a tumor in her abdomen. Doctors dismissed the idea that JoJo had intentionally communicated her knowledge of the girl's condition, but the dolphin experts at the facility disagreed. Though he didn't want to get all New Agey about it, Steve figured there just might be something to the healing and rescue powers of the dolphins.

Once in the water with the sleek animals, Bobby had quickly loosened up. He played with them, returned their affection, splashed them when they slapped the water to douse him. He had his favorite, Bucky, a speedy male with a pink-striped belly. Bobby would stroke Bucky's fluke and imitate his high-pitched squeaks and creaks. He told Steve he understood the dolphin's language. Bucky would say when he was tired or bored or hungry — and specifically whether he preferred smelt or herring for lunch. Bobby said Bucky understood him, too, and Steve wondered whether a relationship with a fifty-million-year-old species called *"Tursiops truncatus"* might be easier than one with a modern woman.

Now the seaplane skimmed over the Gulf, temporarily cooling the simmering dispute between Steve and Victoria. The water color kept changing, from turquoise to emerald to muddy brown to muted rust, depending on the depth and the grasses and coral below. He watched the shadow of the plane as it crossed miniature islands, some little more than marshy savannahs and woody hammocks poking out of the sea.

Steve was still thinking about what Sheriff Rask had told them. Ben Stubbs died without regaining full consciousness. There'd be no "Griffin shot me" statements. Once the Grand Jury handed up the indictment, it would be a purely circumstantial case. Steve still wondered about Stubbs raising two fingers in the ICU. Had he meant there'd been two attackers? Or was he giving the old "peace" sign? Or maybe just waving good-bye?

Even before Griffin was officially charged, there were things to be done. Jury selection didn't begin in the courthouse. It started in the news media and spread to the taverns and beauty parlors and coffee shops. Steve was already planning a statement for his client.

"Harold Griffin, noted builder and philanthropist, deeply regrets the unfortunate accident at sea that claimed the life of a dedicated public servant."

Steve hadn't a clue if Griffin was a philanthropist, but it sounded better than "a rich dude who builds mammoth resorts in environmentally sensitive ecosystems."

"Just a few more minutes, folks," the pilot said over the speaker. He was a man in his forties with wispy blond hair and a sunburned face. Wearing chino safari shorts and a navy blue shirt with epaulets, he spoke with a British accent, telling them his name

was Clive Fowles. Pronouncing it "Foals." He had invited Bobby to sit copilot in what he called his "magic flying boat," but the boy, always shy with strangers, turned him down. Then he'd offered to take them all diving on the reef if their stay allowed it.

"Anything you need, just ring up Captain Clive," Fowles told them as they settled into their seats. "Mr. G told me to take good care of you."

"Mr. G, Senior, or Mr. G, Junior?" Steve asked.

"Only one Mr. G," Fowles said. "That's the boss."

Now, as they neared Paradise Key, Steve glanced at Victoria. She was staring out at the sea, quietly smiling to herself.

"Excited about seeing the hottest boy at Pinecrest?" Steve asked.

"Do you remember the first girl you kissed?"

"Sarah Gropowitz. Beach Middle School."

"You ever think of her?"

"Only when I send a check to the ACLU. She runs the Equal Rights for Lesbians Committee."

Victoria turned to look at him.

"But my kissing her didn't make her that way," Steve defended himself.

"Would you at least concede the possibility of cause and effect?"

"Sharks!" Bobby shouted.

Sure enough, maybe a dozen sharks were cruising the shallow water, the plane's shadow darting over them. Well, why not? They were flying over Shark Channel just off Upper Matecumbe Key. Suddenly two sharks leapt out of the water.

"Spinners, Uncle Steve. A hunting party."

Bad omen, Steve thought, just as Fowles said over the speaker, *"Paradise Key. Dead ahead."*

Dead ahead.

Steve thought of Ben Stubbs, *dead indeed.* He thought of Victoria, upset with him for grievances he could barely comprehend. He thought of his father, angry at him for nothing more than trying to restore his lost reputation. With a sense of uncertainty and foreboding, Steve tried to figure out just what was going on.

Why is Vic so pissed off, anyway?

Hadn't he curbed the habits that offended her feminine sensibilities? He'd cut way down on the scratching, burping, and farting. He'd quit representing hookers, and it had been months since he'd spent all night playing Texas Hold 'Em at the Miccosukee casino. Not only that, he'd been considerate of her foibles, too. Did he say anything last week when she used his razor to shave her legs, then put it back on the sink, where it lay, waiting to maim him like a rusty machete? Not a word, other than "Ouch!" On her birthday, hadn't he written her a sexy poem, working her love of tennis into the last stanza? She didn't seem to appreciate the effort it took to find a rhyme for "Martina Hingis." Did she think the word just popped into his head: "cunnilingus"?

He pressed his face to the window just as the plane banked hard and began to descend. An island shimmered out of the water like a green mirage. Circling the shoreline was a single-lane road that connected to a private causeway linking the island to Lower Matecumbe Key.

The seaplane headed for a horseshoe-shaped cove on the Gulf side. At the far end was a concrete dock where the *Force Majeure* would have been docked if it wasn't being hauled away in pieces from Sunset Key. Next to the dock, a sandy beach studded with saw palmetto trees. Half-a-dozen snowy egrets wading in the shallow water took to the air at the sound of the engines. A sloping lawn rose from the shoreline to a strand of Australian pines that surrounded a large, three-story wooden house. Solar panels on the roof flashed brilliantly in the sun.

"Everyone buttoned up back there?" Fowles asked over the speaker. *"There'll be a bloody big splash when we hit."*

The plane was at thirty feet when it passed through the opening in the cove, and Fowles set it down with the promised *splash,* the windows plastered with streaming water. The plane slowed immediately, the two props on the high wings still whirling, the plane now a boat chugging toward the shoreline.

"Welcome to Paradise," Fowles told them. *"Junior should be waiting in the . . . oh, sod it all! Look at that, off the starboard."*

Steve was already looking out his window, so he caught the entire amazing sight. Maybe it wasn't a pair of dolphins jumping in tandem or a school of sharks in a hunting party. This was both more impressive — and more threatening. Without quite knowing why, Steve sensed that this sight portended a greater impact on his life than the wonders of nature.

A man in skimpy, black Speedos shot out of the water, smooth and sleek as a Polaris missile. He held a lobster in one hand and grabbed the pontoon of the seaplane with the other. With athletic grace, he hoisted himself onto the pontoon and waved the lobster over his head, flashing a smile toward the fuselage windows.

Could he see Victoria through the glass? Steve wondered.

She could surely see him.

And what would she have seen? Or, more important to Steve, what would she have *felt?*

The man was an inch or two over six feet tall, with a swimmer's body. Flat waist, ridged six-pack of abs, carved shoulders, and long, smooth, muscled arms. With his arms raised, his lats flared like stingrays from his sides. His chest was simply too large for the rest of him. Two slabs of meaty pecs, like thick steaks, and an overall impression of chesty, brutal strength. He was suntanned a deep bronze, so deep that his smile looked dangerously bright. His long hair was slicked straight back and darkened from the water, but Steve could see it was sun-streaked. An Abercrombie & Fitch ad come to life, a fucking nightmare of a guy, Steve thought. But even worse, he wasn't just some chiseled waiter-actor or model-poseur or jock–beach bum that infested South Beach like cockroaches in the hotels. No, this guy had a history with Victoria, and with fissures already appearing in the professional relationship of Solomon & Lord, Steve was starting to feel insecure about their personal relationship as well.

"Jun-ior," Victoria breathed, her face pressed to the window, somehow making the name sound pornographic. "My, but he's all grown up."

Was it Steve's imagination, or was her breath fogging the window?

Standing on the pontoon, one arm gripping the strut — all the better to display his undulating muscles — Junior Griffin turned squarely toward the fuselage, and now Steve noticed one final attribute. The sizable bulge in his Speedos. Steve wasn't sure where Victoria's gaze was directed, but he could swear he heard her sigh.

NINE: SPEEDO GUY

The seaplane rolled onto the concrete ramp at the water's edge. Bobby clambered down the stairs, followed by Victoria and Steve. In an instant, Junior appeared, kissing Victoria swiftly on the lips, then twirling her off her feet in a big, wet hug.

"Wow! You're here," he said. "You're really here."

She laughed at his enthusiasm, so straightforward and without irony or sarcasm.

He set her back down on the dock as if she were made of glass and looked into her eyes. "Tori, I've really missed you."

Tori. No one had called her that since she was twelve. In fact, nobody except Junior had ever called her that, and just now it sounded so sweet and lovable that she felt herself blush.

Junior exchanged pleasantries with Steve and Bobby but never broke eye contact with Victoria. Was his smile always this radiant, she wondered, his dimples so deep? His eyes were a deep blue, almost the color of one of her eyeshadows, Adriatic Azure. She watched him towel off and pull a pair of white canvas shorts over his Speedos. The rich golden hue of his skin, the lingering taste of salt water from his kiss, the warmth of the sea breeze . . . so many sensations bombarding her.

Bare-chested and barefoot, like a preppy Tarzan, Junior led his visitors up a flagstone path toward the house, Casa de la Sol, according to a tasteful sign embedded in the wall of coral boulders.

"Dad told me how beautiful you are," Junior said, "but wow. I'm at a loss for words."

"That's so sweet." She was aware of Steve next to her, could feel his discomfort.

"And a big-time lawyer, too. Wow."

"Wow" seeming to be a key component in Junior's verbal arsenal. Okay, so he was never valedictorian at Pinecrest, but he was voted Most Popular. And now that he'd turned into this bronzed Adonis, all she could think was, *Well, being a National Merit Scholar isn't everything.*

"All these years . . ." Junior said, letting it hang there.

"Yes," Victoria said.

"Do you remember Bunny Flagler's costume party at La Gorce?"

She smiled at the memory. "You were Zorro. I was Wonder Woman."

"We sneaked out to the eighteenth green."

"And the sprinklers came on." Victoria laughed. Remembering spiked punch, an Eagles cover band, and sloppy kisses in the humid night.

Steve cleared his throat, the sound of a dog growling. "I once went to a costume party as David Copperfield."

"Great magician," Junior said.

"The Dickens character," Steve corrected him.

"Oh, right."

"He was an orphan, like me."

"You weren't an orphan, Uncle Steve," Bobby said.

"But I wanted to be."

"Why?" Junior asked.

"Not sure you'd understand," Steve said. "You live in Casa de la Sol. I grew up in Bleak House."

"Maybe it just needed some decorating," Junior said, and Victoria's spirits sank. Had the literary reference sailed by him like a catamaran in a gale? But then, Junior laughed and let them know he'd been joking. "Sometimes I wish I had a Dickensian upbringing. Builds character, don't you think?"

"Didn't work with Steve," Victoria said.

How about that, Steve the Slasher? The hottest boy at Pinecrest can go toe-to-toe with you.

The elevation climbed slightly as the flagstone path curled around a stand of coconut palms. "Steve, you move like an athlete," Junior said.

"You staring at my ass?" Steve shot back.

"No, I mean it. The way you walk. Graceful-like."

"Uncle Steve played baseball at U of M," Bobby announced, proudly.

"See," Junior said. "I can tell."

Victoria took stock of the moment. There was Steve, pissy as a skunk, and there was Junior, exuding charm. Guileless and confident. So much to like about him.

"Uncle Steve still holds the record for stolen bases in playoff games," Bobby continued.

"Wow," Junior said. "Ever play in the College World Series?"

"Yeah, but I don't brag about it."

" 'Course not," Bobby said. "You got picked off third in the championship game."

"Really? That's hard to do, isn't it? Getting picked off third base, I mean."

"Bad call," Steve defended himself. "I got in under the tag."

"But Uncle Steve caught hell," Bobby added. "Bottom of the ninth. Probably cost the 'Canes the title. That's why they call him 'Last Out Solomon.' "

"Thanks a lot, kiddo," Steve said.

"That's too bad, Steve," Junior said. "I had no idea."

It struck Victoria then. That "move like an athlete" stuff. Junior had set Steve up. He had intended to draw out the most humiliating moment of Steve's life.

"I had no idea"? Hah. You knew exactly what you were doing.

Meaning he'd researched Steve. And her, too, she supposed. Meaning also that there was far more to grown-up Junior than his suntan and amazing pecs.

"I like solitary sports," Junior said, as they neared the house. "Maybe it's because I'm an only child."

"I wish I were," Steve said.

"Then I wouldn't be here, Uncle Steve," Bobby said.

"Good point. I withdraw the remark. And I'm glad my sister's a nutcase, or you wouldn't be living with me."

The path ended at the house, the highest point on the small island. On one side of the house, a helicopter pad. On the other, a negative-edge swimming pool. And down a slight grade, a private beach of white sand. As they walked, Junior told them of his love of the water. He was a windsurfer and a kitesurfer, a distance swimmer and a scuba diver. But most of all, he loved free diving off Cabo San Lucas, sinking as deep as possible with no oxygen except what you can hold in your lungs.

He told them about his rigorous physical training, claimed he could hold his breath for five minutes and twenty seconds and consciously reduce his pulse rate to twenty beats per minute. He told them about the terrifying thrill of being attached to a weighted sled and descending to 400 feet — the world record was 558 feet, but that diver died — and the searing pain in his chest as his lungs shriveled to the size of a fist. He told them about rocketing back to the surface like a human missile on the air-powered sled, about the hallucinations from nitrogen narcosis, about the fear that his heart would burst, his brain explode. And that was the exhilarating kick, the electrical charge of the sport, the knowledge that every time you slipped into your wet suit, you taunted the angel of death.

And when he was done, it was Victoria

who said, "Wow."

As they approached the coral rock steps leading to the front door of Casa de la Sol, Steve asked: "What was Ben Stubbs doing on your father's boat?"

He asked the question so quickly, Victoria had been caught off guard.

Dammit! Breaking his promise that I take the lead.

"Now, that's a long story," Junior said.

"Does it have something to do with Oceania?" Victoria asked. Trying to seize the momentum from Steve.

"Everything to do with it," Junior agreed cheerfully. "In case Dad didn't explain it, Oceania's going to be a floating hotel."

"Isn't that a cruise ship?" Steve asked.

"Trust me, nothing like it."

"Where would the hotel be built?" Victoria fired off the question before Steve could follow up.

"In the Gulf. Four miles west of Boca Chica."

While Steve and Victoria tried to picture exactly where that would be, Bobby piped up: "That's a marine sanctuary. There's a big coral reef and a zillion fish."

"Right," Steve said. "Federally protected. How can you build out there?"

"That's why Stubbs was so important. He was the EPA guy who could say yea or nay."

"Which was it?" Victoria asked.

"Thumbs-up. He'd already prepared a draft of his report. With all the safeguards to protect the reef, Stubbs was on board. All he needed was to talk to you two about the paperwork for the permits."

"So your father had no motive to hurt him?" Victoria said, as they paused at the top step.

"Just the opposite," Junior answered. "Stubbs was crucial to our getting the project approved. Whoever killed him wanted to stop Oceania."

"Did your father tell you what happened on the boat?" Steve asked.

"Only that he came down the ladder, saw Stubbs with the spear in his chest, tried to get back up to the bridge, then somehow got knocked unconscious. He came to, passed out again. Next thing he knew, they'd crashed on the beach."

Exactly what Uncle Grif told us, Victoria thought. "What about all that money on the boat?"

"That's just Dad. He likes the feel of having lots of cash around."

"The money was in waterproof bags," Steve said. "What was that about?"

Junior shrugged. "On a boat, that makes sense, doesn't it?"

"Actually, there's a lot that doesn't make *any* sense. A hundred thousand on the boat. Forty thousand in Stubbs' hotel room. The spear in Stubbs' chest."

"There's something I should tell you," Junior said. "Something I feel terrible about."

"What?" Victoria asked.

"In a way, I'm responsible for Stubbs' death."

"How?" they asked simultaneously.

"That was my speargun."

■ ■ ■ ■

SOLOMON'S LAWS

■ ■ ■ ■

4. You can sell one improbable event to a jury. A second "improb" is strictly no sale, and a third sends your client straight to prison.

Ten:
The Coral Kisser

"There's something I need to show you that will explain a lot," Junior said.

"The speargun," Steve said, intending to stay on track. "How about an explanation of that?"

"Not a problem. But there's a lot more to this than the speargun."

Junior Griffin was leading the three of them through the foyer of the house, all limestone floors and rich wood paneling. On one wall were brightly colored paintings that seemed to be Haitian in origin. On another, openmouthed, mounted fish, including the largest amberjack Steve had ever seen. Plump and silvery, with a yellow racing stripe, the fellow had to be six feet long. Next to the fat jack was an even more impressive specimen, a blue-striped, scaly-hided, lantern-jawed tarpon that, according to a brass plaque, weighed 271 pounds and was caught by Hal Griffin off the coast of

Cuba on a twenty-pound test line. It must have been a hell of a fight, Steve thought, reading the inscription: *Runner-up, Ernest Hemingway International Fishing Tournament.* For a moment, Steve wondered whether the owner of the *Force Majeure* was ever satisfied with second place.

"I have quite a collection of spearguns," Junior said. "Excalibur, Rhino, Beuchat, plus some classic handmade mahogany and teak guns from the fifties and sixties. And I make my own. Made an eight-bander that can bring down a thousand-pound tuna."

What Steve really wanted to know was who brought down a 160-pound guy with a P-4 Civil Service rating. "The gun that shot Stubbs," he said, "where'd you keep it?"

"In a compartment on the *Force Majeure.* I shoot lobsters with it."

"It's illegal to spear lobsters," Steve said, contemplating a citizen's arrest.

"In Florida waters, maybe. Not in the Bahamas."

So who speared Stubbs, beach boy? That's illegal just about everywhere.

They walked into an open living room with curved walls two stories high. Windows looked out on the cove, where palm fronds fluttered in the ocean breeze. The place was all handcrafted woods. Maple floors, redwood beams, cherry panels. To Steve, the house resembled the interior of a fine yacht. "Did your father know where you kept the gun?"

Junior shrugged and his deltoids rippled as if shocked with a cattle prod. "The gun was mixed in with some fishing gear. I'm sure he'd seen it, but I doubt Dad would even know how to load the thing."

"But you know how."

"Sure."

"In-ter-esting. Very interesting." Steve was trying to sound profound, but managed to sound like a pompous twit, even to himself.

"What's the big deal?" Junior asked.

The big deal, Steve thought, was that he wanted to place the murder weapon in someone's hand, someone's other than his client's. If that hand belonged to Zorro at Bunny Flagler's costume party, well tough shit.

"Yes, Ste-phen." Victoria made his name sound like a streptococcus. "What is the big deal?"

She was pissed, Steve knew. He'd promised to let her take the lead, had even meant it at the time. But once they got here, once the game began, he just couldn't back off. Hey, you don't pinch hit for Alex Rodriguez.

Bobby piped up: "Uncle Steve wants to

pin the murder on the hottest boy at Pine-crest."

"I know, Bobby," Victoria said. "I just wanted to hear Steve say it."

Steve wished that Bobby didn't have the irksome habit of speaking only the truth, a real anomaly in the Solomon household. Turning to Junior, Steve asked: "Where were you when your father and Stubbs took the boat out?"

"Taking a swim."

"By yourself?"

"I'm a big boy, Solomon."

Bobby said: "What Uncle Steve means, do you have an alibi witness?"

Junior laughed. "Only the barracuda who likes to tail me."

"Cool," Bobby said.

"Look, Solomon. I had no motive to kill Stubbs."

"No apparent motive," Steve corrected him.

"Don't be a dick, Steve," Victoria said.

"It's okay, Tori," Junior interposed. "I know you guys have a job to do." As they started up a maple staircase to the second floor, he said: "If you're interested, I've got a theory about what happened."

"What is it?" Victoria asked. Eager now.

Yeah, Steve thought. Show us something

besides your fast-twitch muscle fibers.

"I think Stubbs might have found the spear-gun and started fooling around with it," Junior said. "It's an old pneumatic model. The Poseidon Mark 3000. Works on air pressure instead of bands. If he tried to jam a shaft down the barrel and did it wrong, the spear could fire."

"Why would Stubbs even handle the gun?" Victoria wanted to know.

Junior shrugged again, his lats joining his delts in a little muscle dance. "Why do kids take their fathers' revolvers out of night-stands?"

"So if Stubbs shot himself, who slugged your father?" Steve asked, before Victoria could slip in another question.

"No one. After Dad found Stubbs, he rushed up the ladder to get back to the bridge. Dad had been drinking — they both had — and he was excited. The ladder's wet from spray. He slips and falls, conking his head."

They stopped in front of a wide set of double doors, Junior fishing for a key from a pocket of his shorts. Junior didn't lock up his spearguns, Steve thought, but he needed a key to get into whatever room he was go-ing to show them.

"I can sell swampland to alligators," Steve

said, "but that story stinks like old mackerel. The problem is, you're compounding multiple improbables."

"The hell does that mean?"

"Tell him, Vic."

She nailed Steve with a look that said she didn't like being ordered to perform. Then said: "One of Steve's theories."

"Not just a theory. A law. The Solomonic Law of Compounding Improbables. Vic, you do the honors."

Again, she shot Steve a look. "Stubbs shooting himself," Victoria said, "that's one improbable event. Your dad falling down the ladder and knocking himself out, that's two. A boat without a driver crashing on the exact beach where it was supposed to dock, that's three. There's a multiplier effect. Each improbable event makes the others harder to believe."

"And easier for a jury to convict," Steve said.

"Say a man takes his boat out fishing on Christmas Eve, though he has virtually no history of fishing," Victoria said. "And his pregnant wife disappears the same day. Months later, her body and the baby's body wash up onshore in nearly the same place as the guy went fishing. A place the guy went back to when he claimed he was somewhere else."

"The Scott Peterson case," Junior said, unlocking the doors.

"His defense compounded too many improbables," Victoria said, as they walked into a darkened room that seemed cooler than the rest of the house.

Steve smiled to himself. As much as Victoria complained about his lawyering, she was picking up his techniques.

Why doesn't she realize what a winning team we are?

"Steve's created a mathematical formula around the theory," she continued.

"One of Solomon's Laws," Steve said. "I call it squaring the improbables: 'If you have one chance in three of convincing jurors of an improbable event, you have one chance in nine of convincing them of two, and —' "

"One chance in eighty-one of convincing them of three," Bobby calculated.

"Exactly. In other words, no chance in hell."

Junior flicked on a light switch, and a tiny spotlight in the perimeter of the ceiling came on. They were in a huge, windowless room, bathed in shadows. "What I'm going to show you," Junior said, "only a few people have seen. Stubbs was one of them."

Steve squinted, trying to make out the

shape rising from the middle of the room, but could see nothing but shadows. This was all a bit theatrical for his taste. He had the feeling that Junior was putting on a show for them. Or more likely, just for Victoria.

"You have to know something about my background for this to make any sense," Junior said. With the four of them standing in the half-light of the cool room, Junior spent the next few minutes explaining that over the years, with all the time he spent on the water, he'd become a deeply committed environmentalist.

Save the Whales.

Protect the Reefs.

Ban Tuna Nets.

The whole range of do-gooder ocean projects. Junior said he'd given away chunks of money to environmental groups, probably, he thought now, as penance for his father's actions. Hal Griffin, his son admitted, was a one-man tsunami when it came to ecosystems. Blowing opponents out of the water, literally sinking a Greenpeace boat in Sydney Harbor by ramming it with a barge. His old man was a major-league pillager, an All-Pro despoiler, his projects a dishonor roll of moneymaking, havoc-wreaking, eco-disasters. Eroded beaches from shoreline condos in the Philippines, massive fish kills off Jamaica after dredging a marina, a vicious sewage runoff from a gated community in the Caicos Islands.

"Everywhere Dad goes, environmentalists come after him with elephant guns."

But does Dad go after others with spearguns? Steve wondered. Whereas the son, by his own immodest admission, was Sir Galahad of the Deep.

"You've heard of tree huggers," Junior said. "Call me a coral kisser. I've snorkeled the world's best, and they're all living on borrowed time. The coral reefs are the rain forests of the oceans."

"All of which has exactly what to do with Oceania?" Steve asked.

"A couple years ago," Junior continued, "I was arguing with Dad and said something like, 'You won't be happy till you build a resort right on top of a coral reef.' And Dad took it as a challenge. He asked where there's a coral reef at least three nautical miles offshore from an English-speaking country, with a population center of at least three million people nearby."

"Why three miles?" Victoria asked.

"So it's outside territorial waters," Junior said.

"The cannon-shot rule," Bobby said, and

they all looked at the smartest boy in the sixth grade. "From pirate days. Four hundred years ago, the farthest a cannon could shoot from shore was three miles. That's where the law comes from."

"Thank you, Mr. History Channel," Steve said, then turned to Junior. "If you're outside the three-mile limit, you can run a casino. That the idea?"

"Exactly. But we'd still be within the two-hundred-mile EEZ."

Steve gave him a blank look.

"The Exclusive Economic Zone," Bobby translated, adding sheepishly, "I know most of the federal acronyms. Also most of the personalized license plates banned by the State of Florida."

"Don't start," Steve warned him.

"G-R-8-C-U-M," Bobby said. "I-W-N-T-S-E-X."

"Bobby . . ."

"B-I-G-P-N-S."

"Cool it, kiddo!"

"Because we're in the EEZ," Junior said, "the federal government still has jurisdiction over development. So we need an environmental assessment report to get a federal permit."

"Ben Stubbs of the EPA," Victoria mused.

"Yep. Which is why Dad had to jump

through all the hoops. He was cussing all the way, but he did it. And here's the result."

Junior flicked another switch, and the enormous room was bathed in a soft light. "Behold Oceania," he said.

Looming in front of them was a three-dimensional diorama, maybe thirty feet long by seven feet high. From floor to shoulder level was the ocean — or at least a blue Lucite rendition of it, complete with miniature, plasticized fish. Floating on the surface were three donut-shaped buildings, connected by covered passageways. From the bottom of each building, steel cables angled downward and were embedded in the ocean floor. At the side of the center building was a marina with perhaps two hundred miniature boats, little plastic people waving gaily from the decks. Above the hotel, suspended in the air by a wire, was a seaplane, a larger version of what they had flown to Paradise Key.

"The center building is the casino," Junior said. "Two hundred thirty thousand square feet of slots, blackjack, craps, roulette, keno, poker rooms. The works. And unlike Atlantic City or Las Vegas, no taxes to pay. Or as Dad likes to say, 'Uncle Sam ain't no relative of mine.' "

"How would you get people out there?" Victoria asked. Ever practical, Steve thought.

"Seaplanes, private boats, hydrofoils leaving the mainland every thirty minutes."

"What about hurricanes?" Steve asked.

"We'd evacuate the hotel, of course," Junior said. "But our construction method is revolutionary. Woven steel cables fasten the buildings to the sea bottom, but they're flexible, so the buildings can rise and fall in high seas. Computer models show we can withstand a Category Four storm."

"What about Category Five?" Steve asked.

"Statistically improbable. Only two have ever hit the United States."

Bobby chimed in: "Camille in sixty-nine. Andrew in ninety-two."

The kid watched the Weather Channel, too. "You're not counting the ones before the Weather Service had a numbering system," Steve said.

"We're confident our hotel can take the worst storm that's statistically likely to hit," Junior said.

The worst storm that's statistically likely to hit.

Not bad, Steve thought, giving Junior bonus points for lawyerlike double-talk. The guy was sharper than he looked, greater than the sum of his pecs and traps.

"You haven't seen the best part," Junior

said. "Take a look at Building Three. We call it The Atlantis."

They walked around to the other side of the diorama. The ocean floor sloped upward there, as it neared the largest of the donut-shaped buildings. But it wasn't just a sandy bottom. It was a coral reef in miniature, frozen in plastic, reproduced in startling detail. Staghorn coral, looking like deer antlers; green sea fans waving hello; grooved brain coral, looking like a human cerebrum. A moray eel poked its head out of a skyscraper of pillar coral. Swimming above and through the reef were giant grouper, bright blue angelfish, multihued parrotfish, huge tarpon, sea turtles, and other creatures Steve couldn't name.

"The Atlantis seems submerged." Victoria pointed beneath the building. This donut was more like a floating saucer, with a portion of the building under the surface, portholes beneath the sea.

"My idea." Junior's smile was so wide, his dimples looked like gunshot wounds. "Three hundred hotel rooms underwater. You can watch the fish swim by your window."

And in fact, there were two sharks cruising past a porthole window. Thrill the folks from Omaha without getting their feet wet.

"If you look closely at the passageways connecting the buildings, you'll see the floors are transparent. Stroll from the dining room to the casino and you're walking across the world's largest aquarium."

"Incredible," Victoria murmured. "The hotel is a giant glass-bottom boat."

Junior smiled. "I told Dad that most people will never take the snorkeling or scuba trip. So, if you're going to build a hotel above a reef, why not bring the reef into the hotel? Or damn close, anyway."

"It's really something," Victoria said. Awe in her voice, as if Junior had just shown her the *Mona Lisa* and said he painted it.

Big deal, Steve thought. The rich kid tells the architects to stick portholes in the hotel rooms. What's he want, the Nobel Prize?

"Here's where Dad surprised me," Junior said. "The construction costs will be astronomical, so at first he balked. A real sense of arrière-pensée."

"I hate it when that happens," Steve said. Thinking: *What the hell did he say: "derriere penises"?*

"That means he had doubts," Bobby piped up. "Uncertainty. Reservations."

"But Dad's so smart," Junior continued. "He thought it over and realized that the marketing hook was the reef with underwa-

128

ter hotel rooms right above it. It's the sizzle of the steak. Nothing like it anywhere in the world."

Junior rattled on for a few more minutes about the state-of-the-art desalinization plant, the solar-powered generators, the recycling plant that grinds leftover prime rib into fish food. Steve wasn't giving it his full attention. Instead, he was trying to take the measure of Junior Griffin, prep-school make-out artist turned thick-chested free diver who oozed lethal levels of testosterone from every pore.

"So, what could have been an environmental disaster will be a beacon to the world for safe construction in environmentally sensitive areas," Junior said. "Construction in harmony with nature."

Jeez, he's giving a speech to the Kiwanis.

"You must be so proud," Victoria said in a gushing tone that Steve interpreted to mean, *"You are the sexiest and most wonderful man in the universe, and if I can dump my boyfriend, I'd like to have your babies, starting nine months from today."*

Steve kept trying to size up the guy, which was hard to do objectively because he was growing so aggravated with Victoria. But it occurred to him that maybe he'd been mistaken about Junior. The guy's save-the-planet shtick seemed sincere. Of course, not having to work for a living gives you free time for wholesome hobbies. Back in college, Steve had joined the ACLU. At the time, he had few political opinions, but he figured that left-leaning coeds were easy to bag.

A stray thought began to gnaw at him, a vague notion that there was something wrong with Mr. Right. What was it?

It only took a moment. It's so obvious, Steve thought, all the while realizing that his powers of reasoning might be tainted by jealousy, envy, and fear.

The son-of-a-bitch is just too good to be true.

Which meant that he was a phony. And with any luck, a murderer, too.

ELEVEN:
THE SECRETS
PARENTS KEEP

"Do you remember the time your father took us to that hot dog place on the causeway?" Victoria asked.

"Fun Fair," Junior said.

"You ate ten chili dogs on a dare."

"Twelve. With onions. I got sick in the back of Dad's Bentley."

"And do you remember what we did on your fourteenth birthday?" she prodded.

"Skinny-dipped in the Venetian pool."

"Nope. We carved our initials on a banyan tree."

"Right. Bayfront Park," Junior remembered. "A security guard chased us."

"And we jumped over that concrete wall to hide. . . ."

"But it was a sea wall, and we landed in four feet of water."

Laughter. From two out of three, anyway. Steve's expression was both aggravated and distant, as if fretting about something he could do nothing about, the sliding value of the dollar, maybe. "Could I bring you two back from Memory Lane a second?"

"Sure thing," Junior said.

Do we have to? Victoria thought.

"I never saw anything in the papers about Oceania," Steve began, "never heard anyone in the Keys talking about it."

"Dad didn't want the gambling industry finding out what we were doing until we had the federal permits," Junior explained. "What do you think the lobbyists for Atlantic City and the Gulf casinos would do to stop us?"

"Bribe a congressman or two," Victoria suggested.

"And if that didn't work?"

"Kill Stubbs and frame your father," Steve said. "You're saying a competitor did it."

"Who else would have a better motive?" Junior said.

It had been fifteen minutes since Junior relocked the double doors to the Oceania room. The three adults — if you counted Steve — lay on chaise lounges on an outdoor deck overlooking the cove. A pitcher of margaritas with a platter of tortilla chips and fresh-made guacamole sat on a table in the shade of an umbrella. A man-made waterfall poured over rocks into a small pond stocked with fish and long-necked swans. Bobby was wading in the pond, trying to talk swan language to the big birds.

Junior's cell phone had rung several times, reporters calling. Following their instructions, Junior expressed his father's regret at Stubbs' demise and declined comment on everything else. Helicopters from three Miami TV stations hovered over the island like noisy mosquitoes. One buzzed so low, it stirred the cove into a white froth. The crews got their footage, then powered north again.

Now, as Steve ran through his questions, Victoria sorted out her feelings. She felt slightly decadent, reclining on a wicker chaise lounge, sinking into the cocoa-colored cushions, sipping tequila on a workday afternoon, with two hot guys. One was her lover and potential life mate and the other once seemed destined for that role. Over the years, she had wondered about Junior. What kind of man had he become?

To start with, an awesome hunkalicious man, but he seems so much more than his physicality.

A decent, smart, caring man. All that time and money he spent on worthwhile causes.

And look at Oceania, something that could have been an environmental holocaust, but thanks to Junior could become an environmental showplace, a stunning blend of commerce and nature.

So, Steve, what do you think of Junior now?

Sure, Junior had enjoyed a privileged life. But he wasn't the spoiled rich kid Steve had predicted — and spitefully wanted — him to be.

Now, in the shade of an umbrella, the same cocoa print fabric as the chaise cushions, with Junior's coppery-bronzy tan accentuating his bright smile, with his sun-streaked thatch of hair, with his six-pack of abs rigid as body armor and his carved deltoids rippling with each movement of his bare arms, with his strong jaw with that devilish cleft, he was . . .

Oh, hell, just say it, or at least think it.

If I were standing, my knees would have buckled by now.

Not to get overheated about it, but he was the closest thing to a Greek god she'd ever seen. A modern Adonis, who, if she remembered her course at Princeton, Fables and Myths, got it on with Aphrodite, notwithstanding the lady's marriage to somebody-or-other. Was she feeling a little like Aphrodite, the trampy goddess of passion, who also peeled grapes with Ares, Dionysus, and a few other guy-gods Victoria couldn't remember?

Jeez, am I so superficial that his looks, his luscious total maleness, turns me into mush?

No, of course not. It was just a healthy sexual fantasy, right? Like Steve studying the *Sports Illustrated* swimsuit issue more closely than any appellate court decision. She wondered if Steve was picking up her vibes. Could he tell what she was thinking — and feeling — about Junior?

"Great margaritas," Steve allowed, sipping at his drink.

Okay, she thought, maybe he wasn't tuned to her channel just now.

"Fresh-squeezed lime juice," Junior explained. "No matter what anyone tells you, don't go for the cheaper tequila just because you're mixing drinks. Arette's best. Blanco Suave, if you're willing to spend a hundred bucks a bottle. Now, if you're sipping tequila straight, go for Tres, Cuatro y Cinco, blue agave, but that will set you back four hundred bucks."

"Seems like a lot of money for something that's gonna turn into piss in twenty minutes," Steve countered. Mr. *Savoir Vivre.*

"Depends what's important to you, I guess," Junior said.

What *was* important to Steve? she wondered. His nephew, Bobby, of course. His work. And her. But how important was she? Getting Steve to open up was a lot like opening a jar of martini olives. It helps if you bang on his lid a few times.

Steve's tongue flicked a salt crystal from the rim of the margarita glass. He had a faraway look, and Victoria knew he wasn't thinking about their relationship. Or the Florida Marlins. Or even Bobby. He was getting into the case, and his look told her something was bothering him.

"I still don't get it," Steve said. "A project as big as Oceania. How'd you keep it quiet?"

"Dad's good at keeping secrets," Junior said, "and not just about business."

"Meaning what?"

"After Nelson passed away —"

"Committed suicide," Victoria interrupted the Greek god, preferring plain English to euphemisms. "My father committed suicide."

That silenced both men for a moment. Victoria instantly regretted having altered everyone's mood, especially her own. But she was still furious at her father and probably always would be. The mention of his name, of his death, brought back the pain.

"After your father committed suicide,"

Junior continued, looking at her with tenderness, "I kept bugging Dad to tell me why he did it. The two of them were inseparable. Our mothers were best friends. You and I were, you know . . ."

Destined to be a couple.

She had finished the sentence in her mind while sipping her drink. "What did your father say?"

"Nothing. Except, 'I'm sure Nelson had his reasons.'"

"He didn't even leave a note," Victoria said. "I was twelve, and all these years I've hated him for not even leaving a note. Why couldn't he just write, 'My darling daughter, I'm sorry. Please forgive me. I always loved you.'"

Neither man had an answer. Steve dipped a chip into the guacamole. He wanted to talk about the case but seemed to realize he'd have to wait out the talk about family.

After a moment, Junior said, "What did your mother tell you about it?"

"Not much. There was a Grand Jury investigation. Something about kickbacks and bribes in the construction industry. Dad got subpoenaed and committed suicide right before he was scheduled to testify." Victoria drained the margarita quicker than she had intended. "The Queen never would

137

go into details. So I guess your father's not the only one to keep secrets."

"My theory is that Dad put all the pressure on Nelson to take care of the legal problems," Junior said. "When they had some setbacks, it was too much for him. And ever since, Dad's felt guilty."

"Is that why he stayed away all these years?" she asked.

"Dad didn't stay away. He sent all those checks."

"What checks?"

Junior seemed surprised. "I guess The Queen never told you. For a couple years, Dad sent her checks, but she didn't cash them."

"Why? What'd she tell your father?"

"I don't think they spoke after the funeral. Not even once."

"Maybe she had trouble reaching him. You guys moved out of the country. You disappeared from our lives."

"He wrote her, Tori. Tried to call, too. But no response."

Why? Victoria wondered. And why hadn't her mother told her? That was Irene Lord for you. Secrecy and stoicism were the currencies The Queen traded in. You don't go around whining about your husband's suicide. You don't examine it. You give it a handy label — *"business pressures, your father cracked"* — and you move on.

The Queen had stored away the memories in an attic trunk and kept the key from her only daughter. But Uncle Grif must know what's inside. Now Victoria had another mission, having nothing to do with the murder case. She would learn everything she could from Uncle Grif. This meant spending more time with him, getting to know him all over again. And while she was at it, that applied to Junior, too.

■ ■ ■ ■

Solomon's Laws

■ ■ ■ ■

5. "Love" means taking a bullet for your
   beloved. Anything short of that is just
   "like."

Twelve:
Four Suspects

Maybe it was the tropical sun beating down on Steve or the potent Arette tequila that fogged him in, or the uncertainty — yeah, the *arrière-pensée* — triggered by Junior's muscular presence. Or did it start with Victoria refusing to have sex in the water, then insisting they split up the firm? Steve couldn't tell.

Wasted away again in Margaritaville, he was sprawled on a chaise lounge three feet away from the woman he loved. Three feet on the other side was the suntanned slab of beef who was obviously putting the moves on her. Even worse, she seemed receptive, her eyes shiny with anticipation, her body language open and inviting.

Maybe it was his own fault, Steve thought. Had he driven her away? But how? He didn't have a clue.

In the whole wide world, there were two people he cherished with his lifeblood. Victoria and Bobby. Meaning he'd take a bullet for either of them. Without hesitation, no questions asked. Given the cosmic choice — the voice of God claiming his life or theirs — Steve would sacrifice himself. Deep down, Steve believed he loved his pain-in-the-ass father, too. But giving up his life for the old man was a stretch.

"Another margarita?" Junior offered. "Milagros can make a couple more pitchers." A Spanish-speaking woman in a white uniform stood at a discreet distance on the deck, waiting for her master's instructions.

"No thanks," Steve said. "We've got work to do."

"Anything I can do, just ask," Junior volunteered.

Just how much should he tell Junior? Steve didn't describe how he always broke down a murder case into its component parts. The prosecutorial cliché was that there are three elements to a crime. In a circumstantial case — a case without an eyeball witness — you get a conviction by proving that the defendant had the *motive, opportunity,* and *means* to commit the murder.

In State of Florida versus Harold Griffin, there'd be no trouble proving opportunity. Two men go out on a boat. When it reaches shore — *hits* shore — one man has a spear in his chest. Talk about simple math.

There'd surely be the means, too; the defendant knew there was a speargun on the boat and had easy access to it.

But motive was the state's problem. Griffin had no apparent reason to kill Stubbs. Hell, he *needed* Stubbs alive. Needed him to turn in a favorable environmental report on Oceania. Which, apparently, the man had been ready to do. Weren't they all going to celebrate by feasting on lobster jambalaya at Louie's while toasting Oceania with expensive champagne and Cuban cigars?

So Steve came to the studied conclusion — all the while knowing, this ain't rocket science — that Hal Griffin was probably right.

Whoever killed Stubbs wanted to deep-six Oceania. And to defend Griffin, we gotta find that person.

Or persons. Again Steve remembered Stubbs raising two fingers in his hospital bed.

He squinted into the sun and turned to Junior, who was soaking up rays himself. "We need a list of everyone who knew what your father was planning out in the Gulf."

"Not a problem," Junior said.

"Plus everyone with a financial stake in Oceania."

"You got it."

"And everyone who knew that your father was taking Stubbs out on that boat."

"Easy," Junior said. "They're all the same people."

"Good," Steve said. "Give us their names and addresses."

"I can do better than that," Junior said, stirring from the chaise. "C'mon. Let's go to the movies."

It's nice to own an island, Steve thought. And have your own seaplane. And a mansion built on a cove. And your own cozy little movie theater.

They had gone into what Junior modestly called the "media room," which turned out to be an elaborate mini movie theater with a proscenium entrance, Doric columns, motorized curtains the color of blood, and leather recliners that, according to Junior, rumbled and rattled to enhance big action sequences. They were not there, however, to watch a *Terminator* or *Matrix* flick.

They were there to review the security video shot by mounted cameras on the dock twenty-four hours earlier. As they sank into cushy leather love seats, Junior used a remote to dim the lights.

"Sorry about the decor," Junior said,

gesturing with the remote.

"What's to be sorry about?" Steve asked.

"I wanted more of a Zen design," Junior answered. "Earth tones. Clean lines. A more meditative feel. But you know Dad, Tori."

Victoria laughed. "Uncle Grif's more the Roman Colosseum type."

"Exactly. Years ago, when Caesar's Palace opened in Vegas, Dad thought it was too subtle."

Steve watched as a grainy black-and-white image flickered onto the large screen. There was the *Force Majeure,* tied up at the dock, several hours before it had vaulted ashore and split in two like a coconut. The image on the screen changed. The angle sharper, the distance closer. There was no audio.

"There are three security cameras behind the house on the dock side," Junior told them. "The recording alternates from one to the other every seven seconds."

On the screen, two men were sitting on the fighting chairs in the cockpit of the boat. One was Clive Fowles, the pilot with the British accent. The other was a broad-shouldered African-American man. He wore a flowery islands shirt and khaki safari shorts. He was animated, talking while gesturing with both hands. Fowles nodded, listening, while sipping a drink.

"That's Leicester Robinson with Fowles," Junior said. "Robinson Barge and Tow. A native Conch, fifth generation Key West, at least. Leicester has the Oceania contract to ferry workers and material to the site."

"So no motive to stop the project," Steve said.

"Just the opposite. He would have made a fortune."

"Would have?" Victoria tucked a leg underneath her. "You make it sound like the project's dead."

"Not dead, Tori. But we have to face facts. No more stealth permits. Oceania's gonna come under intense scrutiny. The gambling lobby will line up against us. Indian money. Casino money. And if Dad's convicted of murder, everything stops."

"But if he's acquitted . . ."

"In projects this size, there's a momentum factor. You line up the investment bankers and the foreign investors and the insurance carriers, and you gotta move quickly. Any unfavorable publicity, delays, scandals . . . the bad karma spreads like a red tide."

"Anything else about Robinson we should know?" Steve asked.

"He's a character," Junior said. "He puts on this tough-guy exterior. Wears a skull-and-crossbones ring because his ancestors were supposedly pirates. Pilots tugboats and operates barges and knows how to handle cranes and pile drivers. But he's got an English degree from Amherst, a master's in history, too. If he hadn't come home to take over the family business, he'd probably be some Ivy League professor."

In Steve's experience, history professors were unlikely assassins unless they bored you to death. "What about Fowles?"

"Ex–British Navy. Submariner. Fought in the Falklands. Was living in the Bahamas trying to build two-man submarines when Dad met him. Boat captain. Scuba diver. Pilot. Jack-of-all-trades. He's been with Dad fifteen years."

"Trustworthy?"

"A good man. Drinks a little too much, but down here, who doesn't?"

"What's Fowles' connection to Oceania?" Victoria asked.

"Overall troubleshooter during construction," Junior replied. "Dive master once we start reef tours for the guests."

Again, no motive, Steve thought.

"On his days off, Fowles takes marine biology students out to the reef for cleanup dives," Junior said. "They haul up all the crap the boaters toss overboard. Once a year he takes a fish census."

"What's he do, knock on the coral?" Steve inquired. "Ask how many barracuda live there?"

"He counts fish with a bunch of volunteer divers. It's how you judge the health of the ecosystem. Fowles is an excellent diver, really knows his sea life. He'd be the key man for the underwater tours."

On the screen, the glass door to the salon slid open, and Junior walked out. Wearing his Speedos. Barefoot and bare-chested, as usual. He said something to Robinson and Stubbs, then climbed the ladder to the fly bridge, graceful as a high diver scooting up the ten-meter board. Once he got to the control panel, he hit some switches.

"Checking the NOAA weather for Dad," he explained.

The salon door opened again, and this time, a tall, caramel-complexioned woman with long, dark hair stepped into the cockpit. The woman seemed to blink against the glare of the sun, then put on large, stylish sunglasses. She wore a light-colored, low-cut, spaghetti-strapped sundress, and for just a moment, as she walked across the cockpit, hips in full, fluid motion, breasts straining at the thin fabric, Steve thought she resembled a young Sophia Loren. One difference, though. He had never made love

150

to Sophia Loren.

"Who's that?" Victoria asked. Putting a little disapproval into the "that," Steve thought.

"Ah," Junior said. "That sweet confection is —"

"Delia Bustamante!" Steve immediately regretted the exhilaration in his voice.

Victoria turned toward him, studied his profile in the semidarkness. "You know her, Steve?"

"Last I saw her," Steve said carefully, aiming for nonchalance, "she owned a Cuban restaurant in Key West."

Victoria kept quiet, but he could read her cross-examining mind. *"And just when was the last time you saw her?"*

"Havana Viejo," Junior helped out. "Great Cuban food. Plus, Delia's on the Monroe County Environmental Advisory Board. Dad brought her into his circle, tried to get her support. Even offered her a consultant's job in food services at Oceania. Big bucks, little work."

"In other words, a bribe?" Steve said.

"A well-intended favor," Junior replied. For a beach bum, he had a way with words.

"If I know Delia, she wouldn't go for it," Steve said. Feeling Victoria alongside, shifting onto one hip on the love seat.

"Delia told Dad that Oceania was a blight," Junior continued. "Worse than drilling for oil. She raised all the bugaboos. Pollution in the Gulf. Traffic congestion at the hydrofoil ports. Increase in crime up and down the Keys. Gambling addictions, poor slobs tossing the rent money into the slots. She was gonna blow the project out of the water. Her exact words."

"I can picture Delia saying that," Steve said, "but I don't see her killing anyone."

"How would you know that?" Victoria asked, her tone even.

"Some things you intuitively know about people."

"Just how well do you know her?" Her voice still neutral, so clean as to be positively antiseptic.

"Before you and I met, like a couple years before we met, Delia and I . . ."

What was the word? What was the phrase they were using these days? "Hooked up"? But that was so juvenile, and he was, after all, an adult, at least chronologically.

"Fucked each other's brains out?" Victoria suggested. Ever helpful.

"Well," Steve said. "Not only that."

Aargh. He'd blundered. Because, in fact, his relationship with Delia had been pretty much limited to mutual lust. He lusted for her luscious *lechon asado* as well as her luscious self. He'd gained ten pounds in the short time they'd dated.

Her thing was having sex out-of-doors, something that seemed more enticing in the telling than the doing, once you've rolled bare-assed over pine needles a few times. Their long-distance coupling — it's a four-hour drive from Miami — lasted three months. Either she'd run out of locations to expose her ass to the moonlight, or he'd gotten tired of her roasted pork and sweet plantains. He couldn't quite remember which. So his "not only that" was both misleading and destined to bring another unwanted question.

"What else was it besides sex?" Victoria's tone took on the flavor of the prosecutor she once was. "Just how would you describe the relationship?"

"Brief," Steve said. "I'd describe it as brief."

"Well, perhaps you'll have some insight into Ms. Bustamante when we interview her."

Was Steve imagining it, or did Victoria hit the "we" a little hard?

On the screen, several things happened in the next few moments. Delia seemed to say her good-byes to Fowles and Robinson.

153

Then Fowles offered an arm so she could step onto the dock, showing some tapered calves as she left.

Moments later, the salon door opened again and Griffin walked out, talking over his shoulder to someone following him. Ben Stubbs. Looking considerably better than he had in the ICU. A slim man, in his forties. Skinny legs under baggy khaki shorts, a paper-shuffler's paunch visible under his polo shirt, deck shoes with socks. He actually looked like a Washington bureaucrat on vacation.

A few more flicks of the cameras, and Griffin was gesturing toward Stubbs. One hand, then the other, then both. Were they angry gestures?

Steve leaned forward. "Was your father arguing with Stubbs?"

"Don't know. I was up on the bridge, and the radio was on."

"Did you know your father was stopping at an island to pick up lobsters?"

In the darkness next to him, Junior shrugged. "Never mentioned it to me."

On the screen, Robinson and Fowles stepped onto the dock. That left just three people on the boat, the two Griffins and Stubbs. Then Hal Griffin climbed the ladder to the fly bridge, the captain about to

154

take command. Stubbs stayed in the cock-pit, plopping down in one of the fighting chairs. On the dock, Fowles came back into view, kneeling near the bow, untying a line from a cleat, and tossing it aboard. Back on the fly bridge, Griffin said something to Junior and gave him an affectionate clop on the shoulder. Junior climbed onto the rail and balanced there a moment, looking like some ancient statue intended to deify the human form. He turned to face the water, his profile to the camera. Even on the grainy video, one thing was clear — that damn bulge in his Speedos.

On the screen, Junior reached over his head, flexed his knees. Then he did a perfect swan dive into the water, clearing the starboard side of the boat by inches and disappearing from view.

"Like I told you before, I went for a swim," Junior said, casually.

"Really?" Steve said. "I thought you were auditioning for La Quebrada."

"The Acapulco cliffs? I dived them when I was in college. Spring break. You?"

"I would have but I was getting arrested in Daytona Beach," Steve claimed. On the screen, the boat blocked any view of Junior. "Where'd you swim to?"

"Around the island. Five miles. I do it

every day."

"So when you finished your swim, the cameras would have picked you up again, right?"

"They would, if I'd come back to the dock," Junior explained. "But I always finish at the beach, and there aren't any cameras there."

Meaning an incomplete alibi, Steve thought.

On the dock, Fowles tossed the stern line aboard, and water churned as the engines started up.

And then there were two. Just Hal Griffin and Ben Stubbs on the Force Majeure *as it headed out of the cove.*

Griffin steered the boat toward open water. Stubbs got out of the fighting chair and walked to the rail, smiling and waving to someone onshore. In a moment, the boat was out of camera range.

"So that's it," Junior said. "Everybody connected with Oceania was there."

"But everybody got off the boat, except your father," Victoria said.

"That doesn't rule out somebody finding a way to get back on," Steve said.

"Okay," Junior said. "Then you've got Clive Fowles, Leicester Robinson, and Delia Bustamante. Three suspects."

"Four, actually," Steve said, looking straight at Junior.

THIRTEEN:
VENOMS TO LOSE

The old Caddy was just north of mile marker 106, headed toward Miami. Steve drove, Victoria alongside, with Bobby reading in the backseat. His grandfather had bought a Harry Potter book, but Bobby had left it behind and brought along a collection of John Updike's early stories. The little wizard — Bobby, not Harry — had already gone through his Philip Roth stage.

" 'He was robed in this certainty,' " Bobby read aloud, " 'that the God who had lavished such craft upon these worthless birds would not destroy His whole Creation by refusing to let David live forever.' "

"What the hell's that?" Steve demanded.

" 'Pigeon Feathers,' " Bobby said. "A boy shoots some pigeons in his family's barn. It's all about the inevitability of death."

"Jeez, Vic. Did you give that to him?" Steve said.

"Bobby wanted something challenging,"

Victoria said.

"How about cleaning his room?" Steve suggested. "That seems to be quite a challenge."

"Don't discourage Bobby from reading fine literature," Victoria said.

"Or how about doing your homework for once, kiddo?"

"Bor-ing," Bobby sang out.

"And what's with that note I got from your social studies teacher? Two demerits for insubordination?"

"All I did was ask: 'If vegetarians eat vegetables, what do humanitarians eat?' "

"Nobody likes a smart-ass, kiddo."

"Re-al-ly?" Bobby and Victoria shot back in unison.

One hand on the wheel, Steve grumbled something to himself, stewing over Bobby, or Junior, or even her, Victoria figured. As the tires hummed along the roadway, she thought about the man sitting next to her. Her feelings for Steve were so scrambled. They seldom talked about their relationship, never really defined it. They had drifted into monogamy with no plan for the future.

Where are we headed?

Marriage? Steve never brought it up. He had suggested living together, but she thought that had more to do with cutting driving time than a blossoming commitment. They had gotten together while defending Katrina Barksdale on a charge she killed her husband during kinky sex. At the time, Victoria was engaged to Bruce Bigby, avocado grower and grown-up Boy Scout. She had laughed off Steve's flirtations, rebuffed his advances. In truth, she hadn't much liked him. A shark in the courtroom, a wise guy everywhere else. The idea of getting together with him had seemed preposterous.

But something had happened. Steve burned with a joyous fire. He would burst through the courtroom door like a rodeo rider coming out of the chute. Combat juiced him; injustice angered him. Once he believed in his client, he would do anything to win. Sometimes he crossed the line of acceptable behavior, often even erasing it.

"If the law doesn't work, work the law."

At first, Solomon's Laws offended her. And even now Steve's tactics could shock her sense of gentility. But he was right about so many things. You didn't win cases by sticking to the rules carved in the marble pediments. You didn't win by citing precedent. *"Your Honor, referring to the venerable case of Boring versus Snoring . . ."*

You won by finding your opponent's soft spot and attacking. You won with showmanship and flair and, whenever possible, the truth. A trial lawyer is a warrior, a knight in rusty armor, who would often be bloodied but would never surrender. Steve taught her to conquer her fears.

Don't be afraid to lose.

Don't be afraid to look ridiculous.

Don't be afraid to steal home.

He sometimes won impossible cases. When a burglarious client was caught with his fingers lodged in the cash slot of an ATM machine, Steve not only beat the criminal charge, he successfully sued the bank for the man's mashed knuckles.

Steve had style. Prowling the well of the courtroom like a shark in the ocean, woe unto the fatter, slower fish. Where she was tense in trial and could even feel herself trembling during moments of stress, Steve was totally comfortable. It seemed he didn't just own the courtroom, he leased it out to the judge, the prosecutor, the jurors.

Not that the attraction was all intellectual. Steve was undeniably, if unconventionally, sexy. A thatch of dark hair a bit too long. Eyes a deep liquid brown, brightening with mischief. A sly smile, as if he were playing some joke on the world. A bad boy, a sleek male animal with an almost feral look. And an infectious enthusiasm. He had seemed so exciting compared to Bruce Bigby, the South Dade Avocado Growers Man of the Year.

Then there was the night it had snowed in Miami. Victoria and Steve had gone to Bruce's avocado grove to help the workers protect the trees from the frost. Smudge pots curled black smoke into the air; Christmas lights warmed the avocado trees; Benny Moré's love songs played with a bolero beat. It was a wholly surreal and bizarre night, which still did not explain what had happened.

I made love to Steve Solomon in a chickee hut . . . on Bruce's farm. Wearing Bruce's engagement ring! What a slut!

She had lived a life of rigid propriety, had never even cheated on a boyfriend, much less her fiancé. But what a red-hot connection, her feelings crackling with electricity. Of course, the relationship couldn't sustain the heat of those first encounters. Every *affaire d'amour* has its peaks and valleys, she reminded herself.

And ditches and gulleys and sinkholes and deep, deep canyons.

She asked herself: When would she feel that sizzle with Steve again?

When it snows again in Miami?

Then, an even more depressing thought: Had her first impression of Steve been correct? That he was just wrong for her. That any relationship with him would be a ludicrous mistake. From the start Victoria knew she shared little in common with Steve. She was country club, Chardonnay, and paté. He was tavern, burgers, and beer. She had book smarts, winning awards, making law review. He had street smarts, passing the Bar after three tries. Maybe their different backgrounds and talents combined to make them better lawyers and more complete people. That was Steve's pitch, anyway. And true enough, they had a magnificent synergy, as long as they didn't exhaust each other sparring on the way to the courthouse.

Complicating her analysis, enter Junior Griffin, swimming back into her life. Whatever she now felt for Junior was surely wrapped in the mists of nostalgia, a dangerous and misleading emotion. She vowed to keep the relationship with Junior strictly professional. She hadn't kissed another man since that first night with Steve, and she wasn't about to now. She would get through this case, then reevaluate everything. Her professional life. Her personal life. Hell, even her hairstyle.

She shot a look at Steve. He was on the cell phone with Cece Santiago, their assistant. Setting up a deposition in his father's Florida Bar lawsuit. So typical. Plunging ahead even though his father had ordered him to drop the case. Not listening, always thinking he knew more than anyone else.

She glanced out the windshield and said: "You missed the turn."

He clicked off the phone. "I'm taking Card Sound Road."

"It's longer that way," Bobby piped up from the backseat.

"Few minutes, is all."

"So why go that way?" Victoria asked.

"I want to stop at Alabama Jack's. Stretch my legs. Get a brewski."

Brewski, she thought. Like some college frat boy.

"You didn't even ask me," she scolded.

"You don't like beer."

He was either playing dumb or was truly clueless, she thought. "You just plowed ahead. Unilaterally changed the itinerary."

"What's the big deal? We're not visiting the great museums of Europe. We're driving home from the Keys."

"Just typical you," she said.

"Hold on, Vic. Listen to this." He turned

up the volume. On the radio, a local talk-show host named Billy Wahoo was interviewing Willis Rask.

"Sheriff, what can you tell us about the homicide investigation of that fellow from Washington?"

"Unless you're on the Grand Jury, Billy, that's none of your beeswax."

"C'mon now, Sheriff. You can tell our listeners if that multimillionaire Harold Griffin is an interesting person."

"You mean a person of interest, Billy?"

"Whatever."

"Gotta go now. Couple deer stuck in traffic on the Seven Mile Bridge."

"That was enlightening." Steve punched a button on the radio, searching through the stations. "Now, where were we? What were you busting my chops about?"

"Nothing."

"I remember. You're upset because we're stopping for a beer. Or because I didn't ask if you wanted to stop. One of the two."

"I'm not upset." Thinking it wasn't the beer.

It's just you, Steve being Steve.

"Hey, Vic. You wanted the top up, I put the top up. You didn't want to listen to the Marlins game, I didn't put it on. Now, is it okay if I have one cool one before we hit the turnpike?"

"Are you two gonna fight all the way home?" Bobby said, putting down his book.

"We're not fighting," Steve said.

"We're working on our issues," Victoria said.

"What issues?" Steve said. Flummoxed.

He quit changing stations when the radio picked up Jimmy Buffett wailing "Coastal Confessions." Steve tried to sing along, just another tropical troubadour.

What was the point, she wondered, of glorifying beaches and bimbos and lazy days in an alcoholic haze? The Surgeon General ought to put out warning labels: *These songs could turn your children into slackers."*

The tires were singing, too, buzzing across the bridge over Crocodile Lake when Steve turned to her and said: "Anyway, this road's more scenic."

Why did he always have to have the last word? "It's been a long weekend," she said. "Just take me home."

"Other than being thirsty, did I do something wrong here? Because if I did, tell me now instead of next month. I'd like to have a decent enough recollection to defend myself."

"You didn't do anything wrong. You were just you. Stephen Michael Solomon."

"Stephen Michael Solomon," Bobby said, wrinkling his forehead, unscrambling the words in his brain. "COMPLETE MANLINESS. HO. HO."

"Thanks, Bobby," Steve said, then shot a sideways look at Victoria. "Tell me the truth. What'd I do?"

On the berm, a turkey buzzard was hunched over the remains of a possum, picking at its bones. The buzzard, brazen as a trial lawyer, didn't even move as the Caddy blasted past, Jimmy Buffett confessing his misspent youth.

"I don't want to start anything," Victoria said, "but you acted unprofessionally with Junior."

"Did not."

"You practically accused him of murder."

"You guys *are* fighting," Bobby said.

"Pardon me, partner," Steve said, "but I thought a defense lawyer's job was to suggest to the jury that someone other than his client might have committed the crime."

"Not when the someone is the client's only son."

"Is that it? Or is the problem that the client's only son can't possibly be guilty because you get dreamy-eyed around him."

Dammit, she thought. I *was* giving off

vibes. "I don't get dreamy-eyed around *any-body.*"

"Ouch. Somebody pull the knife from my heart."

"Don't play the wounded lover, Steve. It doesn't become you."

"I'm just making an observation. The way you were gawking at Junior, you were practically secreting hormones."

"Estrogen or progesterone?" Bobby asked.

Just when you think Steve's not paying attention, Victoria thought, when he seems to be daydreaming about the Dolphins or a plate of stone crabs or some game where he stole a base — and maybe the petty cash, too — he surprises you.

She would not be defensive. Like a good trial lawyer, she would attack when challenged. "Face it, Steve. You're jealous of Junior."

"That's ridiculous. What's he have that I don't?"

Bobby leaned over the front seat. "He's rich. He's buff and ripped and totally jacked."

"Hey, Bobby," Steve said. "How'd you like to go back to the orphanage?"

"I was never in an orphanage."

"Never too late, kiddo," Steve said.

They rode in a silence a few minutes.

Then, Bobby yelled: "Hey, look at that!"

Over the water, an osprey, its talons wrapped around a fish almost too big to handle, struggled to stay airborne. A second, larger osprey, hovering like a helicopter, tried to tear the fish away with its own talons.

"Put your money on the smaller, quicker bird," Steve said. "The one that grew up hungry."

"You have this preconception about people," Victoria told him as they passed the entrance to the Ocean Reef Club, home to rich snowbirds. "You think everyone who grew up with privilege is spoiled or lazy or degenerate. So it really bothers you that Junior is a good guy, that he cares about people and the environment."

"You can't be objective about him."

"And what about you and Delia-Big-Boobs Bustamante?" She dipped her voice into a pretty fair imitation of Steve's supercilious tone: *"'I don't see Delia killing anyone.'"*

"I know Delia better than you know Junior. You haven't even seen the guy since he hurled chunks of chili dogs in his old man's Bentley."

"What difference does that make? You saw the video. Junior dived off the boat before it

169

left the dock."

"Right. Then where'd he go?"

"For a swim."

"Did you see him doggy-paddling away from the boat?"

She shook her head. "Once he went over the side, he was out of camera range."

"Exactly. And we never saw him come back."

"Because he swam to the beach, not the dock."

"Convenient, wasn't it? Think about it, Vic. The others, Delia, Robinson, Fowles. We clearly see them leave the boat. No way they can get back on without the camera picking them up. But Junior, who knows he's being filmed, makes a big point of diving off and disappearing."

On the radio, the Monotones demanded to know, *"Who wrote the book of love?"*

"What are you saying?" Victoria asked. "That he climbed back on board?"

"So far, it's the only scenario I know that clears our client. Junior's a champion swimmer. He free dives to four hundred feet. He's like that comic book character . . ."

"Aquaman," Bobby helped out.

"Right. How hard would it be for him to climb up the swim ladder or hang on to the dive platform and hitch a ride?" Steve asked. "When Stubbs goes into the cabin to pee, Junior climbs into the cockpit and goes down the rear hatch into the engine room. He comes up through the salon hatch and shoots Stubbs."

"And I suppose Junior clobbered his father, too?"

"Don't know. He may have. Or he may have just figured his father would be arrested for the murder when they docked at Sunset Key. In which case, the story about Griffin falling down the ladder is true."

"And how did Junior get *off* the boat?"

"Easy. They were never more than a few miles offshore the whole trip down from Paradise Key. Junior swims to shore just like that stowaway in that Conrad book I never read. He picks up a car he's hidden and drives home."

"And his motive for all this? For framing his father for murder?"

Steve shrugged. "To take over the company, probably."

"Junior seem like a corporate type to you?"

"Okay, how's this? Junior's a 'coral kisser.' His term, not mine. He loves the reef. He's wondering if maybe Delia's right. Oceania will be a disaster. When Junior can't talk his father out of it, he goes radical, becomes an environmental terrorist."

"Conjecture piled on speculation and topped by guesswork."

"That's called lawyering, Vic. Which, I might remind you, requires an open mind. Creative thinking. Fresh ideas. Not being rigid."

"Who's rigid?" she fired back.

"No-o-o-o-body I know."

God, how she despised that sarcastic tone.

"I'm not going to let you do this," she announced, firmly. "You're not going to screw up Uncle Grif's case just because you're jealous of Junior."

"The beach boy drooling all over you has nothing to do with it. Your lighting up like a slot machine when he's around does piss me off, though."

"Steve, listen. The only interest I have in Junior is helping win the case."

"Really?"

"That and learning more about my own father. The reasons he committed suicide. The reasons my mother won't ever talk about it."

"And that's all it is for you?" he asked.

"That's all," she said, not quite knowing if it was true.

FOURTEEN:
LEXY, REXY . . . AND
PINKY

The next morning was warm and sticky, with fat gray clouds hanging over the Everglades. A sure sign of afternoon thunderstorms. Steve pointed the old Cadillac east and headed across the MacArthur Causeway toward the beach and the offices of Solomon & Lord. The canvas top was down, the only benefit, as far as he knew, of traveling solo.

Victoria had declined his generous invitation to share his bed the night before. He'd dropped her off at her Brickell Avenue condo before doubling back to Kumquat Avenue in Coconut Grove. Bobby had gathered up the *Miami Heralds,* stained red from the squishy berries of a Brazilian pepper tree, and they'd spent the night by themselves. After Bobby had gone to sleep, Steve sat at the kitchen table, drinking beer — not four-hundred-dollar tequila, Junior — pondering just what the hell was going on. It was a three-beer ponder. First, Victoria wanted to split up the firm. Then, the obvious attraction between her and Junior Griffin, aka The Guy He'd Most Like to Pin a Murder Rap On.

Victoria was wrong about one thing.

I'm not jealous of Junior.

Jealousy was a cheap, tawdry emotion, filled with adolescent overtones and boy–girl gamesmanship. Jealousy implied mere infatuation. Victoria meant so much more to him. If he were a house, Steve thought, Bobby would be his foundation and Victoria his walls. Lose either one, his roof would cave in. For the truth was, he loved them both and could not imagine life without either one.

He pulled up to the building just after nine a.m. There was no sign with fancy lettering proclaiming "Law Offices." No brass plate emblazoned: "Solomon & Lord." Instead, the squat, two-story, faded seafoam green stucco pillbox was decorated with a hand-painted *Les Mannequins.* Hurrying inside, Steve decided to do whatever it took to get to his second-floor office unimpeded. Broken-field running, a buttonhook pattern, even stiff-arm a runway model if necessary.

He kept his head down and moved past

the reception desk, where an attractive young woman with a headset was speaking in a clipped British accent, telling a caller not to send her daughter's school yearbook photos, even if she was captain of the Archbishop Curley cheerleading squad. The receptionist looked up: "Stephen! Lexy and Rexy need you."

He grimaced and plowed ahead, sailing through an interior door, passing a photographer's studio and a makeup room with lights bright enough to blanch almonds. The stairs were in sight when he heard: "Steve!" Followed by an echoing rifle shot: "Steve, wait!"

He didn't stop. Even the wildebeest knew better than to pause for a chat with the lions. He quickened his pace, hearing the *click-clack* of Jimmy Choos, or some other flimsy but outrageously costly shoes. A six-foot-tall blonde cut him off at the foot of the stairs. Her identical twin was a half step behind.

Lexy and Rexy.

Lexy wore spandex hot pants festooned with pink stars and a canary-yellow tank top pocketed with stylish holes, revealing ample portions of bare skin underneath. Her Sunday church outfit, no doubt. Rexy wore a clinging piece of floral silk that might have been a dressing gown or a swimsuit cover-up, Steve couldn't tell. It was slit from ankle to hip and held up by nothing more than Rexy's enhanced breasts, which, now that he thought about it, could doubtless cantilever a load considerably heavier than the wafery dress. Best Steve could tell, Rexy wore nothing underneath, except what God and Dr. Irwin Rudnick had given her.

The twins had blue sapphire cat's eyes and perfect, expensive smiles. Steve noticed they had recently cropped their long flaxen hair very short. It looked like someone had plopped bowls on their heads and put the shears to work, but this was probably some chic new Parisian style that had passed him by. They looked like twin blond Joans of Arc . . . if Joan had been an anorexic hooker.

Lexy and Rexy were on the far side of twenty-five — though they claimed to be nineteen — and probably realized they would never achieve the success of their hero, Linda Evangelista, who long ago said she didn't wake up in the morning for less than ten thousand dollars. Lexy and Rexy earned ten thousand dollars one weekend, but that was thanks to a blond-worshipping Saudi prince who maintained a permanent suite at the Ritz-Carlton on Key Biscayne. Modeling had nothing to do with it, of course, unless the prince brought his own camera.

"We need you," Lexy said.

"A bunch," Rexy said.

"Not now." Steve tried to edge past the twins but was blocked by Lexy's bony elbows. "I'm busy."

"You owe us," Lexy said.

Damn. He was about to be roped into work that was both nonpaying and mind-numbing.

Les Mannequins provided Solomon & Lord with office space in return for legal services for a bevy of lithe young women who frequently sued their plastic surgeons and occasionally their hairdressers. Lexy and Rexy also sometimes ran afoul of the law for forging diet pill prescriptions, parking in handicapped spaces — neither low IQs nor bulimia being recognized by the State of Florida as legitimate handicaps — and once assaulting a TV meteorologist who predicted sun on a day in which thunderstorms ruined an outdoor photo shoot. In the three days that Steve had been away, who knows what legal calamities had befallen these stork-legged, lazy-yet-rapaciously-avaricious young women?

"Lex, Rex, it's gotta wait. Really. I've got a murder case going."

Lexy pouted and lodged an elbow on a shot hip, her skinny upper arm, forearm, and angular pelvis forming a triangle.

"You gotta sue Paranoia for us," Lexy said.

"Paranoia? The club? Why?"

"Our names weren't on the list, and this new bouncer didn't recognize us," Rexy pouted.

"The big stoop," Lexy said.

"So you couldn't get in," Steve said. "What's the big deal?"

"We got in," Lexy said. "But the jerk made us wait, like fifteen minutes, and it was so hot, our mascara melted." She fanned herself to convey just how Hades-like it had been, standing on Ocean Drive, queued up outside a noisy, trendy club where horny young men crawled over one another like scorpions to buy them drinks.

"Matt Damon was there." Rexy picked up her sister's fanning motion, so now they seemed to be performing a Kabuki duet. "I'll bet he'd have cast us in his new movie if we hadn't looked so shitty."

Steve saw an opportunity, and while the twins pantomined, he slipped past them on the stairs. "I'll research the law," he called out.

"Mental anguish!" Lexy blared. "Gotta be worth six figures."

"Sure, Lexy. Sure. A hundred thousand dollars of anguish for a fifty-dollar mind."

"Whadaya mean by that?" Lexy demanded.

There was the *clang* of metal on metal as Steve opened the door to his reception room. Once inside, he heard a grunt, a guttural growl, and an exhaled "*Maldito!* That's heavy." Cecilia Santiago, a thickset young woman in black tights and a muscle tee, was lying on her back on a bench press. She had a café au lait complexion, and three metal studs pierced one wavy eyebrow, which was shaped like the tilde in *"mañana."*

"Morning, Cece."

"Wanna spot for me, *jefe?*" She hoisted the bar and a cobra tattoo curled upward from rippled triceps.

"I'll make a deal with you, Cece. Type up the overdue pleadings and correspondence, and I'll spot for you."

"Slave driver."

"Anybody call?"

"The usual. Xerox says you're three months behind on the copy machine lease. Bobby's teacher called, something about truancy. A couple bimbos from downstairs. They wanna sue Ben and Jerry's. Just discovered there's fat in ice cream."

"What about Vic? Where is she?"

"Queen Victoria? How should I know?"

"Vic's a princess. It's her mother who's The Queen."

"Whatever, *jefe*. She ain't here and she ain't called."

He wanted to see her, wanted to talk to her. Why is it, he wondered, when a relationship feels shaky, you crave the connection even more?

Cece started another set, exhaling on the thrust upward, inhaling on the negative downward motion, the bar *clang*ing into the metal brackets. Steve had hired her not from a paralegal school, but from the Women's Detention Center. He considered her crime a mere peccadillo. Beating the stuffing out of her boyfriend, then driving his Toyota into the bay after catching him fooling around with her cousin, Lourdes. Cece was a decent enough assistant, even though she screwed up Steve's pleadings by typing every word phonetically, when she bothered to type at all. She was particularly adept at keeping the models away, mostly by threatening to break their spindly limbs.

Steve walked to her desk and riffled through the mail. Bills, solicitations, and Cece's muscle mags. Maybe he should lift weights, grow some stingray lats like Mr.

Deep Diver. He opened a magazine called *Big and Brawny*, turned to a photo of a guy in a G-string, his granite torso oiled up, his arms bursting with veins like writhing snakes. The headline: "Do Steroids Really Shrink Your Testicles?" Steve tossed the magazine aside.

"Guy's waiting," Cece huffed.

"Who? Where?"

"In your office. Some old geezer. Said he was a friend of your *papi*'s."

Steve shot a look at the door to his office. Closed. He had no appointments today. Who the hell was in there, and why?

"Dammit, you can't let somebody you don't even know into my inner sanctum."

She looked up from the bench. "You afraid they're gonna steal your great works of art?"

"If you're talking about my Florida Marlins posters . . ."

"Ain't talking about your briefs."

The premises of Solomon & Lord consisted of Cece's reception room/gym and a single office overlooking a narrow alley and a rusting green Dumpster. On warm days, meaning nearly every day, the pungent perfume of rotting vegetables, decomposing ham croquettes, melting tar, stale beer, and fresh piss wafted through the open window. Across the alley, on an apartment balcony within spitting distance, a Jamaican steel band could be counted on for migraine-inducing rehearsals, the musicians smoking giant doobies and occasionally cooking jerk chicken on a hibachi.

The office furnishings were Salvation Army Moderne. Two desks, purchased at police auctions of stolen property; a Jupiter Hammerheads baseball-bat rack, a gift from a grateful client, a minor-league outfielder Steve helped beat a steroids rap; and a fish tank usually stocked with Florida lobster, courtesy of a poacher client. On the wall, instead of diplomas or plaques from the Kiwanis, were posters celebrating the Marlins' two World Series Championships.

The fermenting stench from the Dumpster hit Steve as he stepped inside. Another scent, too, bay rum cologne. Steve knew only one man who used the stuff, and the son-of-a-bitch was here, round and pink, sinking into the sagging client chair.

"Some shit hole you got here, Stevie," Peter Luber said, gesturing with a small pink hand. In his late sixties, Pinky Luber — no one ever called him "Peter" or "Pete" — had a rotund torso with short pudgy legs and a round, bald head with a thin, hooked nose. His face and his scalp were the same carnation pink, as if he were mildly feverish. His cheeks were so chubby that his eyes were reduced to slits of indeterminate color. He wore a jet-black suit, a white shirt with rough-hewn gold nugget cuff links, and a red silk tie as gaudy as fresh blood. On his lap was a black felt hat with a maroon feather and a narrow, upturned brim. The bowler, Steve remembered, was a Luber trademark, as distinctive as an eye patch or a cane, and highly useful for keeping the sun off his already pink scalp. An unlit Cuban cigar, the short, fat Robusto, was clenched in his teeth. On the little finger of his left hand — yeah, the pinky finger — was a black onyx ring set with a glistening diamond.

What's the perjurious pink bastard doing here?

"If I'd known you were coming, I'd have fumigated for vermin," Steve said. "Now I'll just do it after you leave."

A hard look flickered in Luber's tiny eyes, then passed quickly. In that instant, Steve saw the toughness the man tried to hide behind his cherubic pinkness, his bowling ball physique, and his silly English hat.

"If I were you, I'd burn this joint down," Luber said, gravel in his voice.

"If you were me, I'd kill myself."

"Nothing like your old man in the old days. Herb always went for mahogany. When he was first elected judge, he spent his own money to panel his office in the Justice Building."

His father's name coming out of Luber's mouth made Steve want to toss the son-of-a-bitch into the Dumpster.

"Herbert T. Solomon," Luber mused. "Now, there was a lawyer."

" 'Was' being the operative word. Just what the hell are you doing here, Luber?"

"C'mon, Stevie. Call me 'Pinky.' Everybody does."

"Wouldn't feel right. But I got some other names that might."

"You got some attitude, kid. As for your old man, he's better off fishing in the Keys. I wouldn't want to be in that rat race downtown now."

"You don't have a choice. They pulled your ticket when they sent you away."

Luber took the Robusto out of his mouth and waved it like a wand. "Eighteen months in Eglin. No big deal. I worked on my tennis game, got my life master's in contract bridge."

"Didn't know you can cheat in bridge."

"Mind if I smoke?" Luber licked the tip

184

of his cigar with a pink tongue. "Might improve the smell in here."

"I mind."

"Aw, hell, Stevie. Your old man's let it go. Why can't you?"

"I'm not my old man."

"I remember when you'd come to the courthouse and play with your baseball cards in the holding cells." Luber's unlit cigar bobbed up and down as he spoke. "I was Chief of Capital Crimes, your old man Chief Criminal Judge."

Suddenly, Steve felt the room get warmer. Pinky Luber's cologne had turned the air sticky sweet. "You were chief of sleaze. Dad was a public servant. I can't fucking believe what you did to him."

"You blame me for your father's tsuris." Giving Steve some Yiddish for old-times' sake.

"You're the *momzer* who lied under oath." Adding his own Yinglish to the yin and yang of the sparring match.

"Kid, there are things you don't know, and that's all I'm gonna say."

Steve walked to the corner of the room and pulled a Barry Bonds bat from the rack. Gorgeous maple, only twenty-eight ounces, with a thin, whippy handle. Steve took a swing. Wishing he could take batting practice, tee off on Pinky Luber's round, pink head. What did he want, anyway? The bastard still hadn't said.

Pinky was fingering the hatband on his bowler, his look inscrutable. His face was remarkably unlined for a man his age. He appeared much the same as he had twenty years earlier, when he was trying murder cases in front of Judge Solomon. A smooth if ruthless prosecutor, Luber won seventeen capital cases without a loss. Not even a hung jury. Just like the 1972 Miami Dolphins, 17–0, with a sizable number being sentenced to death. About halfway through that Super Bowl run of convictions, the newspapers began calling Luber "the Electrician" and Herbert Solomon "the Frying Judge." In those days, Florida still used the electric chair, affectionately known as Old Sparky in law enforcement circles. The name, Steve knew, was not entirely fantastical, as the condemned would occasionally burst into flame, much to the chagrin of prison authorities.

Then, inexplicably, the Electrician and the Frying Judge parted. Herbert transferred to the Civil Division and Luber, hungry for dollars instead of headlines, left for private practice. He publicly vowed never to "go over to the dark side," as prosecutors called criminal defense. But Luber's foray into plaintiff's work — medical malpractice, auto accidents, products liability — didn't work out. He spent a fortune working up contingency fee cases that he lost at trial. Luber was nearly bankrupt when he returned to the corridors of the Justice Building, a Prince of Darkness working the shadows of the law. He developed a reputation as a fixer, both in court and in City Hall. He turned out to be a master briber and extortionist. A life master, just like his contract bridge, Steve thought.

When the U.S. Attorney's public corruption unit pulled a sting operation, it swept up Luber, some zoning inspectors, and two public works employees in a kickback and bribery scheme. Luber flipped quicker than you could say "minimum mandatory sentence." He signed affidavits implicating several other public officials, including Circuit Judge Herbert T. Solomon.

Steve pleaded with his father to fight the accusations, but the old man caved, quitting the bench and the Bar, even while protesting his innocence. Luber pled guilty to reduced charges, spent his eighteen months at a country club prison in the Florida Panhandle, then came back to Miami. Stripped of his Bar license, he set up shop as a lobbyist. From talk around City Hall, Pinky was making more money than ever, securing lucrative concessions at the airport, rezoning agricultural land for shopping centers, and selling fleets of not-quite-wholesale sedans to the county — all under cover of darkness. It never hurt Pinky's clients in such matters to make substantial, unreported contributions to local public officials. The contributions were always in cash, and usually delivered by Pinky Luber. In Miami politics, the term "lobbyist" was a pleasant euphemism for "bagman."

The sight of Luber, fat and prosperous, stinking of treacly cologne, gave Steve the creepy-crawlies. He took a swing with the Barry Bonds. And then another. Closed his eyes. Visualized a ball on its upward arc leaving the bat, soaring toward the fence, nearing the warning track, then *plop,* into the outfielder's glove. The outfielder's face appeared: round and pink and chomping a cigar. Damn! The bastard even screwed up Steve's daydreams.

"I was there the day you stole home to beat Florida State," Luber said.

Steve opened his eyes. "Who gives a shit?"

"Won five thousand bucks."

"You bet on college baseball?"

"Stevie, I bet whether the next gal to get

on the elevator is a blonde or brunette." He smiled ruefully. "Then I lost ten grand on the College World Series when you got picked off third in the bottom of the ninth."

"Ump blew the call."

"Yeah, a tough break." Luber took a moment to size him up. When he spoke, it was softly and with a touch of sadness. "You were an arrogant little shit. That dancing off third base, that big lead you took in the series. Why the hell do it? You woulda scored on any hit."

"I was trying to draw a bad throw. If the pitcher puts it in the dugout, I score and we tie it up."

"You put the whole team at risk so you could be the hero. Now you're doing the same thing with Herb." Luber rocked forward in the chair and got to his feet. He brushed off his pants, as if he'd just hopped off a particularly dusty horse instead of a relatively clean, secondhand chair. "I gotta get going. Ponies are running at Calder."

Luber had always seemed short, but now, aged and a tad stooped, he was truly pint-size.

Luber started for the door, stopped, and turned. "Getting picked off. There's a lesson in that you never learned. You can't depend on umpires. Same for judges. Same for the whole damn system. That's why it's better to resolve matters informally. Between people."

Steve put the head of the bat on the floor, leaned on the handle. "What are you getting at?"

"That cockamamie suit you filed to get Herb's license back. You drop it, I could give you some help."

"What kind of help?"

Pinky's cheeks crinkled with a chubby smile. "Let's say you had a murder case that's got you stumped."

That caught Steve by surprise. "What do you know about it?"

"C'mon, Stevie. I got friends who say Hal Griffin's been pulling some pretty cute permits down in Monroe County. New docks, hydrofoil service, liquor license for a gulfside terminal. Then a guy from Washington gets whacked on his boat. If I were defending Griffin, I'd be asking myself one mighty big question."

"What's that? Who could you bribe to get the case dropped?"

"The one the ancient Romans asked, wise guy. *Cui bono?* Who stands to gain?"

"Already doing that. Looking for who profits if Griffin takes a fall."

"So let me help you. I know people. I hear things."

"So whadaya know? Whadaya hear?"

"Oy! I should give it away, you gonif?" Pinky Luber sniggered and waddled toward the door. "Got another Roman expression for you. Quid pro quo." He opened the door to the reception room and slipped the bowler onto his head. "Without some *quid,* kid, there ain't no *quo.*"

FIFTEEN:
IN PRAISE OF
INANIMATE WOMEN

"Pinky Luber tried to bribe you?" Victoria sounded skeptical.

"I don't know if you'd call it a bribe," Steve said, "but he implied he'd help us in Griffin's case if I'd drop Dad's Bar petition."

Victoria wanted to ask more, but it was awkward, with all the people staring at them. "This is so embarrassing."

"What's the problem?" Steve said.

They were hurrying along Flagler Street, a woman in a thong bikini slung over Steve's shoulder. The woman's breasts, full spheroids, overflowed her bikini top. Her hair, a blond avalanche — Farrah Fawcett circa 1976 — tickled Steve's neck.

"Everyone's looking at us," Victoria said.

True. Patrons at the *café Cubano* stands, clerks from the discount camera shops sneaking smokes on the sidewalk, Latin-American tourists rolling luggage carts . . .

everyone was gaping, pointing, laughing. Probably because the woman in the bikini was a hundred-pound, custom-made, silicone "love doll," anatomically correct right down to every digit and orifice.

"We should have parked right across the street from the courthouse," Victoria said.

"And pay fifteen bucks? No way."

Steve had parked his old Caddy at a meter around the corner on Miami Avenue. They had three minutes to get to the hearing. Motion for summary judgment in the case of Pullone vs. Adult Enterprises, Ltd., dba The Beav. Long before Steve hooked up with Victoria — professionally and personally — he had represented The Beav, the strip club in Surfside. The cases were usually mundane consumer-fraud actions: selling sparkling cider as champagne for twenty bucks a glass or running multiple credit card charges every time the song changed during a lap dance. There was also the occasional personal-injury suit, including today's case. Clayton Pullone, a middle-aged, married CPA, claimed to have suffered a dislocated hip while wrestling Susie Slamazon, The Beav's famed bikini grappler, in a vat of lime Jell-O. Although the blonde on Steve's shoulder was not Susie, her specs were as close as he was likely to find. Her name was

Tami, according to the instruction manual, which also included helpful hints about washing various parts with warm, sudsy water.

"Cuánto cuesta la rubia?" a man in a guayabera shouted as they passed Castillo Joyeria, a cut-rate jewelry store. Inquiring into the price of the blonde.

"You can't afford her," Steve called back.

In fact, Tami cost six thousand dollars. Custom-made to the buyer's specifications. Skin tone: tan. Hair: honey blond. Nails: French manicure. Pubic hair: lightly trimmed. Breasts: 38DD and jiggly. Articulated hands that can grip. Mouth, vagina, and anal cavity, well . . . in working order. Lubed and suction ready, if you were into that sort of thing. Tami was on loan from Harvey Leinoff, The Beav's owner, who after dating the hired help for years had recently turned to inanimate sex objects for his personal needs. No back talk, no dressing room catfights, no overtime pay.

The three of them — Steve, Victoria, and Tami — headed up the granite steps to the courthouse, Steve beginning to wish they had parked closer. Tami was damn heavy, and as her weight shifted, a perky silicone nipple lodged — like a pencil eraser — in his ear.

Victoria tried to ignore the carnival going on next to her. "So how could Luber help us in Uncle Grif's case?"

"He let on that he knew who stuck Stubbs with that spear. Or could find out. It wasn't clear which."

"Do you trust Luber?"

Steve struggled up the last step. "About as far as I can throw Tami."

They were at the front doors, waiting to go through the metal detector, the guards stifling laughs.

"This is crazy," Victoria said. "There's no way you can force the plaintiff to roll around on the courtroom floor with your rubber doll."

"Don't need the plaintiff. I'm gonna wrestle Tami."

"Oh, please . . ."

"I'm gonna strip down to my briefs —"

"Not the leopard-spotted ones!"

"Of course not. That would be tacky. I'm wearing my Florida Marlins silk boxers. Which you'd know if you'd slept over last night."

Waiting for an overweight bail bondsman to go through the security check, Victoria whispered: "Please try not to get us held in contempt."

"Vic, a lawyer who's afraid of jail —"

"Is like a surgeon who's afraid of blood," she finished. "I know. I know."

They'd reached the front of the line, where Omar Torres, a portly courthouse security guard, was manning the walk-through metal detector.

"Omar, we're late for a hearing," Steve said. "Could you speed it up a bit?"

"No way, Steve," Torres said. "Yesterday, some *santero* sneaked in here with a human skull, cast a spell right in Judge Gridley's courtroom."

Victoria placed her purse on the conveyor belt for the X-ray machine.

"Gonna have to pat you down, honey," Torres said.

"In your dreams," Victoria said.

"Not you, Ms. Lord." Torres pointed at Tami the Love Doll, now standing shakily on her feet — painted toenails and all — leaning on Steve. "*Her.* Gotta check all her body cavities."

"No need, Omar," Steve replied. "I already did last night."

Victoria tried to analyze what Steve had told her, but it didn't compute. "Why would Pinky Luber care about your father's case?"

"Obviously, he's afraid of something."

They were sitting on a black wooden

bench that resembled a church pew in the corridor outside Judge Alvin Schwartz's chambers. Steve had moved Tami between them after two guys in suits walked by and pinched the doll's boobs. Plaintiff's P.I. lawyers, Victoria figured. The insurance guys would never be so bold.

Steve had checked in with the bailiff, an officious young man who would be unemployed if not related to Judge Schwartz through marriage, if not bloodlines. The bailiff carried a clipboard and demanded to know the names of every lawyer and witness who would be appearing in his great-uncle's chambers. Steve dutifully gave their names, choosing "Tami Stepford" for his witness. They settled down to wait. Judge Schwartz was running late, a legalism for reading the morning paper while having his coffee with a bagel and a schmear.

"What's Luber afraid of?" Victoria asked. "He's served his time. There's nothing more the state can do to him."

"Unless something new came out in the Bar case."

"Anything now would be too late under the statute of limitations."

Steve shrugged, and Tami's head slid down his shoulder. "All I know, Pinky's scared shitless about my lawsuit."

"Did you tell your father about his visit?"

"Yep. Dad said Pinky was a wind-belly from way back. And if I got mixed up with him, I'd be hitched to a dead mule that was ass-deep in molasses. Or maybe it was manure, I can't remember which."

"Herb still wants you to drop the Bar case, right?"

"Said if I didn't, he'd write me out of his will."

"Strong words."

"Yeah, I'd lose a leaky houseboat and a collection of empty Bacardi bottles."

"So what are you going to do?"

"I'm not going to be intimidated by Dad or bribed by Pinky. Full speed ahead on the Bar case and to hell with Pinky Luber."

"But if Luber really can help us . . ."

"Forget it. I won't sell out my father."

"Herb doesn't want his license back. Maybe you should listen to him."

"This is what I've been talking about, Vic. You're too close to the Griffins. You can't be objective."

"Me? You won't accept help in Uncle Grif's case because you need to prove something to your father."

"Prove what?"

"That you're just as good a lawyer as he was."

"This isn't about me."

"Yes it is. If *you* were objective, you'd see it."

After that, no one said a thing, not even Tami.

The bailiff called three other cases, whose deep-carpet lawyers customarily gave him cash at Christmas, Halloween, and Bribe-Your-Public-Servant Day. So the partners of Solomon & Lord were still sitting on the hard, wooden pew at ten a.m., Victoria wondering what to tell Steve about her late-night phone call.

Then she just blurted it out. "The Queen called last night."

"Zurich or Johannesburg?"

"Katmandu. She's getting injections of pituitary glands from mountain goats. Supposed to rejuvenate the skin."

"You tell her about the case?"

Victoria nodded. "She was shocked. First time in years either of us mention Uncle Grif's name, and I have to tell her he's being charged with murder."

"She ask about Junior?"

"Only a hundred questions. 'How's he look? What's he doing? Is he married?' "

"She still think he's a dreamboat?"

"And *'terrif.'* She said Junior was a *terrif*

kid, so she's not surprised how he turned out."

"And how did he turn out? I mean, what exactly did you tell her?"

"Nothing much." Which was basically true, she thought. She didn't share her conflicted feelings with The Queen.

"Her Highness hates me, doesn't she?" Steve pried.

"She barely knows you."

"She thinks I'm not good enough for you."

"All parents think that about their children."

"Not my old man."

"You want to make a better impression on The Queen, stop wearing that stupid T-shirt every time you see her."

"What shirt?"

"Don't play dumb. The one that says: *'If It's Not One Thing, It's Your Mother.'*"

"I've tried being nice. She didn't like the watch I gave her."

"If it had been a real Cartier and not a knockoff, she would have loved it."

"If it had been a real Cartier, I couldn't have bought it from the valet parker at jai alai."

"The Queen doesn't hate you, Steve. She just always imagined me with someone . . ." How could she put this? ". . . different."

"A Princeton WASP whose Daddy owned an investment bank. Summer in Southampton, winter in Aspen."

"Actually, she always thought I'd marry Junior."

Steve made an "ow" sound and wrapped an arm around Tami. "I'm beginning to see the benefits of inanimate partners. No mothers-in-law."

Victoria had never told Steve some of her mother's pithier comments about him:

"For the life of me, Princess, I don't know what you see in that ambulance chaser."

And just now Victoria decided not to tell Steve something else, too. Her mother's odd reaction last night to the news about Uncle Grif. The Queen never asked about the case. Victoria would have expected her to wonder — *Who's dead? Did Grif do it? How badly hurt is he?* — but she didn't ask any of those questions. Her first response: *"What did Grif say about me, dear?"*

On second thought, maybe that was to be expected. After all, The Queen's egocentricity was as much a trademark as her couture dresses and salon coiffures. But the question wasn't: *"Did he ask about me?"* More of a concern, an alarm, about *what* was said. And then there was: *"Did Grif mention your father?"*

Again, it wasn't the question so much as the tone, Victoria reflected. Was there just a hint of fear? It seemed as if The Queen didn't want her talking about the family with Uncle Grif. After all these years of silence, what was she afraid of?

Victoria wondered about the secrets parents keep. Both Steve's father and her mother were hiding things. Was it to protect themselves, or their children? But don't all of us keep secrets from our loved ones? After all, she didn't come clean with Steve about just how shaky their relationship was.

What am I afraid of?

There was fear all around, it seemed to her.

The Queen had ended the phone call with another odd note Victoria was still processing.

"Grif was always envious of your father," Irene Lord had said.

"I thought they were best friends," Victoria replied.

"They were. But Nelson had such . . . je ne sais quoi . . . *elegance, such class. Grif always knew he'd be nothing more than . . ."*

Victoria could picture her mother, in her suite at the Shangri-la Hotel, making a dismissive European gesture, to be followed by a French expression.

"Another nouveau riche builder," The Queen concluded.

Victoria kept herself from pointing out that, after her father's death, she and her mother were *nouveau pauvre.* "I don't get it, Mother. Why are you criticizing Uncle Grif?"

"I'm not, dear. I'm only saying, don't take everything he says at face value. Now, I must ring off, darling. I'm late for my mud bath."

Victoria imagined her mother, the phone pressed between shoulder and ear, delicate fingers removing a three-carat diamond stud from the other ear, placing it carefully in her black-lacquer traveling jewelry box. There was so much more Victoria wanted to ask. Why had The Queen never told her about Grif's offers of financial support? And why had she refused all his help? Why shut Uncle Grif out of their lives when they needed him the most?

She decided not to share any of this with Steve, at least not until she could figure out some of it. She glanced at him stuffing Tami's overflowing breasts back into place. Wondering if he was taking longer than absolutely necessary to complete the task.

She thought of her father, remembering a handsome man in an old-fashioned, three-piece suit, a barrel-chested man with a deep voice and a mane of salt-and-pepper hair.

He had seemed so strong. So invincible. But damn him, he'd been weak. He took the coward's way out, abandoning his family. Not even a note, she thought for the thousandth time. How hard would it have been to write of his love for his only child?

Damn him! Damn him for the pain he left in his wake.

A memory came back to her, just a glimpse of her father, scooping her up and swinging her around, her legs nearly parallel to the ground as she shrieked with delight. A merry-go-round of a father. She remembered him as a tall man, but years later, she saw photos of Nelson and Irene Lord together. They were about the same height, and Irene was five-eight. The tricks the mind plays, she thought. What else was distorted in her memory? And what other secrets did her mother keep locked in her black-lacquer jewelry box?

Sixteen:
This Year's Bigby

In the span of seven minutes, Judge Alvin Schwartz — eighty-one years old, near-sighted, absentminded, and cantankerous as a hemorrhoid — threatened Steve with contempt, ordered him to put his pants back on, reserved ruling on his motion for summary judgment, tossed all lawyers out of his chambers, but commanded Ms. Tami Stepford and all her silicone charms to remain behind, while His Honor considered the weighty legal precedents concerning injuries suffered while wrestling bikini-clad women in vats of Jell-O.

On the way out of the courthouse, Steve felt elated. Victoria had made the legal arguments, and he'd handled the single-leg take-down and crotch-and-a-half pinning move. Surely Victoria must realize they were a ter-rific team. "We're gonna win," he predicted cheerfully.

"Great," Victoria said, without enthusiasm. "We'll get more work from . . ." She couldn't bring herself to say it. Even the name sounded dirty. "That place."

"Hey, The Beav pays the bills."

"Not just in lap dance coupons?"

"C'mon, Vic. You know I don't mess around with The Beav Brigade." Referring to the pole climbers, lap dancers, and bartop booty shakers.

It was technically true, thanks to his use of the present-tense verb "don't." It would have been completely true if he'd added "anymore."

From the day he first kissed Victoria — actually, she kissed him on the dock of a yacht club while her fiancé was having avocado vichyssoise inside — he had not been with another woman. Had not even lusted after another woman. In the time they'd been together, he had often told Victoria that he loved her — usually amidst various whoops and snorts while her legs were wrapped around his hips — but even so, he figured he meant it.

"So, how 'bout Nemo for dinner?" he asked. "My treat. You're crazy about their pan-seared yellowtail."

"Ah. Uhh. Ah," Victoria said.

She was either buying time or was in desperate need of a Heimlich maneuver,

Steve thought.

"Actually, Junior's in town," she admitted after a moment.

"No problem. Tell Junior to join us. He can pick up the check."

"The thing is . . ."

"Yeah?"

"He already asked me to dinner."

Steve felt like he'd been slugged in the gut. "You mean, like a date?"

"Not a date-date. Just a chance for us to catch up on old times without you cross-examining him."

"No fucking way."

She shot him a harsh look. He knew she hated the F-word, and he'd curtailed using it as the modifier of choice. No more "fucking hot out there." He'd cut back on the action verb, "fuck him," and the noun, "the fuck you doing?" And he was working on not using it as a suffix of the word "mother."

So when he chose to smack Victoria with a "no fucking way," it was a calculated verbal slap on the kisser to let her know just how pissed he was.

How pissed was he? *Fucking pissed.*

"Ste-phen," she dragged out his name, showing her irritation, "just chill. Having dinner with Junior is no big deal."

"Where you going?"

"Norman's. In the Gables."

"A date restaurant. The most romantic place in town."

"Then why don't you ever take me there?"

"Because we're not dating. We're together. We don't need a dark, expensive place with fancy food."

"Meaning what? Romance is dead?"

He'd walked into quicksand, and struggling was useless, but he flailed about, anyway. "C'mon, Vic. I've taken you there when a client paid."

"Which would make it a business restaurant, correct?"

Touché. The woman was a born cross-examiner.

"That's irrelevant," he scrambled, trying to counterpunch. "You're not going to talk business. You're going to relive the joys of playing strip poker at Bunny Flagler's."

"You're overreacting."

Was he?

No. This is how you react when the woman you're crazy about might jump ship.

He remembered the day he met Victoria, the ultraproper, rigid-postured, long-legged young prosecutor in a conservative glen-plaid suit. She'd had a meltdown when he tried to call Mr. Ruffles, a talking toucan, to testify. Face flushed, she'd lost her cool and called Steve unethical and sleazy, diabolical and dangerous, a disgrace to the profession. How could he not fall for her?

That day in the courtroom, she was still a novice, and he'd caught a tremor in her lower lip as she rose to speak. But when she did speak . . . *Oh, Lordy,* as his father might say. In her tailored suit and velvet-toed shoes, with her short, butterscotch hair tousled just a whisper, with her commanding height, and her voice, growing stronger and more confident by the minute, Victoria Lord conveyed intelligence, competence, and unshakable integrity.

She had what every great trial lawyer desires, something that cannot be taught, bought, or even forgotten; she had *presence.* You couldn't *not* watch her.

Still, Steve the Slasher was the wilier practitioner, and he'd tricked her into a mistrial, which got her fired from the State Attorney's Office. He'd been regretful about that, at first. But no more. Had she not been sacked, they never could have hooked up to defend Katrina Barksdale on charges she'd strangled her husband.

Victoria had been engaged to the Avocado King then, and she'd stiff-armed all of Steve's advances. Until she came to the conclusion — not rationally, Steve figured,

but chemically, magically, hormonally —
that he, Last Out Solomon, was the man
for her. Not Bruce Bigby. Which, at this moment, gave him precious little solace. For it
stood to reason that if he stole Victoria's
heart from Bigby, could not another man
do the same to him? Was he this year's
Bigby?

Seventeen:
The Love Song of Junior Griffin

Victoria felt her cheeks burn as she followed the maître d' past the open, wood-burning oven on the way to the table. Or maybe the warmth wasn't coming from the oven at all. With Junior Griffin's strong hand on her bare skin, just above the top of her sequined silk chiffon ruffle top, was she blushing?

Diners at other tables stared as they walked by. Usually, she was the one who drew the looks, but now it seemed that her companion was the focus of attention. Junior wore an unstructured beige silk jacket, the sleeves pushed up to his elbows, his dark tan a burnished bronze in the subdued lighting. Underneath the jacket, a coral blue silk shirt was open at the neck, the fabric picking up the color of his eyes.

Adonis in Armani.

Sounds and smells filled this room of dark woods, a feel of old-world Spanish architecture. From the open kitchen came the crackle of rum-painted grouper, sizzling in a pan. From the tables, the tinkle of glasses and quiet conversations — in English, Spanish, Portuguese — giving the place an exotic feel.

The maître d' led them to a prime table, and why shouldn't he? They looked like an upwardly mobile young couple, sophisticated and successful.

Except we're not a couple at all.

She felt a moment of confusion as they ordered drinks, tequila for Junior, a Cosmopolitan for her. She was trying to convince herself that she had been honest with Steve. This wasn't a date. This was just a reconnection with her childhood friend. An opportunity to learn more about her father, more about her mother's secrets, maybe even a nugget or two for the murder case.

But not a date. Definitely not a date.

She hadn't let Junior pick her up at the condo. There'd be no awkward moments — *"Want to come up for a drink?"* — at the end of this evening.

So why had she taken such care dressing? She didn't have to change out of the high-collared, pin-striped suit she'd worn to court. But she had showered, washed and blow-dried her hair, then tried on four outfits. First, the conservative blue-green tweed jacket with a fringe trim and matching skirt with a silk scarf tie. No way. She looked like Mary Poppins.

Then the racy Balenciaga criss-cross halter minidress. But she didn't have the nerve for that one. Next, a middle-of-the-road Burberry beige wrap dress with splotches of black spots. Forget it. She looked like a demented schoolteacher whose fountain pen had exploded in her closet.

Finally, she decided on the bare-shouldered, sequined Max Azria ruffle top with the black tuxedo pants. When Junior met her at the bar, he'd cocked his head and said: *Wow, you look gorgeous.* They brush-kissed and she felt a tingle of excitement and a creeping blush that rose like a fever from the back of her neck.

Now, as the waiter served pre-appetizer snacks like little party favors sent from the kitchen — a bite-size flan risotto flaked with lemon and a griddled masa cake topped by a tomatillo sauce — Junior surprised her with a question. "So, you and Solomon, law partners and how much more?"

She told him the story. How months earlier she'd called Steve "the sleaziest lawyer she'd ever met." How they'd shared facing jail cells after being held in mutual contempt for bickering in court. How he'd tricked her into a mistrial, which got her fired, and then how they'd teamed up to try a murder case. She left out the bit about making love in her fiancé's avocado grove. Wildly romantic at the time, it just seemed tawdry in the telling. But as she spoke to Junior, that night kept coming back to her. A snowstorm in Miami, a hurricane in her heart. She could still smell the black smoke of the smudge pots, could see the twinkling Christmas lights warming the trees. One indelible image: Steve's face. Startled . . . because *she* had made the first move. He had resisted — well, hesitated, anyway. The tough guy had been afraid of getting hurt. She was, after all, engaged to someone else.

So I must have fallen in love with Steve, right?

Or was that just her rationalization for what she had done? Now she wondered, had things happened too fast? And that nagging thought returned: Were her first instincts about Steve — the cutthroat, corner-cutting competitor — correct? Were the two of them just *too* different?

But now, another scary thought whipped through her like a chilly wind. Was she about to do something tawdry again?

"We've been together since then," Victoria told Junior. Giving away none of her concerns. Or was she? Was just being here in a darkly lit romantic restaurant in her ruffled top with the bare shoulders . . . was that some signal that she was available?

He nodded and gave her a little smile with a raised eyebrow. As if it just didn't compute, Steve and her. But what he said was: "He's a lucky guy."

"Steve's charms are not always readily apparent. He has a real affinity for the underdog, and he's truly fearless. He doesn't care what people think of him, and if he believes in a client, he'll do anything to win, including risking disbarment and sometimes dismemberment."

"Yeah, he seems a little aggressive."

"Steve actually has a tender heart." Why did she feel the need to defend him? To justify her choice in a man, maybe? "You should see him with his nephew."

"Let's not talk about Solomon," Junior said, even though he was the one who'd raised the issue. "A toast."

He hoisted his glass and swirled the tequila. Victoria held the stem of her martini glass, the Cosmo glowing crimson in the candlelight.

"To old friends," Junior proclaimed, his eyes a deep azure pool. "And new beginnings."

And self-knowledge, Victoria thought. Awareness of who I am and what I want.

She felt her face heat again and sipped her Cosmo, hoping it would cool her, erase the blush from her neck. Then, like an attentive beau, Junior focused the conversation on her.

Not the Marlins, the Dolphins, or the 'Canes, like what's-his-name?

It was fun answering Junior's questions, his eyes never straying from hers. "Tell me about Princeton." Then Harvard Law. "*Wow.* Competitive, right?" Then, prosecuting criminals in Miami. "*Wow,* that takes some *cajones.*" Asking how she'd kept her femininity. Those balls-to-the-wall lady prosecutors he's seen on *Larry King* seemed like man-eating sharks. She told him about the murder case she'd handled with Steve, drawing another *"Wow"* from the Wow-zer.

By the time his third tequila arrived, along with her second Cosmo, Junior was telling her how deeply his father had been affected by her father's suicide. When the Griffins moved to Costa Rica, his father was practically catatonic. Then, a year later, Junior's mother died of a particularly vicious form of stomach cancer. After another year of semiretirement, Hal Griffin got back in the game, building hotels in the Caribbean, then off to the Far East, and back home again. Junior was never able to sink roots, never found a woman he'd want to settle down with. Oh, how he'd missed Florida and his closest companion from childhood.

"I thought about you a lot." His look earnest. "I know we were just kids then, but we had such a natural rapport. Everything was so easy."

"How hard could it be when the biggest issue is ten o'clock curfew?"

An old defense mechanism, she knew. Using humor to deflect serious insight into feelings. So conflicted. Junior seemed to want to unburden himself of his pent-up feelings. Part of her wanted to hear him; part of her was afraid of what he would say.

He smiled and said: " 'Let us go then, you and I . . .' "

She finished the line: " 'When the evening is spread out against the sky . . .' "

They both laughed. "The Love Song of J. Alfred Prufrock." They'd read the poem as children and tried to memorize it, but it was too long. That Junior would remember the opening stanza just now touched her. It was *their* poem. Did she have a poem with Steve? No, but if they did, it would probably be "Casey at the Bat."

Junior reached across the table and placed

a powerful hand gently over her forearm, his thumb making tiny figure eights just above her wrist. "That's why this is such an opportunity," he whispered. "It's horrible, the mess Dad's in, but somehow, it's almost like fate brought us back together." He took a sip of his drink as if to fortify himself for what he had to say. "I've been thinking about this ever since I saw you the other day, and what I want you to know, Tori, is this. You're the only . . ."

He paused. Did he need another drink to say it? No, he was looking over her shoulder at someone. Who?

Then, a male voice, hearty and loud: "Well, well, look who's here!"

Oh, dammit. Dammit to hell!

"My law partner and the lobster poacher!" Steve exclaimed, with mock surprise.

He headed to their table, flanked by those twin blond bimbos, Lexy and Rexy from Les Mannequins. Lexy (or maybe it was Rexy, who could tell?) was dressed in a shimmering, low-cut, red silk dress that would have been ankle-length, had it not been for the flapping pleats — as wide as rubber flaps at a car wash — that opened at the waist, and curled around her long legs with each step. Rexy (unless it was Lexy) wore a simple black tube dress that stopped a foot north of her knees. Both had silicone breasts that were too mammoth for the twins' bony frames. Both were perched on the latest Jimmy Choo skyscrapers, with hundred-millimeter heels, and both moved with that hip-shot, glide-in-the-stride walk of accomplished runway models. Or hungry lionesses.

Victoria painted on a smile like the chef painted rum sauce on the grouper. "Hello and good-bye, Steve."

"What do you mean? Junior, you don't mind if we join you, right?"

"Well . . ."

"Great!" Steve turned to the nearest waiter and cried out, "Garçon. *Camarero.* Three more menus. *Pronto, si'l vous plait.*"

Mixing his languages like a fish stew.

Steve introduced his two props to Junior, then signaled the waiter to take a drink order. Cristal champagne, and sure, put it on Mr. Griffin's check. He positioned Lexy and Rexy on either side of Junior and took a seat next to Victoria.

"Isn't this cozy?" Steve asked.

"And quite a coincidence," Junior replied.

"I eat here all the time," Steve said.

"Hah," Victoria exhaled.

Junior looked at Victoria and shrugged, as if to say: *"What can we do?"* In that moment, she liked him even more. So calm, so confident in himself, he didn't need to rebuff Steve or toss him headfirst across the bar.

"Showing some skin, Vic." Steve nodded toward her décolletage. "New dress?"

"I wore it to the Vizcayans Ball. You forget?" Her voice steely.

"Don't wrinkle your forehead, Vicky," Lexy cautioned. "Those lines will harden like concrete."

"How many carbs, you think?" Rexy mused, examining a rosemary breadstick as if it were a deadly spear.

"So, ladies." Junior smiled, like an amiable host. "What do you do?"

"They're brain surgeons," Victoria said, drily.

"We're mo-dels," Lexy said. *Moe-dells.* "Can't you tell?"

"Cutie here's our lawyer." Rexy pointed a breadstick at Steve.

"We're celebrating," Steve said. "Lexy and Rexy got a TV commercial today."

"Vagistat!" the gals honked.

Lexy looked into Junior's eyes, as if staring into a camera lens: "Do *you* suffer from vaginal itching, soreness, or burning?"

"With a thick, smelly discharge?" Rexy chimed in.

"You may have a yeast infection!" Lexy proclaimed cheerily, as if congratulating a friend on winning the lottery. "So, if you don't want a fungus among us . . ."

In unison, they sang:

"Vag-i-stat your yeast away.
Don't you wait a-nother day.
Buy one tube, get a-nother free,
It won't sting when you pee."

"They say that on TV?" Junior asked.

"Cable," Steve explained. "Spice Channel."

The waiter approached and said: "If you're ready to order, may I recommend the barbecued duck?"

"Fuck that," Lexy said. "I'm a veterinarian."

They finished a second bottle of Cristal and an array of hired hands were clearing empty plates, picked clean of yuca-stuffed crispy shrimp, pan-roasted swordfish, catfish in a pecan crust, and a hearts-of-palm salad, the sole sustenance for the twins, who split the dish, wishing to retain their 112 pounds spread over their whooping-crane frames.

Steve spent the meal sizing up the body language of Junior and Victoria, but what could he tell? He had shattered the dynamics of the table with his intrusion. Maybe he should have worn a disguise and sat at the bar. Then he could have done real surveillance, picking up their vibes, unobserved. In the next moment, he wondered if he was losing his mind.

Hey, relax. Vic deeply cares for me. We're just going through a rough patch.

Steve listened to Junior entertain the table with tales of free diving off Cabo San Lucas — descending to four hundred feet but finishing only third in the competition — and catching a record swordfish off the Caicos Islands, but tossing it back, instead of roasting it for fifty people with black bean muneta. Actually, the guy seemed okay. He wasn't playing footsie with Victoria under the table, and so far, he hadn't speared anyone with his butter knife.

Was Victoria right?

Have I screwed up, trying to pin two crimes on Junior? Killing Ben Stubbs and lusting after my lady — the latter being the true capital crime?

As the waiter applied a blowtorch to the top of Junior's crème brûlée, Steve said: "This reminds me of something, Vic. Remember the case of the flaming toupee?"

"Café Jacquet in Lauderdale." She turned

toward Junior. "Our client's toupee got caught in the duck flambé."

"Wow," Junior said.

"Only his pride was hurt," she said. "His date didn't know he was bald, so Steve sued for his embarrassment."

"Ten grand plus free desserts for life," Steve said.

Another server brought out a medley of tropical ice creams. Guava, mango, papaya. Steve launched into a recitation of restaurant legal cases, including a libelous review that referred to one dish as "veal à la bubonic plague," a collapsing chair that injured a four-hundred-pound diner, and a careless sushi chef who served his own fingertip with the California roll.

Junior laughed, displaying his well-advertised dimples and clefted chin. The discussion turned to the legal system, Steve calling trial lawyers the last hope of the common citizen in fighting megacorporations, incompetent doctors, and insurance companies. This went on a while, Lexy and Rexy sharing their fruit platter for dessert, slicing the skin off the grapes to save calories, Steve ranting that insurance companies were racketeering gangs and their executives were the spawn of Satan who denied coverage to honest policyholders, and when that didn't work, fought dirty against the truly injured, all the while gobbling their expense account beef tenderloin and whining about malingerers and malcontents who file workers' comp claims for having limbs torn off by ten-ton jig grinders.

"I'm with you on the insurance companies," Junior agreed. "You wouldn't believe the hoops they made us jump through on Oceania."

"I can imagine," Victoria said. "What'd you need, a hundred-million-dollar binder?"

"Three hundred million," Junior said.

Steve let out a low whistle.

Across the table, Lexy and Rexy seemed bored with the adult conversation. They were pinching each other's upper arms, testing for fat content. They would have found more by squeezing chopsticks.

"Which carrier did you end up with?" Steve asked.

Junior stroked his chin, Steve wondering if food particles ever got stuck in the little clefted canyon. "A foreign consortium," Junior said after a moment.

"Lloyd's of London?"

Another pause, another chin stroke. "No, a Bermuda trust, actually."

"We sued a Bermuda group," Victoria said. "What was its name?"

"Pitts Bay Risk Management," Steve answered, eyes on Junior. "They had the re-insurance on a Sarasota condo project that failed to meet the building code."

Steve paused. Expecting Junior to say, *"Yeah, that's the one."* Or, *"No, we're using Hamilton Liability, Limited."* Or whatever.

"Now that I think about it, we turned down the Bermuda company," Junior said. "Placed the insurance with a Pacific Rim group."

"Probably Trans-Global out of Singapore," Steve said. Was it his imagination, or did the world's third-deepest free diver have a case of the darting eyes?

"Sounds like it," Junior said. "Yeah. I think that's the one."

Junior signaled the waiter for a refill on his after-dinner brandy — a forty-year-old Montifaud at forty-five bucks a glass — saying something about its masculine, woody taste. Then his cell phone beeped, and he looked relieved, excusing himself from the table to take the call. A moment later, the waiter delivered the check in an embossed leather folder as thick as a book. He placed the handsome package in front of Steve, who tried to slide it over to Junior's empty place, but Victoria blocked it like a hockey goalie, and skidded it back to Steve with a wicked look. Steve peeked inside at the four-digit number, made a croaking sound as if a chicken bone were caught in his throat, then slapped the folder closed.

"I don't care about your dreamboat stiffing me with the check," Steve groused.

"Sure you do," Victoria fired back. "You'll have to take out a second mortgage."

They stood outside the restaurant on this warm, breezy night. Waiting for the valet service, Junior's silver Hummer having been delivered first. He'd already cheek-kissed Victoria and smacked Steve good-naturedly on the shoulder, then drove off, turning north on Ponce de Leon Boulevard with two chattering blondes aboard.

It was Steve's idea that Junior give Lexy and Rexy a ride back to their South Beach condo. After all, Junior was staying at the Astor just a flew blocks away. It was all very logical, especially to Victoria. Steve was trying to set him up. The *bimbos a deux* would report everything to Steve, who was doubtless hoping the pair would make a midnight sandwich out of Junior in their tenth-floor playpen-by-the-sea.

That goofy plan didn't irritate her half as much as Steve's crashing the dinner party. Junior had seemed on the verge of expressing something for her when Steve rode in with the long-legged cavalry.

"What gets me," he grumbled now, "is how evasive Junior was about the insurance company."

"C'mon, Steve. Junior's not a detail person."

"A three-hundred-million-dollar insurance policy isn't a detail. You can't close a construction loan without an insurance binder in place."

"What's the big deal? You heard him. They placed the insurance with Trans-something-or-other."

"Trans-Global."

"Right. Trans-Global from Singapore."

"There's no such company. I made up the name, and he took the bait."

She was stunned. "Why the cheap trick?"

"To see if he was lying. Which he was."

"He was just agreeing with you to change the subject. Who wants to talk about insurance binders at dinner?"

"Lawyers trying to defend a murder trial."

"That's not it." Victoria pointed a finger at him. "You've made it personal. What do you have against Junior?"

"Other than the fact that he'd like to free dive into your —"

"Don't be crude, Steve. Just tell me. What

are you doing? What's the insurance company have to do with who murdered Ben Stubbs?"

"It's a piece of the puzzle that doesn't fit. Oceania's the reason Stubbs was killed. If Junior's lying about Oceania's insurance, what else is he lying about?"

EIGHTEEN:
I GREASE THE SKIDS,
KID

"Please state your name for the record," Steve said.

"Peter Luber." The pudgeball in pinstripes turned toward Sofia Hernandez, the raven-haired court stenographer whose tricolored nails were *click-clack*ing the keys of her machine. "But you can call me Pinky, hon."

Sofia rolled her eyes, but like every good court reporter kept blessedly silent. She was used to men flirting with her, including one Stephen M. Solomon, Esq., with whom — BV, before Victoria — Sofia used to dally.

"Where do you live, Mr. Luber?" Steve asked.

"Penthouse One-A, Belvedere Condos, Bal Harbour."

"And your office address?"

"Front seat of my Lincoln, boychik."

"You have no office?"

"Least my Town Car don't smell like a garbage dump."

Pinky sniffed and made a face. They were in the Solomon & Lord suite, if that's what you could call their second-floor hovel, the air ripe with rotting papaya from the Dumpster below the window. Steve was taking Luber's deposition in the lawsuit to get back Herbert's Bar license.

"Try to keep your answers responsive to the questions," Steve instructed.

Pinky Luber chomped his cold cigar and glared at Steve. Unhappy at being served with a subpoena, unhappy swearing to tell the truth, unhappy giving any deposition, much less one that poked around in his past. "Then let's move this charade along. I gotta get to the track in time for the daily double."

"What's your occupation, Mr. Luber?"

"Consultant."

Luber had tried enough cases himself to know that a smart witness answers as concisely as possible. A sentence is better than a paragraph, one word far better than two.

"Could you be a little more descriptive?" Steve asked.

"No."

Steve got the message. This wouldn't be like pulling teeth. Pulling teeth would be too easy. This would be like passing gallstones.

"Tell me the names of your clients."

Luber shook his head. "Confidential."

Steve was trying to send a message of his own. If he could, he would mess up Luber's business. Lacking a Bar license, Pinky could no longer ply his trade inside the courtroom. But he found life even more lucrative in the chambers of municipal commissions and the myriad agencies of city, county, and state government. If you needed retail space at the seaport — for a rental car company or a gift shop or a pretzel stand — and wanted to avoid pesky complications like competitive bidding, you hired Pinky Luber, influence peddler extraordinaire.

"Fact of the matter, Mr. Luber, you're a fixer, right?"

"Already told you. Consultant."

"You know a lot of people in government?"

"I been around a long time."

"You're pals with county commissioners? Agency heads? Judges?"

"Yeah. Some of 'em even send me Chanukah cards."

"You're too modest, Mr. Luber. Let's say I wanted to put up billboards along I-95. Would I come to you for help?"

"If you're smart. Which you ain't."

"And just what would you do to get me

231

my billboards?"

"I'd introduce you to some people downtown and hope everyone falls in love."

"So, you're a matchmaker?"

"I grease the skids, kid."

"You ever grease the skids in Circuit Court?"

"That's old news. I did my time. What's that gotta do with the price of borscht?"

Just then the door opened and Herbert Solomon barged in, his flip-flops smacking the floor with each step.

"Cessante causa cessat et effectus!" Herbert sounded like a Roman senator but looked like a beach bum in paint-splattered denim cutoffs and an aloha shirt festooned with bougainvillea flowers. "Cease and desist, son."

"Are you drunk, Dad?" Steve asked.

"Ah'm removing you as counsel." Herbert turned to Luber and nodded. "Pinky, you're looking good."

"You look like *Hawaii Five-O*," Luber said.

"You hear me, son?" Herbert said. "Ah'm firing you and dismissing the case."

"You can't fire me," Steve retorted. "You don't have standing."

"In mah own damn case, ah sure as hell do."

"I filed under the private attorney general

232

statute. You're not the real-party-in-interest. The people of Florida are."

"You slippery bastard," his father said. "You think you can get away with that?"

"You did when you sued those phony muffler repair shops."

"Ah should have known you wouldn't have an original thought." Herbert turned back to Luber. "So how the hell are you, Pinky?"

"Jesus, Dad. This is the guy who butt-fucked you."

"Is 'butt-fucked' hyphenated?" Sofia Hernandez asked, typing away.

"Go off the record, sweetie," Herbert ordered, and Sofia's hands flew up like a pianist finishing a concerto.

"*I* say when we go off the record," Steve protested.

"So, on or off?" Sofia asked.

"Off," Steve instructed, "but only because I said so."

She shrugged and opened her purse, looking for a nail file.

"On the nitro, that's how I am, Herb." Luber patted his chest. "Plus Nexium for the acid reflux. And a whole drawerful of pills for arthritis. And you?"

"Feeling good, Pinky. No complaints."

"Like I was saying to your boy, you're better off out of the rat race. But the big *k'nocker* don't listen too good."

Using bastardized Yiddish to brand him a "big shot," Steve knew. "Better a *k'nocker* than an *alter kocker*," he fired back. Calling Luber an "old fart."

"Steve's always been a hard case," Herbert allowed.

"Dad. What are you doing?"

"Pinky and ah go back a long way."

Steve couldn't believe it. Here was the guy who'd torpedoed his father's career, and the two of them were acting like old war buddies. Next, they'd be exchanging pictures of their grandchildren.

"I won seventeen capital cases in a row in front of your old man," Luber said.

"Yeah, yeah, I know," Steve said. "Just like the Dolphins."

"But like Don Shula used to say, you remember the losses more. I'll never forget the last jury before the streak started. They must have come straight from an ACLU meeting." Pinky hacked up a laugh, his body jiggling like a beach ball. "All *shvartzers* from Liberty City and Yids from Aventura."

"Happens that way sometimes," Herbert said. "Luck of the draw."

"Those folks wouldn't have convicted Ted Bundy of littering." Luber turned to Steve.

"See, kid. Jurors will do what they damn well please. I remember one trial, they were all dressed in jeans and sneakers. Gene Miller writes in the *Herald* that times had changed. Used to be, jurors would wear coats and ties, dresses or nice skirts. Now, your old man had instructed the jury not to read the papers, but the day after the story appeared . . ."

"All the men wore suits, all the women dresses." Herbert filled in the rest. "Looked like they were going to church."

"So what's the lesson, kid?" Luber said.

"Don't patronize me," Steve said.

"You can't trust juries. Take it from me."

"You don't believe in the system, that it, Luber?"

"Would you want to be judged by people too stupid to get out of jury duty?"

"You believe that, too, Dad?" Steve challenged.

"I don't think about those things anymore."

"Jesus, we had some cases," Luber said.

"*We?*" Steve shook his head. "You guys weren't partners."

"The law's stacked against the state, so a good prosecutor always gets the judge on his side. Right, Herb?"

Herbert silently walked to the window and

stared across the alley.

"You remember the Butcher of Lovers' Lane?" Luber prodded.

When Herbert didn't respond, Luber kept chattering: "I was at the top of my game. Jury voted in thirty-nine minutes to fry his ass. That still the record, Herb?"

"Ah wouldn't know." Herbert still looked out the window.

Steve was trying to figure out the change that had come over his father. At first, Herbert had seemed genuinely pleased to see this rosy-faced son-of-a-bitch. That was strange enough. But now, with Luber telling war stories, his old man's mood had dipped.

What message is Pinky sending that I'm not getting?

Herbert turned around and faced the two of them. "Son, if you've got some questions for Pinky, why not ask them and get this over with?"

"Fine," Steve said. "Sofia, back on the record."

She stretched her arms over her head, then behind her back, which caused her breasts to strain against the fabric of her silk blouse. All three men — one young *k'nocker,* two *alter kockers* — took a gander at Sofia's knockers. Smiling to herself, she curled her fingers over the stenograph keys and waited.

"Did there come a time you testified to the Grand Jury in a corruption probe, Mr. Luber?" Steve asked, reverting to the formal cadence of a trial lawyer.

"Yes."

"Did you testify that Herbert Solomon took bribes to rezone agricultural property to commercial use?"

"Lemme save you some time, kid," Luber said. "If you're asking me to recant what I said about Herb, I ain't gonna do it."

"So your lies stand, is that it?"

"Go pound your pud, bud."

"Son, just get back to your murder case and drop this, okay?" Herbert pleaded.

"I offered to help the kid out," Luber said. "And this is the way he treats me."

"Don't want your help," Steve said.

"I'll give you some, anyway. You oughta be following the green path."

Steve must have looked puzzled.

"The money trail, kid. Hal Griffin's got a hundred thousand cash on his boat, then the cops find forty grand in Stubbs' hotel room after he croaked. But with Oceania, you're talking hundreds of millions of dollars. So if a hundred forty thousand's floating around, there's gotta be more. Find out who's greasing those skids, kid. Follow the money, sonny."

NINETEEN:
LORD'S LAW

"Not guilty!" Hal Griffin proclaimed in a strong, clear voice. Exactly the way Victoria had instructed him. They were standing in front of Judge Clyde Feathers in a fourth-floor courtroom of the Monroe County Courthouse, three blocks from the harbor in Key West. With Steve in Miami prepping his father's case, Victoria was flying solo, handling Griffin's arraignment by herself. Happy to be in charge.

She had rejected Steve's advice that Griffin sing out: "Not guilty, not guilty. Thank God Almighty, I am not guilty!" All to the rhythm of Martin Luther King's "free at last." Too melodramatic for Victoria's taste.

Lately, Steve had been fussing around with creative pleas, intended to influence the press and prospective jurors. Once he tried "Innocent as the pure, driven snow," an unfortunate choice in a cocaine trial.

But is Uncle Grif really innocent?

For the past two days, at Steve's suggestion, Victoria had been following "the green path," and she didn't like where it seemed to lead. She'd been hauling down mildewy books in the county's Real Property records room, breaking two fingernails and poring over real estate sales. Now she was sure Uncle Grif had misled her, and she planned to confront him as soon as they got back to the hotel.

"Damn it, Uncle Grif. I told you to be honest with me. I can't help you if you lie."

She had been careful all morning not to let Griffin know she was upset. He needed to appear confident and at ease in his first court appearance. Glancing at him now, she thought Griffin seemed dignified and prosperous in a dark, double-breasted suit. But the suit made him even thicker through the chest — more physically imposing — and Victoria made a mental note to have him dress in something slimming when a jury was impaneled.

She wore a double-breasted suit, too. A mauve, Dolce & Gabbana with the extra-wide lapels, a boned bodice, and a fitted skirt. A hip-hugging summer wool fabric made stretchy with a touch of spandex, and no, she didn't need any slimming tricks, thank you very much. Her suede-lined Bottega Veneta woven-leather black purse — large as a satchel — was perfect for carrying a legal file as well as her makeup. What had Sarah Jessica Parker said on *Sex and the City?*

"Purses are to women what balls are to men. You'd feel naked leaving home without them."

Got that right, girl.

Judge Feathers spent a few minutes with housekeeping details. Victoria waived the formal reading of the indictment. Calendars came out, and the judge set discovery deadlines and a trial date. Then he announced bail would be one million dollars. No problem there. The amount had been agreed upon in advance, and the surety was already posted. Griffin would walk out of the courthouse without ever feeling the shame and discomfort of the orange jumpsuit with the Monroe County jail logo . . . unless he was convicted at trial.

A hot blast of muggy air hit her as they left the courtroom, which opened directly onto an outdoor walkway that led to the elevators. Cameras clicked and questions were shouted as Victoria escorted Griffin through the snarling, slobbering, shoving pack of backpedaling jackals and hyenas, aka journalists.

"Any chance of a plea?" one reporter yelled.

"What's your defense?" shouted another.

"Why'd you do it, Griffin?" a particularly rude reporter called out.

"My attorney will answer all questions," Griffin said, serenely.

Victoria put on her lawyer's look for the evening news — confident but not cocky. "We fully believe the jury will conclude this was all a tragic accident."

"Tragic accident."

Steve had given her the tag line and told her to repeat it as often as possible. *"Start drilling your theme into the public consciousness and never let up,"* he'd instructed.

Okay, she had to admit Steve had won a bunch of cases using the technique.

Mistaken identity.

Sloppy police work.

Justifiable homicide.

And now *tragic accident.* Which would have been a lot easier if Uncle Grif had said he was showing Stubbs the speargun when it accidentally fired. But Griffin stuck to his story: He was on the bridge, and when Stubbs didn't respond to the intercom, he put the boat on auto, climbed down the ladder, and found the man with the spear in his chest. So she was stuck arguing to the jury that Stubbs had been messing around with the speargun and accidentally shot himself.

The spear's angle of entry was crucial to support the theory. So far, Victoria had consulted two expert witnesses: a biomechanics professor from Georgia Tech and a safety engineer from a private firm. The professor told her the accident theory was *"not provable to a reasonable degree of biomechanical probability"* and the engineer said his tests were similarly inconclusive. Nothing they could use in court. There was another professor, a human factors expert from Columbia University, but his report wasn't prepared yet.

Steve had been toying with the idea of a courtroom demonstration where he would load the speargun, trying to shoot himself in the chest while wearing a Kevlar vest. He did a dry run in the office and managed to fire the spear out the window and onto the balcony across the alley where the Jamaican steel band was grilling chicken and smoking weed. Victoria was fairly certain it would not help their case if they impaled a juror.

Now she guided Griffin by the elbow, steering him toward the elevator. An odd sensation, this role reversal. She could remember Uncle Grif's protective hand on *her* arm, steering her through crowds at Disney World so many years ago. Now *she* was the protector. She was all that stood between Uncle Grif and life in prison. At least for the moment. When the trial began, Steve would be alongside, jockeying for position.

For now, though, she enjoyed the spotlight, the attention from the press. Amazing, the instant respect a high-profile murder case seemed to convey. Especially when you sit first chair. No wonder Steve was reluctant to give it up. But she'd laid down the law, Lord's Law. *"Your choice, Steve. You can sit second chair. Or take a seat in the gallery."*

"No problem," he'd said. *"You're the boss. That's what we agreed."*

Steve's unconditional surrender made her suspicious — she half expected him to burst through the courtroom door with some headline-grabbing announcement — but he'd stayed behind while she handled the arraignment and soaked up her fifteen minutes of media fame. Now, as she clawed her way past the reporters to the elevator, she still wondered if Steve wasn't lurking nearby, about to call his own press conference.

"Ms. Lord! Mr. Griffin!" a disheveled young man she recognized as a reporter from the *Key West Citizen* shouted at her.

"What happened on that boat?"

"It will all come out in court." She smiled for the cameras.

Of all the sappy platitudes, she thought. Of course it will all come out in court. She just didn't know what the hell *it* would be.

"And in due course," she added, "it will be clear that the death of Mr. Stubbs was simply a tragic accident."

Steve would be proud, she thought.

A fine rain was falling now, and Victoria worried about her makeup running. The courthouse, with its open-air walkways, was one of those designs for the subtropics, where you can get sunburned or rained on while technically still inside the building.

Once in the lobby, they passed a mural of a Spanish galleon, buccaneers landing on a sandy beach, pirates engaged in sword fights. An unusual image in a courthouse, she thought, a celebration of the island's distant — or not so distant — lawlessness.

"This way, Ms. Lord!" one photographer screeched, aiming a still camera at her.

"No. Over here, Ms. Lord!" another belted out.

"Will Griffin testify?" hollered a man in dirty jeans and a wife-beater T-shirt.

They were down here, too. Clogging the lobby, scrambling like cockroaches. A bothersome, boisterous, unkempt lot. But feeling a bit like a star on the red carpet, Victoria figured she'd better get used to the attention. The spotlight, she believed, burned bright but was narrowly focused. Wide enough only for one. Even when they're partnered up, lawyers are lone gunslingers. Who remembers the name of Johnnie Cochran's law partner? Or Melvin Belli's? Or Gerry Spence's?

So, yes indeed, a lawyer who makes a name for herself in a big murder trial had better expect the high-wattage lights. And buy some waterproof makeup, too.

■ ■ ■ ■

SOLOMON'S LAWS

■ ■ ■ ■

6. The client who lies to his lawyer is like a husband who cheats on his wife. It seldom happens just once.

TWENTY:
THE MONEY TRAIL

Ten minutes and a pink taxicab ride later, Victoria and Griffin were in the War Room, her suite at the Pier House. An oak conference table and leather chairs, a wicker sofa, sailing prints on the walls. The miscellany of trial prep filled the suite. Cardboard boxes stacked on the floor; documents scattered across the table; a model of the *Force Majeure* on a sideboard.

Victoria kicked off her velvet-toed pumps, poured mineral water over ice, and sparred with her client. "So where did Stubbs get forty thousand dollars in cash?" she demanded.

"Like I told you before, Princess, I got no idea."

"The state will say you bribed him for a favorable environmental report."

"Let 'em prove it."

"They can subpoena your bank accounts, get all your records."

"Good luck to 'em."

"Meaning?"

"I've lived in a dozen countries. Even I can't remember where all my money is."

Victoria didn't know how to get him to open up. Should she tell him what she knew, perhaps limiting what he would disclose, or should she keep the questions open-ended, hoping he would fill in even more? She sipped at the mineral water, buying time.

Outside the windows, tugboats guided a cruise ship into port. In the hotel parking lot, three TV news trucks sat side by side, resembling giant insects, their antennas poking the air. Victoria had the fear, not entirely irrational, that a TV camera attached to a mechanical arm would appear on her balcony and poke its lens into the suite.

"Uncle Grif, you have to tell me the truth."

"I have, Princess."

"Did you give Stubbs the forty thousand?"

"I didn't. I swear."

She took a deep breath and plunged ahead. "I've spent the last two days going through the county's real estate records. Do you know what I found?"

"They're still selling waterlogged property

in the Glades?"

"Two months ago, Ben Stubbs bought a lot in Key Largo for three hundred thousand dollars. No mortgage. All cash."

Silence. Griffin sat at the conference table, poker-faced.

"Where do you suppose Stubbs got the money?" she asked.

"Maybe he won big at jai alai."

"The money was wired from a corporate account in a Cayman Islands bank to an escrow agent in Key Largo. Want to guess the name on the account?"

"Nah. I bite."

"Queen Investments, Limited." She paused to gauge his reaction. Nothing. "Unusual name, don't you think?"

"The Caymans are British. Maybe they're honoring Queen Elizabeth."

"Or Queen Irene."

"Your mother?" He laughed, but his smile seemed artificial. "What are you getting at, Princess?"

"Uncle Grif, I've got the corporate filings. You're the sole officer of Queen Investments. You wired that money to Ben Stubbs."

He grunted, getting out of his chair, then walked to the window. Outside, the cruise ship eased up to the dock, hundreds of passengers lining the rails. "Nice work, Princess."

"Uncle Grif, why didn't you tell me you bribed Stubbs?"

He turned back and seemed to appraise her. Maybe trying to figure out just how much she knew. Usually, she got that look from an unfriendly witness, not her own client.

"A bribe?" Griffin said finally. "At the time, it felt more like extortion. Stubbs demanded the money."

"Whatever you call it, you lied to me."

"If you knew I paid off a federal employee, would you put me on the stand to deny it?"

"Of course not. That would be unethical."

"Which is why I couldn't tell you about the money. I needed to preserve my ability to deny."

"It won't work. If I found this, the state will, too. Uncle Grif, the truth might be better than a lie. Bribing Stubbs is a lot better than killing him. In fact, it could help the case."

"How?"

"Hypothetically, if you bribed him, you'd have no reason to kill him. You knew his environmental report was going to be positive. You just needed him to file it."

"You're saying we admit I paid off

Stubbs?"

"It'd be ballsy; but without motive, the state can't win."

"Ballsy" bringing Steve to mind. It was just the kind of bungee-jumping tactic he loved.

"Hypothetically," Griffin said, borrowing her ten-dollar word, "let's say Stubbs wasn't happy with the lot in Key Largo, even though that's what he'd been yammering about. A place for his retirement. Let's say we're having dinner and the greedy prick says, *'Hal, you're gonna make millions off Oceania. Tens of millions. But you couldn't make a dime without me.'* "

Victoria frowned, seeing where this boat was headed. "When would this have happened? Hypothetically?"

"A week before we get on the *Force Majeure* to come see you and Solomon. And suppose we're eating red snapper and Stubbs says, *'From now on, I'm your partner, Hal. I want a million up front and five percent of the casino profits.'* " Griffin snorted a laugh. "Like he was some connected guy in Vegas. The stupid shit watched too many movies. No concept what it takes to build something like this. Saying he's my partner. I could have bashed his head in right there."

"Please tell me you didn't."

Seeing her case sink to the bottom of the Gulf.

"I told him to fuck off. But I never touched him. Not then. Not on the boat. What you gotta understand, Princess, people see this kind of money, they all want a piece. A county commissioner threatened to hold up a port license unless I paid him under the table. I told the bandit I didn't need no stinking license. Leicester Robinson, the barge guy, said he'd do his work for nothing up front, but he wanted three points of the gross. Points! Where do they get this stuff?"

"It wouldn't have been a crime to make Robinson your partner. He's not a federal employee."

"I told Robinson to fuck off, too. He backed down and was damn glad to get the barge work at cost plus thirty percent."

"Ben Stubbs," Victoria said, getting back on track. "After he extorted you, after you wanted to bash his head in, what happened then?"

"I calmed down. Decided to toss him some chum. The day before I brought him down on the boat, I'd put a hundred thousand in cash in one of the lobster pots. So now, when I pull up the pot, I say to Stubbs, *'Here's the best-tasting lobster you'll ever eat.'*

Up comes the money and I tell him I'll give him a hundred grand every lobster season the rest of his life. Which, come to think of it, I guess I did."

"What was Stubbs' reaction? He wanted a million and you only gave him a hundred thousand?"

"I gave him an annuity. He was good at math, so he took it."

"You tell anyone you were paying Stubbs off?"

"No."

"Not even Junior?" Thinking if Junior knew and hadn't told her, there were ramifications, both professional and personal.

Griffin shook his head. "I didn't want to implicate my boy."

"You think Stubbs told anyone about your deal?"

"Doubt it. No wife. Kind of a loner. And he didn't need an accomplice to pull this off."

"Anything else about Stubbs I should know?"

Griffin seemed to think something over. Then he said: "The last week or so, he was a little skitterish."

"Skitterish?" Thinking he meant skittish. Or maybe jittery. Or maybe a combination of the two.

"Kind of nervous and paranoid. He started using disposable cell phones so there'd be no record of his calls. Every time I needed to talk to him, I'd have a helluva time because he was using a different phone. He was like a scared rabbit."

"Maybe he wasn't as used to taking bribes as you were at giving them."

Griffin belted out a laugh. "Okay, Princess, you got me there. Maybe all those projects in the islands made me a little reckless. Jeez, in the Caribbean, you gotta put every politician's brother-in-law on the payroll before you even think about moving dirt."

Like an astronaut tethered to a space capsule, Victoria suddenly felt as if she were floating in a vast, dark, dangerous place. She tried to assess the damage. Assuming the cops didn't find a to-do note in Stubbs' hotel room — *eat breakfast; buy Bermuda shorts; shake down Hal Griffin* — there was still a chance the state wouldn't learn what was going on. Or at least not be able to prove it.

Still, any chance of putting Griffin on the stand just sank into the deep, blue sea. She couldn't let him lie, and without knowing what the state had, she could never subject him to cross-examination.

"Anything else? Please, Uncle Grif. Don't hold back."

"There is something that's been bothering me."

Oh, boy. Here we go.

"That lot in Key Largo. The cash from the lobster pots. Those were from me. Bribes. Extortion. Whatever. But I didn't lie to you about that forty thou in Stubbs' hotel room. The money didn't come from me."

"Then where'd Stubbs get it?"

"Damned if I know."

That made no sense, Victoria thought. But neither did lying about it. Two bribes are as bad as three. Without warning, the case had gotten even more complicated. Did the money trail lead to a third party? And if so, who? But could she trust anything Uncle Grif told her?

"The client who lies to his lawyer is like the husband who cheats on his wife. It seldom happens just once."

Another of Steve's laws. He would know what to do. Twisty, complicated cases were his forte. Probably because he preferred the serpentine path to the straight one.

"So, what now, Princess?"

Before she could answer, before she could even admit to herself that she wanted to ask Steve what to do next, there was a knock at the door.

"Room service." A woman's voice with a faint Spanish accent.

"We didn't order," Victoria said, walking toward the door.

"Suite Two-thirty-one," the woman persisted. "Champagne and caviar for three."

"You have the wrong room." Victoria opened the suite's double doors. A young woman in a pink uniform with a name tag reading *"Evelia"* stood there with a cart. A bottle of Cristal lounged in an ice bucket. Three place settings, two covered plates, and a slender vase of lilies as the centerpiece.

"I have the order ticket," Evelia said. "Suite Two-thirty-one. See?"

Another woman breezed by them and into the room. "Of course it's the right suite. Not bad . . . But I would have gotten the southeast corner, for the breeze."

The woman walked with perfect posture. She was in her late fifties but could easily have passed for a refined and elegant forty. Her upswept hair, the same color as the Cristal, reminded Victoria of Princess Grace of Monaco. She wore a corded pink satin jacket, fitted at the waist, and a long matching skirt with a beaded hem. Covering her wrist — and half her forearm — was a John

Hardy hammered-gold cuff bracelet. Altogether too formal a look for midday in Key West, but splendid for a sweeping entrance.

Splendid for The Queen.

"Grif, I hope you still like beluga," Irene Lord cooed.

"Jesus, Mary, and Joseph!" Griffin's face froze somewhere between a smile and a stroke.

"Mother!" Victoria exclaimed. "I thought you were in Katmandu."

"It was quite chilly, dear." As if that explained it. Irene patted her hair. "But this damn humidity. I'll never get used to it."

"Mother, what are you doing here?"

"Do I need a reason to visit my only daughter and my oldest friend?"

"Irene, Irene," Griffin sighed. "After all these years. All this time gone by."

The poor guy looked like he was in a trance.

"Are you two just going to stand there?" Irene said, "or is somebody going to pour me champagne?"

Twenty-One: Caviar on the Carpet

"Irene, Irene," Griffin gushed. "You haven't changed in sixteen years."

"You swine. I look *better!*" Irene laughed, the sound of church bells pealing. She lifted her chin, letting him take in her fine bone structure and the silken skin of her throat.

"How do you do it?" Griffin hugged her tightly.

"Nutrition. Exercise. And a few dents have been pounded out and repainted."

Not to mention a few parts that were brand new, Victoria thought. Her mother's boobs were teenagers and her butt a newborn babe.

"Mother, you still haven't said what you're doing here."

"Grif's in trouble, so I came."

Victoria wished she could cross-examine: *"Really? And when's the last time you walked across the street to help someone, much less flew halfway round the world?"*

Victoria loved her mother but could be coolly rational about her. As a child, there were times Victoria felt like one of The Queen's matched snow-white poodles, Van Cleef and Arpel. At dinner parties, she'd be summoned from her room to perform for her mother's guests. The gleaming baby-grand piano was a prop, Victoria a bit player in the melodrama that was her mother's life.

"Something Chopin, Princess. Nocturne thirteen, perhaps."

Victoria's proficiency as a pianist, her posture and manners, even her well-groomed looks all reflected on The Queen, whose friends *oohed* and *cooed* at the precocious child.

"White wine only, darlings." Her mother's voice flooding back.

With carpets and sofas as white as Van Cleef and Arpel's fluffy pelts, The Queen refused to serve red wine. No wonder, as a rebellious teenager, Victoria was drawn to Chianti, Campari, and Singapore Slings with grenadine. No wonder she had desperately yearned for a *normal* mother. Home-baked cookies, PTA meetings, maybe even a career other than the full-time job of appearing regal. Now, fully grown, Victoria wished they had a closer, warmer relationship. But her mother was an air-kisser, not a hugger. And just how do you embrace a woman who's deathly afraid of smearing her makeup?

"All these years," Griffin murmured, yet again.

"Forgive me, Grif," Irene said. "I should have returned your letters and calls, but after Nelson died . . ."

"I know. I know." They released each other to arm's length, Griffin keeping one hand on Irene's back. It looked as if they were going to fox-trot. "But you should have let me help you."

"It just didn't seem right, Grif. I needed the money, that's for sure. But . . ."

The Queen let it hang there, and Victoria tried to remember the days after her father's death. Her mother had gone from society hostess — what's that corny old phrase, "the hostess with the mostest" — to a social pariah. There'd been whispers among the La Gorce Country Club set. Irene Lord's profligate spending had driven the family into debt. Nelson had cut corners in the business. They sank into the quicksand of legal problems, tax problems, money problems.

How much of it was true?

The Queen refused to talk about it.

Uncle Grif and her mother still stared into

each other's eyes. Victoria was starting to feel like the uninvited guest at another couple's party, a couple she didn't know all that well. Whatever memories were unspooling, she was not privy to them.

"I'm so sorry about Phyllis," Irene offered. "And forgive me for waiting all this time to say so."

"Thank you, Irene. She always thought so highly of you."

They reminisced a few minutes more before sitting down to guzzle champagne and slather caviar, eggs, and onion onto tiny wafers. Irene had signed the check to the room, meaning Victoria would have to pay.

At a lull in the conversation, Irene lowered her voice to a whisper. "You didn't really kill that fellow, did you, Grif?"

"Of course not. And The Princess is going to prove it. She's outstanding, Irene. Smart like her father, beautiful like her mother."

"I hope she's not in over her head."

"Mother. I've handled murder cases."

"For riffraff, maybe," Irene said. "But Grif's family. He should have the best."

"Not to worry," Griffin said. "Victoria's terrific. Her partner, too."

"Solomon?" Irene wrinkled her nose, which had been expensively sculpted upward, like the prow of a fine yacht. "I suppose he's effective in his own déclassé way." She took another sip of champagne, then said, "How's Junior doing? Victoria tells me he's turned into a real hunk."

"Mo-ther," Victoria said in her chiding tone. No surprise that her mother changed the subject from Steve to the only boy — well, man now — considered good enough for her little darling. Oh, how The Queen adored Junior, or at least the memory of him. As for Steve, a few months ago Irene had told Victoria that three things gave her indigestion: raw onions, men in lime velour sweatsuits, and thoughts of her marrying Steve.

"Junior never cared much about making a buck," Griffin said. "But lately, he's taken an interest in the business. Been riding me hard, telling me I spend too much money, take too many risks."

Irene cocked her head and rolled a pearl earring between thumb and index finger. "I remember years ago the six of us were at the Surf Club for dinner. Junior must have been about ten and Victoria eight, and they were feeding each other stone crabs with little cocktail forks. And one of us, I think it was Nelson, said wouldn't it be great if the kids got together someday." She paused, relishing the memory. "I think we all were hoping for a Griffin-Lord wedding."

"Plans," Griffin said. "If there's anything I've learned, it's that man's hopes are just God's toys."

Irene sighed. "Don't I know it, Grif."

Victoria decided to intervene before the discussion turned to her kindergarten report cards, her childhood measles, or her first menstrual period. "Mother, Uncle Grif and I were working on trial prep, so I wonder if you —"

"Go right ahead, dear. I won't interfere." Irene hoisted her flute and finished off the champagne a trifle too quickly. Pouring herself another, she said: "So, have the two of you been talking about *moi?*"

"Mother, the world doesn't revolve around you."

"Since when, dear?"

"You have to leave," Victoria said. "We're discussing the case. You're not covered by the attorney-client privilege, and anything Uncle Grif says —"

"Oh, fiddles! Grif, tell my daughter she can't evict me."

"Now, I-rene," Griffin said with mock exasperation.

"Don't you 'Now, Irene' me."

They both laughed again, and Irene's eyes glistened with pleasure. The way they spoke to each other reminded Victoria of something, but what was it? She tried to dig up a memory but couldn't.

Just what was her mother doing, anyway? She seemed almost flirtatious. But then, flirting was second nature to her. There'd been many men in The Queen's life the past fifteen years, one rich widower or recently divorced tycoon after another. Much like her hammered gold bracelet, Irene was a most presentable trinket. The Queen's modus operandi, Victoria knew, was to show as little interest as possible, which only fueled men's ardor. She clearly enjoyed the fawning attention, the travel, the perks of private jets and five-star hotels.

When Victoria once asked why she didn't marry any of the suitors, her mother dismissed the idea with a wave of the hand. *"Heaven knows, I've been asked, but I've had the one great love of my life."*

Meaning Victoria's father, of course. Or so Victoria always thought. But just now, another suspicion was nibbling away, like a mouse in the larder.

Those pealing laughs.
Those glistening eyes.
The tenderness between them.

Her mother and Uncle Grif? No, it was utterly preposterous, to use one of The

Queen's own phrases.

Or was it?

Uncle Grif was the one who'd christened them The Queen and The Princess. He had always been around, always been attentive to their needs. That day she got lost at Disney World — she couldn't have been more than six or seven — it was Uncle Grif, not her father, who found her. And what about that bank account in the Caymans? *Queen Investment, Ltd.* Why not *Phyllis Investments?* Why not his own wife's name? Did the covert account reveal a surreptitious relationship?

"Now, I-rene."

"Don't you 'Now, Irene' me."

It came back to her then. That's the exchange she remembered between her mother and father. Or was it? Had it been Uncle Grif all along? Was she confusing the two men? And was her mother doing the same?

The two couples had been so close. Until her father's suicide. Logic told Victoria that her mother would have needed Uncle Grif even more in those awful days. So, with such a powerful emotional bond between them, why did The Queen cut him out of her life?

There could only be one reason.

Guilt.

Oh, God, no.

Victoria strained to keep her voice under control. "Mother, you can stay if you'll answer one question."

"Anything to help." Irene neatly knifed a layer of caviar onto a wafer.

"When Dad committed suicide, were you and Uncle Grif having an affair?"

Irene's hand trembled and she dropped the caviar-laden wafer, facedown, onto the carpet.

"Oh, Jesus," Griffin gasped.

Irene forced a smile as brittle as an icicle. "What an astonishingly rude question."

"Dad found out, didn't he?" Victoria's question caught in her throat. "Is that why he killed himself?"

Griffin squeezed his eyes shut and massaged his temples with his knuckles.

Irene dabbed a linen napkin at the corner of her mouth, a dainty motion. "My goodness. For poor Grif's sake, I hope you're a better lawyer than a gossip, dear."

Twenty-Two:
Talk, Hug, Kiss,
Screw

On the Caddy's radio, Roadkill Bill Jabanoski was singing "I Wanna Get Drunk, I Wanna Get Laid, and Monday Morning Seems Like Two Years Away." Even though it was one of Steve's favorite Key West songs, he turned down the volume as he shouted into his cell phone. "What kind of lawyer are you!"

In the passenger seat, Bobby fidgeted, first covering his ears with his hands, then putting a finger to his lips. Unless he was a third base coach signaling a hit-and-run, he wanted Steve to quiet down.

"Don't raise your voice to me," Victoria responded at the other end of the line. Sounding so calm, it aggravated Steve even more. Why couldn't she see past her own family problems?

"The client always comes first, Vic. Not the lawyer's personal needs."

"Then why aren't you here? Why are you

wasting your time on your father's case when he told you to dismiss it?"

"You didn't want me there!"

"Since when does that stop you?"

"Don't change the subject. I thought you could handle one simple arraignment without the client firing us."

"Uncle Grif didn't fire us. He just walked out and didn't come back."

"And won't return your calls."

"You're overreacting," Victoria said.

Steve was driving south on the Overseas Highway, headed to Key West and what was left of their case. Victoria had told him about Griffin bribing Stubbs but continuing to deny that he killed the "greedy prick" — an expression they might want to fine-tune before getting to court.

If we get to court.

The relationship between murder client and defense counsel was as delicate as that between two lovers. Had Victoria destroyed it?

"What the hell happened?" Steve demanded. "I'm the one who breaks the china. *You're* the one who's supposed to get along with people."

"I told you. It all came clear to me about The Queen and Uncle Grif."

"And you couldn't keep quiet about it?"

Steve banged the steering wheel with the heel of his hand. "That's ancient history. Who cares if they were playing hide-the-salami when Bette Midler was winning Grammys?"

"Must you be so crude?"

"Haven't I told you nothing's as important as maintaining your client's trust?"

"Aren't you the one who accused Uncle Grif of murder ten minutes after meeting him?"

"I *implicated* him. I *accused* his son. Besides, that's just my interviewing technique."

It was nearly ten p.m., Steve had a piercing headache, and the drive had barely begun. A misty rain was falling when they left Miami, so the top was up, the wind whistling through a small tear in the canvas above Bobby's head. They zipped past rows of Australian pines that looked like the log pilings of a wooden fort. A pale slice of moon peeked out from a thin layer of scudding clouds. On either side of the road, the turquoise water had turned an ominous black, the tangled mangrove trees melding into one indistinguishable dark mass, and the marshy hammocks — baked all day by the sun — were discharging a brackish smell into the moist night air.

"Why can't you understand my feelings?"

Victoria pressed him. *"Uncle Grif and my mother might be responsible for my father's death. How can I have a relationship with either one of them?"*

"Exactly what Griffin's wondering. He thinks you wouldn't mind seeing him go to prison. We're dead in the water, Vic. He'll have new counsel by the morning."

"Uncle Grif never said that."

The Caddy rumbled over the Jewfish Creek Bridge. Steve always wondered if he should be offended by the name. The jewfish was a giant grouper — some weighed several hundred pounds — and he had no idea why anyone would ascribe an ethnic heritage to the ugly old creature. Was there such a thing as a Methodist moray? A Baptist barracuda? He didn't think so. He hoped the reason behind the name was positive. Maybe jewfish were the doctors or professors or comedians of undersea life. But he feared the name reflected some negative stereotype, like the big fat loan shark dishing out a hundred clams at usurious rates. Shylocks of the deep.

"You gonna bill him for the time you spent calling him a sleaze?" Steve said into the cell phone.

"You billed The Beav for time spent wrestling a silicone doll."

"In Judge Schwartz's chambers? That was a hearing."

"I'm talking about at home, the night before."

"That was trial prep."

Judge Schwartz's clerk had called that afternoon, saying he was drafting an order dismissing the lawsuit against The Beav, but that His Honor would be hanging on to Tami the Love Doll a bit longer.

"I would have expected a little more empathy from you," Victoria said. *"When I told Junior about the two of them, he practically wept."*

"You called Mr. Suntan before me!"

"Why are you so insecure about him?"

Steve heard a throaty roar from behind the Caddy. In the rearview mirror, he saw a motorcycle swoop closer, tailgating them. The road was only two lanes with a solid line, but the chopper — a cherry red Harley — shot past him, the rider in black leather with a Darth Vader helmet.

"You should have called me first," Steve told Victoria.

"Junior has an emotional stake in this. He's sharing my pain."

"What Junior wants to share is your bed."

There was silence on the line.

Steve listened to the Caddy's tires whining across the asphalt. The Harley had disappeared into the distance. He was still waiting for Victoria to say: *"I'm not interested in Junior. You're the only man for me, even if sometimes you are the world's biggest dummy."*

But she didn't say that, not even the "biggest dummy" part. He decided to make a tactical retreat. "Look, I'm sorry — I'm being a real shit."

Still nothing.

"I'll try to be more understanding of what you're going through."

Line static.

"We should talk about the case, Vic, just in case we're not fired."

"I'm tired, Steve. I'm going to sleep."

Avoidance. Steve had never been in therapy or couples counseling or Deepak Chopra seminars, but he intuitively knew that you had to talk through your problems. In his experience, there was a surefire, four-step method for making up:

Talk.

Hug.

Kiss.

Screw.

Occasionally, it was possible to skip a step or two on the way to number four, but women loved to talk as much as they loved to buy shoes, so it was best to start there.

"How 'bout waiting up for me?" he suggested. "It's a beautiful night. Maybe we can walk on the beach, sip some sour mash whiskey."

"I'm really tired."

"It's been a few days and I really miss you."

"Uh-huh."

Okay, he thought, just lay it on the line. "I've got an itch that needs scratching."

"Gross," Bobby said.

"Try calamine lotion," Victoria said, and the phone clicked dead.

TWENTY-THREE:
A THOUGHT BEFORE
DYING

"Why do you always fight with everybody?" Bobby drilled him.

"I'm a lawyer," Steve said.

"I don't mean in court. With Victoria and Gramps."

"I guess 'cause I love them, kiddo."

"So why not tell them that, then just let them do what they want?"

"Objection. Compound question."

"I mean it, Uncle Steve. When's the last time you told Victoria you loved her?"

Steve shrugged. No way he was going to tell a twelve-year-old kid that his "I love yous" were generally confined to moments of priapic, pre-orgasmic bliss. And now that he thought of it, their lovemaking had tailed off recently. Starting the day Hal Griffin's boat went airborne, there'd been a definite slowdown in the hot-and-saucy department. No doubt about it: life would be better if the Griffins — Senior and Junior — had never shown up.

"And why don't you listen to Gramps?" Bobby continued. "He's older than you, so he's gotta know more, right?"

"The old man's being stubborn about his case."

"He says you're an egg-sucking gallywampus."

"I'd deny it if I knew what the hell it was."

They were on the bridge crossing the Spanish Harbor Channel, thirty miles from Key West. On the oldies station, the Zombies were asking, "Who's your daddy?" and inquiring if he was a man of wealth like the singer.

"Victoria says you're overbearing," Bobby said. "What's that mean, exactly?"

"It means sometimes I care so much about her that I invade her space."

"Is that why she threw your autographed Jeff Conine baseball at your head the other day?"

"We were just playing pitch and catch."

"Then how'd the window get broken?"

"I ducked. Look, kiddo. Women act weird sometimes. Once every month, for a few days, they have this hormonal thing going on."

"I know all about that stuff, Uncle Steve."

"Good, but there's more to it. It's probably time I taught you everything I know about women."

"Go ahead. I've got a minute."

"I'm serious, kiddo. You can learn from my mistakes."

Steve was trying to figure where to start when he heard the roar. In the rearview mirror, another chopper. As it pulled around to pass, he saw that it was the same one, a red Harley, the Screaming Eagle, all steel and chrome, with Darth Vader still aboard. It must have pulled off the road somewhere after passing them earlier. Now it came alongside and hung there.

"What's with this cowboy?" Steve said.

"Maybe he wants to race," Bobby said.

"On a two-lane bridge? What a jerk." Steve eased off the gas, but the Harley did, too, hanging with him. They were neck and neck, a mile from Big Pine Key and dry land.

Steve gave the Caddy some gas, and the old speedometer wand wiggle-waggled to seventy, seventy-five, eighty, the engine clearing its throat, then snarling to life. The Harley kept alongside, effortlessly.

"Asshole," Steve muttered.

Darth Vader waved. He seemed to have something in his hand. Then he let go, and sheets of paper flew across the road.

"Litterbug," Steve said.

Darth reached into a saddlebag and came up with something else in his hand. A jar, or a jug, half-gallon size.

"What the hell?" Steve said.

The Harley pulled ahead of them and the object shot from the guy's hand, striking the Caddy's windshield with a *crack*. Seconds later, a black, greasy liquid covered the glass.

"Shit!" Steve flicked on the wipers. That only smeared the gunk. With zero visibility, he hit the brakes, trying to keep the wheel straight, but the front right tire hit the curb of the raised walkway and blew out with a *bang*. Steve steered left, but the exploded tire's rim was grinding into the concrete, throwing off sparks, and dragging the Caddy back into the curb. The car leapt onto the walkway. The right rear tire blew out, the right front fender grazed the railing with the skull-jarring rattle of a dentist's drill.

"Fuck!"

"Uncle Steve!"

Steve's right arm shot out reflexively and pushed Bobby back into the seat. His left hand gripped the shuddering steering wheel. The car bounced off the walkway and back onto the bridge, skidding straight into the oncoming lane. The wipers had cleared enough of the gunk from the windshield to see the Harley was gone. But something far worse was coming at them. Eight beams of light, which Steve hoped was only one car, its headlights quadrupled as the beams refracted through the black goo.

The oncoming car's horn blasted, and Steve yanked the steering wheel right again, but still the Caddy dragged left, screeching across the oncoming lane. As he fought the wheel, Steve was aware of several sounds.

The honking of the car rushing straight at them.

The grinding of the Caddy's rims on the pavement.

His own breathing.

Steve steadied the wheel, but the rear end fishtailed left. He gave it some gas — braking would only heighten the spin — and tried to straighten the wheel. The car fishtailed right, and when the rear end passed the midpoint, they slid backwards toward the oncoming car.

The next five seconds passed in slow motion.

The oncoming car swerved into the left lane and sideswiped the Caddy.

Sliding ass-backwards, the Caddy skipped over the walkway on the left side of the bridge and crashed through the guardrail.

They tumbled toward the water, Steve pressing an arm into Bobby's chest to lock him into his seat. The Caddy flipped over a half turn and landed on its side with a *splash* that was surprisingly quiet.

"I'm okay! I'm okay!" Bobby's voice was ragged as the car sank, the headlights glowing eerily, a greenish yellow, in the murky water.

"Attaboy," Steve said, forcing himself to stay calm. "We're going for a swim."

The car headed downward, nose first. The headlights flickered and went out. The Caddy hit the bottom with a muted *thud.* Steve's chest smacked the steering wheel and his head banged into a metal strut in the canvas top. Pain shot across his skull. He heard the rush of water. His feet and legs were wet. Everything was black, except for the sparks that ricocheted in his brain.

"Bobby?"

He groped across the seat. The boy was gone.

"Bobby!"

Water poured through a gash in the canvas top. Colder than he had expected.

"Bobby! Where are you? Bobby!"

Steve fumbled with the release of his harness and felt it give way. He floated toward the torn roof where water rushed in.

"Bobby!"

Taking a breath, he dived into the back-seat, his hands feeling for the boy.

Nothing.

Stay calm. Think it through. Okay, Bobby is out. That's good. Now, how the hell did he get out? Because if one person can do it . . .

Steve floated into the front seat, sucked in another breath, went under again, and tried to open the door. It weighed a ton.

He came up and kicked at the closed window, but in the rising water, he had no purchase.

He groped at the top. The tear in the canvas had to be there somewhere. One hand broke through. The opening wasn't large enough for him. But Bobby, all skin and bones, must have gotten out. Was he hurt? What about the current? Would it take him toward land or out to sea? With both hands, Steve tried tearing at the canvas, but it wouldn't give. Fear gripped him. He had to find Bobby, get him to shore.

As water rushed in, the air pocket shrank. No choice now. Steve sucked in a breath and rammed his head through the hole in the canvas.

His shoulders stuck.

He tried wriggling through but could not.

He corkscrewed his body, twisting violently. He was jammed tight. He might as well have been in a straitjacket.

His lungs on fire, he thought again of Bobby. He was ready to make a deal.

Okay, God, take me down. Save the boy.

He thought of his father. So many regrets.

Dad, I should have been a better son.

He thought of Victoria and how much he adored her.

Vic, from that first day, I . . .

His lungs gave out and he sucked in a mouthful of water. He choked and gagged. Then as his chest bucked and his throat spasmed, another thought hit. If he had Junior Griffin's lung capacity, he could live another couple minutes. It pissed him off, dying like that, thinking of the son-of-a-bitch who would comfort the woman he loved.

Bobby's question came back to him. When *was* the last time he'd told Victoria he loved her?

I am such a fool.

Now, there's a dying thought for you.

Why hadn't he told Victoria how much he loved her? Why hadn't he told her every damn day?

Twenty-Four:
Gimlet-Eyed

Victoria stood on the balcony of her suite at the Pier House, sipping a vodka gimlet. Just like you-know-who. The Queen drank gimlets. In fact, she was quite particular about them.

"Always squeeze fresh limes, dear. Get your vitamin C with your vodka."

Must have worked. Her mother never came down with scurvy.

It was nearly midnight. The TV trucks were gone from the parking lot, but they would be back. A cooling breeze fluttered from the Gulf, and Victoria was drinking alone. She wondered where her mother had gone. Uncle Grif, too. She hadn't seen either one since they stomped out of the suite, seconds after she accused them of being David and Bathsheba and causing her father's death.

In the hours since, Victoria hadn't left the room, except to stand at the balcony rail, watching a ribbon of clouds dance across the face of the moon. She'd called Junior and told him her suspicions. He seemed shocked and hurt, and in their mutual sorrow, she felt closer to him than ever before. Junior vowed he would talk to his father and demand to know the truth.

Was there some irony at work here? If her father hadn't committed suicide, she would most likely have become Mrs. Victoria Griffin. It's what all four parents had wanted. It's what she herself wanted, at least as an adolescent. So, if her mother's affair led to her father's suicide, which led to the shame and guilt that sent Uncle Grif globe-trotting . . . well, weren't the illicit lovers to blame for laying waste to her fated marriage, too? The domino effect of fate.

It was all too much to contemplate, and definitely called for another gimlet.

Seconds passed. Or minutes. Or an eternity.

If I'm dead, Steve thought, would I feel the passage of time?

It was dark and wet and cold.

Something tugged at Steve, and then he was moving.

Or was he still and everything around him was moving? He couldn't tell.

There was the *slushing* sound of gushing

water. Something *click-clack*ed and tapped him in the chest. Or maybe not.

He tasted salt water and choked and coughed. A thin beam of light cut through the darkness, a slice of an eerily beautiful moon.

Where the hell am I?

Then darkness again.

Victoria went back inside, but left the balcony door open to feel the breeze and catch the pale moonbeams. Earlier, she had scanned the room service menu, decided she wasn't hungry, then raided the mini-bar for the third time. Two little bags of pretzels, a bottle of Rose's sweetened lime juice — *Sorry, Mother* — and a bunch of miniature Belvedere vodkas. Now the bottles were lined up like Lilliputian bowling pins on the conference table where the *State v. Griffin* files were stacked. The bottles were empty, the files unopened and unread.

"What kind of a lawyer are you?"

Steve's question echoed in her brain. A lousy lawyer. Maybe a lousy daughter, too. She could be wrong about her mother and Uncle Grif. She wasn't thinking clearly. Her lips were vodka numb and the moon in the night sky kept disappearing. Either clouds were scudding by, or she was woozy. Or both.

She wondered if Steve, driving down the Overseas Highway, was looking at the same moon. Then she giggled.

He can't be looking at a different moon.

She hoped he wasn't consuming alcohol at the rate she'd been.

At the poolside bar, below her balcony, a band was playing Jimmy Buffett. Something about a big pile of work and the boss is a jerk. If Steve were here, he'd want to go down to the bar and sing along. She wondered if he'd been telling the truth about fishing with Jimmy Buffett. With Steve, you never knew.

She thought back to the day Uncle Grif's boat crashed onto the beach. The day she'd told Steve she wanted to fly solo. Meaning professionally. At least, that's what she had said.

Who's kidding who? Or whom? Or whatever?

The realization hit her along with the ocean breeze. She'd lied to Steve and to herself. She'd been cowardly. What she really wanted was to break up the relationship. Dump Steve. That had to be it, right?

Yes, dammit. I should have followed my gut instincts from the start. And I should have listened to The Queen.

Hadn't her mother — Bathsheba Lord — been right about Steve, even if she'd put it rather badly?

"Leave it to you, dear, to find a Jewish man who's not a good provider."

But it wasn't the material success or lack therof that so aggravated Victoria. It was the fact that Steve was so — what's the damn word? Could she ferret out the damn word through a four-gimlet haze?

Unconventional. Undignified. Unruly. Unpredictable. And a bunch of other *un*-words she couldn't quite grasp just now. *Unsuitable. That's it!*

One of The Queen's words. Growing up, how many times had she heard her mother say about one boyfriend or another: *"He seems a nice enough boy. But unsuitable for you, Princess."*

Steve was fun and challenging and a great lover. And aggravating and overbearing and . . . clearly unsuitable. How could she even think of him as a forever-and-ever mate? No, she needed to break up with him. But how to do it, what to say?

For some reason — maybe because she was just a few blocks from Ernest Hemingway's house or maybe because she studied American Lit at Princeton — she thought of Agnes something-or-other, the nurse who tended to Hemingway's wounds in France. When Agnes broke off their affair, she'd written him, saying they must have been in love, because they argued so much.

Maybe she should write Steve a letter.

No. That's stupid. I'll see him tomorrow and tell him then. "You're wonderful. But unsuitable."

Then she remembered something else. After Agnes broke up with Hemingway, she married a wealthy Italian. A count or something. And just now Victoria had reconnected with Junior.

No, this has nothing to do with Junior.

She told herself she was going to stay away from him, too. Truly fly solo for a while, at least until she got her bearings. Then she wondered if that was true.

The band struck up another Buffett number, "Trying to Reason with Hurricane Season," and Victoria wondered if she should close the balcony door and batten the hatches. Instead, she opened the minibar and pulled out another little bottle of vodka.

"Are you cold, Uncle Steve?"

"Mmm."

" 'Cause you're shivering."

Steve tried to lift his head, heavy as a bucket of concrete. "Ooh."

It was dark, but he could see the faint crescent of moon peeking in and out of a passing cloud. He was lying on his back. The air was sticky with salt, moist and primordial. Water splashed softly against a sandy shore. In the distance, another recognizable sound, tires *whizz*ing on asphalt. He turned his head cautiously to one side. Headlights shot across the bridge, silhouetted in the distance.

"Where are we, Bobby?"

"A little island."

"How'd we get here?" Steve's head throbbed. He touched his forehead. Tender, a bump already forming.

"Bucky."

"Who?"

"Bucky the dolphin."

"Don't shit me."

"Well, not him, exactly. But one of his friends, maybe."

Maybe he was dreaming. Or worse — dead. "A dolphin brought us here?"

"I got through a hole in the top, but you got stuck. I tried to pull you through but I couldn't. Then this dolphin grabbed you by the shoulder and got you out."

Steve ran a hand experimentally over one

shoulder, then the other. "I don't have bite marks. Tell me what happened. The truth."

"I am telling you. When you got to the surface, the dolphin pushed you. And I held on to his fluke till we got to shore."

"Aw, c'mon, Bobby. Did you get me out?"

Somewhere, a police siren wailed. On the bridge, two cars had stopped. Three or four people stood at the railing, looking their way and gesturing.

"I wanted to save you, and you saved me," Steve said.

"*Tursiops truncatus* did it, Uncle Steve."

Steve knew that Bobby's athletic abilities were limited. In a footrace, the boy was all flying elbows and churning knees, a whirlwind of inefficient motion. Unkind kids called him a "spaz." But Bobby was a natural swimmer, his long legs and skinny arms cutting smoothly through the water in a precise cadence. Steve was just the opposite. He ran with his head still and a powerful sprinter's stride. In the water, he flailed and splashed.

Steve rolled onto an elbow. Everything started spinning again, and he eased back down.

"You've got a big bump on your forehead." Bobby gently touched a raw area just above Steve's eyebrow. "I hope it's not a subdural hematoma."

"What the hell's that, Doogie Howser?"

"An intracranial lesion. It's pretty common with blunt trauma to the head."

"So, 'common' is good, right?"

"Unless the cerebral hemisphere is lacerated. Then you shouldn't be buying any green bananas."

"Jesus."

Bobby leaned closer, looked into Steve's eyes. "Your pupils look good, Uncle Steve. I think you're gonna be okay."

Steve did not believe in a grand scheme. There was no general contractor or master architect of the universe. But what about this? When Bobby needed someone to break him out of the commune where he'd been locked up, there was Steve, outrunning half-a-dozen guys with shotguns, zigzagging through the woods, carrying the boy to safety. And now, seconds from drowning, Steve was sure he'd been rescued by Bobby, not *Trunky turnip,* or whoever.

From the bridge, someone was shouting, "Ambulance coming. Hang in there!"

Fine, Steve thought. He wasn't going anywhere.

There was a soft *splash* in the water, and Bobby said, "There! The dolphin jumped."

Steve painfully turned his head, but it was

gone. Sure, it could have been a dolphin leaping in that parenthetical shape. Or a plain old fish. Or a little asteroid hitting the water, for all he knew. "I didn't see anything, kiddo."

"You never do, Uncle Steve."

Twenty-Five: Head Case

The headache floated away on a sea of Demerol and Steve dreamily wondered why his sense of smell had suddenly become so acute. When the paramedics had loaded him into the ambulance, the salty evening breeze seemed to blossom like a fine tequila. When the orderlies wheeled him into the ER at Fishermen's Hospital, his nose was on sensory overload, inhaling a mixture of iodine and limestone dust, crushed shells and wet mud. Then, in the hospital, the harsh metallic tang of cleansers and solvents.

Later, sedated in his room, he sensed the sweetness of English Leather cologne. He'd known that aroma since childhood. Opening his eyes, he found the room dark, but heard a familiar Southern drawl. Saying Bobby was fine. *"Not even a scratch. Don't worry about a thing. Sleep well, son."*

Now, with the morning sun peeking

through the blinds, he dreamed he was on a Hawaiian beach, a Polynesian girl draping a lei of fresh gardenias around his neck, the fragrance as intoxicating as a wahine's smile. For some reason, he thought the girl's name was Mauna Loa, but that could have been the jar of macadamia nuts in his cupboard at home.

A few minutes later, Steve's eyes half opened and he saw a bouquet of flowers on the sideboard.

Aha. White gardenias.

He wondered if he could get a job as a police dog, sniffing luggage at the airport. Maybe his other senses had sharpened, too. Maybe the knock on the noggin had made him smarter. Then he drifted back to sleep. A minute later, or maybe an hour, another aroma. Something spicy but with a hint of vanilla. A woman's perfume. He thought he heard a soft voice calling his name, but that could be a dream, too.

"Steve, are you awake?"

"Mauna Loa?"

He opened his eyes. Victoria was standing over him. Little vertical lines creased her forehead. She looked at him with such tenderness and care that he nearly choked up with emotion.

"When's the last time I told you how

beautiful you are?" he asked.

"You okay, Steve?"

"And that I love you. I really, really love you. And cherish you. I really cherish you." He began singing, *"Cherish is the word . . ."* and the lines in Victoria's forehead deepened.

The goofy smile was so un-Steve-like, Victoria thought. His sharp-featured face was almost cherubic and all the rough edges of his personality seemed rounded off.

"You're beautiful," Steve said. "Have I told you that lately?"

"Thirty seconds ago."

"And I love your outfit," he continued.

"This rag?" She looked down at her wrinkled, spaghetti-strapped tank dress. She'd pulled it on hurriedly when Herbert called. And she wasn't feeling beautiful. She'd splashed on a drop of Must de Cartier but hadn't taken the time to put on makeup, and she felt pasty and dry-mouthed from the river of gimlets the night before. "I've had this dress since college. You've seen it a hundred times."

"It picks up the color of your eyes."

"The dress is red and white, Steve. Just which color does it pick up?"

"I don't know. Today, everything looks

gorgeous."

She sat on the edge of the bed and gingerly touched his forehead. A bump, purple and blue, rose from beneath the hairline.

"Bobby," he said. "Where's Bobby?"

"At your father's. Sleeping. He's fine."

"I love that kid. I couldn't love him any more if I were his father."

"I know. He knows, too."

"I've been lost and confused, Vic. In a fog. But I see clearly now."

Please don't, she thought. Please don't sing.

Too late. He was already into it: *"I can see clearly now . . ."*

A nurse had told her that Steve had a Level 2 concussion. But not a word about him being possessed by aliens.

Shortly after the rain had gone, Steve stopped singing and blurted out, "I'm gonna change, Vic."

"Really? How?"

"I'm gonna talk less. I'm gonna listen more. I'm gonna focus on you. I'm gonna be nicer to everybody."

"I think I wandered into the wrong room."

"We need to do more things together. Maybe a cooking class. Or join the opera society. What about the ballet? You love ballet."

"But you hate it."

"Doesn't matter. I want to do things for you."

"What's in that IV, anyway?"

"I dunno, why?"

"I'd like to order a case."

There was a knock at the open door, and Willis Rask walked in. A holstered gun jiggled on the sheriff's hip. "Am I disturbing anything?"

"Not at all, Sheriff," Victoria said.

"Willis," Steve said. "I love you, man."

"That's great, Stevie. I been talking to your doctors."

"I have doctors?"

"Post-traumatic amnesia. It'll come back to you." Rask grinned at them. "They did a brain scan and found nothing."

"Is that good?" Steve asked.

"I think it's the sheriff's little joke," Victoria told him.

"I see you got the flowers." Rask nodded in the direction of the sideboard.

"They're from you?" Steve gave him the goofy grin that looked like it belonged on someone else's face.

"I ordered them, but only on instructions. You see the card?"

Steve rolled onto an elbow, then settled back down hastily. "Vic, you do it."

Victoria picked the card off the plastic spear and read it aloud. " 'Come Monday, it'll be all right. Get well quick, and we'll chase some wahoo.' It's signed, 'Jimmy B.' "

"That's nice of him," Steve said. "Damn nice."

"So you really know Jimmy Buffett?" Victoria said.

"I love him so-o-o-o much," Steve cooed.

With Victoria looking on, Sheriff Rask spent a few minutes trying to take a statement from Steve, who kept interrupting with wild-hare statements about how much he loved the Keys, including all the fishes and the birds and each and every gator, and how Bobby saved his ass, claiming it was a dolphin, and isn't Bobby the greatest kid and old Herbert the best dad in the world, and did Willis know that Victoria was an incredible lover, even better than that double-jointed little gymnast from Auburn he'd met during the college baseball playoffs all those years ago?

Rask took notes, but Steve didn't provide much useful information. He hadn't gotten a license number on the motorcycle. He couldn't identify the rider. Unable to see past the space helmet, Steve couldn't even tell if the bottle thrower was a man or a woman.

"And I got no idea who would want to kill me."

"If he wanted to kill you," Rask pointed out, "he would have used a gun, not a jar of used motor oil. This seems more like a warning."

The sheriff asked if he'd pissed off anyone lately, and Steve mentioned Pinky Luber, but he didn't think the little bowling ball spent much time riding Harleys.

Rask told him that a bunch of leaflets were scattered on the road where the Caddy went off the bridge, and Steve remembered Darth Vader tossing papers from the saddlebag.

"They're all about Oceania," Rask said. " 'Stop the polluters. Stop destroying the reefs.' That sort of thing. They've all got the logo of Keys Alert. You know the group?"

"Delia Bustamante," Steve crooned. "Sweet girl. Owns a restaurant."

"Didn't you used to bake her frijoles?"

"Ancient history," Steve said.

"Once the news broke about Oceania, Delia's been the biggest mouth in the South. She's leading the opposition to the project."

Victoria adjusted the blinds to let more sun into the room. Outside, a breeze from the Gulf riffled the fronds of a towering royal palm. "You think Steve was nearly killed because we're defending Hal Griffin?"

Rask shrugged. "If you get Griffin off, Oceania gets built. If you don't, the project sinks. But those Keys Alert folks aren't eco-terrorists."

"You're sure?"

"Mostly, they're just people who like to wade in the surf without tar sticking to their feet."

"Delia Bustamante was on the *Force Majeure* just before it left the dock," Victoria said. "What about it, Steve? You still believe she's not capable of violence?"

Steve's answer was a peaceful snore. His eyes were closed and he still had the goofy smile in place.

"You think after the medication wears off we'll get the old Steve back?" Rask asked.

"Not for a while, I hope," Victoria said. "I kind of like the new, improved model."

A few minutes later, Rask said his good-byes — one to Victoria, one to his snoring buddy — and departed. Victoria sat in the chair next to Steve's bed, thinking through the day's events. She had already decided this was no time to break up with Steve. It was bad form to dump a boyfriend when he's hooked to an IV. Not only that, they had too much work to do. Uncle Grif had called her cell phone as she crossed the Seven Mile Bridge on the way to the hospital. He'd heard about Steve and asked if he could help. A private plane to take him to Miami or to bring specialists to the Keys . . . anything, just name it. And he said he wanted Solomon & Lord to continue with his case. He trusted her and hoped she trusted him.

When she hesitated, Griffin had added: *"Your mother and I had a special relationship, Princess. We were dear, close friends. As close as people who aren't lovers can be. We did nothing to be ashamed of. And that's the truth."*

Did she believe him? Uncle Grif's relationship with the truth was proving to be more a distant cousin than a blood brother. Still, she apologized for making the accusations, and he *shush*ed her, saying he understood; he knew the stress she'd been under.

Her mother and Uncle Grif. Another issue to table until after the murder trial. Then she would use all her skills to delve into that "special relationship." She would learn exactly what happened and why her father committed suicide. If her original suspicion proved correct, she would surgically remove both of them — Uncle Grif and The Queen — from her life.

Tabled, too, was Steve. Saved, temporarily, by a Level 2 concussion. But when this case was over, she'd reconsider him, too. De novo review, as the courts say. A brand-new look from page one onward. If she needed to use the scalpel on that relationship, too — well, it would be painful but not without an upside. There would be a loss of a connection, but a gain of independence.

But in the midst of a murder trial, it's best not to make any irrevocable decisions.

There was a snort from the bed. "You say something?" Steve asked, blearily.

"Delia Bustamante. Is she capable of violence?"

"Only against pork chops."

"I'm serious, Steve. We've finally got a possible defense. Is there any chance she's behind the attack on you and the murder of Ben Stubbs?"

Steve touched his forehead, sizing up the bump. "Delia's a sweetheart. I mean, she's emotional, but in a good way. She's warm and funny and a great cook, and —"

"Okay, I get it."

Steve leaned back and closed his eyes. Before he could fall asleep again, Victoria asked, "So who the hell was that double-jointed gymnast from Auburn?"

■ ■ ■ ■

Solomon's Laws

■ ■ ■ ■

7. When meeting an ex-girlfriend you dumped, always assume she's armed.

Twenty-Six: Bonnie Vouches for Clyde

The doctor was in his mid-thirties, both too young and too suntanned for Steve's taste. The tattoo on the doc's forearm — a windsurfer jumping a wave — did not exactly inspire confidence, either. "The scans are clean. Your reflexes are fine. Now, what's two plus two?"

The doctor seemed to be in a hurry, Steve thought. Maybe the wind was coming up. An old joke came to mind. A priest, a physicist, and a lawyer are all asked: *"What's two plus two?"* Lowering his voice to a whisper, Steve gave the lawyer's punch line. "How much do you want it to be?"

The doctor forced a smile and scribbled on a clipboard. He was releasing Steve, with instructions to call if he experienced any headaches or dizziness. Along with some pain pills, the doctor gave him a tip: A posse of reporters and photographers were sniffing around the hospital lobby like vultures after roadkill. Wanting a statement, photographs, some link between the bridge attack and the Griffin murder case. Steve thought it over. What would he say?

"There are forces out to stop Hal Griffin any way they can, including assaulting his lawyer."

But was that true? He had no idea. For the first time in his professional life, Steve decided to forgo a chance at free publicity — mother's milk to a trial lawyer — and he ducked out the employees' entrance.

Victoria picked him up in the hospital parking lot, threaded her Mini Cooper between two TV trucks, and headed south toward Key West. They were going to pay an unannounced visit on Delia Bustamante.

"Why are we sneaking out like this?" she asked. "You never met a camera you didn't love."

"Anything I say would just be a guess. I don't know enough to make an intelligent statement."

"Usually, that doesn't stop you."

"I'm trying to be more circumspect."

Oh. Just how long would that medication last? Victoria wondered again.

Steve called Bobby on the cell. The boy felt terrific. He was going shrimping with his grandfather. No, he didn't need more rest. He'd slept half the day and was mega-bored. The resilience of kids.

When they reached Key West, Victoria parked on Duval Street. First stop, Fast Buck Freddy's to get Steve some clothes. Within fifteen minutes, his new fashion statement was complete. Black sneakers, green camouflage pants, and a T-shirt with the slogan:

Twenty-four beers in a case.
Twenty-four hours in a day.
Coincidence?

He put on the shirt and paraded around the store, but *GQ* didn't call to set up a photo shoot. Victoria paid the bill and insisted on carrying his packages, which was fine with Steve. He was playing his concussion for all the sympathy he could get.

They passed through Mallory Square just before sunset. The place was jammed with tourists, plus the usual collection of jugglers, mimes, balloon twisters, and a guy with a sign, *I Read for Food.* He mildly entertained the crowd by reciting passages from Hemingway's *Islands in the Stream.*

"How do you feel?" Victoria asked for the tenth time.

"Kind of funky, but nothing a couple margaritas couldn't cure."

"No alcohol. You heard the doctor."

Steve didn't argue. He liked being pampered by Victoria, and he was still in the post-traumatic, post-Demerol glow of goodwill and affection.

They walked along the waterfront to Havana Viejo, Delia Bustamante's restaurant.

On the porch, several patrons hung out at a raw bar, and Liz O'Connor, a local musician, strummed her guitar and sang, "I'll Know It's Time to Go When the ATM Says No."

"How 'bout some key lime garlic oysters before we talk to Delia?" Steve asked Victoria.

"Didn't you hear the doctor say only bland foods?"

"Yes, ma'am. Whatever you say."

She gave him another of those *who is this guy?* looks, and Steve just smiled and held the door for her as they walked inside. Like a lot of Keys' eateries, Havana Viejo had a nautical theme — all anchors and buoys and sharks' jaws — plus black-and-white photos of pre-Castro Cuba on the walls. The air was fragrant with curry sauce in a conch stew. At a nearby table, under a framed photo of a yacht club in Old Havana, locals in shorts, T-shirts, and sandals devoured swordfish glazed with mango and Scotch peppers. Delia Bustamante, owner and chef, maintained a passionate, sensuous relationship with food. She was, as Steve recalled, pretty damn hot in the bedroom, too.

"You hungry, Vic?" he asked, as they headed for the kitchen.

"You think Delia's gonna cook for you?"

"Why wouldn't she?"

"Didn't you break up with her?"

"I always manage to stay friends. It's part of my charm."

"Really? What's the rest of it?"

They entered the kitchen through swinging doors. Delia stood in front of a gas range, stirring sliced papayas and apples in a saucepan that emitted the aroma of brown sugar and cinnamon, papaya applesauce, the side dish for one of her specialties, spicy barbecued salmon.

"What's cooking, babe?" Steve spread his arms, as if to hug her from twenty paces.

Delia looked up from the range, her black eyebrows arching. She wore spandex yoga pants and a pink tank top with a lace-up front. The laces were undone and the tops of her caramel breasts were slick with perspiration. Her dark hair was pulled straight back, setting off her cheekbones.

"Bastard son-of-a-bitch! *Y que carajo tu haces aqui, cabron, hijo de la gran puta, descarado?*"

"My mother was no such thing," Steve said.

"Come mierda!" She threw the spatula at him, missing by two feet, but pieces of sautéed papayas splattered his T-shirt.

"Delia, sweetheart. You gorgeous babe. What's the matter?"

"Bastard!" She scooped up a meat cleaver and hurled it across the kitchen. Steve would have ducked, but the throw was high and wide, like an overanxious catcher tossing the ball into center field when trying to catch a runner stealing second.

The cleaver smacked into a wooden support piling with a *thunk* and stuck there. Then Steve realized he hadn't been the target. His photograph was tacked to the piling. A shot of him at the restaurant's raw bar, his head thrown back as he tossed down an oyster. Someone had drawn a Salvadore Dali mustache on the photo, so it appeared he had inhaled a mouse into each nostril, stringy tails curling out. A black eye-patch, also the artist's touch, gave him a sinister, piratical look. And now the meat cleaver split his forehead in two.

"If that's the way you feel, I'm gonna pass

on the mushroom-dusted snapper," Steve told Delia.

Five minutes later, the three of them sat at a redwood picnic table on the wharf just outside the kitchen door. Victoria tried to calm down Delia with a sister-to-sister chat. Sure, Steve could be incredibly aggravating. Heaven knows, there had been many times she'd longed to brain him. "But he speaks highly of you, Ms. Bustamante, and we're here on court business. So if you could just answer a few questions . . ." But before Victoria could start her interrogation, Delia launched her own.

"That bump on the bastard's head, did you hit him with a frying pan?"

"I've been tempted to, but no."

"Too bad. You sleeping with the *puerco?*"

"That ain't kosher," Steve said, "calling me a pig."

"We're law partners," Victoria said, "and . . ."

Just how should I put it? Lovers-for-now?

"C'mon, Delia," Steve broke in. "We're here on business. Leave the personal baggage out of it."

Delia loosened the clip that held her hair back and shook her head. Long, dark tresses cascaded over her bare shoulders. She turned to Steve with a look as sharp as the meat cleaver. "Is this tall, cold *cerveza* better in bed than I am?"

"Ah, Jeez," Steve said. "Why not ask what's better, stone crabs or filet mignon?"

"Because you said I was the best lover you ever had."

"I think I said the 'loudest lover.' "

"You said the best! *Tu eres el mejor amente que he tenido en toda mi vida.*"

"That was before I met Victoria."

"So she is better!"

"I didn't say that."

You did to me, Victoria thought.

"Lighten up, Delia," Steve continued. "Making love isn't an Olympic contest. No judges give style points. It's physical and chemical and emotional and the feelings come from deep inside."

"What would you know of feelings?" Delia demanded.

"All I'm saying is that in the moment, everyone is the best lover with the one they're with. In that moment, you can't imagine ever being with anyone else. But things change. People move on."

Delia looked at Victoria with sympathy. "*Ay,* he'll break your heart, too, *chica.*"

"Delia, I didn't break your heart."

She pressed one hand to her ample

bosom. "I gave you everything."

"You gave me mango flan. And what's with the theatrics?"

"Steve, why don't you go for a walk and let us girls talk?" Victoria suggested.

"Delia, be honest," Steve blasted ahead. "We just had fun. We never even said we loved each other."

"When I made you bouillabaisse, was that not love?" Delia's eyes glistened.

"You make bouillabaisse for parties of eight."

"Not with sourdough croutons I bake myself."

"Okay," Victoria interposed. "Let's agree on something: Steve's an insensitive jerk."

"No I'm not."

"And look at you now," Delia said, with disgust. "Ass-licking *lambioso!* Doing Griffin's dirty work. Will you lie to the jury the way you lied to me?"

"I never lied to you," Steve said. "Not once."

"You said you could eat my grilled pork chops forever and ever. *Siempre y siempre.*"

"I could. Your chops are delicious. That shallot glaze, I've never tasted anything like it."

"So why did you leave me?"

"It was a long drive. We drifted apart." He

shrugged, as if searching for more. "I started eating sushi."

"*Cabrón!* Bastard!"

Victoria wanted to steer the conversation out of Delia's kitchen and as far from her bedroom as possible. "Ms. Bustamante, you're a potential witness in a murder case, and we really need to find out what you know."

A pelican landed on the dock nearby and stared at them over its pouch.

"I know nothing except that your client harpooned that man from Washington," Delia fired back.

"Really," Steve said. "You know what a good defense lawyer would say to that?"

Delia laughed without smiling. "How would you know?"

"A good lawyer would say you had a helluva lot more reason to kill Ben Stubbs than Griffin did. Put that in your bouillabaisse."

"Steve, be quiet," Victoria ordered. Apparently, the painkillers were wearing off.

"If I were going to kill anyone, it would have been Griffin, not his government flunky," Delia said. "Griffin's the one who's going to destroy the reef and pollute the coastline. It's his casino that will steal grocery money from hardworking people."

"It's all perfectly legal. Griffin was getting

316

the permits and licenses."

"A license to steal!"

"You were on Griffin's boat before it left the dock that day," Victoria persisted.

"He fed me cheap champagne and soggy hors d'oeuvres. Then he tried to bribe me with a job at his hotel. A hundred thousand a year to do nothing except shut up. I told Griffin what he could do with his job and left the boat."

"Where did you go?"

"You mean, do I have an alibi?" Delia smiled slyly. "My lover met me at my home. We devoured each other all day. At midnight, we ate four dozen oysters and drank two pitchers of sangria, then made love the rest of the night."

"Obviously, she's not talking about me," Steve said to Victoria.

"We'll need his name and address," Victoria told Delia, "so we can interview him."

"If he's not too exhausted," Steve added.

"He is the greatest lover I've ever known." Delia fanned herself with one hand. "Sometimes I faint with ecstasy."

"He's probably putting roofies in your sangria," Steve suggested.

Victoria shot her partner a *shut up* look and said: "Delia, do you know anyone who would have killed Ben Stubbs and tried to pin it on Hal Griffin?"

"No."

Victoria slid a leaflet across the table. "Have you ever seen one of these?"

"Of course. The Keys Alert flier about Oceania. I wrote it."

"Any idea who would have tossed these flyers all over the bridge at Spanish Harbor Channel?"

"None of my friends. That would be littering."

"How about somebody on a motorcycle who ran me off the road last night?" Steve asked.

Delia shrugged and seemed puzzled.

"My nephew was with me. He could have been killed."

"Bobby?" Delia said. "If you had half his humanity, Solomon, you'd be *un santo*. A saint. No one I know would threaten Bobby. Or you, no matter how rotten you are."

Victoria took inventory of Delia Bustamante and immediately came to two conclusions. One: the woman seemed to be telling the truth. And two: She was still in love with Steve.

Just what is this effect he has on women?

"Hullo, luv!" A man came out the restaurant's kitchen door onto the wharf. He looked familiar, Victoria thought, and the

British accent clinched it.

Clive Fowles.

Uncle Grif's seaplane pilot, boat captain, and dive master. Fowles wore a blue short-sleeve shirt with epaulets and chino safari shorts. His fair skin, which probably never took on a true tan, was scorched pink.

"Well, bugger me! It's the barristers. You all right, Solomon? They're talking about you on the radio."

"I'm fine, Fowles."

Delia leapt from the table and threw her arms around the oyster-eating Brit, squashing her breasts against his chest, kissing him on the lips a little longer than necessary, purring like a kitten. Victoria figured she was putting on a show for Steve.

"Ms. Lord, I see you've met my bird," Fowles said. "I know Mr. Solomon's already acquainted." He said it with a trim smile and no rancor.

"Mr. Fowles," Victoria said, "we'd like to come see you tomorrow and take a statement."

"Outfitting a new boat for Mr. G tomorrow. Day after's fine though."

Delia was still draped over him like a leopard on an antelope. "If you'll excuse us," she purred, "I have to cook something *very* special for my man."

"Hang on a sec before you grease the pans," Steve said. "Fowles, does Griffin know about your love of Cuban food?"

"You mean Delia, mate?" Fowles shrugged. "I don't ask Mr. G who he shags and he doesn't ask me."

"What the *cabrón*'s really asking," Delia said, "is whether I got you to frame Griffin for murder."

The Englishman barked a laugh. "You're good in bed, darling, but no one's *that* good." He turned to Steve, his eyes losing the laughter. "You take me for a sodding idiot, Solomon? Mr. G's been good to me. Bought me my own boat. Treats me with respect."

Steve gave him the Solomon stare. Accompanied by silence, it was intended to make a witness keep talking. Instead, Fowles laughed again. "What's up, mate? Got a touch of the sunstroke?"

"Just thinking about the curious case of Clive Fowles. The day we meet, you offer to take us diving. You do a fish census every year. You take students on dive trips. You love that reef. Maybe you love Delia, too. She hates Griffin, hates what he's planning, and I can only imagine what she whispers across the pillow. She's your alibi, and you're hers. Which is like Bonnie vouching for Clyde. You're what trial lawyers call a 'reasonable alternative scenario.' You know what that is, Fowles?"

"Sure, mate. A bleeding fall guy. Now bugger off and we'll talk day after tomorrow. I'm hungry, and not just for fried snapper."

Delia giggled and snuggled Fowles' neck. If either of them were worried about just being accused of murder, they didn't show it.

Victoria got to her feet. "See you, Mr. Fowles. Nice meeting you, Delia."

With Delia clutching Fowles' arm, the pair headed toward the kitchen door.

"Good night, lovebirds," Steve said.

"Adiós, cabrón," Delia retorted. "Are you man enough to admit you're dying for another taste?"

"Don't talk dirty, Delia."

"I'm talking about my mango flan."

"Your flame's too hot," Steve called out. "You always curdle the cream."

Minutes later, Steve and Victoria walked silently along the docks, seabirds squawking above their heads.

"What are you thinking about?" she asked. "Besides Delia's culinary specialties."

"You."

"Yeah?"

"I've been trying to figure out what's been bothering you."

"You noticed. So what's your reasonable alternative scenario about me?"

Testing him. He'd been so clueless about Delia's feelings for him. Were his instincts better with her?

"You've been unhappy for a while," Steve said. "But I've been so wrapped up in my own stuff, I didn't see it."

"Getting warmer. Keep going."

"You're reassessing everything in your life. Including me."

"Burning hot," she said. "And what are you going to do about it?"

"Work on our relationship before you throw a meat cleaver at me. Or worse, before you walk away without throwing it."

"Three-alarm fire," Victoria said. Wondering if it was possible for the flame of a relationship to burn just right. Hot enough to cook, without curdling the cream.

Twenty-Seven:
To Snoop or Not
to Snoop

Standing in the galley of his houseboat, Herbert Solomon crushed fresh mint leaves while he peppered Steve with questions. "Did you know Billy Wahoo's been talking about you on the radio?"

"Billy Wahoo's a moron."

"A caller asked why you didn't get eaten by sharks when you went into the channel, and Billy said it had to be professional courtesy."

"A moron who needs new material."

It was the day after the visit to Havana Viejo and Steve's brain trust — his father and his nephew — were dispensing their opinions. As he talked, Herbert used a handpress to squeeze a stalk of sugarcane, dribbling sweet *guarapo* into a glass filled with ice cubes. "Billy asked his listeners if they thought you had an accident or if someone was out to get you because of Griffin's case."

"Yeah?"

"Majority think you're just another lousy driver from Miami." Herbert poured a healthy portion of rum into the glass, added some fresh lime juice, a splash of club soda, and mint leaves. "So did that Cuban gal have something to do with attacking you?"

"No way," Steve said.

"No way, José," Bobby agreed.

"Delia's emotional but she wouldn't resort to violence."

Herbert tasted his concoction, nodded his approval. "What's Victoria think?"

"She says any number of women would like to run me off the road."

"That why she didn't stay here last night?"

"Vic sleeps better in the hotel."

"Uh-huh. How long's it been?"

"What?"

"Since you two humped?"

"Jeez, Dad. There's a child present."

"Steve humps Victoria," Bobby said. "Wanna see what I can do with that?"

"Don't do it, Bobby. No dirty anagrams today."

"HIS STUMP OVERACTIVE!" Bobby rearranging the letters almost as fast as Steve told him not to.

"He wishes." Herbert took a pull on his drink and turned to Steve. "When ah was your age, your mom and ah did it every day. Some men sneak out for nooners with their mistresses. Ah'd go home for lunch and have a quickie with mah wife."

"If it's okay with you, Dad, I'd rather not picture you and Mom in the bedroom."

"Wasn't time for the bedroom. We'd do it standing up in the kitchen." Herbert polished off the mojito. "Son, you be careful you don't lose that gal."

Sitting at the galley table, working on his laptop computer, Bobby pretended not to listen. He had found a website with live satellite photos of the Florida Keys and was looking for nude beaches. Steve was sprawled on a love seat. His headache had gone from a roaring avalanche to a dull thud. Overhead, a paddle fan stirred the moist air.

"You told me Pinky Luber had some scary friends," Steve said. "Any of them ride Harleys?"

"You're digging in the wrong pea patch," Herbert said. "Pinky would never jeopardize a child."

"Meaning *me,* Uncle Steve. Not you." Bobby clicked the mouse, zoomed on a satellite photo. "Look, I got a shot of Pirates Cove. You can see the top deck of Gramps' houseboat."

For a moment, Steve wondered if Bobby could get a photo of the Pier House, peer into the windows of Victoria's room, look into the deepest corners of her heart. If technology couldn't do that, Steve wondered, how could he? But he didn't want to dwell on his personal life just now. "Dad, how come you keep sticking up for that scumbag Luber?"

"Ain't gonna talk about Pinky." Herbert handed Steve a drink. "This'll cure what ails you."

"A little honesty would be better than a mojito."

"Nothing's better than a mojito." Herbert peered over Bobby's shoulder at the monitor. "Well, look at that. There's the channel. Bobby, you think the shrimp will be running tonight?"

"Shrimp can't run, Gramps."

"Good, they'll be easier to catch. Turn that off and go fetch the nets and lanterns."

Changing the subject, Steve thought. A lifetime habit of his father's. Hit and run. First the crack about losing Victoria, then the evasion about Luber.

Just what is the old man hiding?

"Uncle Steve, you going shrimping with us?" Bobby asked.

"Nah," Herbert said, before Steve could

respond. "Uncle Steve needs to rest."

To snoop or not to snoop.

That was the question facing Steve.

Along with the bigger question.

Why is Dad so protective of Pinky Luber, the guy whose perjury ruined his life?

The questions were coming faster than the answers. Mellowed out by rum and Demerol, Steve leaned back on a plastic chaise lounge on the stern deck, gazing at the calm water. An unseen bird trilled in a gumbo-limbo tree, sounding remarkably like a ringing cell phone. Herbert and Bobby had taken the Boston Whaler to Sugarloaf Key. Once they anchored near the bridge pilings, they'd be scooping up shrimp for hours.

Like the incoming tide, Steve's thought processes moved slowly but inexorably in one direction. He could poke around like a cop without a warrant.

No . . . I can't snoop through Dad's things.

But . . . if Dad doesn't find out . . . what's the harm?

So . . . where do I start?

If his old man had ever been involved in anything nefarious, he sure as hell didn't make any money from it. Otherwise, why live on this rust bucket, a fourteen-by-forty foot rectangular chunk of fiberglass sitting askew in the marshy water of Pirates Cove?

Steve began his search on the top deck. It was an open party deck with a fly bridge at the bow. Not even a hiding spot. On the main deck, the lockboxes were filled with fishing gear, gaffs, flashlights, and coiled lines. He heard an outboard motor chugging in the cove. A couple kids in a center-console fishing boat headed toward open water, the bow up on a plane.

Steve slipped into Herbert's stateroom, sifted through the built-in cabinets, riffled a pile of khaki shorts and faded T-shirts.

Just what am I looking for, anyway?

A small desk was mounted into the bulkhead. Some bills were stuffed into wooden slots. In a drawer, a box of stationery and his father's checkbook. Steve scanned the check stubs. Small amounts. Electricity, liquor store, phone bill.

Phone bill.

Paid yesterday.

Steve dumped the rubber trash can under the desk. Junk mail. Real estate flyers. A notice from Monroe County about mosquito spraying. And there . . . the Verizon bill.

He went through the numbers, recognized

a few. His own, of course. And a Coral Gables number he knew as Teresa Toraño's, a client and friend Steve inherited from his father. There were a cluster of calls to a Miami number Steve didn't recognize. Five calls the day he deposed Pinky Luber. Judging from the time code, two calls made before the depo and three after. Probably nothing, but . . .

Steve dialed, waited.

A woman answered crisply: "Mr. Jones' office."

Jones. That narrows it down.

"May I speak to Mr. Jones, please?"

Whoever the hell he is.

"Who's calling?"

"Mr. Darrow. Clarence Darrow."

"Will Mr. Jones know what this is regarding, Mr. Darrow?"

I doubt it. Even I don't know what it's regarding.

"It's personal," Steve said, figuring that was true.

"If it's not court business, he won't return the call until after six p.m."

Ah, court business.

"Actually, I got this jury summons in the mail. . . ."

The woman laughed. "And you're calling the chief clerk to get you out of jury duty?"

Chief clerk. A name popped into Steve's head. *Reginald Jones.* Chief Clerk of the Circuit Court for Miami-Dade County. Steve had seen the name hundreds of times. It was printed on every subpoena, administrative order, and other official document that came out of the courthouse.

"I wanted to tell Mr. Jones they misspelled my name."

"I'll pass that along, Mr. Darrow. Good day."

Steve had another mojito, though he doubted that's what you call it when you skipped the sugar, soda, lime, and mint. Sipping the rum straight, he wondered what was going on between his father and Reginald Jones.

Jones was one of those anonymous bureaucrats who run local government. An executive with a handsome six-figure salary, his name would rarely appear in the newspaper unless there was a bomb threat at the courthouse or the janitors went on strike. Jones' job was to manage several hundred deputy clerks, bailiffs, and lower level administrators. They, in turn, ran the whole creaky mechanism of the justice system. Civil Court, Criminal Court, Juvenile Court, jury pools, adoptions, marriage licenses, real estate records, tax liens. All the mundane governmental intrusions into our lives.

But Herbert Solomon didn't have any court business. Not now. But *then* . . .

A memory came to Steve. He was still a kid, one who loved visiting the courthouse, loved basking in the glow of his father's power and authority. Herbert Solomon was Chief Judge of the Eleventh Circuit. Pinky Luber was Chief of Capital Crimes in the State Attorney's Office, head prosecutor in Herbert's courtroom. And the deputy clerk sitting in front of the bench, stamping exhibits, running the courtroom with brisk efficiency, was a trim African-American man in his twenties with a neat mustache. Judge Solomon seemed to like the young man, would invite him up to sidebars and into chambers. Steve could even remember his father talking to the man in chambers.

"Reggie, you best tell Juror Three to start wearing panties to court."

"Reggie, that witness' testimony had more holes than the Loxahatchee Road."

"Reggie, you find Mr. Luber and tell him if he's late again, ah'm gonna put him in the cooler."

Young Reggie had to be Reginald Jones, now Chief Clerk of the Court. He had been in Herbert Solomon's life long before the judge's fall from grace. But what the hell was he doing there now?

Twenty-Eight: Rude Awakening

Like a winged goddess, Victoria arched her back, spread her arms, and sank deeper into the salty, inviting sea. What a luxurious sensation. The turquoise water like warm velvet swirling between her bare legs, cupping her exposed breasts.

Suddenly, a man — sleek and naked — swept below the surface and scooped her into his strong arms.

Junior Griffin.

She was in twilight sleep, vaguely aware she was dreaming. Fine with her. Better to remember the dream in the morning. Judging from the trailer, it would be a hell of a movie. R-rated.

Steve was spending the night on the houseboat; she was alone in her king-size bed at the Pier House. Well, almost alone.

Now, where the hell did Junior go?

Ah, there he was, free-diving to the bottom, arms extended, legs kicking, and . . .

oh, God . . . that sledgehammer between his legs. Cutting through the water, creating its own wake, a keel on a sloop.

Come back, Junior. It'll be morning soon, and my dreamy self is horny as hell.

Victoria pondered just how was she breathing, being underwater and all. Then, figuring she might be a mermaid, left it at that.

Junior zoomed back into view, rising like a missile from the deep. With something in his hand. An oyster.

Victoria's mind drifted like kelp in the current. Steve loved oysters with beer. The Queen loved oysters with pearls.

Dammit, forget them; go with the flow of the dream.

Junior pried open the oyster with his bare hands. Said something to her. *Glug-glug,* bubbles bursting from his mouth. Inside the oyster, a gorgeous ring. Dainty triangular gems surrounding a hefty square diamond.

Princess cut. Naturally.

Junior opened his mouth and *glug*ged something again. The underwater acoustics were lousy.

"What is it, Junior? You want to marry me?"

"I want an underwater hump-a-rama," Junior enunciated clearly, but in Steve's voice.

Damn him. Trespassing in my dream!

She heard something then. A slapping sound. Not the slap of a leaping fish smacking the water. Something landlocked and familiar. A quiet thud, the sound of something flat hitting carpet.

Something moved. Her bed was on an elevated portion of the room. One step down and twenty feet away was her worktable, covered with files. Beyond that, the sliding door to the balcony. She could see the silhouette of a person outlined against the glass door, backlit by torches on the pool deck below.

Oh, Jesus. I'm awake, and this is real!

The figure bent, picked up a file from the floor, replaced it on the table.

Should I scream? Jump up? Fight?

Heart racing. Paralyzed with fear. Holding her breath, then exhaling, so loud that surely the intruder could hear her breathe.

A weapon. She needed a weapon. Scissors. A pen. Anything. But what did she have? A clock radio. A paperback book. A pillow.

Defenseless. Lying under a sheet, wearing only a satin camisole that stopped above the waist.

A rustle of papers. The intruder opening a file. A narrow beam from a miniature flashlight.

Go ahead. Steal whatever you want. Then leave!

Her ears seemed to twitch like a cat's, her sense of hearing on high alert. The bed had become a furnace. In an instant, she was bathed in sweat. Beads of perspiration, like salty tears, trickled down her face and neck. She could barely breathe, her throat dry and constricted.

Oh, God. Don't cough.

An involuntary spasm shook her, and she barked a cough. The miniature flashlight clicked off. For an eternity, no movement, no sound. The silhouette a statue at the table, Victoria frozen under the sheet.

Breathe. Dammit, breathe, or you'll cough again.

She watched the figure walk silently toward the bed.

Oh, God, what now?

Her muscles were locked so tightly, she was terrified she wouldn't be able to move. Her joints petrified wood.

C'mon. You've got to fight.

She would not let herself be raped. Or beaten. Or killed. Furious now. The intruder just a few steps away. When he was close enough, she would spring at him. *Go for his eyes. Gouge!*

She curved her hands into claws.

Another step closer. Two more steps and . . .

Scream and spring.

She would shriek to startle him, then tear his face off.

One step away, the intruder stopped. She heard breathing, this time not her own. In the dark, could he see her eyes were open?

The intruder turned and walked past the table. She heard the balcony door sliding in its track. She counted five seconds, then leapt out of bed and raced to the door. Slammed it shut, locked it, inserted the pin in the slot in the track.

Breathing hard, she peered through the glass. Tiki torches burned on the deserted pool deck. The fronds of a palm tree swayed in the ocean breeze. Nothing else moved. The intruder could have crawled down from her second-story balcony — maybe even jumped — to the ground.

The adrenaline flow had stopped, but her mind cranked at the speed limit. So much to do. Call the police. Call Steve. Wash her face. Get dressed. Pee . . . don't forget to pee.

Okay, slow down. Relax.

Think.

The digital clock on the nightstand read 3:17 a.m. She turned on the lights and checked the worktable. Nothing seemed to be missing. A chilling thought.

Someone left. That doesn't mean someone else isn't still here.

She ran to the closet, threw open the door. No one inside except Calvin Klein and Donna Karan. Whoops, Vera Wang, too.

She considered waking her mother, just a few feet away in the adjoining room. No. She'd be a mess. Let The Queen get her beauty sleep. Tell her about this in the morning.

Victoria sat on the edge of the bed, picked up the phone, and dialed Steve's cell. She had to tell him three times before he was sufficiently awake to understand. Then he came unglued.

"Oh, Christ! Are you okay?"

"I'm fine. I'm going down to the front desk as soon as I get dressed."

"No. No. No. Stay in the room. Check all the locks again. I'll call Rask at home. He'll have cops there in ten minutes. Sure you're okay?"

"I'm sure."

"Stay calm now." His voice rising.

"I'm calm."

"You get a look at the guy?"

"No."

"I should have been there. I'd have clobbered him with my Barry Bonds."

True, Steve slept with a baseball bat under his bed, but the only thing he ever clobbered was the occasional palmetto bug. On the phone, she heard what sounded like drawers slamming and muttered curse words.

"What are you doing, Steve?"

"Looking for Dad's car keys. Dammit. Where the hell . . . ?"

"Steve . . ."

"Yeah?"

"Calm down."

Five minutes later, Victoria pulled some cotton sweats from a drawer, but sticky with sweat, she decided to clean up before dressing. She slipped out of the camisole and padded into the bathroom, nearly tripping over a halter sandal she'd left on the floor by the sink.

She opened the shower door and turned on the water, hotter than usual, the steam rising like a cleansing cloud. Once inside, she let the water stream over her body.

Water. The sea. My dream. Junior.

Or half Junior, half Steve. A Minotaur of a dream lover. If dreams represent repressed desires, as she had learned in Psychology 101, just which man did she desire?

She grabbed the soap and lathered up,

pondering the question.

Suddenly, something grabbed her bare leg.

A snake!

It tightened on her calf and circled higher, gripping her knee.

She screamed, the sound echoing off the tile, the loudest sound she had ever made. Thick as her wrist, the snake coiled around her thigh. Its head solid black. Stripes of yellow, red, and black along its five-foot length.

Coral snake!

Slithering up her leg, tongue flicking in and out.

She screamed again.

Dammit! Do something!

She shot a hand out and grabbed the snake near its head. Tugged at it, tried to pull it off her leg. The damn thing was impossibly strong. She braced a foot against the shower wall, yanked as hard as she could. The snake flew off her leg and coiled around her arm, its tail flapping in the air. She shook her arm, but the snake stayed put, opening its mouth to an impossible dimension. Wide enough to swallow an orange. Fangs showing, the head darted toward Victoria's face. She jerked sideways, slipped on the wet tile, and crashed through the shower door, falling to the floor.

Her hip took the fall, and pain shot down a leg. The snake flew off her arm, slid across the tile, and coiled in front of the bathroom door. Blocking her exit. The reptile's head bobbed, left to right and back again, tongue flicking, daring her to move.

Naked. Wet. Hip throbbing. Afraid. Victoria stayed on the soapy floor, her eyes searching for a weapon. What was there? A bar of soap? A towel? A tiny bottle of perfume.

A shoe!

She'd nearly tripped over it. An ankle-strapped, halter sandal with fuschia pom-poms. One of the Manolo Blahniks filched by a client. Nothing more than flimsy scraps of leather, weighing a few ounces. What she needed was a work boot with steel toes.

But look at the heel. A solid three inches. You could pound nails with it. The shoe was three feet away, halfway between her and the damned serpent.

The snake's head swung back and forth, seeming to size up the space between them. Then lowering itself to the floor, the snake slithered toward her.

"Princess! Princess! Are you all right?"

Her mother's voice. From the bedroom. She must have come through the connecting door. The snake stopped. It turned its head toward the sound.

Now!

Victoria's hand flew out, grabbed the sandal, swung as hard as she could. The heel caught the top of the snake's snout, pierced its hide, and slammed it to the tile. The snake coiled and shook its entire body, the sandal staying put.

"Princess! Are you in there?" Her mother getting closer.

"Stay out!" Victoria commanded, scrambling to her feet.

On the floor, the snake writhed, and the sandal tore loose. Victoria grabbed the tail and cracked the snake like a bullwhip. There was the *crunch* of breaking cartilage. She whipped the snake again, its head smashing against the tile wall. Then she dropped it, motionless, onto the floor.

"Princess! What's happening? Why'd you scream?"

The Queen came through the doorway. She'd taken the time to put on a swirling white silk gown and fluffy slippers. A beauty mask was propped on top of her head.

"Omigod!" Her mother shrank back, keeping her distance from the snake. "Those red stripes. Coral snake?"

Victoria sank to the cold tile floor, trembling. "Yeah, I think so."

"Are you all right?"

"I fell pretty hard, but I'm fine." Victoria rubbed her hip; there'd be a bruise within hours.

"Thank God. I should get some ice —"

"It's okay, Mom. Don't worry about me."

"Not for you. For the snake."

Oh. Her mother thinking more clearly than she was. "For evidence. That's a good idea, Mother."

"Evidence? What evidence? I've got a craftsman in Miami who can make a killer handbag out of that beauty."

Twenty minutes later, her mother had gone back to sleep and Victoria had changed into pink cotton sweats and sneakers. Outside, Monroe County deputies roamed the pool deck and parking lot. Inside the hotel suite, Sheriff Willis Rask stood astride the dead reptile and hefted Victoria's fuschia pom-pom sandal.

"You killed that monster with this little-bitty thing?" The sheriff wore a quizzical look.

Victoria shrugged.

When Steve arrived from the houseboat, he hugged her tightly and expressed all the right concerns, saying if he caught whoever did this, he'd pulverize the guy. Break every bone in his body, starting with his knees. Rask told Steve to chill out, then asked Victoria to tell him everything that had happened that night. She did as instructed, skipping the nude-coed-in-turquoise-water dream.

"Snake in a shower's a new one on me," Rask admitted. "Saw a toilet filled with mud puppies and scrub lizards once. Men's room at Charlie Harper's Arco on Tortuga Drive. Molly Alter's boy dumped the poor creatures there after Charlie caught him stealing cans of tire glue. Boy was a sniffer."

"Lizards and mud puppies won't bite you," Steve said.

"Maybe not, but if one licks your butt, you might trip over your own drawers and bang your head on the wall. Happened to Charlie."

Victoria pointed a sneakered toe at the carcass. "That's not a mud puppy, Sheriff. It's a coral snake. Someone tried to kill me."

"Maybe. Maybe not," Rask mused.

A little too mellow for Victoria's taste. The sheriff carried the scent of cannabis with him. Either Rask had just captured a freighter stuffed with marijuana or he'd smoked a joint on the drive over.

"Willis, I gotta agree with Vic," Steve said. "Whoever broke in planted the snake in the bathroom."

"Most likely true," Rask agreed, "but Ms. Lord could have gotten to the hospital in ten minutes. Plenty of time, and they're damn good with snakebites. If a local did this, he'd know that."

"What are you saying, Sheriff?" Victoria demanded. "This was just a practical joke? Like lizards in the toilet?"

"Ever see a baby gator bite a woman in the ass?" Rask asked.

A breathtaking non sequitur, Victoria thought. Weed will do that.

"Trailer park on Stock Island." Rask nodded at the memory. "Woman gets in the bathtub, plans to soak a while, file down her corns. Her husband neglected to mention he'd caught a baby gator that morning. Don't know if he planned to eat it or raise it. Woman's ass took thirty stitches, as I recall."

"Sheriff, someone ran Steve off a bridge. Now someone puts a poisonous snake in my shower. You don't see a pattern here?"

"Pattern, yes. Attempted murder, no. Like I told Steve before, if someone wanted to kill him, they wouldn't just toss glop on his windshield. And whoever was in your room tonight could surely have killed you if they wanted."

"They want to mess with our heads," Steve said. He walked to the mini-bar and tried to open it, but Victoria had hidden the key to keep her mother from charging booze to her room. "They want to foul up Griffin's defense."

"Which means," Victoria broke in, "that whoever's doing it is also trying to frame Uncle Grif."

"And is probably the real killer," Steve said.

"Can't comment on that," Rask said. "My position's gotta be that your guy's the one."

"Vic, you're not spending any more nights alone," Steve advised her.

"The houseboat's too small," she replied. "I need room to work."

"Then I'll move in here."

She didn't immediately reply.

How to say it?

"I need my space, Steve."

"Nice try, tiger," Rask needled him.

"Then give her official protection, Willis. Two deputies here all night. One in the corridor, one under the balcony."

"I dunno, Stevie. We got a budget crisis down here. . . ."

"Willis. This is important to me, okay?"

"Jeez, Stevie."

"My dad would want you to."

Playing that card, Victoria thought. Did Willis Rask owe his career to Herbert Solomon, getting him out of trouble all those years ago?

Rask sighed. "Okay, you got it."

"I don't want it," Victoria said.

"I don't care," Steve said.

"Are you listening? I don't want police protection."

"Not your call, cupcake."

"What did you call me?"

"Keep your cops here, Willis," Steve instructed. "Send in the National Guard, too, while you're at it."

"You can be so damn controlling." Pretending to be annoyed, but deep down, appreciating the way Steve stepped up to the plate for her. The concern in his voice. With all the doubts she had about their relationship, there was something about which she was always certain: Steve truly, deeply cared for her.

The sheriff crouched down and straightened the snake to its full length. "Think there's enough skin for a pair of boots, Stevie?"

"I was thinking more of a briefcase," Steve replied, crouching down beside him.

"Forget it, both of you," Victoria ordered. "Someone else already has dibs."

Twenty-Nine:
V for Victory

An hour later, Sheriff Rask carted off the dead snake in an Igloo cooler, promising to FedEx it to Irene's leather craftsman as soon as it was measured, photographed, and analyzed for evidentiary purposes. By nine a.m., Victoria and Steve were driving north toward Paradise Key.

Steve felt a stew of conflicting emotions. Relief that Victoria was okay. Guilt that he hadn't been there to protect her. Guilt over something else, too. His deception.

He hadn't told her about rooting around in his father's trash. He knew she would disapprove; the phrase "invasion of privacy" came instantly to mind. So, not a word about uncovering his father's mysterious phone calls to Reginald Jones, Chief Clerk of the Circuit Court. That was something he would have to investigate by himself.

Jones to Luber to Solomon.

Sounded like a double-play combination,

with his old man the first baseman. But what the hell really went on two decades ago in all those capital cases? Back then, the courthouse was a beehive of little fiefdoms, with sleazy lawyers, greedy bail bondsmen, and corrupt cops buzzing in the corridors. Presiding over the messy business, perched on a higher plane in each courtroom, were the robed lords of the manor, some decent, some incompetent, and some nakedly opportunistic.

"A den of treachery and mendacity that ah'll clean up," Herbert Solomon announced when his fellow jurists named him Chief Judge of the Circuit.

But what had happened? What did Herbert do then that made him fear Luber now? Reginald Jones was the link between the two men, literally sitting between them in the courtroom. But what did Jones — a baby deputy clerk at the time — have to do with it?

Today, Steve had intended to find out. He had planned to rent a car, drive to Miami, and drop by Jones' office. Pound the table and get some answers. Or not. But after the episode in the hotel room, Steve was not about to leave Victoria alone. And she insisted on interviewing Clive Fowles. Jones would have to wait.

Steve figured that Fowles was a man with conflicts of his own. Torn between his love for Delia Bustamante and a coral reef on one hand and his duty to Hal Griffin on the other. Just who won that tug-of-war, Steve couldn't be sure.

Victoria turned off her cell phone as they approached the causeway to Paradise Key in her metallic silver Mini Cooper. Reporters had been calling since dawn with questions about the snake attack. The car radio was tuned to a talk show hosted by Billy Wahoo, the self-proclaimed "prime minister of the Conch Republic."

"These two Mia-muh lawyers seem mighty accident prone. First Solomon drives off a bridge, then Lord nearly gets bitten by a snake. Those two are the mouthpieces for that carpetbagger Hal Griffin, and trouble follows him like skeeters on a sweathog. You ask me, Solomon and Lord are gonna be up the creek when they get to court."

"This bastard's polluting the jury pool," Steve complained.

"Don't worry. I'll weed out the bad ones on voir dire."

Steve looked over and laughed.

"What?" she asked, without taking her eyes off the road.

"That was terrific. Your confidence. If there's a problem with the venire, you'll fix it. I love that."

"I learned that from you. Don't you know that?"

"Sure I do. I just like to hear you say it."

At mid-morning on this breezy, sunny day, Fowles droned on about his courageous grandfather and Steve pretended he gave a damn. It was a classic lawyer's trick. You don't just come out and ask: *"Did you see my client holding a smoking gun over the victim's body?"* You buttered up the witness like a toasted bagel until he was convinced the guy with the gun didn't look anything like your client, and even if he did, he was acting in self-defense, and even if he wasn't, the victim was a son-of-a-bitch who deserved to be killed.

You accomplished this by putting on your sincere listener's face and trying not to doze off while the witness rambled from one inane subject to another. His prize-winning butterfly collection. Her mouthwatering s'mores recipe. Or in this case, the heroic exploits of Horace Fowles, Royal Navy submariner in World War II.

Victoria was terrific at the game. Probably because she actually cared about people and didn't have to feign interest in their banal lives. In the car, she had announced she'd take the lead in questioning Fowles, Steve still seeming a bit woozy and all. Her roundabout way of saying she was better at getting people to talk. Steve didn't disagree. They needed to learn just why Fowles, Griffin's trusted boat captain, was conveniently absent when the boss took Stubbs on the fatal cruise. How solid was the Englishman's alibi? Was he really delving into Delia's oysters — garlic and otherwise — when a spear impaled Ben Stubbs?

They had found Fowles in the boathouse on the far side of the island. An open-sided garagelike building that straddled a narrow inlet, the boathouse caught the easterly breeze and was filled with light. In stained coveralls, Fowles wore an eye shield and heavy gloves and aimed a welding torch at what looked like an old rusted torpedo with two seats built into it. The contraption was suspended from an overhead rack by a pair of heavy chains. Sparks flew as Fowles seared the tail assembly with a blue flame.

Catching sight of the visitors, he had turned down the gas and flipped up his eye shield. "Bet you don't know what this is."

Even had he known, Steve would have

kept quiet. *Always let the witness have his fun.*

"My grandfather's chariot," Fowles said proudly. "Without the warhead."

Chariot? Warhead?

"Wish I had his midget sub," Fowles continued. "But that's at the bottom of a fjord in Norway."

"Has to be a story in that," Victoria said.

And hurry the hell up and tell it, Steve thought.

Fowles offered them each a Guinness Stout from a cooler. Steve accepted; Victoria frowned and declined. Fowles' blond hair was mussed. His sunburned face brighter than usual, probably from the heat of the welding torch. Leaning on a sawhorse, Fowles began telling tales of his grandfather.

Horace Fowles had helped design the Royal Navy chariot, basically a torpedo with a six-hundred-pound warhead on the bow. Two men sat atop the chariot on seats sunk into its hull. Horace was an early charioteer, perhaps the most dangerous job in World War II, other than kamikaze pilot. Wearing a bulky dive suit, Horace would pilot the craft underwater, aim it at a German warship, then hop off, hoping to be picked up by a friendly ship or submarine. Later, he graduated from the chariot to four-man midget submarines called X-craft. He named his *Fowles' Folly.*

"Bloody floating coffin is what the midget sub was," Fowles told Victoria and Steve. "Or *sinking* coffin may be more like it. Glands leaking, batteries dying, pumps useless. Grandpop would patch her up with chewing gum and twine. Makes my service in the Falklands seem paler than piss. Not like fighting Nazis in the North Sea."

Fowles finished his story. Horace led the raiding party that went after the biggest prize of the war, the *Tirpitz,* a Bismarck class battleship. To get into the Norwegian fjord where the German ship was anchored, Horace swam out of the *Folly* in freezing water and cut through submarine nets with a knife. Sailors on the *Tirpitz* spotted the X-craft but thought it was a porpoise.

"That's how small she looked when you're on the deck of a fifty-thousand-ton battleship," Fowles explained. "Grandpop gets through and brings up the *Folly* amidship. Picture it, now: three British lads, looking up at this behemoth, twenty-six hundred German sailors aboard. Enough armaments to blow up all of London. But the big bastard can't fire her guns straight down, so the Krauts are using rifles and pistols and there's my Grandpop in the water, attaching charges to the hull. He gets back in and as they're pulling away, *ka-boom,* the *Tirpitz* lifts five feet out of the water. Hauling ass out of the fjord, the *Folly* gets tangled in the net, and a German cruiser sinks them."

Clive Fowles took a pull on his stout, doubtless picturing the midget sub going to her watery grave. "They gave my Grandpop the Victoria Cross. Posthumously, of course."

He reached inside the top of his coveralls and pulled out a medal dangling from a chain. A cross with a crown and lion and the inscription *"For Valour."*

"Churchill himself presented the medal to my grandmother." Fowles raised a hand above his head and spread two fingers in the fashion of the wartime prime minister. " 'V for Victory.' That's what Winnie told my grandmom."

"You must be so proud," Victoria said.

"Doubt if anyone in the war showed more guts than my grandpop." Fowles lowered his voice into a deep Churchillian baritone. " 'I have nothing to offer but blood, toil, tears, and sweat.' " He smiled sadly and continued: "That was Horace Fowles. Which makes me a lucky bloke. The man I look up to most is my own flesh and blood."

It was more than that, Steve thought.

Clive Fowles seemed to be measuring himself against his grandfather. Desperate to be a hero. But how could a man compete with those memories? In the warm turquoise waters of the Gulf, just what could a man do to earn his own medals?

Ten minutes later, they sat on the edge of the concrete seawall, soaking up the morning sun. Victoria wore an orange Lycra bandini top with floral pants that tied in front and stopped at mid-calf. Her long, tanned legs dangled over the water. Steve wore denim cutoffs and a T-shirt that read: *"Could You Come Back in a Few Beers?"*

Fowles turned up the bottoms of his coveralls and now resembled a sunburned Huck Finn. He had carried his cooler from the workshop, and Steve accepted a second cold stout, even though it wasn't yet noon. Half a mile offshore, a sailboat headed downwind, its bright orange spinnaker puffed off the bow like an umbrella in a storm.

"Did you know Griffin was taking Stubbs to Key West?" Steve asked.

" 'Course I knew," Fowles said. "I cleaned the boat and fueled it for Mr. G."

"You had drinks at the dock," Victoria elbowed in. "Then you went ashore. Why weren't you driving the boat?"

"When Mr. G has company, he likes to handle the *Majeure* himself. Show off a bit."

"Even though he was stopping to pull up lobster pots?" Victoria asked.

"Especially then. He gets to play Great White Fisherman. Anchor the boat, get out the gaff, pull in his supper. It's a macho thing."

"You get the feeling Griffin didn't want you along?" Steve asked.

"Not really, mate. Mr. G just gave me the rest of the day off. I'd busted my hump the day before. Hauled ass out to Black Turtle Key to bait the lobster traps, plus all my other work back here."

Victoria and Steve exchanged glances. There was a question someone had to ask without giving up too much. The pots had been baited with more than chum. But did Fowles know that? Victoria chose her words carefully. "I thought Hal Griffin baited the traps himself."

"He tell you that?" Fowles laughed. "Yeah, I can hear him saying it. *'I baited the traps.'* Same way he'd say: *'I flew the Grumman to Nassau.'* Or *'I reconditioned the diesels.'* I suppose it's true because Mr. G pays for it, but good old Clive Fowles does the flying and the reconditioning."

"And that baiting," Steve said. "What'd you use? Redfish? Crab?"

Another laugh. "Don't sod about, Solomon. Just ask it. Yeah, some crab and a big bag of currency."

Sloppy, Victoria thought. Uncle Grif involving Fowles like that. Now the boat captain would be a prime prosecution witness. Fowles could help the state establish the bribes, or at least one of them.

"Griffin tell you what the money was for?" Steve asked.

"Nope."

"And you didn't ask?"

"I don't get paid to ask questions."

"But you wondered," Steve said. "Wondering's free."

"I figured Ben Stubbs was gonna be richer stepping off the boat than stepping on."

"Make you angry, knowing your boss was paying the guy off?"

"Just reinforced my beliefs about the way of the world, Solomon. Money talks. Bullshit walks." *Bull-shite.*

Fowles tossed an empty beer can back in the cooler. He scooped up one of the plastic bands that ties a six-pack together. It was lying on the seawall and would blow into the water in a light breeze. The plastic bands strangle fish that get caught in them.

No way Fowles would ever toss junk into the water, Victoria decided. Or tolerate those who did. His heart would be with Delia in the battle to save the coral reef, but his pocketbook would be with Uncle Grif. So just where did he stand?

"Any idea who would want to frame your boss for murder?" she asked.

"I figure someone who wanted to stop Oceania."

Victoria dropped a line into the water. "Someone like Delia?"

"Strike me pink! You're still on that? Delia's a lover, not a killer. Just ask your partner."

Steve smiled, agreeably. Annoyingly.

"Ever tell Mr. Griffin how you felt about Oceania?" Victoria asked Fowles, ignoring Steve.

"I told him how development killed the big reefs off Honolulu and Singapore and Hong Kong. I told him how pile driving so close to the reef would dislodge sediment that would clog up the coral. How the gas pipeline and the conduits for water and electrical would mess up the ocean floor. But he had a study to rebut every one of my arguments. Like I told Delia from the start, it's Mr. G's decision, not the guy who drives his boats and flies his planes. In the end, my opinion didn't count any more than Junior's."

"What's that mean?" Steve jumped in. "What was Junior's opinion?"

"All I'm saying is that father and son don't always see eye to eye."

"Mr. Griffin told you to be open with us," Victoria reminded Fowles. "But you're holding back."

When the Englishman didn't respond, Steve said, "Just what's Junior got to do with this?"

Fowles rolled his pants legs back down. "Nothing much, except when the financing fell through, Mr. G and Junior had a row. A real argy-bargy."

"When the financing fell through . . ."

What did that mean? Griffin had a huge construction loan in place. He had his financing. So what the hell did Fowles mean? Steve shot Victoria a look that warned: *"Don't let on we're clueless."*

As if she would give that up. She tried to remember something Junior told them. Jesus, what was it? Had her knees been so wobbly from seeing him that she'd forgotten? The word "hoops" came back to her. Junior complained about "all the hoops" the insurance companies made them jump through to get their financing. He'd been evasive about just who issued the binder, some double-talk about a foreign consortium. Then Steve made up the name of a Pacific Rim company that Junior seemed to agree was the one.

Victoria cautiously baited another line, cast it. "Did the financing run into trouble because of the insurance problem?"

"It did indeed."

"But Griffin landed insurance somewhere," Steve added, "or he couldn't have gotten a construction loan."

Fowles barked out a laugh. "You don't know shit, do you, mate?" *Shite.*

"Tell us," Steve said.

"Oceania couldn't get insurance. The computer models showed the hotel would capsize in a Category Five hurricane. Mr. G argued that the chances of a Category Five hitting one tiny spot in the Gulf were infinitesimal, but it didn't matter. No one would insure the place."

"So how'd he get a construction loan?"

"By putting up everything he owned as collateral. Every last piece of real estate. Every stock and bond, all his spare cash, too. That's what the row was about. Junior was ranting and raving that his father's ego had run amuck. That he was building a monument to himself that was sheer folly and he'd lose everything."

Victoria remembered something Uncle Grif had said the day The Queen showed up. *"Lately, Junior's taken an interest in the business. Been riding me hard, telling me I spend too much money, take too many risks."*

"So Junior was scared shitless he'd lose his inheritance," Steve emphasized, as if Victoria didn't get the point. As if she didn't know he was already pushing Junior to the head of the Reasonable Alternative Scenario class of suspects most likely to create reasonable doubt.

"And Mr. G was yelling right back," Fowles continued, "giving Junior a real bollocking, calling him a prima donna and a playboy."

"A playboy," Steve repeated, just in case Victoria had missed it.

"Mr. G said it was his money and he'd do whatever the hell he wants with it. So if you ask me, Junior Griffin had a helluva lot more reason to deep-six Oceania than Delia or me. Millions more, you might say."

Steve's smile was so smug, Victoria longed to slap it right off his face.

THIRTY:
CROSSING THE
BRIDGE

"Junior's not a killer," Victoria said as they approached Big Pine Key.

"No way you can be certain."

"But you know Delia's harmless, even though she throws a mean meat cleaver."

Victoria was at the wheel of her Mini Cooper, headed south on U.S. 1. The car would have fit into the trunk of Steve's old Eldo, although the trunk was probably currently occupied by families of grouper and snapper. They were on their way to meet Junior, Steve insisting they confront him with Fowles' accusations.

"Look at the facts," he said. "Junior was angry that his father was going to build a hotel on top of a coral reef. But it gets worse. The old man's gotta put up everything he owns to secure the financing. Now Junior's afraid the fish aren't the only ones who are gonna be homeless. The two men argue, but no way Dad's gonna change his mind. Junior wants to stop the project, but how? He won't kill his father. And maybe he didn't even want to kill Stubbs. Maybe he just wanted to threaten him but things escalated."

"Couldn't happen unless Junior miraculously gets back on the boat while it's under way."

"No problem for Aquaman. You saw him climb on a seaplane that was under way."

"The security video clearly shows Junior diving off the *Force Majeure*."

"But not swimming away from the boat. He could have climbed up the dive ladder when no one's looking. He hides below, then confronts Stubbs in the salon, tries to get him to change his report. Stubbs says no. He's being paid a fortune to whore for Oceania. Junior threatens to expose the bribes, but Stubbs figures he's bluffing. If Stubbs is guilty of taking bribes, Griffin's guilty of paying them. Stubbs doesn't think Junior will take his old man down."

"You're making this up as you go along."

"That's what creative lawyers do, Vic. Now, just hear me out. Junior threatens Stubbs with the speargun. Maybe Stubbs tries to take the gun away and it discharges accidentally. Or maybe Junior just flat-out shoots him. Either way, Junior dives off the boat and swims to shore."

"Too many maybes. And Uncle Grif? Who knocked him out?"

"I don't know yet. But remember that cruise ship that got smacked by a forty-foot wave on a calm day?"

"Yeah."

"Maybe a rogue wave hits the *Force Majeure* as Griffin's going back up the ladder. He falls to the deck and is knocked out."

"*Way* too many maybes."

"Jeez, Vic. I'm just playing poker with ideas here. All I'm saying, we can toss Junior's Speedos at the jury and create reasonable doubt."

"Uncle Grif will never go for it."

"You're assuming he doesn't already think that's what happened."

"If Uncle Grif thought all that, why wouldn't he tell us?"

"Because he wants us to win the case without involving his son."

When they hit Big Pine Key, Victoria turned left onto Long Beach Road. Before leaving Fowles at Paradise Key, Steve had called Junior, who was looking at dive boats for sale in Marathon. Then he was heading to the Polynesian Beach Club to unwind.

Unwind from what? Steve wondered. The

guy didn't work. What would wind him up in the first place?

Junior invited them for lunch at the club, which he said served a fine grilled ahi. So now Steve looked forward to tuna followed by cross-examination.

Junior said the club was reachable only by a private bridge from the southern tip of Big Pine Key. He'd lowered his voice to tell Steve the password, "Kon-tiki," which they were to say to a guard at the gatehouse. It was all a little too Skull and Bonesy for Steve's taste. A rich man's private retreat, fat cats congratulating one another over rum and colas. Junior chuckled on the phone, saying he was sure they'd enjoy the "ambience."

Ambience, my ass. The phony bastard.

"So what's your plan?" Victoria asked.

Steve gave her a smile. "I'm going to tell Junior to be a man. Save his father by turning himself in. Plead to manslaughter. Ten years, out in seven. Not too bad. Of course, he'll lose his tan."

The man in the gatehouse wore a pith helmet and a navy shirt with epaulets. He smiled broadly when Steve whispered, "Kon-tiki."

"Have a good day, sir, ma'am," the guard

said. "And watch out for sunburn."

They crossed the bridge, and Victoria parked the Mini Cooper next to a silver Hummer with a trailer hitch. Junior's, she told Steve, as he unfolded himself from the little car. On the back bumper of the Navigator was a bumper sticker: *"Divers Do It Deeper."*

"Tacky," he said. "Very tacky."

"You're one to talk. With those juvenile T-shirts."

"Mine have meaning. They're not idle boasts."

"You're all adolescents," she said. "All of you."

They headed toward a clubhouse with bamboo walls and a thatched palm roof. Standing by the front door was an eight-foot carved wooden tiki, the Polynesian god. A long red tongue hung from his open mouth, looking distinctly obscene.

Steve heard the *thwack* of racket on ball. He took a closer look, first seeing a flash of movement, then a flash of flesh. Half hidden behind a row of sabal palms was a tennis court, two middle-aged couples playing doubles.

"I think the laundry workers are on strike."

"What are you talking about?"

"The tennis players aren't wearing shirts. Or shorts, for that matter."

Victoria peered between the trees.

A man shouted, "Out? Out, my ass!"

Then a woman's voice, "C'mon, Al. It was out. Forty love."

"They're naked," Victoria whispered, as if the tiki god might be eavesdropping.

"That's what I'm telling you. Junior wants us with our pants down. You, anyway."

"Don't freak out. It's got to be one of those clothing-optional resorts."

"Nothing optional about it," said the young woman behind the rattan counter in the clubhouse. Woven tapa cloths hung on the bamboo walls, and in the corner, a red-and-blue mynah was perched on an artificial tree. "Everyone's in the buff. Members, guests, staff."

The woman had one of those Disney World smiles, as if she'd overdosed on nitrous oxide. Her name tag said *"Honey"* and hung on a cord that snaked through the cleavage between her oversize, suntanned breasts. In Steve's estimation — based both on firsthand experience and defending Dr. Irwin Rudnick on med mal charges — Honey's grapefruit-shaped boobs had been surgically enhanced. "Once you cross the bridge, it's all nude, all the time," Honey emphasized. "Even the luncheon buffet."

"We're meeting a member," Victoria said, and Steve refrained from making a really bad pun.

"Who would that be?" Honey inquired.

"Junior Griffin."

"Oh, Mr. Grif-fin," Honey purred. "He's a big man around here."

Again, Steve stifled himself.

"I'm an intern," Honey volunteered. "Hotel management at Florida State. Mr. Griffin is my mentor."

"You're in good hands," Victoria said.

"Both of them," Steve remarked. A man can only resist so much temptation.

Honey pointed toward the locker rooms. After they disrobed — Honey confided that Junior-the-Mentor advised her never to say "stripped" — they should follow the Tahiti Trail across Volcano Bridge and the Koi Lagoon. They'd pass the swimming pool and find Junior Griffin on the croquet court.

"Mr. Griffin swings the best mallet at the club," Honey breathed, dreamily.

"Golly, is there anything that man can't do?" Steve said, agreeably.

"When he's got a clean shot, he always scores," Honey said, her eyes aglow.

■ ■ ■ ■

Solomon's Laws

■ ■ ■ ■

8. If a guy who's smart, handsome, and
   rich invites you and your girlfriend to a
   nudist club . . . chances are he's got a
   giant *shmeckel.*

THIRTY-ONE: SIZE MATTERS

"Do you think I'm flat-chested?" Victoria said.

"Absolutely not. You're well proportioned."

"Is that like saying a plain girl has a good personality?"

"You're tall and sinewy and athletic with boobs that are perfect for the rest of your bod."

"But small."

"Not small, not big. Just the way I like them."

"You're sure?"

"More than a handful is a waste."

"So why were you staring at Honey's humongous bazooms?" she demanded, having trapped him on the road of cross-examination.

"Because looking away would have stamped me as a rookie." Slipping out of the trap.

Naked and self-conscious, they passed a row of stone tikis that Victoria thought resembled the Easter Island gods. The path cut through a stand of mangrove trees, providing cover and a sense of security, for now.

"If a woman's a nudist, she *wants* you to look," Steve continued. "Proper etiquette requires a gaze. Not a long stare, but a look sufficient to appraise and appreciate."

"Great excuse. You really *are* a good lawyer." She'd been staring straight ahead, but now glanced at him. "What's with the newspaper?"

"It was in the locker room."

"And why are you holding it over your crotch?"

"No reason. I've been meaning to catch up on world affairs."

"Really?" She grabbed the paper. *Diario Las Américas.* "What's new in Tegucigalpa?"

A noise startled her. Just off the path, a woodpecker — as naked as they were — hammered at a bottlebrush tree. Victoria tried breathing deeply, inhaling the moist air laden with salt from nearby tidal pools.

She never considered herself an exhibitionist. If anything, she was shy about her body. But this posed a test, like competing for a spot on the law journal. She was determined to overcome her inhibitions, to win whatever was at stake.

I have a good body. And there's nothing wrong with nudity, right?

She was starting to convince herself. What was there to be embarrassed about?

Junior.

Junior would be naked, too. One gorgeous hunk of a man. What would *he* think of her body?

God, why am I thinking of him?

Victoria tossed the newspaper into a trash receptacle and glanced at Steve, whose right hand covered his groin.

"Now what?" she asked.

"It's shrinking."

"Oh, stop."

"Do you think I'm small?" Remembering Aquaman in his Speedos. Knowing they were moments from encountering Junior's jumbo Johnson.

"I think you're well proportioned for your body."

Touché.

"I mean it, Vic. Am I a little . . . *little?*"

"I don't have a sufficient sampling to answer. But yours is fine. It's cute."

"Cute? Cute is for kittens. A man wants to be a monster. A leviathan. A colossus."

"Okay, it's a cute little colossus."

"An oxymoron if ever I heard one."

"It's fine. You also have a great tush. You look terrific in jeans."

"I'd kill for a pair right now," Steve said.

The path ended at a rope bridge suspended over a peaceful lagoon. Lily pads and water flowers on the surface, fat Japanese koi swam below. From unseen speakers, music played. Dark and mysterious, heavy on the drums. Jungle music.

A man and woman, both naked, both in their sixties but fit and tanned, padded across the bridge, headed their way. They would all have to pass sideways.

Okay, good test, Victoria thought. Act normal. Reach a comfort level.

"Hullo there!" the man called out.

"Hi! Hi!" Victoria was too loud.

The woman looked them up and down, and Victoria felt herself reddening. "You two need some sun," the woman advised.

Victoria told herself to keep her eyes above waist level, but maybe Steve was right. If you're going nude, you *expect* people to look. As they scooted sideways, she let herself check out the man. The rope bridge was swaying back and forth and, *omigod,* so was the man's oversize scrotum. A low-hanging, loose sack that resembled a burlap bag with a couple onions inside. Victoria turned away so quickly, she could have suffered whiplash.

What am I doing here? This isn't me.

On the other side of the bridge, the path opened onto a wide expanse of grassy lawn. The pool was fifty yards away, and they could hear the yelps and cheers from a water volleyball game. They passed nude couples on chaise lounges, soaking up the afternoon sun.

A panorama of bare butts. A smorgasbord of exposed navels and glistening loins. Breasts heavy and pendulous, perky and firm, round and conical. Nipples puffy and nipples flat, nipples like raisins, nipples like raspberries. Forests of pubic hair, some wild and untamed, others as carefully tended as a putting green. Then the slack penises, draped on thighs like dead squirrels on logs. An array of sleeping male organs, ludicrous in their frailty. Did God play a trick on mankind with those distended pieces of droopy, feeble flesh?

As they approached the pool and refreshment stand, smells of coconut oil mixed with grilling meat from a barbecue pit. An aroma both sensuous and carnivorous.

Then Victoria felt the beginning of a piercing headache. "Maybe this isn't such a good idea."

"That's what I've been saying. Junior's trying to throw us off. How can we cross-examine him when . . ."

Just then, two petite women in their twenties with taut gymnasts' bodies jogged toward them. Perfect bods, Victoria thought. Slick with oil, defined deltoids, small breasts barely moving with each powerful stride. Steve, of course, was mesmerized.

"When what?" she said.

"Huh?"

"You were saying something. How can we cross-examine Junior when . . . something. *When* what?"

Steve turned to watch the women's perfect tight butts disappear into the foliage. Ten million years of evolution, Victoria thought, and men still act as if they had just crawled, web-footed, from the swamp.

"We're fine here, Vic. Just fine."

Several couples played cards at poolside tables. Others waded through the shallow end of the pool toward a waterside bar. People were staring at them, Victoria thought. Staring at her. Appraising her.

This is insane.

"Steve, I'm really not comfortable here."

He was looking around at the nude women sprawled on the chaises. "I'm not shrinking anymore. I might even be growing."

"I just feel so strange."

"We have work to do."

But his voice wasn't in work mode. Deeper now, his mellow mode.

How could he have relaxed just like that? To her, it seemed like a thousand eyes were drilling into her, and she felt herself blushing.

"Thank God my mother can't see me now."

"Princess! There you are."

That voice. It couldn't be.

"Join us for a piña colada, darling. Then for God's sake, get some sun."

In the second row of chaise lounges, reclining like royalty, there she was. The Queen held half a coconut shell festooned with two straws and a little purple umbrella.

Naked! In front of all these strangers.

Just look at her! An all-over tan. Her tucked tummy flat as an ironing board, her siliconed breasts as buoyant as floating beach balls, her skin tighter than the head of a snare drum. The Queen's bare legs, stretched out on the chaise, were slim and evenly bronzed, all the way up to . . .

Omigod. My mother, my fifty-eight-year-old mother, has shaved her pubic hair into a champagne-colored stripe the width of an emery board. At the spa, they had a name for it. What was it?

"Wake up! Look's who here." The Queen issued commands to the heavyset older man with hairy shoulders on the adjacent chaise. "Grif, wake up and say hello."

Uncle Grif! God, this can't be happening.

Victoria felt her throat constrict. Could she even speak? "Mother, what are you doing here?"

"Oh, don't act so surprised. I was going nude in Monaco when you were still in boarding school."

Landing strip.

That was the name of the neat little swath of pubes. Perfectly groomed in every way, her mother proudly displayed a landing strip, while she still had a jungle, a woolly rain forest.

Hal Griffin awakened and sleepily scratched his private parts. He extended the same hand toward Steve, who tried pounding — rapping knuckles — instead of shaking. "Hey, Solomon, how they hanging?"

When Steve seemed stuck for an answer, Griffin barked out a laugh. "Relax. Enjoy what you got now. As a man gets older, his dick gets smaller."

"But his boat gets bigger," Irene Lord chirped, happily.

Griffin looked tanned and healthy, a streak of reddish scar tissue on his forehead the only evidence of the boat crash. "Welcome to Polynesia, Princess."

Again she fought the urge to cover herself. "We were expecting to see Junior, Uncle Grif."

"And you will, but I have something to say first. Something important."

"They just got here, Grif," Irene said. "Why not talk business later?" She propped herself on one elbow and tucked her legs under her firm butt. "Princess, I hope you don't mind my saying so . . ."

Dear God. I don't have cellulite. Pilates keeps my abs tight. I don't need plastic surgery. What could she possibly say?

"Have you ever thought about a bikini wax, darling?"

Thirty-Two:
Adiós, Steve

Griffin began giving orders. Telling Irene to take a swim, the lawyers to sit down, and the waitress to bring a round of beachcombers.

Irene sashayed into the shallow end of the pool, giving everyone a chance to admire her newly tucked tush. Steve and Victoria took seats at a bamboo-legged table shaded by a thatched palm umbrella. And the nude waitress jiggled off to get their tall lemonades spiked with rum and triple sec.

"Clive Fowles called me right after you left him," Griffin told them. "All worked up. Afraid he'd given you the wrong idea about Junior."

"Maybe you're the one who gave us the wrong idea," Steve said. "Why didn't you tell us you and Junior fought about Oceania?"

"Ever argue with your father, Solomon?"

"Only for the last thirty years."

"Ever kill him as a result?"

"Not yet."

An unfamiliar sensation, Steve thought, the breeze between his legs. But not unpleasant. These naturists might be onto something. In the pool, two young women — barely old enough to drink — screamed as they sailed down the water slide. Maybe there'd be time for a coed volleyball game before they left.

Griffin turned toward Victoria. "Princess, you don't go along with this nonsense about Junior killing Stubbs, do you?"

"I'm trying to keep an open mind."

That's my partner. She doesn't think Junior did it, but she won't split ranks outside our little family. Lawyers and mobsters follow lessons learned from The Godfather.

"But it makes no sense to me, Uncle Grif," she continued.

So much for the Sonny Corleone rule.

"Because it's bullshit," Griffin said. "Junior had nothing to do with Stubbs' death."

"I'd like you to hear me out," Steve said.

"Hey, guys!"

Coming toward their table was the killer hunk himself. Twirling a croquet mallet, chest out, shoulders back, smiling with those Chiclet teeth. And between his legs . . .

Oh, shit. The Monster.

Angled out a bit, surrounded by tufts of blond hair, was a happy, confident, hey-look-at-me salami. The son-of-a-bitch could play croquet without a mallet.

"How'd you do, son?" Griffin called out.

"Good enough to win." Junior grinned and swung the wooden mallet by its blue suede handle. "Twenty-six to fourteen in the final."

"Attaboy."

"Hi, Tori." Junior leaned over the table and kissed Victoria on the cheek.

Jesus, did his pendulous pendulum just brush her bare shoulder?

"Hey, Junior." She smiled up at him.

"Steve." Junior nodded.

"Nice mallet," Steve replied.

"Son, why don't you swim some laps while I finish up with my lawyers?" Griffin suggested.

"No problem, Dad. I'll do five hundred meters of butterfly."

Junior bounced toward the pool, Victoria staring after him.

Griffin sipped at his lemony drink. "Go ahead, Solomon. Make your pitch."

"To win your case, we need to point the finger at someone else."

"Not at my son, you don't. Jesus, Junior

384

wasn't even on the boat."

"You're sure?"

"I was there, dammit."

"You were up on the bridge. No way you could see what was going on below."

"I'm not buying it, Solomon."

"Junior thought Oceania might bankrupt you," Steve barreled ahead. "If he thought that killing Stubbs would stop the project —"

"Bullshit. *I'm* the only one mad enough to kill the bastard."

Victoria wrinkled her forehead. "Uncle Grif, I don't understand that."

"What's not to understand?" Steve shot back. "He's sticking up for his kid."

"Listen to me for once, Steve," she ordered. "That's not what I'm talking about. That day on the boat, Uncle Grif, what were you mad at Stubbs about?"

"Like I told you before, he was extorting me for a million bucks."

"No, that was a week earlier. On the boat, you settled everything. You gave Stubbs the hundred thousand from the lobster pot with a promise of more. You told me he accepted it."

There was an unspoken question hanging in the humid air, Steve knew.

"If you'd told the truth, if you'd reached a

deal with Stubbs, why were you still mad enough to kill him?"

Doing good, Vic. Steve felt a sense of pride. She was using skills he'd taught her. Always precise with time lines, she'd picked up an inconsistency he had missed. Now he'd just settle back and follow her orders; he'd shut up and listen.

"Were you lying to me before, Uncle Grif? Did you have a fight on the boat over money?"

Griffin waved at Irene, who was hanging on to the side of the pool, doing leg kicks. The reluctant witness buying time. Then he sighed and said: "What I told you was true as far as it went. Stubbs took the hundred thousand. But only after trying to hold me up for more. The dumb shit told me he had a better offer."

"A better offer for what?" Victoria asked.

"Another 'bidder' is what he called it. *'I got another bidder soliciting my services.'* Someone promising him a million bucks to write a negative environmental report. To kill Oceania."

"Who?"

"Stubbs wouldn't say, and the more he refused, the madder I got. So, I pulled that old speargun of Junior's out of the lockbox and aimed square at Stubbs' chest."

Victoria's hand flew to her own bare breasts. "Uncle Grif, no."

"Hold on, Princess. I yell at Stubbs he'd better tell me who my enemies are or I'll nail his hide to the bulkhead. He laughs at me. I look down and see there's no spear in the gun. That breaks the tension a bit, and we both calm down. We talk, and I tell him I'll pay him a hundred thousand every year. He chews it over, then says fine, he'll be *loyal* to me. As if the asshole knows anything about loyalty. Anyway, we got a deal, so I go back up to the bridge and head for Sunset Key to meet you two. Maybe half an hour later, I put her on auto, come down the ladder, and he's got a spear sticking in his chest."

For a moment there was no sound but the joyous chatter of the naked volleyballers.

Victoria pursed her lips. Attuned to her expressions, Steve knew she was framing a diplomatic reply. Whereas he might blurt out: *What a load of crap!* she chose words like a florist picking roses, right down to pruning back the rotting leaves.

"That's a pretty tough sell, Uncle Grif," Victoria said, evenly.

"Pretty tough?" Steve broke his vow of silence. "Tell that story in court, better bring your toothbrush, because you're taking a long vacation."

"What are you saying?" Griffin asked. "You don't believe me, or a jury won't?"

"I believe you can't see the truth because you're blinded by love for your son."

"That again?"

"Ste-phen, don't." Victoria's warning tone.

Steve gave them his victory smile. "Don't you get it? You solved the case. Junior's the other bidder. He gave Stubbs forty thousand as a down payment but didn't trust him. The day you're coming to see us, Junior dives off the boat then comes back on board and hides below. When he hears Stubbs accept your offer and turn him down, he waits till you go back up to the bridge. Then he comes out and kills Stubbs."

"That's ridiculous." Griffin laughed but there was no joy behind the sound.

"There is one more possibility."

"There damn well better be."

"None of this is news to you. You come down the ladder and find Junior standing over the bloody Mr. Stubbs. Sure, you're angry. Your son just offed the one guy you need to build Oceania. But he's still your son and you love him more than a floating casino. So you put Junior ashore, fake the hit on the head, run the boat onto the beach, and hope your lawyers can get you off. And why shouldn't they? You're an innocent man."

Steve sat back, triumphant. He felt like lighting up a cigar, except he didn't smoke. But he savored this moment, distracted only by the discomfort caused by the cedar slats of the lawn chair sticking to his bare butt.

Griffin leaned forward, his neck seeming to lengthen, like a tortoise extending from its shell. "How you gonna represent me if you don't believe me?"

"I represent liars all the time. I just like knowing the truth."

"Uncle Grif, Steve's been under a lot of strain. He suffered a concussion."

"Don't make excuses for me, Vic," Steve commanded.

"This is just the way Steve's mind works," she continued, ignoring him. "He comes up with different scenarios. Maybe Junior killed Stubbs. Maybe it was an accident. Maybe you were there. They're just guesses and theories."

"Dammit, Vic." Steve didn't want her help. "I know what I'm doing."

"Then do it somewhere else," Griffin barked.

"Meaning what?"

"Meaning you're fired."

"You might want to think that over," Steve

said. "Trial's set and you won't get a continuance."

"I don't give a shit. You're fucking fired."

Steve stood, aware his private parts were
now at eye level. "Fine. C'mon, Vic. We're
out of here."

Griffin stabbed a finger at him. "I said
you're fired, Solomon. Victoria's still my lawyer."

"Doesn't work that way, Griffin. Vic and I
are partners. One goes, we both go."

Steve was aware of the crashing silence at
the table. From the pool, he heard splash-
ing, Junior plowing through his laps.

"Vic? You coming?"

"Uncle Grif is *my* client. I let *you* come
along for the ride."

"Aw, shit, don't do this."

"You promised to sit second chair, to let
me take the lead. But instead, you steam-
rollered me. Like always."

"We're a team. Ruth and Gehrig, Gilbert
and Sullivan, Ben and Jerry."

"I've given you every chance, but you —"

"Big mistake, Vic. You need me."

"What!"

"You're good, but you'll never be great on
your own."

"That's it. I've had it with you." Her voice
a serrated blade. "We're done. There is no

more Solomon and Lord. Good-bye, Steve."

"You can't mean it."

"What part of *adiós* don't you understand?"

Steve's mind went blank. He needed a retort. An exit line. Something that would set them both straight. Show them that Steve Solomon was The Man. That Victoria would fail and Griffin would be convicted. But he couldn't come up with a thing, so he stood there a long, ego-crushing moment, until . . .

"Hey, Solomon." Griffin grinned at him. "You're shrinking."

THIRTY-THREE: DREDGING UP THE PAST

"What a horse's ass! What a damn fool!"

"Thanks, Dad."

"You *putz*." Herbert Solomon's diatribe shifted to Yiddish with a Savannah accent. "How could ah have raised such a *schmendrick?*"

Steve knew a tongue-lashing was the price of hitching a ride back to Miami. Herbert piloted his old Chrysler north on U.S. 1, taking Steve and Bobby home. The car — underbelly rusted and carpets mildewed — was redolent of bait fish. The night air smelled of moist seaweed and crushed shells. A three-quarter moon cast a milky glow across the smooth inky water of the Gulf.

"You ever think that maybe you're jealous of this guy?" Herbert prodded. "What's his name?"

"Junior Griffin." Even saying his name left a rancid taste.

"IF RUN JOIN FRIG!" Bobby contributed from the backseat. Making an instant anagram out of the bastard's name.

"I'm not jealous. I just can't stand him."

Herbert had a three-day growth of white stubble. He wore tattered khaki shorts, a gray T-shirt with permanent sweat stains in the armpits, and his white hair was crusted with salt from an early-morning snorkel run. To Steve, his old man looked like a cross between a pirate and a serial killer.

"You're afraid he's gonna take away your gal," Herbert said, "so you got no credibility when you accuse him of murder."

"I've got logic and evidence on my side."

"You got jack shit."

"Junior's as likely the killer as his old man. In a reasonable-doubt case, I have an ethical obligation to tell the jury that."

"Since when did you start caring about the ethical rules?" Herbert hacked up a wad of phlegm and spat out the window. "Ah see right through you. You're running scared with Victoria so you lash out at this Junior Griffin."

"JUROR IN FIG FIN," Bobby proclaimed, still working on Junior's name.

"Doesn't make any sense, kiddo," Steve said.

"I JOIN RUFF RING. 'Ruff' is with two 'f's.'"

"Doesn't count. There's no such word."

"Yes there is. It's a big ruffled collar. Everybody knows that."

"Are you listening to me?" Herbert said. "You haven't learned self-control. You open your big mouth and *boom!* You lose your paramour and your client."

"But I still have my principles."

"Gonna sleep with your principles?"

"Hey, maybe Vic doesn't want to practice with me. But she didn't break up with me."

"Schmegege." Herbert doled out another insult.

"Uncle Steve, you don't understand women."

Double-teaming him now, the grouchy old judge and the smart-ass savant. "And you do, squirt?"

"You and Victoria are really different," Bobby said. "She likes that, up to a point."

"How would you know?"

"Because she told me."

"What! When?"

"When we talk about relationships and sex and stuff."

"You're too young for that kind of talk."

"I'm twelve!"

"I'm gonna report her to Family Services."

"Shvayg!" Herbert commanded. "Shut and listen to the boy. Maybe you'll learn something."

Bobby leaned over the front seat. "Women can't compartmentalize the way men can."

"What the hell does that mean?"

"A guy argues with his girlfriend, then ten minutes later wants to do her," Bobby explained, patiently. "Women aren't like that."

"You get that from Victoria?" Steve turned to face his nephew.

"Dr. Phil."

Herbert slapped a hand on the steering wheel. "You got nothing, son. No car. No client. No partner. And no gal!"

The Queen was going through Victoria's closet at the Pier House, making faces as she shuffled hangers and critiqued her daughter's wardrobe.

"A denim mini?" Irene arched her eyebrows. "I suppose you've taken up country music, too."

"Do you think, Mother, that you could be a tad more supportive?"

"You asked me to skip the luau and I did. Now, how much more support do you need?" Irene held up the mini, made a *cluck-cluck*ing sound. "A ragged hem and rhinestones? Haven't seen that since *Urban Cowboy*."

"Mother, we need to talk."

"So talk. Do you suppose room service will deliver martinis?"

"Dammit, listen to me!" Victoria balled up a beige tank top and threw it at her.

"Wrong color for you, darling," The Queen said. "Go with something brighter, or you'll be all washed out."

Victoria sighed and sat on the edge of the bed. "I'm so humiliated."

"About going nude? I find it liberating."

"That's not it. I watched you and Uncle Grif today. You're lovers, I can tell."

"So?"

"You lied to me. You said you didn't cheat on Dad."

"I didn't. Grif and I made love for the first time last night."

Victoria shook her head. "You must think I'm a child."

"I think you act like one. It was wonderful, by the way. Grif is extremely giving."

"You expect me to believe the two of you weren't having an affair when Dad was alive?"

"Don't use that Nancy Grace tone with me."

"Why not just admit it? Dad found out

and killed himself."

"Still singing that song?" The Queen held up a saffron cotton twill jacket. It must have met her approval because she didn't make a face. "Your father had problems. Emotional problems. Business problems. And, of course, his drug use."

"Dad a druggie? You're making that up!"

"Your father abused barbiturates. He was probably manic-depressive."

"I don't remember him that way."

"You were too young." Irene smiled ruefully. "And he was happier around you than he was around me."

Outside the windows, the band on the patio was kicking up. More Jimmy Buffett, damn them. "Simply Complicated," the singer bemoaning the challenges of family life.

Victoria thought of Steve. Maybe she had treated him cruelly, but it was for the best. She should never have brought him into Uncle Grif's case. Look at the trouble he'd caused. She had planned to split up the firm at the end of the trial, anyway. So it was no big deal, right? As for the rest — their relationship — well, let's be honest. That wasn't going so hot, either.

Earlier today, after Steve left the all-nude all-the-time beach club, Junior had asked her to stay overnight in one of the cottages. A hammock strung between palm trees, the gentle caress of the sea breeze, Bahamian lobster steamed inside palm fronds.

No, thank you. Not yet. I don't jump from one man's hammock into another's.

Seeing her mother — all of her — lounging with Uncle Grif had convinced her she'd been right about them. Tonight, Victoria hoped her mother would come clean. Show herself naked in more ways than one. But no, she still claimed to have been the faithful wife, the innocent widow.

"Steve told me to stop asking you about your relationship with Uncle Grif," Victoria said.

"For once I agree with him."

"He said, when you dredge up the past, you never know what you're going to unearth."

"He's not stupid, your Steve. Arrogant and uncouth, but not stupid."

"He's not *my* Steve." Victoria picked up the phone and punched the button for room service. Maybe they *did* make martinis.

Three generations of Solomons traveled in silence until they hit the plug-ugly stretch of Cutler Ridge lined with muffler shops, discount furniture stores, and fast-food joints. Herbert kept the radio tuned to NPR, which was airing an endless interview with the oboe player of the Seattle Philharmonic. A thrilling account of how to make your own reeds.

Steve felt himself growing crabbier by the moment. He was angry at the Griffins, father and son. He was angry at Victoria for choosing them over him. Angry, too, at Irene Lord. He could only imagine what direction she was pushing her only child.

"Princess, why go halfway? For heaven's sake, get out of his bed, too."

But most of all, Steve was angry with Herbert. Why couldn't his father ever take his side? Naturally, the old buzzard had stuck up for Victoria. Then there was the Bar license case. He could have shown some appreciation. Instead, he tried to sabotage the case. Not knowing why only pissed off Steve even more.

Maybe I should just drop the lawsuit. But if I do, I'll never know the truth.

What dark secrets were buried in Judge Herbert Solomon's courtroom? A courtroom staffed by Pinky Luber and Reginald Jones. What could his father have done that would make him quit the bench and Bar without a fight?

And now, two decades later, what's my old

man so afraid of?

Which gave rise to another thought. *Why am I banging my head against the wall?* The answer came quickly, though not without embarrassment. Deep inside, Steve knew he wanted to be a hero to his father. That unquenched thirst for approval.

Hell, no, I won't drop the Bar case. I'll show him. I'll get his license back and protect him from harm along the way.

With no murder case to try, he could just double his efforts in the case of *In re: Herbert T. Solomon.* "So Dad, how's Reginald Jones doing?"

"Who?"

"The guy who used to sit in front of your bench stapling, spindling, and marking."

"You mean Reggie. Nice kid."

"The kid's Chief Clerk of the Circuit now."

"Good for him. How's he doing?"

"That's what I'm asking *you,* Dad."

"How the hell should ah know? You think ah'm filing papers these days?"

The NPR station went to a fund-raising spot, the announcer insisting that civilization would crash and burn if each listener failed to fork over fifty bucks for a coffee mug. Steve reached for the dial, but his father swatted his hand away.

"What's Reginald Jones have to do with you and Pinky Luber?" Steve asked.

Herbert Solomon kept his eyes straight ahead, Steve studying his profile. A craggy-faced jawline, some speckling from the sun, fuzzy tufts of white hair sprouting from his ears.

"Don't know what you're talking about, son."

"Then why are you still talking to Jones? Five calls the day I deposed Luber."

"You little pissant! You been snooping."

"Twenty years ago, when Luber won all those murder trials, Jones was your clerk. What the hell were the three of you up to?"

"Not a damn thing. And if ah were, it'd be none of your business."

Alternative pleading. The old lawyer trick. I never borrowed your lawn mower. And if I did, it was broken when you lent it to me.

"I'll subpoena Jones, take his depo."

"Why don't you spread manure in your garden and stay out of mine?"

"Because you owe me answers."

"Ah owe you shit. It's mah life, not yours."

"It's the legacy you left me. I'm Steve Solomon, son of the disgraced judge."

"Live with it. Ah do."

"Just tell me why you won't let me get your license back. If you're as dirty as Pinky,

I want to know it."

Herbert hit the brakes and swerved into a gas station, squealing to a stop just inches from the pumps. "Git out!"

"What?"

"You heard me. You can walk home."

"You nuts? We're ten miles from the Grove."

"Tough titties. You show me no respect, get the hell out."

Steve looked around. Six lanes of traffic. A nudie bar and a hubcap store on one side of the street, a strip mall with a palm reader, a video rental store, and a U-Wash-Doggie on the other. Trendy South Beach, it wasn't.

He opened the door, then turned back toward his father. "I'm gonna find out what you did."

"What for? What the hell for?"

Steve didn't say it. Couldn't say it aloud. But he thought it just the same.

To prove to you that I can.

■ ■ ■ ■

SOLOMON'S LAWS

■ ■ ■ ■

9. The people we've known the longest
are often the people we know the least.

THIRTY-FOUR:
PUBLIC SERVANT

At the wheel of his new car, Steve raced Lexy and Rexy along Ocean Drive. He drove the egg-shaped Smart — larger than an iPod, smaller than an offensive lineman's butt — as the twins Rollerbladed. An unfair race. Lexy and Rexy were ahead by two limo lengths.

It was the morning after Steve had thumbed a ride home, helped by an amiable but odoriferous septic tank truck driver. Now, headed to the office, Steve put the pedal to the metal — or was it plastic? — and the little German car pulled even with the long-legged Rollerbladers.

He got to the Les Mannequins building first, thanks to a Miami Beach bicycle cop, a lifeguard type in cargo shorts and epaulet shirt, who pulled over the twins. The official charge was reckless skating, but the cop obviously wanted to meet the leggy speeders, who wore cutoffs with bikini tops.

Steve wheeled the Smart to a stop, perpendicular to the curb, where it fit into a parking space without sticking out into traffic. The two-seater was on loan from Pepe Fernandez, a client whose primary occupation was stealing cargo containers of frozen shrimp from the Port of Miami. The enterprise lost money because Fernandez seldom could sell the booty before it melted into a disgusting crustacean slime. Lately, Fernandez and two buddies had begun boosting imported cars by physically picking them up from the dock and tossing them into waiting trailer trucks. This naturally limited the size of vehicle they could steal and resulted in their inventory of Smarts, cars that made Mini Coopers look like Mack trucks. Ordinarily, Steve would have felt guilty driving a stolen car, but the Smart got approximately five times the mileage of his old Eldo, so he rationalized his actions as good for the environment.

Moments later, he was at his second-floor office overlooking the Dumpster. He'd been planning on putting a plaque on the door:

SOLOMON & LORD
ATTORNEYS AT LAW

But he'd never gotten around to it. Now

it was too late.

"You got checks to sign," Cece Santiago announced as Steve came in the door.

Cece was in her customary position, grinding out bench presses in front of the desk she seldom used. Wearing her uniform, Lycra shorts and a muscle tee, with the requisite three studs through one eyebrow.

"What checks?" Steve asked.

"Court reporter. Credit cards. My salary."

"Didn't I just pay you?"

She eased the bar into the brackets and sat up. "Two months ago. For services two months before that. You owe me like a gazillion dollars."

"You get me an appointment with Reginald Jones?"

"No can do. His assistant says he's in conference all day."

"What about tomorrow?"

"County Commission meeting."

"Thursday, then?"

"Public hearings on a new courthouse in Sweetwater."

"He's scared."

"He's busy." Cece lay back on the bench and began her stomach crunches.

"They're in it together. My father. Pinky. Reggie."

"In what, *jefe?*"

"I don't know. Something bad."

"*Malo?* Not your father."

"I wouldn't have thought so. But I'm starting to think that our parents — the people we've known the longest — are the people we know the least, Cece."

"When that stinky old car of yours went off the bridge, just how hard did you hit your head?"

"Don't you start with me."

"You want to lose your *papi,* too?"

"What do you mean, 'too'?"

"Victoria. Chasing her away. Stupid. *Muy stupido, jefe.*"

That afternoon, Steve sat in the chief clerk's waiting room, reading a stimulating article, "Managing Cubicle Space in the 21st Century Office," in a magazine called *Municipal Administrator.* The walls were covered with plaques from the Rotary and the Kiwanis and photos of a beaming Reginald Jones with numerous politicos, all wearing their pasted-on, ribbon-cutting, power-brokering smiles. Governor Jeb Bush here, Senator Connie Mack there. Local movers-and-shakers, too. Jones was an African-American man who seemed fond of Italian suits and silk jacquard ties, with kerchiefs in his coat pocket that matched his shirts. The word "dapper" came to mind.

Jones had manned the clerk's desk in Judge Solomon's courtroom all those years ago. Pinky Luber had captained the prosecution table, long before he became a fixer and a perjurious witness. Now Herbert Solomon was covertly calling Jones and mad as hell about Steve finding out about it. Just what was going on with these three, the Bermuda Triangle of the courthouse?

Steve had already downed two cups of motor oil from the coffee machine in the corridor. He'd checked his cell phone for messages from Victoria. *Nada.* He was camped out with no appointment, but he'd been rehearsing what he would say to Reginald Jones, should he ever get the honor of seeing him. Steve might start off with the bluff:

"I know all about you and Pinky and my old man."

Or maybe the good son approach:

"You can trust me, Reggie. I'm just trying to help out my dad."

Or even a threat:

"You wanna talk to me or the Grand Jury?"

But so far, there'd been no chance to talk to anyone. Mr. Jones was in conference, according to the receptionist charged with keeping vagrants, terrorists, and wayward lawyers out of the chief clerk's inner sanctum.

After what seemed like long enough for most statutes of limitations to expire, an attractive woman in a beige business suit appeared and asked Steve to follow her. They were buzzed into a corridor teeming with deputy clerks parked in front of computers, doing whatever it is that runs the local justice system. At the end of the corridor, the woman dropped him off at a corner conference room with an easterly view. Walking in, Steve could see Biscayne Bay, with Fisher Island and Miami Beach in the background. He could also see two turkey buzzards. One buzzard was perched on the railing outside the window, one was inside, sitting at the conference table. The one inside had a round pink face, a shiny pink head, and a diamond pinky ring.

"Pinky, what the hell you doing here?"

"Same thing I've done for years," Luber said. "Helping my friends."

Outside the window, the buzzard flapped its wings and took off. Steve took a seat. "Where's Reggie Jones?"

"Forget him. He's got nothing for you. But I do." Pinky leaned across the table. "I got a name. Conchy Conklin."

"Who's he?"

"Conklin was in Alabama Jack's the other night, drinking his ass off, throwing hundred-dollar bills around."

"So what?"

"Did I mention he was bowlegged from riding a red Harley he'd parked outside?"

"Keep talking."

"He's flapping his gums about the easiest ten grand he ever made. Messing up some guy in an old Caddy."

"Conchy Conklin," Steve muttered to himself. Trying to find something in the name to spark a memory. Coming up empty.

"Unless his parents were morons, which I don't rule out," Luber said, "I figure 'Conchy' is a nickname."

"Anything else?"

"Yeah. He was bragging about how quick his hands are."

"Quick hands? I don't get it."

"Says he catches snakes barehanded, sells them to reptile farms. Claimed he caught a whole nest of coral snakes on Crab Key last week."

"The son-of-a-bitch." If it was true, Conklin was the guy who ran him off the bridge and planted the snake in Victoria's hotel room. "What else? What about a description?"

"Thirties. Beard. Sunburned. Like he does

411

outdoor work, not a sunbather. He's not a regular at Alabama Jack's. Left the impression he lives farther south in the Keys."

"How do you know all this?"

"Like I told you before, I grease the skids, kid."

"So who hired this Conklin?"

"I give you the moon, you want the stars, too? That's all I know."

Steve would call Sheriff Rask, give him the information, see what he could come up with. "Pinky, why you telling me this?"

"Because I remember you when you were a snot-nosed kid. Before you became a snot-nosed lawyer. And I like your old man."

"What do you want in return?"

"What do you think?"

"I'm not dropping Dad's case. I'm gonna get his license back."

Pinky sighed. "Herb thinks you're a helluva fine lawyer."

"No he doesn't."

"Maybe he doesn't say it. But he admires you. Your damn stubbornness probably reminds him of himself. Problem is, you're too close to this one. You got your feelings all wound up in it." Pinky showed a grin that crinkled his cheeks and slitted his eyes. "Just like Hal Griffin's case."

"For a guy barred from every courthouse

in the state, you seem to know a lot."

"I know Griffin fired you. And you deserved it. You looked at Griffin's case through your dick, and all you could see was that playboy son. Nothing fouls up the brain cells like a woman."

"How do you know . . . ?" But then it came to him. There could only be one way. "Dammit, Dad's been talking to you."

"Aw, lay off Herb. He loves you more than you deserve." Luber pulled out a Cuban cigar, the Robusto, and licked the tip with a pink tongue. "What makes you think that waterlogged beach boy is a killer?"

"Go ask my father." Sounding pissy. Feeling confused. His father leaking info about Griffin's case. Reggie Jones refusing to see him but getting Luber to toss him a bone. Just what the hell was going on?

"I know your theory," Luber said. "The son's afraid his rich old man's gonna lose the family fortune if Oceania sinks. That's a negative motive. Damn tough to convey to a jury. Someone with no criminal record offing a guy to prevent a potential future event that might or might not take place. Too iffy. Jurors like evidence they can lay their hands on."

"So who do you think killed Ben Stubbs?"

"Damned if I know. Did you follow the

green path, like I told you?"

"I tried. The forty thousand in Stubbs' hotel room is still unaccounted for."

"If you ask me, boychik, whoever paid Stubbs that dough is the same shitbird who hired Conklin to run you off the road and scare the panties off your lady. And whoever that is had a positive motive, not a negative one."

"Someone who would make a ton of money if Oceania sank," Steve said.

"That's what I'm saying."

"So if I find who hired Conklin, I'll find who murdered Stubbs."

"I'd bet on it."

"And you don't want anything in return for this information?"

Pinky grinned, pushed his chair back. "Sure I do, kid. When the time comes, I want you to do the smart thing."

THIRTY-FIVE:
"A PUPPET,
A PAUPER,
A PIRATE . . ."

"Do you know how much money your crazy client cost me!" Leicester Robinson thundered. "Millions!"

"You're assuming Hal Griffin is guilty," Victoria said.

"Who else could have done it? I have no problem with Griffin bribing that paper-shuffler Stubbs. It's done every day. But kill him? What in Hades was Griffin thinking?"

"Who said anything about bribes?" Fishing to see what he knew.

"This is the Keys," Robinson said. "You can't take a piss in Tavernier without rattling the plumbing in Marathon."

Victoria had watched Robinson on the security video at Griffin's home. Along with Delia Bustamante, Clive Fowles, and Junior Griffin, he was aboard the *Force Majeure* just before it left for Key West. Technically that made Robinson a suspect in Stubbs' murder. But, like the others, he was seen leaving the boat before it churned away from the dock.

In his mid-forties, Robinson wore workingman's heavy boots with grease-stained shorts and a flowery aloha shirt. An African-American with the reddish-brown complexion of polished mahogany, he had a neatly trimmed mustache and salt-and-pepper hair twisted into short dreadlocks. As he spoke, he jabbed his thick fingers in the air, as if providing punctuation marks.

"Didn't matter to me if Oceania ever made money. I had cost plus thirty percent on the barge work." He gestured toward a pegboard with schematic drawings of a craft that looked something like an oil tanker. "Now what do I have? With all the money I sunk into the plans, all the work I turned down, I'll be lucky to stay out of bankruptcy."

He shrugged his broad shoulders as if to say: *What can a man do?*

They were in the warehouse office of Robinson Barge & Tow Co., hard by the Key West docks. A long, low building of corrugated steel, the place had a slick, metallic smell, the cluttered interior filled with machinery Victoria could not identify. The warehouse was also littered with hundreds of small items like a curio shop. Antique naval artifacts, sculptures, artworks. Along one wall, floor-to-ceiling bookshelves. On another, a vintage map of the Caribbean, with Cuba far larger than in reality, larger even than in Fidel Castro's dreams. Alongside, an oil painting of an enormous pink house with turrets and towers. Behind Robinson's desk hung a collection of rusty muskets, cutlasses, and broadswords.

In the middle of the warehouse, an ancient dugout canoe sat on sawhorses. It looked Native American and seemed to be undergoing restoration. Scattered on the concrete floor, an eclectic collection of maritime items: the glass housing of a lighthouse, a barnacle-encrusted anchor that looked hundreds of years old, open buckets of resin, a binnacle containing a vintage compass, and a rotted-out dinghy that might have been used by Captain Ahab. Victoria hoped that Robinson's barges and tugboats were more modern than the relics he seemed to collect.

"Before you settled on a cost-plus contract, you asked Griffin for a piece of the project."

"A man can ask, can't he?"

"I just wonder if that's customary in your business."

"I had a line of credit for barge construction at Southern Shipyards. No money up front. I could have done the work and waited for profits from the hotel and casino. But Griffin said he wasn't giving away shit. Didn't matter to me. I was going to make money either way. But now . . ." He waved a meaty hand toward the barge schematics on the pegboard. "I can burn those."

Victoria glanced at the bookshelves. Biographies of Theodore Roosevelt, Alexander Hamilton, John Adams. Books on pirates and colonialism in the Caribbean. Some fiction, too. Kafka, Dickens, Hugo. Even a few volumes of English poetry. The burly barge operator seemed to have a fondness for Tennyson.

She remembered Junior saying that Robinson had a bachelor's degree in English and a master's in history from Amherst. The most literate man with work-hardened hands in the Keys. Maybe the most literate person, judging from the end-of-the-road burnouts you run into down here.

"Did you see anything unusual on the boat that day?" she asked.

"Griffin and Stubbs were arguing. Hadn't seen that before."

"Arguing about what?"

"Couldn't tell you. They were in the salon. I only saw it through the glass. But Griffin shoved a finger in Stubbs' chest. Pushed him a bit, the way bullies do."

"That's it? A little shove with a finger?"

Robinson let out a derisive laugh. "Man does that to me, he'll be eating through a straw."

"What about Clive Fowles? Ever see him argue with Stubbs?"

"No."

"What about with Griffin?"

"Fowles wouldn't have the balls. Oh, I heard him tell Griffin maybe they should just do a tour business to the reef. Forget about the floating hotel and casino. Of course, Griffin didn't listen. You want my opinion, Fowles thought too small and Griffin too big."

"Why would Hal Griffin kill Ben Stubbs?"

"No good reason I can think of."

"And yet, you seem to think he did."

"Two men were alone on a boat at sea. One ends up dead."

A concise summation of the state's case, she thought. "There could have been a stowaway."

"Not unless Griffin put him ashore on the way down the coast. Like that book by Conrad."

The Secret Sharer." Victoria smiled to herself. Yes, this was one literate barge operator. She'd mentioned the book to Steve, but he hadn't heard of it. Now, if Jimmy Buffet were the author and the book described island hopping and rum guzzling, Steve would be able to quote entire passages.

"You know the story, then?" Robinson seemed pleased. The usual visitors to Robinson Barge & Tow probably didn't study English at Ivy League universities, Victoria figured.

"A captain hides a stowaway who's accused of murder," she said. "The captain somehow identifies with the stowaway and risks his ship to get the man to safety."

"It's about the duality of good and evil in all of us," Robinson explained. "Maybe your client's a bit like that."

"Hal Griffin is not a murderer."

"Whoever did it, I'd like to wring his neck." Robinson made a twisting motion with those powerful hands. "You know my history at all, Ms. Lord?"

"I know your family's been in Key West for generations."

Robinson barked out a laugh. "That doesn't begin to describe it. There were black Robinsons here long before Thomas Jefferson started playing footsie with Sally Hemmings. I can track my ancestors back to a slave ship attacked by Sir Henry Morgan. He sunk the ship and grabbed the strongest slaves to join his crew. My great-granddaddy times ten or so became his first mate."

"Rescued by pirates," Victoria said. "Ironic."

"Morgan would have run you through with a sword if you called him a 'pirate.' He preferred 'privateer.' Had a license from England to plunder Spanish ships and settlements."

"A license to steal." Victoria laughed. "That's what Delia Bustamante called the EPA permit to build Oceania."

Robinson allowed himself a pinched smile. "Maybe there's a parallel. Maybe those who *can* remember the past are *privileged* to repeat it."

Remodeling the Santayana line. Leicester Robinson, Victoria thought, may actually have read all those books on his shelves. But surely he didn't go around quoting Conrad and Santayana in his daily work. What was such a man really like?

"You have a fascinating background, Mr. Robinson." Her way of saying: *Tell me more.*

"My family's been wealthy and poor, owned castles on some islands and been

421

jailed on others. Sort of like that Sinatra song. " 'I've been a puppet, a pauper, a pirate . . .' "

" 'A poet, a pawn and a king,' " she finished the lyric.

Robinson smiled. "Exactly, all of them. More than a hundred years ago, there were Robinsons in Key West with their own salvage sloops. Licensed by the federal government. A cargo ship gets torn up on the reef, the salvors would race out there. The Robinsons had the fastest sloops, so they'd beat their competitors to the reef. Once you staked your claim, you got forty percent of what you salvaged."

"Just like contingency fee lawyers," Victoria said.

"With even worse morals. Some salvors set false lights, actually lured ships onto the reefs."

"The Robinsons do that sort of thing?"

He smiled and got up from his desk. "Let me show you something, Ms. Lord."

He put on a pair of wire-rimmed glasses and led her to a framed document on the wall. Handwritten in fancy script was a salvor's license signed by a federal judge and dated October 1889.

She read the stilted legal language aloud: *"Know all men by these presents that Walter*

J. Robinson, owner and master, is hereby licensed to employ his Sloop Satisfaction *in the business of wrecking and salving along the coast of Florida."*

"My great-great-grandfather. Do you know why he named his ship *Satisfaction?* That was Sir Henry Morgan's warship. The one that rescued the first Robinson and led to generations of black pirates, leading straight to Walter J. Robinson. So you ask whether my great-great-granddaddy was a tough customer? Let's just say he kept up with the competition. People said he'd save bales of cotton and let stranded sailors drown. A cutthroat business, it was."

"A cutthroat era."

"Aren't they all?"

Victoria wished Steve were here. He would have insights into Robinson she lacked. The man seemed disarmingly open with her. She knew he was trying to create an impression. Friendly and transparent. Was it an act? One of Steve's lessons involved witnesses too eager to talk:

"If they're filling all that dead air, it's because they want to control the conversation."

Robinson went on for a while, tracing his family history. Walter Robinson ran the town's cockfights and owned a brothel and a saloon that catered to both blacks and whites. He also built the grandest house in Key West. There it was, the oil painting on the wall. In the Queen Anne style, with a double veranda, balustraded railings, and a widow's walk, the pink house had been an extravagant showplace overlooking the ocean. There were conflicting stories of how the house was destroyed, Robinson said. His father told him it was demolished in a hurricane. But he'd later heard that his grandfather, Walter's grandson, having lost the family businesses, torched the property for the insurance. After that, it was downhill for the Robinsons. Leicester's father crewed on a shrimp boat and scraped up enough money to buy a leaky tugboat. Leicester went off to college in New England, intending to teach history, but returned home to rescue the business when his father died.

The powerful gravitational pull of family.

Her own. Steve's. Maybe Junior Griffin feared the loss of the family fortune, and maybe Leicester Robinson was obsessed with restoring his. But even if that was true, she still had no idea who murdered Ben Stubbs. And as for Leicester Robinson, no idea if he was a poet or a pirate.

THIRTY-SIX: MAXIMUM HERB

Steve lay in wait like an assassin . . . if assassins surveilled their prey from the front seat of the ultramini Smart car.

He scanned the grassy terrain through binoculars. There was his target, in houndstooth slacks, a black polo shirt, and black leather gloves. Steve could pick him off easily with a scoped M-16. Or pop him in the head with a nine iron. Or just call him on his pager. Reginald Jones was driving a golf cart. Next to him, riding shotgun, some fat-assed business type. The fat guy looked familiar, but Steve couldn't quite place him.

Earlier that morning, while spooning papaya pulp into the blender with yogurt to make Bobby's smoothie, Steve had scanned the *Herald*'s sports section. The Marlins had been rained out, a seventh-grade soccer coach was caught selling steroids, and there was a charity golf tournament at Doral. Athletes, semi-celebrities, and local politicos would be teeing up. Including Reginald Jones, Chief Clerk of the Circuit Court.

Before setting out for the Doral, Steve's phone rang, Willis Rask calling. The sheriff had run the name "Conchy Conklin" through the computer.

"Full name's Chester Lee Conklin," Rask said. "Got the nickname because he's dumb as a conch shell. And that's his friends talking. Guy's got a record. Couple B-and-E's. Couple DUI's. On probation for an ag assault in a bar. Settled an argument with a broken beer bottle."

"If he's on probation, you gotta know where he is," Steve said.

"We would, except he missed his last two appointments. Probation officer went out to the trailer he was renting in Tavernier. No sign of him. Neighbors say they haven't seen him or his Harley in a month."

Rask said he'd start the paperwork for the probation violation, see if they could find Conklin, bring him in.

Now, with the midday sun high in the sky, the air was muggy with fat, puffy clouds building over the Everglades. Steve was slick with sweat, partly from the humidity, partly from the tension. His car was tucked into a strand of sabal palms along the narrow fairway of the eighteenth hole of the Doral

Gold Course. While stalking Jones, he'd cruised past other foursomes, waving as if he were the head groundskeeper in a vehicle only slightly larger than their own carts.

Jones and his partner both put their tee shots in the middle of the narrow fairway. The eighteenth hole was just a shade under four hundred yards and straight, but with an island green totally surrounded by water. Jones' second shot was a beauty, hitting twenty feet from the pin and dying there, like a quail felled by a hunter. The son-of-a-gun must have been sneaking out of the courthouse early to practice. His chunky partner plopped three shots into the drink and cursed loud enough for Steve to hear every syllable from his camouflaged position.

The two golfers climbed back in their cart and headed for the green. Steve tore out of the palms after them. The men were nearing the bridge to the green when Steve beeped the horn and overtook them.

"What the hell!" Jones jerked the golf cart to the right and skidded off the path, heading straight for the water hazard.

An image came to Steve, his beloved Caddy crashing through the guardrail and plunging nose-down to the bottom of Spanish Harbor Channel. The golf cart slid sideways in the moist grass and splashed to a stop in the shallow water.

"The fuck! The fuck!" Jones stepped out of the cart and sank up to his knees in mud. Not looking quite as dapper as he did in the framed photos in his office.

"I'm sorry, Mr. Jones," Steve told him. "But it's the only way I could get to see you."

Jones waded to the shore, his shoes sucking at the mud. His passenger, the heavyset man, waddled toward Steve, brandishing a sand wedge. "You crazy bastard. I'm gonna scramble your brains —"

"Hold on, Jack." Jones held up a calming hand then turned to Steve. "You're Herb Solomon's son, aren't you?"

"Guilty as charged."

"I know you!" The heavyset man wagged the sand wedge in Steve's face. "You're that ambulance-chasing shyster."

"Before you call anyone a shyster, I'd like to see your scorecard," Steve shot back.

"What are you implying?"

"If you put in for any of the prizes, I'm calling the cops."

"Mr. Solomon," Jones interrupted, "say hello to Police Chief Jack McAllister."

All things considered, Steve thought the

chief clerk and the police chief were down-right hospitable, as soon as he offered to buy them new shoes. After Jones two-putted for a par and the sheriff gave himself a five despite at least nine strokes, not including penalties, Steve sat at the bar in the Nine-teenth Hole with the chief clerk.

"Your father was a mentor to me," Jones declared.

"He was always terrific with other people's kids," Steve conceded.

They drank beer and munched burgers. Steve was paying for lunch, too. He was happy he didn't have to pick up their greens fees.

"I was going to community college part-time when I started clerking for your father. The judge talked me into getting my bach-elor's then helped me get a scholarship at FIU for my master's. Government adminis-tration. All the while telling me I could be whatever I wanted if I applied myself."

"Funny, he used to tell me I'd never be half the lawyer he was."

Jones chuckled. "Half of Herb Solomon is still a helluva lawyer."

When they'd run out of small talk, Steve said: "I need to know what my father was involved in when Pinky Luber ran Capital Crimes."

"Judge Solomon was involved in the pursuit of justice."

"Aren't we all?"

"All I'll say is this: You keep this up about Herb's Bar license, you're gonna open a can of worms. Just let it go."

"Not until I know what's in that can."

Jones sipped at his beer, glanced out the window to where other golfers were finishing up. "You remember the early eighties, after the Mariel boatlift?"

"I was still a kid. But I remember the Pacino movie *Scarface*."

"Well, that wasn't far off. Cocaine cowboys. Shantytown under the expressway filled with Castro's mental patients and criminals. Machine-gun shootouts at the Dadeland Mall. Highest murder rate in the country. Tourism down, businesses leaving."

"What's that have to do with my old man?"

"Herb was chief judge of the criminal division. He decided to do something about it."

"What could he do that he wasn't already doing? Maximum Herb was always tough."

"Before you can sentence them, you've got to convict them."

"Meaning what? A judge has to be impartial."

"If you examine your father's rulings,

you'll find he was. The appellate courts must have thought so, too. Lowest reversal rate in the Eleventh Circuit."

"What aren't you telling me? What the hell do you mean my father decided to do something about all the crime?"

Jones slid his plate away. "The judge always had a pure heart. And cleaner hands than most."

"You're talking in riddles, Mr. Jones."

"And one more thing. Your father loves and respects you."

"So I'm told." By everybody except him.

■ ■ ■ ■

Solomon's Laws

■ ■ ■ ■

10. Choose a juror the way you choose a lover. Someone who doesn't expect perfection and forgives your bullshit.

THIRTY-SEVEN: WINNING STREAK

"You win cases in voir dire."

Steve had told Victoria that when they tried their first case together, defending Katrina Barksdale in a murder trial.

"Lawyers think they win with closing argument. Wow the jury with their oratory. But it's too late then. Jury selection's the most important part of the trial. Not opening statement. Not cross of the state's chief witness. And not closing argument. Voir dire! Pick right, win. Pick wrong, lose."

One of his many lectures. He could be so irritating when pontificating. But he was usually right. Which was even more irritating. Ever since she'd left the State Attorney's Office, Victoria had picked juries with Steve at her side. Now, on a rainy Key West day, she was standing alone. Okay, not quite alone. Her mother was perched like a snowy egret in the first row of the gallery. Virginal white the predominant color of her outfit. The Queen apparently trying to send subliminal messages of purity and innocence to the prospective jurors. A Max Mara skirt with a white jasmine floral design and an asymmetric hem, a white linen jacket with a tie front, and gunmetal sandals. The suede bag with lizard trim picked up the gunmetal color and provided what she called the *"accènto."*

The Queen passed the time scribbling her observations about each potential juror, then handed the fine linen stationery to the bailiff, who slipped the pages to Victoria. Her helpful hints were confined to criticizing skirts that were too short, shoes that were out-of-date, and the mortal sin of carrying a knockoff faux-leather Prada handbag.

Hal Griffin sat at the defense table, trying to smile at each potential juror without appearing obsequious. His son slouched in the single row of chairs in front of the bar that separated the well from the gallery. Junior had warned Victoria that he was likely to fidget, as he was unaccustomed to being cooped up indoors. Would she mind if he dropped to the floor for eighty push-ups in the middle of voir dire? Yes, she would. Not wanting the defendant's son to be seen squirming in his chair, she advised Junior to run up and down the staircase to the ground floor if he started feeling antsy.

He'd passed her a note, too. Asking her out to dinner. She'd shaken her head and pointed at her briefcase. *"Work to do."* Junior had given her a sad smile, as if she'd broken his little heart.

Does he have any idea of the pressure of defending a murder trial?

With his father in the dock, shouldn't Junior be a little more understanding?

Now, she was annoyed with both Steve and Junior. Maybe with *all* men.

Reporters packed the first two rows of the gallery. Off to one side, the pool TV camera and a single newspaper photographer, all that was permitted under the rules of court. They would share their video and photographs with all the others.

Victoria forced herself to listen as Richard Waddle, the Monroe County State Attorney, made his introductory remarks to the jury panel. Nicknamed "Dickwad" by defense lawyers, the prosecutor was a jowly man whose pencil mustache combined with seersucker suits gave him a 1940's look.

"The jury is the cornerstone of justice, the bedrock of freedom," Waddle intoned. "Samuel Adams called the jury the 'heart and lungs of liberty.' "

Actually, it was John Adams, Victoria knew. His cousin, Samuel, was the patriot who ignited the Boston Tea Party, probably so people would drink his beer.

Waddle strolled alongside the jury box, pausing at each occupied chair like a train conductor punching tickets. "And when old Ben Franklin wrote the Declaration of Independence . . ."

Thomas Jefferson, Dickwad.

"He guaranteed us the right to trial by jury."

Actually, that's in the Constitution. But close enough for government work.

When did she become so sarcastic? Victoria wondered. Easy answer.

When I hooked up with Steve.

"The jury is what separates us from the uncivilized world," Waddle prattled on.

And I thought it was pay-per-view wrestling.

Yep. Definitely Steve's influence.

"Without you good folks coming on down here, we'd have no justice system. So, on behalf of the state, I say thank you, kindly. Thank you for leaving your jobs and your homes, your friends and your families, putting your lives on hold to see that justice is done."

Trying to be folksy. Next he'll chew on a piece of straw.

"To make certain that no crime goes unchecked, no murder —"

"Objection!" Victoria was on her feet. "That's not the purpose of the jury system."

"Sustained." Judge Clyde Feathers didn't look up from his crossword puzzle. On the bench for thirty-two years, he had mastered the art of half listening. "I don't mind your speechifying, Mr. Waddle, but save your arguments for closing."

"Thank you, Your Honor." Waddle bowed slightly, as if the judge had just complimented him on the cut of his suit. Courtroom protocol required thanking the judge, even if His Honor had just chastised you, threatened you with contempt, and called you the anti-Christ.

"You good folks are the judges without robes," Waddle rambled on, oozing his charm over the jurors like syrup on waffles.

Victoria concentrated on memorizing the names of the panel so she wouldn't have to look down at her pad when questioning them. Steve again.

"Let them know you care enough to learn their names and where they live. 'Morning, Mr. Anderson. They fix the road on Stock Island, yet?'"

"What is your occupation, Ms. Hendricks?" Waddle asked.

Helene Hendricks, the heavyset woman sitting in seat number four, smiled back. "Dick, you see me driving the skeeter truck out of the county garage every day. You know darn well what I do."

Small towns, Victoria thought.

"It's for the record, Helene."

"I spray mosquitoes for the county. Been doing it twenty-two years."

"Ever been in trouble with the law?"

"Willis busted me for DUI a couple times." She looked into the gallery where Sheriff Rask was sitting. He gave her a little wave. "I told him any alcohol I drink is purely medicinal. When I sweat, it cleans out the pores of that damn insecticide."

An hour earlier, the sheriff had greeted Victoria warmly in the courthouse lobby. *"Tell Steve I said howdy. Doesn't seem like Margaritaville without him."*

Victoria said she hadn't seen Steve in several days, though he had called to tell her about the search for Conchy Conklin. She thanked him for the two deputies who'd been hanging around the Pier House, keeping an eye on her room. Then Rask scratched his mustache with a knuckle, lowered his voice, and allowed as how he was sorry if there were problems between Steve and her. *"You two go together like whiskey and soda."*

Or a fish and a bicycle, she thought. Remembering her American Feminism course at Princeton and the essays of Gloria Steinem.

"You tell Steve that Jimmy's been asking about him, too," Rask said. *"Wants to chase some bonefish soon."*

Rask walked away humming "Come Monday," the old Buffett song about missing your lover, then getting back together. Lobbying for his pal.

Now Victoria studied Helene Hendrick's body language. Something else she learned from Steve. Answering Waddle's questions, the woman appeared comfortable, slouching a bit, arms relaxed. If she folded into a protective ball when Victoria stepped up, she'd be spraying mosquitoes by the afternoon.

"The fact you work for the county," Waddle asked, "would that make you more inclined to favor the government?"

"They don't pay me that much," Ms. Hendricks said.

Victoria looked at Hal Griffin's notepad. He'd written a large "NO!" across Helene Hendricks' name. Wrong end of the socio-economic scale for his tastes. Problem was, it's hard to find a jury of peers for a multimillionaire.

The first people who filed into the box were typical Key West. A retired naval officer, a time-share saleswoman, a cigar roller, a shrimper, a tattoo parlor owner, a pole dance instructor, and someone who called himself a "pharmaceutical tester."

"That's a new one on me," Waddle said to the young man. "Didn't know there were any pharmaceutical companies in the Keys."

"There aren't," the man replied. "I just test the stuff my buds make in their garage."

Then there'd been a "wingwoman," who earned commissions accompanying men to bars and introducing them to women. Or in Key West bars, to other men.

There was the city rooster wrangler, a man hired to keep the free-ranging chickens to a manageable level. Like Ms. Hendricks, he was a government employee. Then there were two failed businessmen, one who went bankrupt with a shoeshine parlor at the beach and another who lost everything with an ill-conceived fast-food restaurant called "Escargot-to-Go."

Waddle addressed the entire panel. "This case involves circumstantial evidence. That means there's no eyewitness to the crime. No one's coming into court to say, 'I saw the defendant shoot poor Benjamin Stubbs with a speargun.' Now, you may not know this, but eyewitness testimony is notoriously flawed. In fact, circumstantial evidence is the higher-grade testimony. Yes, indeed, circumstantial evidence is sirloin and eye-witness testimony is chuck meat."

"Objection!" Victoria figured Waddle was testing her. Either that, or he thought she'd fallen asleep. "Misstatement of the law."

Judge Feathers nodded his agreement. "Sustained. Misstating the law is my job."

That evening, Victoria was alone in her hotel room, nibbling a Cobb salad and working on her opening statement. Judge Feathers had told everybody to be back at eight a.m. to resume jury selection. Junior had cheek-kissed her good night, saying he'd be at the bar at the Casa Marina if she changed her mind and wanted to join him. Uncle Grif and The Queen were enjoying his-and-her massages at the hotel spa.

Victoria believed The Queen had lied about her past relationship with Uncle Grif, but what could she do about it? If she fret-ted over that — or pestered them with more questions — she'd do a lousy job in court.

She forced herself to focus on the case and turned to Willis Rask's police report. But that only brought Jimmy Buffett into her head, and soon she was humming "Come Monday," which led to thoughts of Steve. What was he doing? Hitting the South Beach nightspots? What songs were playing in his head?

Standing at the kitchen counter in the little house on Kumquat Avenue with Bobby at his side, Steve wondered where Victoria was having dinner. Louie's Backyard? World's most romantic restaurant, waves lapping the shoreline just yards from the table? *With Junior Big-Dick Griffin?*

Drinking champagne and exchanging tender whispers? Steve briefly considered driving to Key West and crashing their party, again. This time without Lexy and Rexy. They wouldn't fit in the Smart, anyway.

No. Victoria wouldn't be doing that. With her work ethic, she'd be slogging away tonight, preparing for court. He wondered how jury selection was going. He'd taught Victoria a lot about voir dire, but she had one quality that didn't need any instruction. Likeability. Jurors responded to her. More than to him. Still, he felt he could spot a devious juror better than she could.

Dammit, I should be there.

He was Victoria's biggest fan, and part of

him wanted her to win the Griffin trial. But another part wanted her to get in trouble and call him for help. Until she did, he would stay in Miami working on his father's case.

Another nagging thought. Their personal relationship.

Where the hell are we? Did she break up with me and I don't even know it?

"What are you thinking about, Uncle Steve?"

"Work."

"Uh-huh." Bobby peeked under the lid of the panini grill, where a grilled-cheese sandwich sizzled. "I miss her, too."

"Who?"

"Victoria. You're thinking about her, aren't you?"

"Sometimes you scare me, kiddo." Steve rotated the sandwich 180 degrees to cross-hatch the ciabatta roll. "Finish your homework?"

"Bor-ing."

"C'mon, Bobby. You have to do your math homework."

"I'll bet you don't know the only even prime number."

"Don't mess with me. I'm tired of your teacher calling."

"Two." Bobby opened the grill lid. If the

ciabatta burned, even a tiny scorch, he wouldn't eat the sandwich. "What's the largest number divisible by all numbers less than its square root?"

"I see summer school in your future."

"Twenty-four."

"And where are your shoes?" The skinny kid wore a Shaquille O'Neal Miami Heat jersey that hung to his knees. Maybe he had shorts on underneath, maybe not. "Remember the rule? No going barefoot in the kitchen."

"Dumb rule. My feet don't have boogers."

"Lots of rules are dumb, but you still have to follow them."

"*You* don't." Bobby used a spatula to take his grilled cheese out of the grill. "What's the largest prime number?"

"A hundred bazillion. Are you listening to me? I'm worried about your schoolwork." Steve thought he sounded like his own father, except Herbert never checked a report card in his life.

"It's over six million digits long, so it doesn't really have a name. But I can show you on the computer."

"And all this time I thought you only looked at Paris Hilton's anatomy."

"You know what we're studying in school? Algebra for dummies."

"Do your homework first, then come up with a new theory of relativity."

Bobby grabbed a Jupiña pineapple soda from the fridge and sat down at the kitchen table. "Can I help on Gramps' case?"

"Sure." Steve grabbed a slice of cheese — cheddar with jalapeños, great with tequila. "What do you think Reginald Jones meant when he said your grandfather decided to do something about all the crime?"

"Maybe Gramps was like Bruce Wayne. At night he became Batman."

"More like Bacardi Man."

"I know what you think. You think Gramps cheated."

"It has occurred to me. That's why I need to read the old transcripts."

"I already did, Uncle Steve."

"When?"

"This week. Instead of going to school, I took the bus downtown to the courthouse."

"Aw, jeez. You're a truant, too? We're gonna catch hell."

"I read Mr. Luber's murder trials. Seventeen convictions, no losses. Nothing was amiss."

" 'Nothing was amiss'? Who talks like that?"

"Rumpole of the Bailey. On PBS."

"Okay, so Pinky Luber tried seventeen

murder cases and won them all. That's how he made his bones."

"He asked for the death penalty in eleven trials, and the jury recommended death every time."

"Helluva batting average."

"Gramps went along with the jury. Eleven death sentences. Six life sentences."

"Maximum Herb. I need to look at the appeals."

"No reversals. Not even one."

Amazing. Bobby had all the numbers. If only he were as thorough with his homework. "So whatever your grandfather was doing, the Third District and the Florida Supreme Court never figured it out."

"You said that Mr. Luber was a good lawyer before he got all twisted. Maybe he just got hot."

Steve poured two fingers of the Chinaco Blanco and grabbed another slice of cheese. A well-balanced dinner. Protein from the cheese. And tequila came from the agave plant, so that counts as a vegetable, right? "Nobody wins seventeen straight capital cases. Twelve jurors in each one. That's . . ."

"Two hundred and four."

"Two hundred and four jurors you have to convince without one dissent. Can't be done."

"Maybe if you figured in the losing streak, it all averages out."

"What losing streak?"

Bobby took a bite of his sandwich, a string of melted cheese sticking to his lip. "In Mr. Luber's last five trials before the winning streak started, he lost three and had one hung jury. He only got one conviction."

"Holy shit." The newspapers never talked about the losses. It was always, *Luber's Super Bowl streak.* Seventeen wins, no losses. So how'd he turn it around?

"Maybe we're looking at the wrong cases, kiddo. We need the ones Pinky lost. See what he did differently. See what that paper shuffler Reggie Jones did. And most of all, see what your grandfather did."

THIRTY-EIGHT: COUNTING FACES

"Do you watch Leno or Letterman?" Richard Waddle asked.

That old one? Leno fans favor the prosecution, Letterman the defense.

The State Attorney needed to update his repertoire along with his wardrobe, Victoria thought, as they started day two of jury selection.

"I don't stay up that late," said Angela Pacheco, temporarily ensconced in slot seven of the jury box. She was a married woman in her early forties who sold time-share condos from an office in Islamorada. "I never miss *Desperate Housewives,* though."

Victoria processed the information. Did Ms. Pacheco identify with Bree, the uptight Republican housewife, a sure prosecution juror, or Gabrielle, the cheating, conniving — and therefore defense-oriented — hausfrau?

But Waddle must not have watched the show, because he moved on. "Does your car have any bumper stickers, Ms. Pacheco?"

Bumper stickers. Straight out of the prosecutor's cliché bag.

A prosecution juror boasts: *"My child is an honor student at Dolphin Elementary."* The defense juror: *"My kid can beat up your honor student."*

"Only one," Mrs. Pacheco said.

"And what's it say, ma'am?"

" 'If It's Called Tourist Season, Why Can't We Shoot Them?' "

Ooh, good. A defense juror, even if she's only joking. In fact, anyone with a sense of humor is a likely candidate for the defense.

"This is a homicide trial," Waddle said. "The charge is second degree murder. If convicted, the defendant faces life in prison."

"This is a homicide trial," Pinky Luber said. *"The charge is first degree murder, and the state seeks the death penalty. So I have to ask all of you a very tough question. If we prove beyond every reasonable doubt that the defendant is guilty of a vicious premeditated murder, with malice aforethought, can you render a verdict that may result in his execution?"*

451

The words in the transcripts were beginning to blur. Steve had been sequestered in a corner of the musty records room of the courthouse for two days. He'd skimmed thousands of pages of transcripts. The words had melted together like the cheese in Bobby's panini. Nothing in the cold, black type to indicate anything different in Luber's losing trials from the winning ones. Nothing remarkable in Herbert Solomon's rulings. The judge seemed evenhanded on objections, and his jury instructions were right out of the book. As for Reggie Jones, the transcripts seldom mentioned him at all, except when he responded to questions concerning an item of evidence.

Just like Bobby said, "Nothing was amiss."

There was one oddity in the records, but it didn't seem to have any relevance. One of the defendants was tried twice. His name was Willie Mays, his parents doubtless hoping he'd become a baseball star instead of a drug dealer with a homicidal streak. Mays was the last murder defendant to walk out of Judge Solomon's courtroom a free man, the last person acquitted before Luber's famous hot streak. A year later, Luber had a second shot at him. Charged in a new case — killing his ex-girlfriend and her infant child — Mays was convicted and sentenced to death. And no wonder, Steve thought, studying the man's hefty rap sheet. Willie Mays had been arrested exactly twenty-four times, equaling his namesake's uniform number. The Florida Supreme Court unanimously affirmed both the conviction and Judge Solomon's sentence.

The second Mays trial had been televised back when that was still a rarity. The local public station had broadcast the trial with expert commentary from various lawyers eager for TV exposure. In the era before Court TV and twenty-four-hour cable stations, this was pretty hot stuff, at least in the legal world.

Now Steve riffled through the appeals papers. One of the public defender's appellate arguments was that the cameras deprived his client of a fair trial. Jurors are intimidated; there's more pressure to convict; the courtroom is turned into a theater. All routine arguments in the 1980's and all routinely denied by Florida's courts.

Steve looked through the exhibits attached to the PD's appellate brief. A bunch of courtroom photos. Several showed TV technicians setting up their equipment. In others, the lawyers were smiling, either for the jury or the cameras. One photo taken just before the trial began caught Steve's attention. The entire jury panel, ninety strong, sitting in the gallery, waiting to be called to answer questions. It struck him then.

Where are the black faces?

He counted five apparent African-Americans. Way underrepresented.

In a capital case in which a black defendant was accused of killing his white ex-girlfriend and their infant daughter, the defense lawyer would crave black jurors.

Steve found a photo of the panel actually seated. Twelve jurors plus two alternates. Two of the African-Americans made it onto the panel, and a third was an alternate. Okay, that seemed to cure the problem, evening out the statistics somewhat.

A nice trick, getting three of five black jurors on the panel, Steve thought. He turned back to the transcript of voir dire. Hank Adornowitz, the defense lawyer, was a veteran of the PD's office. He'd long since retired, but at the time, Adornowitz was considered the top capital crimes defense lawyer on the public payroll.

Steve dug deeper into the transcript and matched up jurors' names with faces in the photos from their position in the jury box. Juror Two, an African-American man wearing a short-sleeve shirt and a tie, without a jacket, turned out to be Leonard Jackson.

He owned his own home, worked security at a downtown department store, and served in the military as an MP.

Holy shit. Sure, he's black. But you couldn't ask for a more pro-prosecution juror.

Unless you had an immediate family member killed by violence. Juror Seven, Martha Patterson, an African-American cook in a North Miami restaurant, lost a teenage sister to a drive-by shooting. And the alternate, Charlene Morris, worked as a paramedic and dated a cop.

Other than their skin color, these three could give prosecutors wet dreams.

So, what gives? Why did Adornowitz leave them on? Steve could think of only one answer. With the sea of white faces he had to work with, the PD must have been happy to get any blacks seated.

Still, there was something haunting about that first picture. Steve wished he could study the racial composition of all seventeen trials in Luber's winning streak. But the photos were in the Mays file only to bolster the argument about the prejudicial effect of cameras in the courtroom. Lacking the same appellate issue, the later cases would have no photographs. And there's no way to determine each juror's race from the bare transcripts.

But the transcript of voir dire would reveal something. Home addresses.

Miami was among the most segregated of cities. Twenty years ago, if you lived in Liberty City or Overtown or the Grand Avenue section of Coconut Grove, there was a high probability you were African-American. Bobby, the little statistician, could easily put the numbers together for him.

And there was one more thing to examine. The videotape of the second Mays trial. Gavel to gavel on the public TV station. An eerie look into the past. A chance to stare through the knothole at his father two decades earlier. That gave Steve a moment of pause.

Just why am I doing this?

Sure, he wanted to get his father's Bar license back. Partly to rehabilitate the old man's reputation. Let people call him "Judge" again without irony or footnotes. And partly just to prove to his father that he could. It didn't take a shrink to figure out what a son will do to seek his father's approval. But there was something else, too.

If his father was dirty, Steve wanted to know.

If there was to be a wedge between them, he'd prefer it deep enough and wide enough

that there'd be no way to bridge the distance.

Thirty-Nine:
Dead Dummy

Richard Waddle propped an elbow on the rail of the jury box. "This is a story about greed and corruption, bribery and murder."

A strong start, Victoria thought, sitting with perfect posture at the defense table, taking notes. Using the rule of primacy. *Jurors remember best what they've heard first.*

"Greed and corruption. Bribery and murder."

The four horsemen of a murder trial. Waddle would drill the jury with the phrase every chance he got. Some lawyers believed in the rule of recency. *What you hear last stays with you longest.* Steve taught Victoria to use both theories because the best lawyers opened strong and finished strong.

"What I'm about to tell you is not evidence," Richard Waddle said. "It's a preview of what the evidence will be. It's a shorthand version of the story you are about to hear."

Opening statement. What lawyers like to call the "curtain raiser." They had their twelve jurors plus two alternates, all of whom had just raised their hands and promised to follow the law and the evidence and render a verdict just and true.

"And what's that story about?" Waddle asked rhetorically.

Victoria thought she knew the answer.

"Greed and corruption, bribery and murder," he answered himself.

Yep. Thought so.

"It's a story about a wealthy man with no links to the Keys and no respect for our beautiful string of islands, this emerald necklace reaching into the sea. You folks who live here know we've got to protect the beaches and the mangroves, the turquoise waters and the fragile life beneath the sea. But this defendant came here for another purpose. He's a big man with big plans and he doesn't let anything get in his way. Environmental laws? He'll find a way around them. Bribery laws? He'll violate them with impunity. It's the way he's always done business."

Victoria had never heard an opening statement quite like it. Waddle hadn't even gotten to the alleged murder and he'd already crossed way over the line into character assassination. She could object, but Steve's advice rang in her ears.

"You piss off the jurors when you object in opening. They want to hear each side's story. Sit quietly. Smile sweetly. You'll get your chance."

Waddle approached the defense table and pointed at her client. "That's him, Harold Griffin, sitting with his Miami lawyer." *Mia-muh loy-yuh.*

Ordering up some home cooking from a dozen local chefs.

"The defendant roared into town like a wave of napalm hitting a row of shotgun shacks. Shock and awe. That's Harold Griffin. He blasted into the Keys with his private planes and his fancy boats and all that money and he says, 'The rules don't apply to me. I'm Harold Griffin. I do what I want. I bribe public employees, seduce them with greenbacks, and when they don't do exactly what I want, I kill them!' "

The jurors were transfixed. Next to her, Griffin squirmed in his chair. Victoria placed a calming hand on his arm.

Waddle walked to the clerk's table, picked up the speargun with one hand and the spear with the other. Gesturing with both weapon and projectile, he looked dangerous. That was the idea, Victoria supposed.

"With this deadly weapon, Harold Griffin impaled a living human being. Under our laws, you're not even allowed to spear a lobster. But Harold Griffin used this to puncture another man's vital organs. A man named Benjamin Stubbs, a loyal civil servant who was first corrupted and then callously dispatched by the defendant for refusing to do his dirty work."

Waddle droned on, painting a portrait of the deceased man, humanizing him. He was trying to create sympathy, Victoria knew, as soon as he said: "I'm not looking for sympathy. I'm looking for justice."

While Waddle prattled on, Victoria scanned the courtroom. Sheriff Rask was in his usual position in the front row. Junior had taken the day off. He needed to practice free dives in the Tortugas, saying he'd been letting himself get out of shape. The Queen played hooky, too. She needed a shopping fix, but with no Nieman-Marcus for 150 miles, Victoria knew she'd be back at the hotel spa by noon.

"Now, the defense is going to say that Mr. Stubbs might have accidentally shot himself with that speargun. They're going to bring in an expert witness with charts and diagrams to tell you about the angle of entry and velocity and a lot of other mumbo-jumbo they'll say creates reasonable doubt."

"Objection!" Maybe Steve would let it go,

but she'd had enough. "Your Honor, I'd prefer to be the one to discuss our evidence. I probably know a little more about it than Mr. Waddle does."

A polite way of saying, "Mind your own briefcase."

"Overruled. Mr. Waddle's entitled to speculate, and the jury's entitled to hold it against him if he's wrong."

Damn.

"You know what an expert witness is?" Waddle smiled at the jurors. "A hired gun. Now, maybe you can't buy an expert witness, but you can sure as heck rent one. According to papers filed with the court, the defense has rented a 'professor of human factors . . .' "

Making it sound like "charlatan with rank and tenure."

". . . from Columbia University in New York City. I don't know why they had to go all the way to New York City, unless they couldn't find anyone in Florida to do their bidding."

Oh, shit.

Victoria knew she should object. She should pound the table and act outraged. But she was gun-shy after losing the first objection.

"In case you don't know it, a human factors expert is somebody who'll tell you that a curb is too high or a guardrail too low. I'm not sure what this professor from New York City knows about spearguns, so I'll have a few questions for him when he gets down here for his little paid vacation."

Waddle went on, speculating that the professor probably didn't know Manhattan Island from Green Turtle Key. Griffin drummed his fingers on the defense table and scowled. His look, Victoria thought, combined with his bull neck and broad chest, made Griffin appear belligerent. Victoria scribbled the word "smile" on her legal pad and slid it in front of her client.

The State Attorney was better on his feet than she had expected. And yes, Steve had warned her about that, too.

"Don't let Dickwad fool you with that aw-shucks routine. He's smarter and meaner than he looks."

Buried in the middle of Waddle's opening was the admission that no usable fingerprints were found on the speargun. Smart, Victoria thought, hanging a lantern on what might be perceived as a weakness in his case. The proliferation of forensics shows on TV has created what lawyers call the "CSI factor," jurors expecting fiber and hair and blood spatter evidence in every case, all accompanied by techno-hip computer graphics.

"There are no fingerprints," Waddle explained generously, "because the ridged polymer pistol grip on the speargun is not susceptible to prints."

As Waddle wound down, one of his assistants walked into the courtroom carrying a dummy, which he placed in an empty chair at the prosecution table. Unlike Tami the Love Doll, this sack of sawdust lacked name and gender. It resembled one of those crash-test dummies that gets knocked ass-over-elbows when broadsided by a weighted sled.

"Yes, ladies and gentlemen, you're going to hear a bunch about this speargun. It's an old pneumatic model, powered by a blast of air from a carbon dioxide cartridge. You load it like this." Keeping the barrel pointed at the ceiling, Waddle leaned over and jammed this spear into the barrel until it locked. "Not hard to do. As you can see, it'd be darn near impossible to accidentally shoot yourself. But shooting someone else — well, that's as easy as . . ."

Waddle wheeled toward the prosecution table and fired. The spear *whoosh*ed across the courtroom and plugged the dummy in the chest with a sickening *thwomp!* The dummy's arms spasmed and its head whip-lashed. The jurors gasped.

"Imagine the shattering of bones and the bursting of vessels. Imagine the pain and the horror. Imagine Ben Stubbs watching himself bleed nearly to death before he lost consciousness."

Victoria was furious. She could object. But the damage had already been done. Now, for the remainder of the trial, whenever the speargun was mentioned, the jurors would not be listening. Their minds would be focused on one horrific sight and sound. The spear *thwomp*ing into Ben Stubbs' chest.

"Now, I'm going to sit down," Waddle declared, the spear still vibrating. "And I want you to pay as close attention to Ms. Lord as you did to me. All the state wants is for justice to be done. A fair trial for all."

"All the state wants is a fair trial," Pinky Luber said. *"Fair for the defendant, but fair for the people of Florida, too."*

Steve hit the PAUSE button and the picture froze. The videotape from WLRN-TV was twenty years old, but Pinky didn't look much different. Bald, pudgy, pink-faced. Like all the good trial lawyers, he was comfortable in front of the jury box. It was his turf, and before he surrendered an inch of it to the public defender, he was going to get his licks in. Even in voir dire.

Steve put his feet up on his cocktail table, poured himself a tall glass of Jack Daniel's — it was going to be a long night — and hit the PLAY button.

"Mr. Willie Mays is accused of a horrific crime," Luber continued. *"A vicious double homicide, the murder of an innocent woman and her baby. Now, I've got some questions to ask each of you to help us seat a jury that will be fair to both sides."*

On the screen, Luber stood within arm's length of the jury box, close enough for eye contact but without invading anyone's space. "Juror One. Mr. Connor, let's start with you."

The video cut to a shot of the bench and Judge Herbert T. Solomon. Unlike Pinky, he had changed considerably. On the screen, he was a handsome man in his forties with an expensive haircut and aviator eyeglasses. His jawline had not yet gone soft, his hair was not yet gray, but there was something else different, too. An expression Steve could barely remember. As Herbert looked toward the jury box, the judge wore a relaxed and confident smile. He seemed *happy.* This was his courtroom; he was doing a job he loved. What must it be like to lose all that? How deep were his wounds?

Reginald Jones sat at the horseshoe-shaped desk below the bench, a supplicant before his king. Jones' tools were neatly arranged in front of him. Notepads, evidence stickers, a stamping device, and the court file itself: State of Florida versus Willie Mays.

Steve sipped his sour mash whiskey and watched Juror One explain that he had no moral or religious objections to capital punishment. "The Bible says an eye for an eye."

Bobby, barefoot as usual, padded into the living room, toting a legal pad and a guava smoothie. "I've broken down all the stats, Uncle Steve, but I don't know if they help you."

"Let's see what you've got."

While Luber asked his questions on the videotape, Bobby explained how he put together the demographics of the jurors in seventeen murder trials. Sometimes, the questions themselves would reveal the person's race. *"As an African-American living in Liberty City, were you ever mistreated by Anglo police officers?"* Sometimes, the answers were the key. *"What those cops did to poor Mr. McDuffie was a crime, but I didn't* take to the streets and riot like some of those fools." And other things, like membership in the African Methodist Church, civic organizations, and a residential address could help.

"Of the two hundred and four jurors seated in all the trials, twenty-three were African-Americans," Bobby said. "That's about eleven percent, which is less than the population but not, like, really outrageous."

"Not low enough to show systematic exclusion."

"That's what I mean, Uncle Steve. Every trial had at least one black juror and some had two."

"But never more than two?"

"Nope. Unless you count alternates."

"Anything else?"

"The African-Americans were almost never tossed off. Whatever ones got into the box were accepted by both sides."

"Just like the Mays case. Only five on the panel, and three got seated, one as an alternate. Unbelievable odds."

"Maybe it's because the African-Americans were such solid dudes."

"Meaning?"

"The black jurors all seemed to have good jobs."

Bobby handed Steve his notes. Next to the name and address, his nephew had listed the black jurors' occupations. Postal worker. Dentist. Accountant. Homemaker. Paramedic. Dentist. Probation officer.

Probation officer?

"This isn't a jury pool!" Steve thundered. "It's a Rotary meeting. A Republican convention. These guys drive Buicks. Where are the people on work release? On food stamps?"

"Did you watch the beginning of the tape, Uncle Steve?"

"Nothing to watch but an empty courtroom. I fast-forwarded to voir dire."

"You've gotta let it play a while. Mr. Jones came in and was doing something, but I don't know what it was."

Steve rewound the tape to the beginning. Just as before, the camera was on, but the courtroom was empty. Minutes passed.

"Who says trials are boring?" Steve asked.

"Let it play."

A few seconds later, a uniformed bailiff led several dozen people into the courtroom. They wore plastic name tags identifying them as jurors. At the moment, though, they were only *potential* jurors. Veniremen. More minutes passed. The civilians sat on the hard benches, some reading newspapers, most looking bored.

Reginald Jones walked in, pushing what

looked like a grocery cart filled with files. He took his seat below the bench, smiled toward the gallery, and began speaking. No audio here, so Steve couldn't tell exactly what he said. But soon, a line formed in front of Jones' desk, and Steve knew what was going on.

"Jones is asking who wants out of jury service on hardship grounds," he told Bobby.

In a few moments, half the panel queued up in front of the deputy clerk's desk. Apparently a lot of people were caring for dying aunts. It only took another few moments for a pattern to begin emerging.

"He's letting the black jurors go home," Bobby said, just as a young man with dreadlocks hurried out of the courtroom.

"Not all of them. He's keeping the older African-Americans and the better-dressed ones, along with most of the whites."

"But there's a white juror getting excused." Bobby pointed to the next man in line. "He's so big, maybe Mr. Jones was afraid of him."

True, the guy was a load, his shoulders nearly filling the screen. Jones smiled broadly, energetically pumped the man's hand, then handed him a slip of paper. The man nodded and headed for the door.

Jurors in the gallery applauded, and the man waved at them, stopping when someone offered a pen and a piece of paper. An autograph hound. Then Steve recognized him.

"Ed Newman," Steve said. "All-Pro guard for the Dolphins in the eighties."

"Maybe he had a Monday night game and couldn't sit on the jury."

"Keep watching. It's getting interesting."

The next person in line, who appeared Hispanic, wore a blue mechanic's jumpsuit, and Steve could make out the logo of the late and lamented Eastern Air Lines. Sorry, no excusal. Behind him, a well-dressed middle-aged white woman. Sorry, ma'am. You gotta stay, too. Then a white middle-aged man in a suit. Another smile from Reggie Jones. He stamped a slip of paper; the man bowed in gratitude and headed out. The camera picked up the black yarmulke on the man's head.

"The guy's a rabbi or something," Bobby said.

"So's Ed Newman. Jewish, I mean."

Newman, one of those brainy football players of a generation ago, went on to law school and had become a fine judge himself. But that's not what Steve was thinking about. The pattern was taking on another dimension, Steve thought.

"A Jewish football player?" Bobby said. "Cool."

"The Dolphins have had a few *landsmen*. Steve Shull was a linebacker at the same time Newman played. And you remember Jay Fiedler?"

"The quarterback?" Bobby said. "He stunk."

"So did A. J. Feely, and he's not a member of the tribe."

"So what's with Mr. Jones, anyway? Why's he letting off Jews and blacks?"

The blacks and the Jews.

Something came back to Steve, something from the day he'd deposed Pinky Luber. The slippery bastard was complaining about the jury in the first Willie Mays trial, the last case he lost.

"They must have come straight from an ACLU meeting. All shvartzers from Liberty City and Yids from Aventura."

It didn't mean anything then, but it did now. Something else Luber said that day, too.

"You can't trust juries."

Now Steve knew exactly what Luber and Jones were doing. "Bobby, what's the most important part of trial?"

"Jury selection. You always say so."

472

"Reggie Jones is helping Pinky Luber stack the jury. Knocking off blacks and Jews, the most defense-oriented jurors. The blacks he leaves on are all establishment guys. The defense lawyer has no choice but to accept them. Otherwise, he'll have an all-white panel, and God knows what'll go on in the jury room."

Jones' conduct was illegal, of course, a deprivation of the defendant's constitutional rights. But why was he doing it? No way the young deputy clerk came up with this scheme on his own. This had Pinky's sweaty palms all over it. But so far, it didn't seem to involve Steve's father.

There had to be something more. Something Dad was doing. Otherwise, what's he afraid of?

Steve fast-forwarded the tape to the beginning of voir dire. He'd seen it once, but this time he wouldn't take his eyes off his father. He'd study his old man, watch every gesture, listen to every word. Part of him hoped that his father had been unaware of the conspiracy taking place right under his gavel. But another part, coming from a dark place of repressed anger and alienation, yearned for something altogether different. Part of Steve wanted proof that he was right and his father wrong. Proof that the Honorable Herbert T. Solomon was considerably less than he held himself out to be and his son was considerably more.

FORTY: THE PRINCESS VS. THE QUEEN

The sliding door to the balcony was open and the night breeze, moist and smelling of brine, swirled the drapes. Somewhere in the room, a mosquito buzzed.

On the pool deck below the window, a sheriff's deputy leaned against a palm tree. Another deputy sat on a chair outside her door. Victoria's personal bodyguards, courtesy of Sheriff Rask.

Victoria's feet ached and her head throbbed. Her black Prada pumps had been a half size too small when she bought them, and after a day waltzing back and forth in the courtroom, she felt like a victim of Chinese foot binding. The headache came from sitting at the defense table with her shoulders scrunched.

If Steve were here, he'd rub my shoulders. And my feet.

But she was alone in her suite at the Pier House, the sole soldier in a War Room filled with files, books, and the remains of room service conch chowder and Caesar salad. The adjoining suite was dark and quiet, her mother out to dinner with Uncle Grif. It was past midnight. Where were they? Parked at the beach in Uncle Grif's Bentley, listening to Barry White sing "Can't Get Enough of Your Love, Babe" and French kissing in the moonlight. The thought made her cringe.

She was angry at both of them. Uncle Grif should be here, helping her prepare for court. Her mother should be here, just for emotional support. Instead, they were . . .

God, why does it bother me so much? They're entitled to their lives, aren't they?

She sipped a glass of Cabernet and tried to concentrate on the witness files spread in front of her. Tomorrow, the state would start moving the pieces on the chessboard. Six people on the boat, three exit stage left, one dives into the water, leaving the defendant and victim alone for the last cruise of the *Force Majeure.* The "death cruise," Waddle called it. A phrase he'd added to "greed and corruption, bribery and murder."

She knew the state's order of proof for its circumstantial case. Clive Fowles would set the scene — the cocktail party on the deck — then Leicester Robinson would describe an apparent argument between Griffin and Stubbs.

Victoria had not yet decided how aggressively to handle Robinson. She could object if Waddle tried to elicit his impressions of what was going on.

"Now, Mr. Robinson, would you say that the defendant appeared belligerent with Mr. Stubbs?"

"Objection. Leading and calls for a conclusion."

But you don't object to everything that's objectionable.

"Don't make the jury think you're hiding something."

Steve again. He'd know what to do, just like he'd know how to rub the kinks out of her neck. She missed him.

No, dammit. I don't need Steve. I don't need anyone.

Feeling like a gladiator. A sole practitioner of the art of legal warfare. She surveyed the files spread across the conference table. An uneasy feeling spread over her. She always prided herself on trial prep. Unlike Steve, she believed you won cases in research and investigation, organization and preparation. Master the details. Color code the exhibits. Cross-index the depos. Know the file forward and backward. Steve the Slasher was a big-picture guy. Give him a rough idea of the facts and he'd wing it in court. That's why they made a good team, he always told her. Their skills were so disparate that they made each other better.

"You two put the sin in synergy," a prosecutor once raged at them.

Not that I can't do this alone.

But right now, she could have used Steve's improvisational skills, especially since her preparation had been lacking. With everything going on — her mother's unexplained reappearance, Junior's advances, the break-in of her room, the split with Steve — she hadn't been operating on all cylinders.

Victoria heard the door open in the adjoining room, and in a moment, her mother peeked through the connecting door. "Princess, you're still up?"

"I'll be working most of the night." She tried to see around the door. "Are you alone?"

Irene came into the room. "Grif went straight to bed, if that's what you're asking. Poor man's so uptight he wouldn't be any use to me, anyway."

"Bummer. The guy's on trial for his life, and you're upset you're not going to get off tonight."

"You have it backwards. I thought giving

478

Grif a little release would be good for him."
Irene walked over and eased into a chair at
the worktable. Her flowery silk chiffon dress
was low-cut and form-fitting. How many
women her age could get away with that?
For a reason Victoria couldn't quite understand, the thought of her mother's youthful-
ness irritated her.

"Pour me a glass of wine, Princess. And
maybe another one for you."

"Serve yourself. I've already had my
limit."

"You seem so tense, dear."

"Really? I guess trying a murder case will
do that."

Irene unhooked the ankle straps and
kicked off her metallic-gold wedge espa-
drilles. "Does this damn humidity make
your feet swell? It does mine."

"Next time you go in for repairs, have
your ankles liposuctioned."

"Have I done something wrong, Princess?"

"You mean lately?"

"Oh, Jesus, you have become so tiresome.
How long since you've gotten laid?"

"I don't remember you being so crude."

"Nor you so much a prude. On second
thought, yes, I do." Irene got up and closed
the balcony door. "It's like a steam bath in

here. What's the A/C set at?"

"Aren't you too old for hot flashes, Mother?"

"You've gotten bitchier since you dumped that insufferable Solomon." She barefooted back to the table and poured herself a glass of wine. "As for your catty remark, I'm barely middle-aged."

"Only if you live to be a hundred sixteen."

"I know what ails you, Princess, and I have a suggestion. Go out with Junior. He's gaga over you, and I'll bet he's fabulous in bed."

"I have things on my mind. Why don't you service both the Griffins?"

"If I were your age, don't think I wouldn't give Junior a ride. You saw his tool, didn't you?"

"Mother, why don't you go take a cold shower?"

"Not that size always equates with performance. I remember a Spaniard I met in Monaco. *Mucho grande.* Like a salchicon sausage."

"I'm not having this conversation."

"But a real dud in the sack. Then there was this Frenchman who wasn't carrying much more than a cornichon, but oooh-la-la."

"You're doing this just to aggravate me,

aren't you?"

"And you're bitchy because I'm happy."

"That's ridiculous."

"But I am happy, darling." She managed to sigh and smile at the same time. "Grif and me, connecting after all these years."

"*Re*connecting, you mean."

"That again? I told you the truth. We never had an affair."

"But Father thought you did. Is that it?"

"No, dammit. Don't you see what's happening? You've been angry with your father all these years. But you can't yell at him, so you take it out on me."

Victoria was quiet a moment. She swatted futilely at the damn mosquito, now buzzing around her ears. "I am angry at him. That part's true."

"Understandable, dear."

"You know what drives me crazy?"

"The suicide note thing?"

"I've asked myself a thousand times. Why couldn't he write something? 'I'm sorry, Princess. Forgive me. I love you.' "

Irene reached out and gripped her arm. "He did love you, dear. He loved you very much."

"A little note. Is that too goddamn much to ask?"

Irene's voice was little more than a whisper. "He wrote a note."

"What?"

"He said he loved you very much."

"You're making this up. Lying to make me feel better."

"Nonsense. I only lie to make *myself* feel better." She sipped the Cabernet, made a face. "Your taste in wine is really abysmal."

"Jesus, Mother. Was there really a note?"

"Your father wrote that he loved you more than he could express and his biggest regret was that he'd never know the woman you would become."

Suddenly, her mother was right: The room had gotten very warm. "All these years! Why didn't you tell me?"

"I had my reasons." For the first time Victoria could remember, The Queen almost looked her age.

"Why? What else did it say? Did Dad accuse you of having an affair with Uncle Grif? Why not just admit it, after all this time?"

"There was no affair."

"Then why did you destroy the note?"

"Who said I destroyed it? It's in my safe-deposit box. I thought someday you'd be old enough — mature enough — to read it. Apparently, that day has not yet come."

Irene stood, smoothed her dress, and

glided to her room, carrying her shoes. Without looking back or saying good night, she closed the door between the suites and slid the bolt shut.

Two hours later, Victoria lay in bed, listening to the palm fronds slap against the balcony wall. She longed to talk to Steve, but it was too late to call him. No matter the problems between them, he was the closest person in the world to her. At this moment, at this awful, heart-aching moment, she had never felt so alone.

She heard the buzzing again, the damned mosquito. Now where was it?

Ouch. She felt the sting on the side of her neck.

FORTY-ONE:
A SOLOMON
Shlimazel

Suicidal lovebugs — coupling in the air — smacked the windshield, dying instantly in one last orgasmic splat. So many peppered the Smart that Steve swore the miniature car swerved with each machine-gun burst of pulverized bugs.

Just after two a.m. they approached Sugarloaf Key, Bobby asleep in the passenger seat, a good trick in the tiny cockpit. On the way south, Steve rehearsed what he would say to his father, but he still didn't know quite how to do it.

Just how do you say to your old man: "Gotcha"?

It had taken several hours and three run-throughs of voir dire to tie Herbert Solomon to the conspiracy. At first, Steve had made a mistake focusing solely on his father when watching the video. As with a football game, you can't just keep your eye on the quarterback.

His father's role in the scheme was subtle. It did not require him to speak a word. After questioning each prospective juror, Pinky Luber had paused and scribbled a note to himself. Nothing unusual there. Most lawyers jot down their impressions before being called on to accept or challenge. Studying Luber, Steve discovered a "tell." Like the poker player who fingers his chips or stares down his opponent before bluffing, Pinky had a tic, too. Just before writing his note, Pinky always shot a look at the bench. Herbert Solomon never returned the look. Invariably, at this moment, the judge poured himself a glass of water. His old man must have had an iron bladder, because he took a drink each time Pinky finished with a prospective juror.

It wasn't until the third viewing that Steve saw the signal.

The lid of the pewter water pitcher.

When Herbert left the lid up, Pinky kept the juror on the panel. When Herbert closed the lid, off went the juror. Each and every time.

Steve remembered that pitcher. It sat on his father's bench for years. There was a matching tray with an inscription from the Florida Judicial Conference. *Distinguished Circuit Judge of the Year.* Maybe there was still time for a recount.

Herbert Solomon was hip-deep in the conspiracy. Pinky Luber had won seventeen straight murder trials with help from a clerk who stacked the panel and a judge who pruned an already bloodthirsty group into a lynch mob.

It was a brilliant, if blatantly illegal scheme. Herbert Solomon had presided over hundreds of capital cases. He could read jurors better than any prosecutor, and his help would be invaluable to Luber. The poor defense lawyer, meanwhile, was out-gunned, three to one.

There was little chance the conspiracy could be discovered. As long as there were some African-Americans on the juries, who would notice that the larger panels themselves were skewed? Not the ever-changing cast of defense lawyers. Only the judge, the prosecutor, and the clerk who hatched the scheme. But why did they do it? And why, years later, did Pinky Luber implicate Herbert in a zoning scandal? There seemed to be no connection between the rigged murder trials in which Herbert was a player and the zoning bribes where he wasn't. And just what was the link between those two events and the suit to get back Herbert's Bar license?

When Steve was a rookie lawyer and was stumped by a case, his father told him: *"Whenever you find a loose thread, pull it to see where it leads."* Steve had done that. It all led back to the stacked juries and his father's startling willingness to break the law. Still, Steve had more questions than answers. Turning the little car onto the gravel road that led to his father's houseboat, his mood plunged. There would be no joy in proclaiming "gotcha." Herbert was already a broken man. But what took him down that path? Why did he violate his oath? Why did he risk everything?

"Jesus, Dad. Why?"

"Why!" Herbert Solomon fumbled with the drawstring of his ratty old terry-cloth bathrobe. "You drive all the way down here and wake me up to ask why'd ah do it? What kind of a *shlimazel* are you?"

"A Solomon *shlimazel.*"

"Go home! Don't bother me."

"Quiet. You'll wake Bobby."

Steve had carried the boy to the hammock, where he was purring contentedly.

"Ah know what you're doing," Herbert fumed. "You want to show how smart you are. Well, congratulations. Top of the class."

"I'm not so smart. I still can't figure out

why you rigged those juries. And years later, why did Luber say you took bribes in those zoning cases?"

They were in the galley of the houseboat. Herbert poured some rum over ice but didn't offer any to his son. "His son, Barry, that's why Pinky lied."

"I didn't know Luber had a son."

"Barry's dead of an overdose. Back then, he was a punk, in and out of trouble. The state had him on drug charges at the same time the corruption task force was all hot and bothered about Pinky. If he didn't cooperate, they'd come down hard on his boy. Pinky flipped on some small fry in the zoning department, but the government wanted more. Problem was, Pinky didn't have more."

"So he gave them the Chief Judge of the Circuit," Steve said, figuring it out. "Pinky nailed you to protect his son."

"Barry Luber got probation, Pinky got eighteen months, and ah got what you might call a life sentence."

"That son-of-a-bitch," Steve said.

"Blood is thicker, son. Blood is always thicker."

They both chewed that over a moment. Then Steve said: "That leaves only one question. Why'd *you* do it? Twenty-some years ago, why'd you stack those juries?"

Herbert sipped at his rum. After a third sip, he sighed: "Two words. 'Willie Mays.' And ah don't mean the Say Hey Kid. Ah mean the stone-cold killer."

"I read the transcript and watched the video. Pinky had more than enough evidence to convict. He didn't need to cheat."

"That right, smart guy? Then how'd Mays walk the first time, when there was an eyeball witness? Ah'll tell you how. It was right after the McDuffie riots. Everybody in Liberty City thought white cops killed blacks just for the fun of it. The black jurors wouldn't believe a white man who said 'Good morning,' and they sure as hell weren't gonna send a black man to Old Sparky on a white cop's testimony. Ah can't say as how ah blame them, but ah had other fish to fry, if you'll pardon the expression."

"You were supposed to be the *judge.* Not the prosecutor."

"The prosecutor needed help. The Florida Supreme Court just came down with State versus Neil. Kentucky versus Batson was on the horizon at the U.S. Supreme Court. A prosecutor couldn't exclude jurors solely on account of race, even though jurors would *acquit* solely on race. Ah did what ah had to do. If we hadn't nailed Mays, he'd have just gone out and killed someone else."

"If that's the way you felt, you should have quit the bench and become a cop. Or a vigilante."

"Did you see the crime scene photos? The bastard slit his ex-girlfriend's throat and strangled their little baby. Then he walked down the street and bragged about it to his homies."

"So Pinky asked you to rig the jury?"

"Hell, no! It was mah plan from day one. Soon as the second Mays trial fell into mah division, ah called Pinky and Reggie into chambers. Ah laid it all out for them. Reggie like to faint when he heard it. But he was a good kid and did what ah told him. He was perfect for the job. He knew half the families in the old Central Negro District. He didn't just exclude blacks we didn't want. He got us black folks who could help get a conviction."

"I don't see how that's possible."

Herbert downed the rest of his drink. "Reggie cherry-picked the master venire list before it came upstairs from the clerk's office. Assigned folks he figured were pro-prosecution to my courtroom. Anyone Reggie thought would hurt the prosecution got shifted to County Court for misdemeanors. Before voir dire, he'd do more trimming.

Toss off anyone who wanted out if he didn't like him. Then, right before we're about to pick that first jury, Pinky says: 'While we're at it, let's throw the Jews off, too.' "

Herbert laughed as if Pinky were the new Billy Crystal.

Steve shook his head. "Very funny. A Jewish judge and a Jewish prosecutor acting like Nazis."

"Aw, go call B'nai B'rith and spare me your indignation. You know as well as ah do that Jews are defense jurors. Ever try to get a couple *landsmen* to go for the death penalty? Good luck, boychik."

"And even after stacking the panel, you still had to signal Pinky which jurors to challenge?"

Herbert poured himself another drink. "He asked me to. Ah was better at seating a jury than he ever was, and Pinky knew it. Funny thing is, we were gonna stop after Mays was convicted. But it worked so damn well . . ."

"You did it sixteen more times."

"Looking back now, with the benefit of hindsight . . ."

"You wish you'd never done it?"

"Hell, no. Ah wish we'd started earlier. They were all guilty, son. Every last one."

"I'm sure lynch mobs feel the same way."

"Give it a rest. Ah feel a helluva lot better than those damn fool prosecutors who let O. J. Simpson walk. Damn fools tried the case in downtown LA because they wanted a diverse jury. Wanted to be politically correct. Ended up with nine blacks when they would have had one or two, tops, over in Santa Monica. The case was over before it began. The Mays case might have been, too, if we hadn't been proactive."

"Proactive? That a new word for corrupt?"

"Aw, fuck it, Stevie. I know the rules you play by, and they ain't the Marquis of Queensberry's."

"Don't compare what I do with this shit."

"Anyway, ah'm glad you know. I don't have to tiptoe around it anymore. And now you can drop that damn fool lawsuit."

"Why should I? What you did was scummy and made you unfit to be a judge, but you're not going back on the bench. And no one has to know."

Herbert burped out a laugh. "Spoken like a true advocate. Problem is, you're wrong about one thing. That part, 'No one has to know.' "

"Not following you."

"How do you plan to get my Bar license back?"

"By proving that Pinky lied when he accused you of taking bribes in the zoning cases."

"He did, indeed. But when Pinky cut his deal with the state, they made him waive the statute of limitations on perjury. If you prove he lied, he'll go to jail. So he's got to stop you from taking my case to trial."

"How's he gonna do that?"

"He's gonna go back in time, son."

"Meaning what?"

"How many of those seventeen defendants we convicted are still alive?"

"Eight were executed. Three are still on death row. Six were sentenced to life." Steve did the math, maybe not as quickly as Bobby could have. "So nine are still breathing."

"Pinky knows the number, too. Read their names to me. Told me, if you take him down, he'll fess up as to what we did twenty years ago. What do you think happens then?"

"Nine guys get new trials."

"Nine *murderers.* Worst of the worst. Ah can't let that happen, son. Witnesses are gone. Evidence is degraded. Files are lost. How many of those nine do you think would walk?"

"No way to tell. Some, I guess."

"Even one is too many. Especially the one named Mr. Willie Mays."

FORTY-TWO:
Deus Ex Tsunami

Quick, crisp, and efficient.

That's the way Richard Waddle tried his case, and it had Victoria worried. Lousy prosecutors take too much time, put in too much evidence, narcotize the jury with repetition and detail. The nuggets of damning evidence get lost in the blabber and the blather. But Waddle seemed to realize that jurors have attention spans of eight-year-olds. A solid prosecutor with a seemingly solid case, he asked direct questions and received concise answers.

"Detective, what did you find in Mr. Stubbs' hotel room?"

"A briefcase containing precisely forty thousand dollars in hundred-dollar bills."

"Did you also investigate his recent financial transactions?"

"He purchased a waterfront lot in Key Largo for three hundred thousand in cash less than three months before he was killed."

"And the source of that money?"

"The funds were wired from the account of a shell corporation in the Cayman Islands."

"Who owns that corporation?"

"The sole shareholder is the defendant, Harold Griffin."

Slam, bam, thank you, Detective.

Sitting next to Victoria, a silent Hal Griffin was not looking chipper. A little gray in his usually ruddy cheeks. He'd told Victoria he wasn't sleeping well.

Welcome to the club, Uncle Grif.

Delia Bustamante swiveled into court wearing an ankle-length, espresso-colored peasant dress that would have been demure had she not left the drawstring untied at the neck. The curvaceous cook and activist jiggled to the witness stand, and when she raised her right hand to take the oath, her right boob peeked out of the tiered dress top. After some preliminaries, Waddle asked whether Griffin had offered her a job, and the answer lifted Victoria out of her chair.

"Mr. Griffin tried to buy me off to shut me up about Oceania."

"Objection, and move to strike! Ms. Bustamante cannot testify as to my client's intentions."

"Sustained. The jurors will disregard the witness' last statement. Ms. Bustamante, just tell

us what the defendant did and what you did."

"Okay, Judge. He offered me more money than even I thought I was worth. But I wouldn't take a cent from that man."

Leicester Robinson, the well-read barge operator, testified he saw Griffin and Stubbs arguing. Watching through the salon window, Robinson couldn't hear what was said, but claimed he could tell from the animated gestures that both men were angry. And yes, Griffin shoved Stubbs. Victoria cross-examined.

"What you're calling a shove was really just a finger to the chest, correct?"

"Stubbs took a step back. I call that a shove."

"But there was no striking, no blow with the fist, isn't that right?"

"Where I come from, you don't raise your hand to another man unless you can back it up. Unless you can go all the way. But then, maybe your client did go all the way."

"Your Honor, I move to strike the unresponsive answer."

Clive Fowles testified that Griffin instructed him to place a waterproof bag filled with cash — he didn't know how much — in a lobster trap near Black Turtle Key the day before Stubbs was shot. Usually all business, Richard Waddle had some fun with Fowles.

"Were lobsters in season, Mr. Fowles?"

"No, sir. It's only a two-day season in July."

"So, among other things, your boss is a poacher, a lobster mobster?"

"Objection. Argumentative."

"Sustained."

"All that cash is pretty unusual lobster bait, isn't it, Mr. Fowles?"

"I suppose."

"Mr. Griffin tell you what the money was for?"

"No, sir."

"But you figured it was for Ben Stubbs, didn't you?"

"Objection. Calls for a conclusion."

"Overruled."

"I thought the money might be for him, sir."

"So, even though lobsters aren't in season, public officials are?"

Waddle tried to get Fowles to corroborate Robinson's version of the argument between Griffin and Stubbs, but the boat captain had developed a case of witness blindness, aka three-monkey disease. He heard no evil, saw no evil, spoke no evil.

"Come now, Mr. Fowles, are you telling the jury you didn't observe the exchange of words between the two men?"

"I have a habit of tending to my own business."

"You like Mr. Griffin, don't you?"

"He's a good man."

"A good man who signs your paychecks, correct?"

Okay, point made, Victoria thought. Fowles was being loyal to his boss, and the jury would see that.

All three witnesses agreed that the others had gone ashore before the boat left the dock. Standing on the dock, Leicester Robinson and Delia Bustamante watched Junior dive off the bridge and swim away.

The lunch recess was just minutes away when Victoria spotted Steve in the gallery, sitting next to Sheriff Rask. She hadn't known Steve was coming. No calls, he just showed up.

After the judge called the noon recess and Griffin hurried to the outside patio to sneak a smoke, Steve sauntered up to the defense table. "Hey, Vic. How's it going?"

She shrugged. "You know how it is. Some moments are better than others."

"Getting crucified, huh?"

"I see you're making nice with the opposition."

"Willis keeps me updated on Conchy Conklin."

"They find him yet?"

"He's disappeared. But if he's still in the Keys, they'll get him. There's only a finite number of bars."

"A *large,* finite number."

"How 'bout lunch?"

"Oh, I'm meeting Junior."

"Ah."

"I need to prep him."

"Can never prep enough. Especially dim witnesses."

Too tired to fight, she let it go. "Have you been working on your father's case?"

"Don't want to talk about it." Like a proper gentleman, Steve grabbed her briefcase and walked her out of the courtroom. "How's your mom?"

"Don't want to talk about her."

Not now, she thought. Later, when the trial was over, she'd tell Steve about her mother's latest dramatics. Her father's suicide note and the mystery around it.

Father's alleged *suicide note.* Wondering if she could believe anything her mother told her.

They rode the elevator in silence. In the lobby, Steve seemed to want to hand over her briefcase but didn't know quite when and how to do it. It was like a lousy first date that neither party knew how to end. They left the building, and as they passed the kapok tree on the courthouse lawn, Steve said: "Look, this is ridiculous. If you need any help . . ."

She stopped in the shade of the tree, which bloomed with red flowers.

Sure I need help. With the case. With my mother. With my life.

"Thanks, Steve. I . . ."

"Excuse me, mate." Fowles approached, looking a little bashful at the interruption. "Ms. Lord."

"You've been excused, Mr. Fowles," Victoria said. "If you want to go home, you can."

"Oh, I know that. I just . . ." He was fumbling with his hands as if he didn't know quite where they belonged. "How's it going, do you think?"

"Too early to tell. But you did fine. Really."

"I hope it turns out okay. For Mr. G, I mean. No way he would have killed that arse-wipe."

"Now, there's a closing argument if ever I heard one," Steve said.

"Good luck, then." Fowles raised his right hand, two fingers spread, in his Winston Churchill mode. "V for Victory, Ms. Lord."

"Thank you, Clive."

Fowles seemed to have run out of things to say. "Think I'll go have a pint."

"Bar's right across the street," Steve said.

"The Green Parrot."

"Don't I know it." Fowles let himself smile. As if on cue, a bell clanged inside the old bar, signaling that someone had just tipped the bartender.

Fowles nodded his good-byes and headed across Whitehead Street.

"What's with him?" Steve asked.

"If Uncle Grif is convicted, he's out of work."

"Yeah, maybe." Steve watched Fowles disappear into the bar, passing under the sign in the doorway: *No Sniveling Since 1890.* "Anyway, like I said, Vic, if you need anything, I'm here for you."

Do I need anything? Let's make a list. Peace of mind. Self-confidence. And a stunning cross-examination wouldn't hurt, either.

"I'm fine," she said.

"How are your experts coming along?"

"The prof from Columbia will say it's possible Stubbs shot himself loading the speargun. The angle of entry is a little problematic, but it might work."

"Except . . . ?"

"What you said that first day. We can sell one improbability to the jury, but when we start compounding improbables, we lose."

"Griffin being knocked unconscious being the second improbable."

"Without an explanation, it kills us. If we're saying Stubbs shot himself, then there's no assailant hiding on board who also knocks out Griffin. We're stuck arguing that Griffin fell down the ladder and conveniently knocked himself out. No one will buy it. Hell, I don't buy it."

"You check the weather for that day?"

"I remember the weather. It was warm and clear. We were standing in the surf, and you were trying to get into my bikini."

"The way I remember it, you were putting the moves on me."

"Just one of our many differing observations."

"You really should check the weather with NOAA."

"Eighty-one degrees, sixty-nine percent humidity. Southeast wind at ten to twelve knots. Light chop on inland waters. Three foot seas." She gave him her best smart-ass smile. The smile she'd picked up from him. "Like to know the barometric pressure?"

"What about the Coast Guard?"

"What about them?"

"Any boats capsize? Any rescues in the area? Maybe there was a rogue wave. A mini-tsunami."

"A mini-tsunami? Why not Moses parting the Gulf? You want to add another improbable? I know you're trying to help, Steve. Sorry if I'm being bitchy."

"No problem."

She took the briefcase from his hand. "Thanks. I've got to go. Meet —"

"Junior for lunch," Steve said. "I know."

Forty-Three: Looking into the Past

"The Coast Guard rescued a couple fishermen off Raccoon Key, but nothing else that day," Bobby said.

"The fishermen report any rogue waves?" Steve asked.

"They reported drinking a case of Bud and one guy hooking the other's ear with a shank barb." The kid gave him a told-you-so smirk. "Then they ran the boat onto a sandbar."

"It was worth a shot."

They were aboard Herbert's sagging houseboat, Bobby working at his laptop computer, a printed map of the Eastern Gulf spread in front of him. As soon as Steve stepped onto the creaky deck, Herbert took off, claiming he had to run errands. Steve wondered if his father was avoiding him, but in truth, the cupboards were bare of Bacardi.

"I checked the satellite photos, Uncle

Steve. No tidal waves, no tsunamis, no flying saucers."

"Don't you start with me, too. Victoria already gave me grief."

"So maybe Mr. Griffin just fell down the ladder."

"Dammit, don't give up so easily."

"You mad at me about something, Uncle Steve?"

"Sorry. I missed lunch. I'm just hungry."

"You're horny. You miss Victoria."

"Mind your own business." Steve leaned over Bobby's shoulder. "What's that on the screen?"

"A shot from the NOAA Eastern Gulf satellite. The day of the boat crash." Steve peered at the monitor: green islands in a turquoise sea. Bobby pointed to a white speck on the screen. "There's the *Force Majeure.*"

"No shit?"

"Cool, huh? I followed it all the way to Key West, except for when it got cloudy around Big Torch Key."

"The picture on the monitor now. Where is that?"

"Just west of Black Turtle Key. The island there . . ." He pointed at a tiny green speck. ". . . it's got no name. That's where Mr. Griffin stopped to pick up the lobsters."

"And the money. Don't forget about the money." Steve studied the image. There was another boat visible on the screen. Thinner and nearly as long as the *Force Majeure.* "How far away is that boat?"

"Little more than a mile. You can tell from the grid lines."

"Can you back up the pictures? Follow the *Force Majeure* all the way from Paradise Key?"

"I know what you're thinking, Uncle Steve. Did that other boat trail them out there and somebody come aboard and shoot Mr. Stubbs. But that boat got there first, then just sort of stayed in the same spot for a while."

Steve strained his eyes, staring at the long thin boat, a blade in the water. It wasn't a typical fishing boat. More like a speedboat. A Fountain Lightning, or a Magnum, or a Cigarette. Capable of astounding speeds. What was it doing anchored or idling in the middle of nowhere? Of course, the answer could be innocent. The occupants could have been having a picnic or a nap or an orgy.

"Where'd the boat come from? Did you track it back?"

Bobby shook his head. "I told you, it got there before the *Force Majeure,* so I didn't think it meant anything."

"Do it now."

Bobby made a face, hit some keys, and the screen flicked with dozens of images. Time was being reversed, the long skinny boat heading back to wherever it departed shore. The photos finally stopped at an overhead view of scores of boats lined up at several parallel docks.

"Where are we?" Steve asked.

Bobby checked the coordinates against his map. "A marina on Lower Matecumbe Key."

"What time is it?"

In the corner of the screen was the digital readout: *15:51 GMT.*

"Ten-fifty-one a.m, our time," Bobby said.

"The *Force Majeure* left Paradise Key fourteen minutes earlier," Steve said. Remembering the time code on the security cameras. "Start it up again, Bobby. Let's see how close the mystery boat comes to Paradise Key."

The images clicked by again, the boat nearing the tip of Griffin's island.

"Does it stop anywhere?" Steve asked.

"I don't know. I just speed-clicked through these before. I mean, it didn't seem important. There's no way it followed the *Force Majeure.*"

"Don't get defensive. You're doing a great job, kiddo. Now, please slow it down."

Bobby hit more keys. On the screen, the boat remained in the same place inside one of the grids. Then it started moving again. "There, Uncle Steve. It's stopped, but only for like thirty seconds."

"And that's Paradise Key." Even from high altitude, he could spot the lagoon with the huge house on the small island. "Maybe two miles away, right?"

"I know what you're thinking, Uncle Steve."

"Oh, you do?"

"Yeah. You think Junior Griffin swam out to meet the boat. It picked him up and took him to the no-name island. He waited for the *Force Majeure,* sneaked aboard, and shot Mr. Stubbs with the speargun."

"The thought crossed my mind." He gestured toward the screen. "Keep going."

Bobby clicked to fast-forward mode. After a blur of images, the photos slowed to a crawl. Now both boats were on the screen. "This is where the speedboat passes the *Force Majeure.*"

"How fast they going?"

"Really fast. Like maybe fifty knots."

"In a big hurry to go nowhere."

The mystery boat slowed as it approached

Black Turtle Key. Precisely where Griffin's lobster traps were submerged just offshore a no-name island. Bobby had been partly right. The boat hadn't *followed* the *Force Majeure.* It didn't have to; it got there *first.*

"Look at that." Steve thumped the monitor with a finger. "The bastards stopped. Just like they did off Paradise Key." He watched the seconds tick away on the digital clock on the screen.

Twenty-three seconds.

Long enough to let somebody slip into the water. Somebody like Junior Griffin, who could wait for the *Force Majeure* to arrive. The mystery boat moved away from the no-name island, then stopped about one mile away. The *Force Majeure* came into the picture and neared the island.

And suddenly, Steve knew. "Oh, shit!"

"What?"

"Junior didn't swim out there to meet the fast boat. He's not the one they picked up. He's not the one they dropped off."

"But you said —"

"I wish the son-of-a-bitch was the guy, but he's not."

"How do you know?"

"Because Junior didn't know the *Force Majeure* was stopping there. Griffin swears he never told Junior. And there's no reason to lie about it. Four people got off the *Force Majeure* before it left Paradise Key. They all knew the boat was going to Key West. But only one knew it was stopping to pick up lobsters and money."

"Who?"

"The guy who baited the traps and put the money in the pots. The guy who's in love with a woman who sautés snapper with bananas. The guy who could get off Paradise Key without being seen, riding his underwater chariot."

"Clive Fowles? Are you sure, Uncle Steve? Maybe Junior and Fowles did it together. Remember when you got thrown out of the hospital?" Bobby held up his right hand and spread two fingers, just as Stubbs had done in the ICU. "Two men attacked Stubbs. Isn't that what he meant?"

"Higher."

"What?"

"Stubbs was trying to raise his hand higher, but he couldn't."

Bobby raised his hand over his head. "Like this?"

The boy didn't look exactly like Winston Churchill, but close enough.

" 'V for Victory,' " Steve said. "The British submariner's favorite expression. Stubbs was trying to tell me Fowles killed him."

"Wow," Bobby said. "What now?"

"I've got to see a man about a chariot."

FORTY-FOUR: THE HUMAN TORPEDO

The device looked like a torpedo with two seats cut into it. Horace Fowles' sixty-year-old underwater chariot. His grandson, Clive Fowles, was hoisting the rusty cylinder onto the platform at the stern of his sparkling new dive boat.

"Need a hand?" Steve walked up to the dock on Paradise Key.

"Thanks, mate. Wouldn't hurt."

Steve hopped onto the rear deck of the boat and put both hands on the nose of the chariot. Fowles turned a winch handle, and two ropes unfurled from a double-sheaved block, lowering the old contraption toward the dive platform.

"Easy now," Fowles urged, giving up a little rope as Steve guided the chariot into place. The craft settled into an indentation in the dive platform, as snug as a gun in a holster.

"Pretty good fit," Steve said.

"It better be, after what Mr. G spent customizing the boat to my specs."

"And your grandfather's specs." Steve pointed at the lettering on the stern of the dive boat: *"Fowles' Folly.* Wasn't that the name of his midget sub?"

"Right. After Horace graduated from chariots. You remembered."

"Hard to forget. A Norwegian fjord. Your grandfather captains a little tin can that takes on a massive German battleship."

"The *Tirpitz.*"

"David and Goliath."

"It was a miracle he even got into the fjord. Did I tell you Grandpop had to crawl out of the sub and use his knife to cut a mine off the tow line? Can you picture that, Solomon?"

"Not without breaking into a sweat."

"The North Sea's got all these freshwater layers, so it's hard as hell to maintain a trim. The *Folly* keeps popping out of the water like a crazed porpoise. When she gets to the *Tirpitz,* there's my grandpop, in the water again, attaching explosives to the big bastard's hull with German sailors firing at him. How would you describe a man like that?"

"The words 'bravery' and 'courage' don't seem to do him justice."

"You're damned right, Solomon. You understand." He swung the block and tackle out of the way and offered a hand to Steve to pull him back onto the dock. "Some people, I tell the story and they don't get it at all."

"I guess I'm attuned to the legacies our fathers leave us. Grandfathers, too, for that matter."

"I tried to live up to mine. Did my part in the Royal Navy."

"But like you said before, the Falklands and the Argentines weren't exactly the North Sea and the Nazis."

Fowles sat down on the edge of the dock and pulled out a small cigar. He put it in his mouth but didn't light it. "What are you getting at, Solomon?"

Steve sat down next to him. "Yesterday, when I was coming out of the courthouse, you wanted something."

"A Guinness Stout. The Green Parrot, mate."

"You asked about the case. You seemed worried about Griffin."

"Sure, I am. I hope he gets off."

"Because you know he's innocent."

Fowles took his time lighting the cigar. A breeze whipped off the water and the flame wouldn't catch. "I *think* Mr. G's innocent, but how would I know?"

Steve nearly said it then. Nearly said: *"You know because you headed underwater on your chariot just like your grandfather in his midget sub. You know because someone in a fast boat picked you up and followed your directions to a nameless island just off Black Turtle Key. You know because you were there."*

But Steve's instincts told him not to attack this battleship head-on. Another problem, too. This decent man who worshipped the memory of a courageous grandfather seemed to regard Hal Griffin as a father figure as well as a generous boss. While admiring Griffin, Fowles despised the Oceania project. But would the boat captain, a man who loved all the fishes in the deep blue sea, kill someone and frame Griffin for the crime?

"I think you're a good man," Steve said.

Fowles laughed. "And how would you know that?"

"It's what I do for a living. I make judgments about people."

Fowles tried to light his cigar again. Steve leaned over and cupped his hands, creating a windbreak. The flame caught. Fowles inhaled deeply and looked out over the Gulf.

"If you'll excuse me, Solomon, it's my day off, and I'm gonna take my boat out."

"To the reef?"

"Thought I'd scoot around it a bit."

Steve gestured toward the chariot. "On that human torpedo?"

"Once the *Folly* gets me there, yeah, I'll take the chariot down. Want to go along?"

"Me? Underwater?"

Fowles blew a trail of smoke into the humid air. "Not scared, are you?"

"No way. I love the ocean and everything in it. Except sharks."

A white heron with matchstick legs strutted along the dock and watched the *Fowles' Folly* head out to sea. After the boat cleared the dock, a brown pelican dive-bombed just off the port side, flipped over backward, and hit the water with a resounding *splash.* The bird scooped up a fish and swallowed it whole.

The cigar clamped in his teeth, Fowles manned the wheel, his thinning blond hair whipping in the wind. Steve stood alongside, watching the diamond-studded sea, the sun sparkling off the waves.

"You scuba, right?" Fowles shouted above the wind and the twin diesels.

"Don't worry. I'm certified."

"One of those two-day wonders in some hotel pool? Arse-over-tits a couple times and you think you're Jacques Cousteau?"

"Hey, c'mon. I've dived the Little Bahama Bank. Maybe I'm a little rusty, but so's your grandfather's chariot."

Fowles laughed and nodded toward a cooler. "Beer if you want it."

Steve declined. He hated burping into the regulator.

"So, mate, why'd you really come see me today?"

"I told you. I thought there was something else you wanted to tell me. Something about you and Griffin. Maybe having a falling-out."

"Maybe you're not as good at judging people as you think."

"You were mad as hell about Oceania. I'm betting you did something about it."

"I made no secret how I felt. I told Mr. G that Oceania was a mistake."

"But you couldn't convince him not to do it."

Fowles checked the compass, turned a bit more northwest, and gave the throttles a little more juice. "Like I told you before, the boss heard me out. I asked him to consider scuttling the hotel and casino. Maybe just do a tour business. Glass-bottomed boats and catamaran trips to the reef. Mr. G said I was talking about a rowboat while he was building the Queen Mary."

"That had to piss you off."

"The man's been good to me." Fowles ran his hand across the polished teak wheel. "A custom forty-two-footer titled in my name. Everything state-of-the-art. I take Delia's coral kissers out to the reef for cleanups and census-taking. I got no complaints."

"Ever think Griffin was paying you off just to go with the flow?"

The boat passed through a channel between two small islands. "A man makes certain compromises."

"What'd Delia say when you told her about the new boat?" Steve asked.

"She told me to turn it down. We had a bit of an argy-bargy about it."

Not surprising. Delia Bustamante would no more take a bribe than cook her plantains in margarine.

Steve decided to cast a line in the water. "You violated your principles. Then you felt guilty, so you tried to stop Oceania."

"What in bloody hell are you talking about?"

They were in open water, the boat riding on plane, smoothly hopping the three-foot seas. Steve was amidships the *Tirpitz* with nowhere to go. "At the dock that day, after everybody got off the *Force Majeure,* I think you took the chariot out. I think you were picked up by someone in a fast boat, and you led them to that little island near Black Turtle Key where you knew Griffin would stop."

"What for? To kill Stubbs?"

"If you thought that would stop Oceania, maybe. Chances are, the next guy wouldn't be so easy to bribe. And with all the scrutiny he'd be getting, Griffin probably couldn't even try."

"You been in the sun too long, Solomon."

"Okay, how's this? Maybe you didn't shoot Stubbs. Maybe the guy who picked you up was the shooter."

"Setting up my defense for me? Going to be my barrister?"

"C'mon Fowles. You *want* to tell me. Who'd you take out there? Who did the shooting?"

"You're cracked, mate." He slowed the boat as they neared a stretch of shallow water that shimmered red from coral underneath. "Maybe the reef will mellow you out."

Fowles cut the engines, opened a compartment, and began hauling out wet suits, masks, and fins. "The tanks are below. You gotta carry your own. I'm not your valet."

They slipped into the gear in silence. Fowles' demeanor had changed, Steve realized. Not so surprising. He'd just accused the man of being an accessory to murder, if not the murderer himself.

They were untying the chariot from the dive platform when Steve said: "No last-minute words of advice?"

"Watch out for sharks," Clive Fowles said.

■ ■ ■ ■

Solomon's Laws

■ ■ ■ ■

11. If you're afraid of taking a big lead, you'll never get picked off . . . but you'll never steal a base, either.

FORTY-FIVE:
DID YOU DO IT FOR LOVE?

Steve somersaulted backward off the dive platform and spent a few moments flutter-kicking along the surface, orange seaweed tangling in his fins. He hit a valve on the buoyancy compensator, deflated his vest, and let the weight belt take him under. Water trickled into his mask, tickling his nose. He exhaled through his nostrils, and the water drained through the purge valve.

Hey, I remember how to do this.

He listened to the sound of his own breathing, felt the bubbles rising around him, let himself relax. He descended to thirty feet, luxuriating in the water, warmed by his own body heat, encapsulated in the wet suit. And there it was, spread out in front of him, what Fowles wanted him to see.

Steve knew all the clichés. Coral reefs were stone castles. Cities beneath the sea. Underwater rain forests. Living animals, millions of them, growing on top of the limestone skeletons of animals that had come before, this reef perhaps twenty thousand years old.

He'd snorkeled the state park in Key Largo. He'd scuba-dived in the Bahamas and off the coast of Grand Cayman. Could he have forgotten the infinite beauty, or was this reef simply more spectacular than those?

He was mesmerized by the kaleidoscope of colors. Yellow sea fans waved in the current. Angelfish, pulsating with neon blues and greens, darted around mounds of grayish brain coral. Rising from the sand, stately cathedral coral resembled the pillars of an ancient temple in a miniature Atlantis. The tentacles of purple gorgonian whips moved with the current.

Fish everywhere. Hundreds . . . no, thousands. Tenants of the coral condos. Sleek parrotfish with the yellows, reds, and greens of a bird's feathers. A school of silvery jacks, staring at him with huge eyes. Smallmouth yellow-striped grunts that are supposed to make a *grunt-grunt* sound, but Steve couldn't hear anything over his own breathing and bubbles. A moray eel poked its head out of a crevice, didn't like what it saw, then vanished inside.

A large shadow passed over him. The biggest, fattest grouper he'd ever seen. The one called the jewfish, to Steve's consternation. A jewfish bigger than Ariel Sharon and Harvey Weinstein put together. Maybe seven feet long, at least six hundred pounds, with that underslung jaw. It passed, then turned, its tail scattering a dozen smaller fish. Then headed straight for Steve. Not that it was dangerous. More like a fat lawyer, waddling down the courthouse corridor. Taking up his allotted space, and yours, too. Steve didn't know if the fish would swat him with its powerful tail or serve him with a writ, so he moved to one side.

Steve swam deeper along the slope, the water growing cooler, the surroundings darker. He was at sixty feet when it occurred to him.

Fowles. Where the hell was Fowles?

Looking up, he couldn't see the boat. Would he have heard the engines if it had moved?

What if Fowles left me here?

Steve's breathing became louder, heavier. How long had he been down here? How much air did he have left? He checked the gauge. More than two thousand pounds. Plenty of time, unless his heart started racing.

Okay, calm down. Fowles is a good man,

remember? You said it yourself. Yes, and you also said he's possibly a murderer.

Nearby, a steel-gray barracuda swept by and looped back, circling him. Steve swam over a stand of staghorn coral that resembled the antlers of a deer. The barracuda followed like a P.I. on surveillance.

Suddenly, Fowles brought the chariot alongside, motioning Steve to hop aboard. Battery-powered, the chariot had approached stealthily. Unheard by German U-boats in the North Sea, unheard by Steve above the reef. Two seats were sunk into its cigar-shaped body, one in front of the other, like the cockpit of an old biplane. Steve climbed into the second seat, his back resting on the ballast tank near the stern.

Fowles eased the throttle forward, and off they went, a two-man human torpedo. They skimmed the edge of the reef and moved deeper. As the water cooled and the light diminished, the coral thinned out, and there were fewer fish. Then, abruptly, they moved along an upward slope into warmer, brighter waters. Spiny lobster crawled along the bottom, and a school of red copper sweepers whisked by. The coral patches thickened again. Whether it was a continuation of the same reef or the beginning of another one, Steve couldn't tell.

No wonder Delia and her crowd want to protect this. C'mon, Fowles, tell me what the hell went down that day. Did you kill Stubbs because Delia wanted to save the reef? Did you do it for love?

Fowles turned around in the front seat and lifted a magnetic slate from a compartment. With a stylus, he wrote something, then held the slate in front of Steve's face: *"12 o'clock high. Stay calm."*

Steve looked straight up. Four sharks circled twenty feet above them. He couldn't tell a tiger shark from a nurse shark, though he had a pretty good idea these weren't the thick-bodied bulls known for attacking swimmers. He wondered what two guys riding an old metal tube looked like to the sharks.

Fowles erased the slate, wrote something else: *"Nurses. No problem."*

Steve appreciated the sea mail. Nurse sharks were usually not aggressive. Fowles released some ballast and brought back the joystick, and the chariot ascended steeply. Straight through the pack of sharks — *C'mon Fowles, is this necessary!* — but the nurses parted and let them pass.

They surfaced moments later, and both men pulled off their masks and spit out their mouthpieces. Even from the short dive,

Steve's jaw ached. He'd been clenching hard as they came up through the sharks.

"Well, mate, what do you think?"

"Spectacular. I see why you love it, why you want to protect it."

"I knew you'd get it. Delia told me."

"She talked about me?"

"Said you were a decent chap but a lousy boyfriend. . . . I really love her, mate."

"I thought you might."

"You live like I have, hot-tailing from island to island, dallying with a bunch of spunk buckets, when you meet someone like Delia . . ." He paused as small waves broke over the bow of the chariot. "I tried to do the right thing for her."

"How, Fowles? What did you do?"

C'mon Fowles. Tell me about you and Delia and Oceania.

But the Englishman just shook his head and said, "You know where we are now?"

It ain't Kansas, Steve thought.

"Right in the middle of Oceania, if it's ever built," Fowles said. "Building Two, the casino, would be right here, with cables running at an angle eight hundred yards that-away." Fowles pointed into the distance. "The cables would fasten to pilings driven four hundred feet into the ocean floor. You know how much drilling and pile-driving that would take, how much sediment would be displaced?"

Steve recalled the diorama in Griffin's house. The hotel and casino were made up of three floating saucers, anchored to the sea bottom. The saucer nearest the reef had underwater rooms with portholes. In the diorama, the fish had been plexiglass. Here, they were living creatures. "Griffin's studies said the prevailing currents would carry sediment away from the reef."

"Sure, best-case scenario. Doesn't take into account storms or oil spills. And Delia's got some contrary studies."

Delia again. Okay, go for it. If you don't take a lead, you can't steal a base.

"Delia lied, didn't she?" Steve said. "You weren't with her that day, eating oysters and drinking sangria, were you?"

For a moment there was no sound but the *slosh* of waves against the chariot. Then Fowles said: "I didn't want anyone to get killed. I thought, if someone else paid Stubbs more than Griffin was offering, Stubbs would stop Oceania, but it didn't work out that way."

"How did it work out?"

They both heard it then, a boat in the distance. Steve shaded his eyes from the glare of the sun. He could barely make out a craft in silhouette.

"So how did it work out?" he repeated. "Who paid Stubbs to turn him around?"

Fowles squinted into the sun, trying to get a look at the boat. "Headed our way, isn't it?" Sounding like a man trying not to sound concerned.

"You expecting company?"

Fowles looked back toward the *Fowles' Folly,* anchored maybe a thousand yards away. He seemed to be measuring the distance and time it would take to get there.

"What's going on, Fowles?"

The chariot rose and fell in the gentle swells. With each dip, the approaching boat disappeared. With each push upward, it appeared closer.

"Talk to me, Fowles."

"I'm a little nearsighted." Fowles gestured toward the oncoming boat. "What can you see?"

"Moving fast on a high plane. Long and thin. Built for speed."

Just like the boat on the satellite photos, the one tailing the Force Majeure.

"Should we get back to the boat, Fowles?"

"Wouldn't make a difference. We can't outrun it." His voice was tight.

The roar grew louder. Steve remembered the *Force Majeure* approaching the beach at

Sunset Key. The sound of an avalanche. This was more of a whine, like a jet engine.

"Jesus, Fowles. What the hell's happening?"

"Shut your gob and listen, mate. We don't have much time. It happened pretty much the way you said. I took the chariot into the Gulf. A Cigarette picked me up, a Top Gun Thirty-eight. Then dropped me off near Black Turtle Key. I stayed in the water till the *Force Majeure* got there. When Mr. G was pulling up his lobster traps, I climbed aboard. I went down the hatch to the engine room. In a few minutes, I could hear them both through the salon hatch. Mr. G hands over the hundred thou and Stubbs says it's not enough. Someone else has been bidding for his services. Someone who'll pay ten times that if he'll sink Oceania."

Just what Griffin said when he'd finally told the truth.

"They'd both been drinking all day and were bloody snockered. Mr. G demands to know who's the bidder, but the little bugger won't say. There's yelling back and forth. Mr. G must have pulled out the speargun, because Stubbs laughs and asks if maybe he forgot something. Then Mr. G laughs. The gun didn't have a spear. They both settle down and Stubbs says he'll turn down the other guy and take Mr. G's money with another hundred thou every year. That seemed to settle it. Mr. G goes back up to the bridge and heads toward Sunset Key."

Again, just what Griffin told them, Steve thought, looking toward the *Fowles' Folly*. The speedboat was alongside the dive boat. Maybe the guy at the wheel hadn't seen them yet, bobbing in the waves. "So when Griffin leaves, Stubbs is healthy and breathing," he said.

"But white as a ghost when he sees me coming up through the hatch. I ask Stubbs if he's forgotten he just took forty thousand dollars as a down payment from someone else."

"The money the police found in Stubbs' hotel room."

"Right. Now the fucknugget tells me he'll give it back. Thinks he can return a bribe like a pair of pants that don't fit." Fowles turned and watched the speedboat move away from the *Fowles' Folly* and head toward them. "I tell Stubbs I'm there to make sure he doesn't back out of his deal or to throw him overboard if he does."

"On whose instructions? Who were you working for?"

"Doesn't matter who. Those were my orders, but I was bluffing. I never would have killed the man."

The speedboat was five hundred yards away and moving straight at them.

"Now the little bugger goes bonkers," Fowles said. "Grabs the speargun, jams a spear in the barrel against the air pressure, but he must not have cocked it right. He's waving the gun around and I grab it. We tussle, and the damn thing fires. Puts the spear right into his chest. I panic. I get the hell out of there and jump overboard. Tread water till the Cigarette picks me up."

"If you didn't intend to shoot Stubbs, you might have a defense."

"Morally, I'm guilty. I killed Stubbs as surely as if I'd pulled the trigger."

They both looked toward the oncoming boat, down off its plane, puttering toward them at less than ten knots. A Cigarette Top Gun 38 with a sleek white hull decorated with orange and red flames. One man was visible standing in the cockpit, a rifle propped on top of the wheel.

"That's the guy who picked you up, right?" Steve said.

"That'd be him."

"Why's he got a rifle?"

"To kill me. You, too, probably."

"Jesus, Fowles! Do you have any weapons?"

"Not even a speargun," the Brit said with a sad smile.

The sound of rapid-fire gunshots crackled across the water.

Steve ducked lower into his seat. "What now?"

"How much air you have?"

"Maybe fifteen minutes. Less if I'm scared shitless, which I am."

Gunshots ricocheted off the steel hull of the chariot.

"Crew, prepare to dive!" Fowles ordered, sounding no doubt like his grandfather in a Norwegian fjord.

Steve pulled down his mask and readied his mouthpiece and regulator. "You still haven't told me. Who is that guy?"

"Name's Conchy Conklin."

Fowles bit down on his mouthpiece, opened the ballast tank, and pushed the joystick forward. The chariot took them under just as another gunshot *ping*ed off the rusty old craft.

FORTY-SIX:
LIFE IN PAST TENSE

Who the hell is Conchy Conklin?
And why does he want to kill me?
Killing Fowles, Steve could understand. The Brit was a poached egg, ready to crack. When he did, he'd implicate Conklin and whoever hired them both. From everything Willis Rask had said, Conklin was a lowlife without the brains to pull off a sophisticated bribery scheme. His boss was the one who wanted Griffin convicted of murder and Oceania buried at sea. But who was his boss? Fowles never said.

As the chariot descended, bullets streaked through the water. Dying with a *whoosh-whoosh* above their heads. Steve felt his heart racing, and he had a case of cotton mouth from the tank air. Then another sound, the rumble of the Cigarette's props, plowing overhead.

They were at twenty feet and descending at a steep angle. Safe as long as their air held out. But no way to outrun the boat. Or to sneak away. Their bubbles could be followed as surely as Hansel's trail of bread crumbs.

When they reached the bottom, Fowles put the chariot down hard. The craft bounced twice in the sand, scattering some spiny lobsters. The sounds above them dimmed, the speedboat idling, Conklin waiting for their next move.

But there was no move. Nothing to be done. The chariot was their metal coffin. Wasn't your whole life supposed to flash before your eyes when you faced death? But no. Steve was thinking they should try something. Anything.

In the front seat, Fowles craned his neck, looking up. Steve tapped him on the shoulder, then gestured with both hands. He pointed toward the boat above, then touched Fowles' chest and pointed one direction, then touched his own chest and pointed another.

Send the chariot up toward the boat, and you and I swim off in different directions.

Fowles' eyes seemed to squint behind his mask. Then he shook his head.

Steve checked his air gauge. The needle was at the red line. Maybe five hundred pounds of air. God, had he been sprinting?

Just a few minutes left.

Now, images did appear to Steve. Quick ones, flashing by. His mother, dead all these years from a vicious cancer. His father, young, handsome, and prosperous. Bobby the day Steve carried him out of the hellhole where Janice kept him caged. Herbert would have to take care of the boy now.

I can live with that. Or die with it. My old man's a better grandfather than he ever was a father.

Then Victoria's face floated by. He smiled and almost laughed, exhaling through his nostrils and momentarily fogging his mask.

She made me laugh. So upright and uptight. From that first day in the jail cells together, she made me laugh.

Realizing that he was thinking in past tense, that his life would soon be discussed by others, if at all, in past tense.

Fowles was banging something against the metal hull. Trying to get his attention.

The magnetic slate.

Okay, what?

Fowles wrote something on the slate, showed it to Steve.

"I killed Stubbs."

Yeah. Yeah. We've been through that, Steve thought. You *sort-of* killed Stubbs. You're morally responsible. What of it? Why now?

Steve shrugged and raised both hands, palms up, showing his confusion.

Fowles scrawled something else and held up the slate.

"Clive A. Fowles."

I get it now, buddy. A signed confession. To help Griffin. That's great. But only if someone is alive to haul it into court.

Fowles grabbed Steve by the shoulder and motioned for him to get out of the chariot. When Steve didn't move, Fowles grabbed his air hose and pulled.

Okay. Okay.

Steve unbuckled and floated out of the chariot. Fowles punched his fist toward the sandy bottom: *"Stay here!"* Then he thrust the slate at Steve and made one final gesture. Raising his right hand above his head, he flashed the V for Victory sign. A second later, he purged the ballast tank and pulled back on the joystick. The chariot flew upward at a sharp angle.

Maybe it was the fatigue or the fear or the oxygen-nitrogen mixture that fogged his brain. Whatever the reason, it took Steve several seconds to figure out exactly what Fowles was doing.

He was attacking Conklin the same way his grandfather had attacked the *Tirpitz*.

Gripping the slate, Steve swam after the chariot.

Why? He didn't know exactly. Except it seemed unmanly to sit on the bottom of the ocean while Clive Fowles chased the Victoria Cross his grandfather had won.

Steve kicked hard but, above him, the chariot rapidly picked up speed, putting distance between them. Without a heavy warhead in the bow, without Steve's weight, and with its ballast tank blowing, the chariot could burst from the water like a Polaris missile. Except it was headed straight for the hull of the Cigarette.

The chariot's propeller churned white water, and Steve didn't have a good view. Still, he knew Fowles was aiming for a spot where the fuel lines came out of the Cigarette's lightweight aluminum tanks.

He felt the explosion before he heard it.

The shock wave compressed his chest.

The sound pounded at his eardrums with a thunderclap of pain.

He tumbled toward the bottom with terrifying speed.

Arse-over-tits. That's what Fowles would have called it if he could have survived the explosion and fireball. That was Steve's last thought before his head crunched into the sandy bottom, and everything went dark.

FORTY-SEVEN: THE DRAMA QUEEN

"How long have you worked for Poseidon?" Victoria asked.

"Twenty-three years," Charles Traylor said. He was a portly man in his fifties who looked as if he never left the Jacuzzi, much less dived to the bottom of an Atlantic trench. On direct examination, he'd testified that it was "highly unlikely" the Poseidon Mark 3000 speargun, powered by a pneumatic blast of air, could accidentally discharge while being loaded.

"Another two years, you'll get that nice pension."

"Not sure I follow your drift."

"You're a loyal employee, Mr. Traylor. You run Poseidon's quality-control department and you've certified the Mark 3000 as safe. Wouldn't you be fired if it proved to be defective?"

"Objection!" Richard Waddle leaned over the prosecution table, palms pressed into the mahogany. "Counsel's testifying, not interrogating."

"Sustained," Judge Feathers said. "Ms. Lord, I give counsel some room to roam on cross, but you've just passed the county line."

"I'm sorry, Your Honor," Victoria said, though she wasn't sorry a bit. She'd gotten the point across to the jury.

Victoria held the speargun — state's exhibit three — in both hands. "In the instruction manual, your company warns that the shaft should be pointed away from the person attempting to load the spear. Obviously, you anticipated a person shooting himself."

"Oh, the lawyers put that in."

Those darn lawyers.

"But we've never had a lawsuit," Traylor added hastily.

A lawsuit would have been nice for the defense, Victoria thought. A class action even better. *"Everybody shish-ka-bobbed by the speargun, raise your hands."* But you have to play the cards you're dealt.

The courtroom door squeaked open, and her mother swept in. The Queen had disappeared two days earlier, her final words chillier than the frozen margarita she'd been drinking at the time. Lunch at a Mexican restaurant near the courthouse. Victoria had been working on her order of proof at a secluded table when her mother breezed over, carrying her slushy drink. Barely past noon, but the drink wasn't her first of the day. Skipping pleasantries, The Queen berated Victoria for being "bitchy and judgmental and no damn fun," saying it's no wonder she couldn't hold a man.

"Do you ever consider my happiness?" Irene demanded.

"I didn't think it was necessary, Mother, with you spending full time on the job."

"You're a little icy for my taste, darling. Comes from your father's side."

"If only he were here to defend himself."

"I'm entitled to happiness, too." Her mother pirouetted toward the door, the hem of her pink cotton Cynthia Steffe bubble skirt swirling around her hips.

The Drama Queen.

"Good luck in court, dear," her mother tossed over her shoulder. *"Even if you don't care about my happiness, please win for your uncle Grif."*

Happiness seeming to be the topic of the day.

Her mother's Manolo Blahnik sandals *click-clack*ed on the tile floor as she exited.

Now the sandals were back. Well, different

sandals. The Blahniks — open-toed, ribbon-tied, T-strapped — had been a present from Victoria, courtesy of Steve's larcenous client who'd hijacked a cargo container of the Italian beauties. Today's sandals weren't Blahniks and must be new. At least, Victoria hadn't seen them before. Snakeskin with silver buckles, side cutouts, and three-inch heels.

Where did you go, Mother? And why are you and your reptilian shoes back?

Angry at her for leaving, and for coming back, too.

There was something about those snakeskin sandals, she thought. What was it? Gorgeous, really, with vivid red-and-yellow stripes on a black background.

Red-and-yellow stripes! A coral snake. My coral snake.

"Anything else, Ms. Lord?" Judge Feathers asked.

Dammit. Stay focused.

"Just one more question, Your Honor."

"Good. Unless it's the old plumbing I hear, I think some stomachs are growling in the jury box."

Victoria gestured with the speargun. "Mr. Traylor. Just because no one sued doesn't mean no one's been impaled while loading the Mark 3000, isn't that correct?"

"Objection," Waddle said.

"On what grounds?" the judge asked.

"The question has a double negative. Maybe a triple."

"Overruled. I think the jury got it."

"I wouldn't know if anyone's ever been injured," Traylor said.

Avoiding the word "impaled" and the gory image that conveyed.

"So you can't rule out that, on some occasion, the Mark 3000 has fired while being loaded?

Breaking the promise to ask only one question.

"I can't rule it out."

"No further questions, Your Honor."

"Then let's eat lunch," the judge said.

"I need to tell you about Grif and me," The Queen said.

"I'm in trial," Victoria said. "Give me a continuance, okay?"

The Queen persisted and persuaded her to take a walk. Ten minutes later, they were on the docks, passing a row of fishing boats, when Irene said: "I'm in love with Grif."

"Congratulations."

"But I wasn't when your father was alive."

"So you told me. You only did Grif the first time the other night. What else is so important it can't wait?"

"Yesterday, I drove up to Miami and went to the bank. My safe-deposit box. I took out your father's suicide note."

Victoria stopped short next to a stack of wooden slatted lobster traps. "Now! After all these years, you have to do this now? Why?"

"I can't stand your hating me."

"Please, Mother. I can't deal with this now."

A fisherman hosing down his deck looked over at them. Not often did two well-dressed women bark at each other in front of his trawler.

"I know the pressure you're under, Princess, and God knows I want you to win, but —"

"You don't know anything! I don't want to see the note."

"You don't have a choice."

"I'm not twelve years old anymore, Mother. I make my own decisions."

The Queen reached into her burnt-orange leather handbag. Victoria started walking away as soon as she saw what came out of the bag. An old-fashioned manila envelope with a string tie.

The Queen hurried after her in those damn snakeskin sandals. "I adored your father. I never cheated on him. Grif and I were just friends. Bridge partners. We enjoyed the same things. Sinatra. French movies. Postmodern art."

"Mother, I don't care, okay?"

"I never slept with him."

"Fine. Now, just drop it."

"It's your father who cheated."

Victoria wheeled around. In the direct sun, in her pin-striped trial suit, her face heating up, she thought she might faint. "Liar!"

"I knew you'd say that. That's why I brought Nelson's note."

Irene tried to hand her the envelope, but Victoria backed off as if it were on fire. "It's probably a forgery. I wouldn't put it past you."

"I don't wear faux pearls, I don't use paper plates, and I don't forge suicide notes. It's time you knew the truth. Your father was having an affair with Phyllis."

"Phyllis Griffin?"

"It wasn't Phyllis Diller. Yes, Phyllis Griffin. They were sneaking around those last few months."

"Now I know you're lying."

Uncle Grif's wife, Junior's mother. The idea was preposterous.

"When I found out, I told your father I

wanted a divorce. He begged me to forgive him, but I wouldn't. He got all psychological. Said he didn't love Phyllis. It was the pressure of the business, the Grand Jury investigation, maybe even animosity toward Grif for getting them into legal trouble. Nelson offered to get counseling, anything to save the marriage. I told him to go to hell. Said I'd divorce him and take you away. My pride was wounded, and I wouldn't give him another chance. So I am guilty, dear. Guilty of being rigid and unforgiving. Guilty of being so self-directed I couldn't see how damaged your father was. He committed suicide the night after our blowup."

Victoria felt the slightest puff of a breeze. The boats groaned in their moorings, the air heavy with putrid fish. "Give it to me."

The note was handwritten on Griffin-Lord Construction Co. stationery.

Dearest Irene,

I cannot express the depths of my love for you and Victoria, but it's all become too much to bear. I fear the business will go under, and I don't see a way out. I have wronged you deeply, and nothing I can ever say or do will make that right. My biggest regret is that I will not live to see the woman Victoria is destined to become. I beg both of you to forgive me.

Nelson

Overhead, a seabird *caw*ed. Victoria was aware of the sound of diesel engines kicking up, water boiling at the stern of a fishing boat.

"I'm sorry I didn't tell you earlier," Irene said. "I wanted you to remember your father differently. And maybe part of me was humiliated."

"Why?" Suddenly, everything had changed. Her mother was a victim in the marriage, not its villain. "Dad's the one who cheated, the one who took the coward's way out."

"Nelson felt he needed someone else. Not something for me to be proud of. And all these years, I've wondered. If I'd handled it differently, would he still be alive?"

"You can't blame yourself."

"I've told myself that, too. But I'm the only one who could have saved him. And I didn't." She took the note back, tore it up, and tossed the pieces off the dock, where they fluttered in the breeze like wings of herons.

Victoria needed to clear her mind. At the

corner of Southard and Duval, she stepped off the curb and into the path of a pink taxi. The driver squealed to a stop, banged the horn, and cursed in Creole.

Victoria tried to fathom the depths of her feelings. Her mother, who could be so shallow and superficial, had now gone the other direction. She shouldered moral complicity in her husband's death. But what did she expect of herself? What superhuman powers of understanding and compassion did she think she lacked?

"Oh, Nelson darling, don't be depressed. I forgive you for screwing my best friend."

No, the betrayal and shameful abandonment were all her father's.

And the note I so longed for?

Now that she'd seen it, now that she'd held in her hands the last item he'd touched before the swan dive off the condo roof . . . the note made no difference.

You regret not seeing me grow up? Damn you! You could have been here.

Now that she knew what had happened, the truth had not set her free. No peace came with the knowledge, just one pain replacing another. What was it Steve said his father had told him? Something about being careful when turning over rocks. There'll be snakes, not flowers, underneath.

In this moment, more than any other, she wished Steve were here. As she passed under the kapok tree on the courthouse lawn — the last place she had seen him — she pulled out her cell phone and dialed his number. There was no answer, but she listened to the entire leave-your-number message just so she could hear his voice.

Dammit, Steve. Where are you?

FORTY-EIGHT:
THE DEEP BLUE
ALIBI

A very loud woman shouted something at Steve.

He couldn't see her because his eyes were glued shut. At least, that's the way they felt. He forced his eyes open, a salty crust cracking along his lashes.

Ouch. He was staring into a broiling sun. Suddenly aware of noxious fumes. Burning fuel, melting plastic.

"Wave your arm if you can hear me!"

That voice again. Amplified. Authoritative.

If I'm dead, then God could be a woman. But then, that sun is hot as hell, and who's to say the devil's not a chick? Now, just where is my arm?

Steve managed to wave, water pouring down his wet-suit sleeve into his face. His mask was gone. So was one of his fins. He was floating, lifting and falling with every swell. The top-of-the-line buoyancy compensator — *thank you, Stubbs* — was rigged to float an unconscious man on his back.

Fowles. Where are you?

"Just stay calm, sir. We'll get you in a minute."

Steve lifted his head out of the water. It weighed about the same as that giant jewfish.

Maybe heaven is a giant spa, and I'm in the Jacuzzi. Maybe that's where the good Jews go. The others are made into gefilte fish.

Bobbing in the water, smaller than a cutter, was a boat. He recognized the red, white, and blue diagonal stripes. Coast Guard. Most beautiful boat he'd ever seen. A woman in uniform stood at the bow rail, a bullhorn in her hand. Most beautiful woman, too, though he couldn't make out a single feature. He gave her the thumbs-up sign.

"That's it, sir! Don't try to swim over."

Swim? Going back to sleep is more like it. What time's my massage?

He was aware of the *putt-putt* of a small yellow inflatable craft coming to his side. Two men in uniforms leaned over, barking instructions. They seemed very young and pimply but their voices were strong. Best he could understand, he was to do nothing. They'd get him aboard. He tried to say something, but his throat was raw with salt water, and he vomited all over the guardsmen as they hauled him into the inflatable.

"Another man," Steve croaked. "Scuba gear. Where is he?"

"Just relax now, sir."

They seemed extremely competent for twelve-year-olds, Steve thought, hazily.

The inflatable headed toward the boat, dodging pieces of fiberglass and aluminum, the remnants of the Cigarette. Fuel burned, black and orange, on the surface. Bouncing in the waves nearby, without its rider, the rusty old chariot. The bow charred black, but seemingly indestructible.

As they neared the boat, Steve saw another inflatable in the water. Two more Coast Guardsmen. A lifeless body, a man in jeans and a bloodied T-shirt, lay facedown in the craft.

Conchy Conklin? Who else could it be?

With a net, the guardsmen were fishing something out of the water. What was it?

An arm! From the elbow down, an arm in a torn wet suit.

Fowles.

God, he'd done it. He'd sacrificed himself. He'd destroyed his own personal *Tirpitz* and saved Steve's life. How do you repay a debt like that?

You don't. Maybe you make a vow to be a better man, but the debt goes unpaid.

As a young guardsman helped Steve up the ladder of the larger craft, he had the vague notion that he'd lost something. The mask, of course. And one fin. And . . .

The slate.

Fowles' confession. His dying wish had been to settle up, to clear Griffin's name. The slate was Griffin's deep blue alibi and now it was at the bottom of the deep blue sea.

Forty-Nine: Visiting Hour

The ER staff at Fishermen's Hospital appeared happy to see Steve. A couple jokes about discounts for repeat customers, a couple suggestions to stay away from bodies of water. They promised to let him out after a few hours' observation as long as the various probes and scans all came back normal.

Steve's face was the color of a broiled lobster with a ghostly white outline from the mask. His neck was wrapped in a soft brace, but all moving parts seemed to be in semi-working order. Soon, the doctors and nurses dispersed, and his little cubicle was filled with people in uniform, with guns on their hips. Steve refused to make any statements, until he heard someone belting out the chorus of "Trying to Reason with Hurricane Season."

"C'mon in, parrothead," Steve rasped as Sheriff Willis Rask poked his nose through the curtain.

"Jimmy B. says howdy. Wow, you look like shit."

"Thanks, Willis. Why don't you clear everybody out of here so we can talk?"

Rask shooed out the others, pulled up a chair, and Steve told him everything that had happened since showing up at Paradise Key that morning. The chariot ride, the reef, Fowles' story about sneaking aboard the *Force Majeure,* fighting with Stubbs over the speargun, the spear firing, and finally the attack by Conklin in a Cigarette with flame decals.

"It matches up," Rask said. "One body's Chester Lee Conklin. Body parts of the guy in the wet suit are a little harder to ID, but from what you say, it's got to be Fowles."

"What about the Cigarette? Who owned it?"

"Registered to a shell company in the Bahamas. We're trying to track it back, see who pays the annual fees."

"Find anything on the boat?"

"You mean what's left of it? Coast Guard's still sifting through the debris. We did find Conklin's Harley, though. At a marina on Lower Matecumbe."

Steve propped himself up on the pillow. "You inventory the saddlebag? Interview people at the marina? Find out where Conklin was staying?"

"I dunno, Steve. I'm not supposed to share investigative materials with civilians. Especially defense lawyers."

"Give. Or I'll tell the mayor you're still growing pot in your backyard."

"Hell, so's he." He scratched at his mustache. "Nothing but a carton of Marlboros and a traffic ticket in the saddlebag."

"Ticket for what?"

"Expired tag, is all."

"What aren't you telling me, Willis?"

"Nothing I can make heads or tails of. The ticket was issued in Jacksonville. Ten days ago."

Jacksonville? You couldn't get any farther away and still be in Florida.

"Long ride," Steve said. "Any idea what Conklin was doing up there?"

Rask shrugged. "Could have been visiting friends or family. 'Course, it's not like Miami." Rask hummed a little of "Everybody's Got a Cousin in Miami."

Sure, Conklin could have been visiting or vacationing or bodysurfing. But he might also have been working for whoever hired him to run Steve off the road and threaten Victoria. Steve asked for the address where the ticket was issued, and Rask gave him a block on St. Johns Riverway Drive. Then

Steve told him about Fowles signing a confession on a magnetic slate, now lost at the bottom of the sea.

"Wait a sec, Steve. What confession? You said Stubbs got shot accidentally, struggling over the speargun."

"He did. But Fowles took moral responsibility."

Rask tugged at an earlobe. "That muddies the water a bit."

"The truth often does."

"Fowles say who he was working for?"

Steve shook his head, a painful movement. "Only that Conklin worked for him, too. They were supposed to force Stubbs to take their boss's offer of a million bucks. Toss him overboard if he turned them down."

Rask lowered his voice. "I like the confession. And I'll find out who their boss was. But now that I think about it, I can't have you telling the Grand Jury the shooting was an accident."

"Why not?"

"Because if you do, I'll never nail the boss for conspiracy to kill Stubbs."

"So you want me to lie under oath?"

"Just smudge the fine print a bit. Say Fowles admitted killing Stubbs on someone's orders. I'll provide the *someone* as soon as I have it."

"Aw, jeez, Willis. I bend the rules here and there, but you're asking me to commit perjury."

"Sometimes you gotta break the law to do justice, Solomon. Didn't anybody ever teach you that?"

Only my father, Steve thought, sinking back into his pillow.

Ten minutes after Rask left, a nurse came by to tell Steve they were releasing him: "But don't be a stranger, hear?"

A moment later, the curtain parted and Junior Griffin poked his head inside. He wore denim cutoffs, a muscle tee, and even through the curtains Steve could see the entire contingent of nurses staring at him.

"Steve, I came as soon as I heard."

"Thanks, Junior. C'mon in before the nurses drool all over the bedpans."

Junior sat on the edge of Steve's bed. "I just spoke to Tori. She's worried to death. Says to please call her."

One positive development today, at least.

"I brought you something to wear." Junior handed over some faded jeans and a polo shirt. "If there's anything I can do . . ."

"My car's at Paradise Key," Steve said.

Junior offered to drive Steve there; he could use the cell to call Victoria and his

561

father and Bobby; there'd be a hot meal waiting if he wanted it; and wasn't it a shame about Clive Fowles?

"I owe you an apology, Junior."

"What for?"

"For accusing you of killing Stubbs."

"It's okay. Didn't bother me."

"I'm usually pretty sharp about things like that, but with you . . ."

"It got personal. I know."

"Well, I'm sorry about it."

"Like I said, everything's cool." Junior flashed that cover-boy smile. "I was crowding your turf with Tori." He shrugged in a way that tossed a lock of blond hair across his eyes. "It wouldn't have worked out with her and me, anyway."

What's this? Is he throwing in the towel?

"I need someone who'll travel with me. Follow the sun. Hit the dive spots in the summer, the ski resorts in the winter. Tori really enjoys her work, wants to be the best lawyer in town. Hard for me to relate to, but that's cool. We'll always be buds, but we're just very different. Now, you two . . ."

Steve laughed. "Yeah, like flint and steel."

"Sparks are good, right? She really loves you."

He said it so matter-of-factly, like it was a given. Like any idiot could see it.

"She told you . . . ?"

"No offense, Steve, but I know a little more about women than you do. And I know Tori loves you."

Okay. Two positive events today.

Steve's headache seemed to fade away as he pulled on Junior's polo shirt, not even minding it was two sizes too big.

■ ■ ■ ■

SOLOMON'S LAWS

■ ■ ■ ■

12. When a man and woman are in total sync — thinking each other's thoughts, making each other laugh, bringing each other joy — they've hit the sweet spot, and just being together is ~~better than~~ . . . almost as good as sex.

FIFTY:
THE STUFF
MURDER'S MADE OF

"Does it hurt?"

"Only when I look at the hospital bill."

They were in Victoria's hotel room, Steve propped up on her bed. Bobby sat at the worktable, bent over his laptop. It was dark out, and the Jimmy Buffett cover band churned out tunes on the patio.

Victoria kept refilling bags of ice for Steve's neck and taking his temperature, though she wasn't sure exactly why. Despite his brush with death, Steve seemed oddly at peace.

If only I could keep him on codeine and Demerol, we'd get along a lot better.

"You can stay here tonight," she said.

"Here?" Steve patted the comforter on the king-size bed.

"The adjoining room. The Queen's gone back to Miami."

At his computer, Bobby laughed. "I knew you weren't getting any trim tonight,

Uncle Steve."

"Get back to work, kiddo," Steve said, "or I'll report you as a habitual truant."

"You're the one who'll go to jail," Bobby shot back. "What's it called, Victoria?"

"Contributing to the delinquency of a minor," she said.

"The kid was already a delinquent when he moved in," Steve defended himself.

"I'm hungry," Bobby said. "When do we eat?"

"After we solve a murder." Steve had already told them about the trip on *Fowles' Folly* and the aftermath. Everything except for Fowles' sort-of confession. He'd smoothed out the edges on that, telling Victoria simply that Fowles had confessed. Steve hadn't yet decided whether to tell a blatant lie, as Willis Rask had asked, but he wanted to keep his options open.

After Steve finished his tale, with Bobby downloading satellite images of Jacksonville, Victoria gave an update on the trial. The state had rested. Tomorrow morning, she would call her first witness. On the patio, the band played "We Are the People Our Parents Warned Us About."

Steve must have been listening. "So what's with you and your mother?"

"We've reached a new understanding. I

didn't know all the facts. Now that I do, I think I was way too judgmental. What about you and your father?"

"Once I learned the facts, I became more judgmental. You want to tell me what happened?"

"Later. When the trial's over. You?"

"Same."

They were silent a moment before Steve said, "Not that I don't love Dad."

"I understand."

"I mean, that's what love is, right? Accepting the person, with all their flaws."

"Just like they accept you."

Bobby cackled again. "Jeez, you two are a couple of scaredy-cats. Why don't you just come out and say you want to bone each other?"

"I'm warning you, kiddo," Steve growled. "You've got military school in your future."

"Yeah, sure. If you want to see where that scuzzball Conklin got a traffic ticket, come over here."

Victoria got there first; Steve eased himself out of bed and moved slowly to the worktable. They both peered at the satellite shot.

"The St. Johns River in Jacksonville," Bobby said, pointing at the screen. "And that's St. Johns Riverway Drive at Commodore Point. That's where Conklin got the ticket."

"All those ships," Steve said. "Looks like a port."

Bobby clicked the mouse, and the image zoomed closer. There was lettering on top of one of the buildings fronting the river. *Southern Shipworks.* Victoria said it aloud, wanting to hear it. "Southern Shipworks."

"What about it?" Steve asked.

"I know that name. Let me think."

"Work on it a sec," Steve said, going to the mini-bar. "They have Jack Daniel's in here?"

"Robinson!" Victoria said. "Leicester Robinson. That's where he was building his barges for the Oceania work."

Steve stopped short. The Jack Daniel's could wait. "Makes sense if Conklin was working for Robinson."

"Not ten days ago. Robinson said he cancelled the barge work right after Stubbs was killed."

Then it happened. Two runners in sync, stride for stride.

He said: "Unless Robinson lied . . ."

She said: "Because he needed the barges for something other than Oceania . . ."

He said: "Something that could make money only if there was *no* Oceania . . ."

She said: "So Robinson hired Conklin and Fowles . . ."

Together then: "To stop Oceania!"

Total synergy, Victoria thought.

The sweet spot of our relationship.

That's what Steve had called it during the Barksdale trial. They didn't hit it every day, but when they did, well, it was just better than anything else. They completed each other's thoughts, finished each other's sentences, filled each other's lives.

"So what's Robinson planning?" she asked.

"We've got a loose thread. So . . ."

"Let's pull it and see where it leads," she finished. "Fowles told Griffin he should forget about the hotel and casino. Just take people out to the reef on glass-bottomed boats and catamarans."

"Griffin said Fowles was talking about a rowboat while he was building the *Queen Mary*," Steve contributed.

"And Robinson said Griffin thought too big and Fowles too small. So Robinson . . ."

"Planned something in between."

"You know what it is, don't you, Steve?"

"After Stubbs was killed, Robinson wouldn't have needed the barges for Oceania. But if he changed their configuration . . ." Steve stuck a finger under his neck brace and wiggled his chin. "Bobby, zoom in on every ship under construction."

"I will if you order room service. Club sandwich, extra mayo."

"Later. Do your magic first."

On the patio, the band was breaking into "Apocalypso."

"Vic, we don't have time to subpoena the shipyard," Steve said, "but if I'm right, Robinson's building one helluva barge. Tomorrow, you'll have to bluff him. Act like you have his blueprints."

"Robinson's not my first witness."

"He is now."

She nearly said something about her order of proof but stopped herself. She'd have to be more flexible. Steve was always telling her that. "Okay, we call Robinson as an adverse witness, and . . . ?"

"I gotta see the photos to be sure. Bobby, what's happening?"

"In a sec, okay?"

Victoria said: "Steve, maybe you should cross Robinson. You have a handle on this."

He cocked his head as far as his stiff neck would allow. "C'mon, Vic. You wanted the hot seat. I vaguely recall the words 'first chair' and 'autonomy' coming up in the conversation."

It could have been vintage sarcastic Steve,

but his smile was warm, his words soft to the touch.

Yes, painkillers definitely take his edge off.

"But Robinson's the big enchilada," she said.

"I'm hungry," Bobby whined.

Steve smiled at her. "You'll be terrific. I know it."

"I really wish you would take Robinson," she continued. "You're the best cross-examiner I've ever seen."

"That's only because you never watch yourself."

She groaned.

"I mean it, Vic. You're a natural. Robinson will never know what hit him. Besides, I'm not counsel of record anymore. I withdrew, remember?"

"So file a new appearance in the morning."

"A lawyer can't be a witness, too. After you're done with Robinson, you're calling me."

"What? Why?"

"Here's your barge," Bobby said, pointing at the monitor.

Victoria leaned over Bobby's shoulder. Rectangular pods seemed to be stacked on the deck of a long, flat craft. From the satellite, the pods looked like giant children's building blocks. "What is it?" she asked.

"The stuff murder's made of." Steve gave Bobby a hug. "Let's get this boy a club sandwich. Extra mayo."

Fifty-One:
Son of a Son of a Sailor

She was all alone.

Oh, the courtroom was filled. Reporters in the front row, a still photographer alongside. There were the regulars, retirees who cruise the building looking for cheap entertainment. A few local lawyers occupied the back pews, waiting for their own cases, grousing about handling D&Ds — drunk and disorderlies — instead of a juicy murder trial. There were unkempt old-timers, leathery as lizards, who wandered inside just for the air-conditioning. The jurors were stuffed into their box like eggs in a carton, their expressions ranging from bored to bemused to bitchy: *"Prove your case, and entertain me while you're doing it, lady."*

Alongside Victoria at the defense table sat Hal Griffin, not nearly as tan or hearty as when the trial began. Judge Feathers swiveled in his high-back chair, his clerk huddled over her desk below the bench. A paunchy, sleepy bailiff stood just inside the door, the courtroom's Medicare-eligible centurion. Sheriff Rask, placid as ever, sat directly behind the prosecution table.

But I'm all alone.

One gladiator. A hundred lions.

Steve would know that feeling. It was part of their bond, the trial lawyer's steaming brew of terror and exhilaration.

"Never let them see your fear."

One of his first lessons. Closely followed by: *"Act like you own the courtroom."*

Leading up to: *"Make the jury comfortable and your opponent squirm."*

I'll try, she thought, knowing it would be easier with Steve by her side. But he was outside, pacing in the corridor. With the witness rule in effect, he was barred from the courtroom while another witness testified. And right now Leicester Robinson was striding toward the witness stand. He wore pleated black pants and a silk coral shirt open at the neck. His mustache was neatly trimmed, his twisted dreadlocks short and tidy. Wire-rimmed glasses gave him a scholarly appearance, but his broad shoulders and thick, callused hands did not fit the image of the history professor he had nearly become. No, this was a working man. Educated and articulate, but a man comfortable with heavy machinery and dirty boots.

At breakfast, Griffin had reacted with disbelief when Victoria told him about Fowles and Robinson.

"Clive would never betray me," Griffin had said, shaking his head. "And Robinson? That would take some *cajones.*"

Victoria didn't think the tenth-generation grandson of pirates and salvors lacked the balls. Or the brains. Or the "duality of evil." The phrase Robinson used to describe the ship captain in Conrad's *Secret Sharer.*

Now, as Robinson paused in front of the clerk's table, Judge Feathers instructed: "Just take your seat on the witness stand, sir. You're still under oath."

Victoria stood and smoothed the skirt of her Philippe Adec suit. A color so dark, the saleswoman had called it "anthracite." Fitting for the gravity of the day's proceedings. And the difficulty of the task, turning coal into diamonds.

She scanned the courtroom. Junior was missing from his usual spot behind the defense table. Sheriff Rask caught her eye and winked. His second wink of the morning. Earlier, when she was draining a cup of coffee from a machine in the lobby, the sheriff had strolled over and goodmorninged her.

"Good luck with Robinson today." He winked and walked off whistling "Son of a Son of a Sailor."

Now Victoria walked to the far end of the jury box. She didn't want to be in the jurors' range of vision. Let them concentrate on Robinson, who sat waiting, staring at her.

Sometimes, with an adverse witness, you start slowly and softly. Nonthreatening. A neutral tone, a pleasant demeanor, a sunny path strewn with rose petals, concealing the sharpened bamboo in the pit below. Steve likened cross-examination to lulling a pitcher to sleep by taking a short lead off first, then stealing second with a furious, unexpected burst of speed. But early this morning, he'd said that Robinson would know what they were after.

"He just doesn't know how much we know. Act confident. Hold a folder stuffed with papers, as if we have the specs on the barges. Keep the questions short. Don't give him time to think between answers."

"Do you own a Cigarette Top Gun Thirty-eight, Mr. Robinson?" she asked.

"Not personally," he answered.

"In a corporate name, then. Does your Bahamian corporation own the boat?"

"It does."

"And what's the reason you hide your ownership of that boat?"

"Objection. Argumentative." Waddle couldn't know where she was headed but wanted to block the path getting there.

"Overruled," the judge said.

"I didn't hide anything, Ms. Lord. The lawyers titled the boat that way for tax purposes."

"Where's that boat today?"

"It was stolen from a marina yesterday. I've been told it was involved in an accident in the Gulf."

An accident. Sounds better than "My hired killer got his ass blown up."

"Did you report the boat stolen?"

"To tell you the truth, Ms. Lord . . ."

A witness is almost always lying when he says: "To tell you the truth . . ."

". . . I didn't know the boat was gone until the Coast Guard told me it had sunk."

"Do you know a man named Chester Lee Conklin, also known as Conchy Conklin?"

"Apparently, he's the one who stole my boat."

"A stranger, then?"

"I didn't say that, ma'am. He's a welder, used to work for me."

"Used to?"

"Conklin was unreliable. I fired him a few

weeks ago."

"Then what was he doing in Jacksonville less than two weeks ago?"

The question seemed to surprise him. Robinson wouldn't know about the traffic ticket, wouldn't know they could place Conklin near the shipyard.

"Did you hear the question, sir?" the judge asked.

"You'll have to ask Mr. Conklin what he was doing in Jacksonville," the witness replied.

"Come now, Mr. Robinson," Victoria said. "Surely, the Coast Guard also told you that Mr. Conklin's body was found in the wreckage of your boat."

The jurors seemed to perk up at that bit of news. No one was snoring or staring at the clock.

"Sorry, it was just a figure of speech. I don't know what he was doing there."

"Was he checking on your barge at Southern Shipworks?"

Robinson blinked. Maybe he didn't bend at the waist as if he'd been gut-punched, but his eyes flicked twice.

So far, Steve had been right. He'd studied the satellite photos. He'd cobbled together all the bits and pieces from Griffin and Fowles and handed her this shiny new toy.

But Victoria still needed to wrap the toy in colorful paper and tie it up with a pretty ribbon.

"Ms. Lord, as I told you in my office, after Mr. Griffin was charged with murder, I had no choice but to cancel the barge order."

"I wonder if 'cancel' is the right word," Victoria said. "Didn't you simply *change* the order?"

Robinson studied her, as if asking: *"Just how much do you know?"* She opened a folder and angled it so that he could see the four-inch-high letters: "SOUTHERN SHIPWORKS." Inside was the Sak's catalog with this season's resort-wear. Rayon halter dresses seemed to be making a comeback.

"Certain changes were made, that's true," Robinson said, carefully.

Victoria picked up the poster board she'd had made at 8 a.m. A blowup of the satellite photos showing a barge under construction. The flat steel deck was piled high with those giant children's blocks. At least that's what they looked like from low-earth orbit. "Is this the barge you've commissioned?"

Another pause. She could tell from his expression he was looking for a safe passage. A way to navigate the channel between perjury and conspiracy to commit murder.

"It's hard to tell, but yes, that could be mine."

Victoria strolled past the jury box, holding up the poster. "What's that on deck, Mr. Robinson? It doesn't look like heavy machinery or construction equipment."

"Prefabricated steel pods."

"Hundreds of them, right?"

"Five hundred fifty, ma'am."

"When you've cornered the witness, keep the questions simple. Force 'Yes' and 'No,' and pick up your pace."

Thank you, Steve.

"Each one about four hundred to five hundred square feet?"

"Yes, ma'am."

"With conduits for plumbing and electricity and ventilation?"

"Yes, ma'am."

"But no cranes or Mud Cats. No pile drivers or heavy drills?"

"That's correct, ma'am."

"Because this isn't a work barge, is it?"

"No, it's not."

"What is it, then?"

"Well, it's a multi-purpose craft, really."

A fine line of perspiration was visible on Robinson's forehead. She'd made witnesses sweat before, and it was always a thrill. Steve boasted he'd once cross-examined a witness into heart palpitations, firing questions even as paramedics wheeled the man from the courtroom.

"Multipurpose?" A raised eyebrow, a sarcastic tone, idiosyncrasies she'd picked up from Steve. "Would those purposes be gambling and vacationing?"

"You could say that, yes."

She raised her voice. "*You* say it, Mr. Robinson. Those steel pods are prefab hotel rooms. You're building a floating hotel and casino, aren't you?"

"What if I am?" Robinson shot back. "I'm a businessman. I'm not doing anything illegal."

"And if he gets feisty, kick him in the nuts."

"Nothing illegal," she repeated, "unless you conspired to frame Harold Griffin for murder so you could steal his idea at a fraction of the cost."

Waddle jerked to his feet. "Objection! Counsel's testifying." Like all prosecutors, he hated surprises, and now he looked as if he'd just walked into a plate-glass window.

"Sustained," the judge ruled. "Ms. Lord, please frame your accusations as questions."

Victoria circled in front of the jury box, moving closer to the witness. "If my client built Oceania over the reef, your barge hotel would be barred from the area under maritime safely laws, correct, Mr. Robinson?"

"The immediate area, yes."

"You needed access to that reef. If Oceania were built, your barge hotel would be dead in the water, correct?"

"I'm sure it would affect business somewhat, but who is to say how much?"

"And a luxury hotel and casino like Oceania would really take the luster off your floating Wal-Mart, wouldn't it?"

"That's a matter of opinion."

"Your opinion was that you had to stop Griffin from building Oceania."

"No." Robinson glared at her. "Our projects were completely different."

"Just so the jury understands," she continued, "you were hired by Hal Griffin to do the barge work required in the construction of Oceania. But without informing Mr. Griffin, you began surreptitiously planning a competing project?"

"Like I said, I'm a businessman, Ms. Lord."

Victoria paused, which gave the judge time to leap in. "Anything further, Counselor?"

Victoria had run out of steam. She had established motive. Now Steve would have to link Robinson to Fowles and Stubbs actual shooting. She was ready to sit down, but realized she'd also violated one of Steve's numerous rules for cross-examination.

"Always end strong."

"Just one more thing, Your Honor." She turned back to the witness. "Mr. Robinson, that speedboat of yours. What did you name it?"

She hoped the newspaper photographer was clicking away. Robinson's face burned with all the anger he'd been bottling up.

"The *Satisfaction*," Robinson said.

"You a Rolling Stones fan?"

That sarcasm again. I hate it when Steve does it, but sometimes I can't help myself.

"It was the name of one of Henry Morgan's ships," Robinson said through gritted teeth.

"Morgan the Terrible?" Feigning surprise.

"Some called him that."

"Didn't he sink ships and burn villages? Plunder, pillage, and rape?"

"You have to understand history, Ms. Lord. In those days —"

"History or not, wasn't Morgan the Terrible a pirate?"

"He had letters of reprisal from the Crown. He would have considered himself a privateer."

"Right," she said, smiling demurely. "And you consider yourself a businessman."

FIFTY-TWO:
THE WHOLE TRUTH

The corridor leading to the courtroom was out-of-doors, really a fourth-floor catwalk. Waiting to be called to testify, carrying his suit coat over an arm, rivulets of sweat ran down Steve's face into his neck brace. The tropical heat seemed to roll waves of pain through his skull.

The door to the courtroom banged opened and Leicester Robinson barreled out. Muttering profanities, his face set in a snarl. Head down, he nearly plowed into Steve on his way to the elevator.

This is good. This is very good.

Victoria must have skinned him and hung up the pelt, Steve thought. She was a better lawyer than he'd been at the same age. Part of Victoria's effectiveness was that she didn't know how good she was. That tiniest bit of insecurity kept her ego under control. Her need to be liked — an affliction he did not share — made her more . . . well, likable.

There were other differences, Steve thought. He had street smarts, she had real smarts. He wielded a broadsword, she struck with a rapier.

Maybe that's why we're so good together. Maybe when this is over, we'll be a team again. And maybe we'll share the bedroom as well as the courtroom.

As Steve was thinking of all the possible "maybes," the bailiff poked his head out of the courtroom door and made like the town crier: "Mr. So-lo-mon! Stephen So-lo-mon!"

"That would be me," Steve said.

Steve promised to tell the truth, the whole truth, and nothing but the truth.

He'd heard the oath administered thousands of times, but taking it yourself was different. As a lawyer, you weren't supposed to blatantly lie. But you could straddle that fuzzy fine line between light and shadow. You could tap dance with a top hat and cane, distracting and entertaining. "Razzle dazzle 'em," as lawyer Billy Flynn sings. You could shade meanings and color the truth. But when you're a witness, you're bound by . . .

The whole truth.

An acknowledgment that there were different levels of truth.

And nothing but the truth.

Indicating it's possible to tell the truth in the main, but fudge a bit around the edges. As he sat down, Steve still didn't know just what level of truth he was going to dispense.

Victoria's face was flushed as she stood and approached the witness box. "Please state your name and occupation for the record."

"Steve Solomon. Trial lawyer."

"Attorney" always sounding pretentious to him.

"What's your relationship to the defendant Harold Griffin?"

"I represented him until he fired me. Or maybe you fired me. It was hard to tell."

We were naked at the time, but no need to tease the jurors with that tidbit.

"Why were your services terminated?"

"I accused Mr. Griffin's son, Junior, of committing the murder. Mr. Griffin didn't like it. Neither did you. And by the way, I was wrong."

"Why did you accuse Mr. Griffin's son?"

"Do we have to go into that?" Steve pleaded. "It's embarrassing."

"Please."

"It had to do with you. I was jealous of Junior Griffin."

Waddle spoke up. "Your Honor, is this a murder trial or couples counseling?"

"I'll tie it up," Victoria said.

"Do it quickly," Judge Feathers advised.

"Mr. Solomon, did there come a time when you were run off a bridge in an incident with a motorcycle?"

"Did there come a time . . ." One of those expressions lawyers carry in their satchels: "Isn't it true that . . . ?" "Drawing your attention to the night of . . ." "What do you mean my bill's too high?"

"Yes," Steve said. "My old Caddy convertible drowned."

"Did the police determine who was responsible for the attack?"

"A man named Chester Lee Conklin. Goes by 'Conchy.' "

"Did there come a time when you encountered Mr. Conklin again?"

"Yesterday. He was shooting a rifle at me. And at Clive Fowles."

Several jurors stirred. Testimony about shootings will do that.

"Why would Chester Conklin have tried to kill you?"

"Objection! Calls for a conclusion." Waddle needed to make some noise just to disrupt the flow. "And as far as I can see,

Mr. Conklin is irrelevant to these proceedings."

"He became relevant," Victoria said, "the moment Leicester Robinson admitted that Conklin was his employee and the defendant Harold Griffin was a business rival."

"Overruled for now," the judge said.

"Mr. Conklin," Steve said, "did not want Clive Fowles to tell me who really killed Ben Stubbs."

"Objection and move to strike," Waddle said. "That's guess-timony, not testimony. Your Honor, I don't know how they do it up in Miami, but I've never tried a case where the defendant's lawyer takes the witness stand and —"

"Ex-lawyer," Victoria said.

"Whatever. The lawyer takes the stand and opines on who killed the decedent."

"The State Attorney has a point." The judge turned to his bailiff. "Take the jury out for a spell. We're gonna figure this out without mucking up the record."

After the jurors had filed into their little room, Judge Feathers asked Victoria, "Just what is it you're trying to elicit from your partner?"

"Ex-partner," Victoria corrected. "Your Honor, may I voir dire Mr. Solomon in the absence of the jury?"

"Be my guest."

"Mr. Solomon, did Clive Fowles tell you who killed Ben Stubbs?"

"He did."

"I knew it," Waddle said. "There's hearsay coming round the bend."

"Keep your britches on, Dick," the judge said. "Just because I'm hearing it doesn't mean the jury will. Keep going, Ms. Lord."

"What did Clive Fowles tell you?"

"He worked for a third party, someone he wouldn't name. The third party wanted Stubbs to sink Oceania by writing a negative environmental report. Fowles' job was to convince Stubbs to go along. And to kill him if he didn't."

So far, all true.

"And what did Mr. Fowles do in response to these instructions?"

"He sneaked onto the *Force Majeure,* and when Stubbs refused to do what he was told, Fowles did what he'd been ordered to do."

Sort of the truth.

"Could you be more specific, Mr. Solomon?"

Steve took a deep breath. There was nowhere to run. Telling the literal truth — that Stubbs had been shot accidentally — would get Griffin off the hook, if the jury ever heard the testimony. But the truth wouldn't nail Robinson. "Fowles said he shot Stubbs with the speargun. He killed the man, just as he'd been instructed."

Now, that didn't hurt, did it? Actually, yes it did.

"Besides *saying* he killed Mr. Stubbs," Victoria said, "what else did Mr. Fowles do?"

"He wrote a confession and signed it."

"Where and when did this happen?"

"Yesterday. On Fowles' World War Two chariot."

"His what?" the judge asked.

"A two-man underwater craft that looks like a torpedo with seats. You ride it in scuba gear. We were on the ocean floor at the time."

"The ocean floor?" Waddle laughed. "Sounds like the witness has a case of nitrogen narcosis."

"And how did Mr. Fowles write this confession underwater?" The judge was intrigued.

"On a magnetic slate. The kind divers use."

Waddle cleared his throat. "Best evidence rule, Judge. Where's this alleged written confession?"

"Lost at sea," Steve said. "I dropped the slate when Fowles rammed Conklin's boat and they were both killed."

"Jesus on the cross." Judge Feathers let out a low whistle.

"Your Honor, I move to bar all of Mr. Solomon's testimony," Waddle announced. "The alleged confession is a hundred percent hearsay, pure and simple."

"State Attorney's right," the judge said. "Ms. Lord, if you had that slate, I'd be inclined to let Mr. Solomon authenticate it and get it into evidence. But without it . . ."

"Thank you," Waddle smirked. "Now may we bring the jury back in and try this case according to the rules?"

Just then, the courtroom door opened, and a tall, handsome, suntanned man barged in. Junior Griffin wore flip-flops, chinos, and a muscle tee, and his long blond hair was wet and slicked back. To Steve, he looked like one of those men's cologne commercials.

But what's he holding?

"Hope I'm not too late." Junior was waving a mesh bag. Inside the bag was the magnetic slate.

Steve couldn't believe it.

I'm supposed to be the hero. Not Junior Friggin' Griffin!

"It was only in eighty feet of water," Junior said, nearing the bench. "But the Coast

Guard coordinates were a little off. It took me five dives. No tanks, of course."

The court reporter, a young woman in open-toed sandals and a short skirt, was gaping at Junior as if he were a butterscotch sundae. "Could I get your name for the record?" she asked.

"Harold Griffin, Jr."

"And your phone number?" she continued.

"Let's see what you've got there, young man," Judge Feathers said.

Junior opened the bag and handed the slate to the judge. The message was still there: "I killed Stubbs." With Clive A. Fowles' signature.

"Mr. Solomon, is this the written confession you were talking about?" the judge asked.

"It is."

"And you saw Mr. Fowles sign this?"

"I did."

"All right, then. Let's bring in the jury. I believe Ms. Lord has some evidence to introduce."

FIFTY-THREE: FORGIVEN BUT NOT FORGOTTEN

Two days later, in a blissful daze of Tylenol with codeine, Steve was semi-snoozing in the rope hammock strung between two sabal palms along the shoreline at Sugarloaf Key. He would have fallen asleep if his father hadn't been spouting profanities as he crab-crawled across the roof of his houseboat, wrestling with his satellite dish.

"Suck egg, cornholer!" Herbert yelled, then banged the dish with a wrench.

The Solomons were genetically impaired in home improvement genes, Steve knew.

"Still snowing," Bobby called out from inside the living salon. He was watching the TV screen as his grandfather tried to realign the dish.

"Hey, lazybones!" Herbert growled. "You might give us some help over here."

Steve rocked back and forth in the hammock. "If you'd fix the leak, so the boat wouldn't list to starboard, you wouldn't have to keep moving the dish."

"Like you know electronics."

"So why ask me to help?"

Bare-chested, wearing paint-splattered shorts, Herbert was glistening with sweat. He grunted as he tried to muscle the dish a few millimeters.

"Dad, why don't you come down before you have a heart attack?"

"Don't go spending a fortune on the funeral," Herbert ordered. "Not that you would."

"A blizzard now," Bobby reported from inside.

"To hell with it." Herbert climbed down the ladder to the rear deck.

Bobby stuck his head out a window. "Uncle Steve, can you fix the TV?"

"Do your homework. Television's bad for you. Especially Fox News."

A few minutes later, Steve heard the unmistakable *clink*ing of ice cubes in a glass. He opened his eyes to see his father approaching the hammock. He carried two large glasses swirling with golden liquid.

"May I assume that's not root beer?"

"Ain't gator sweat, neither." Herbert sat down in a plastic chair alongside the hammock. "Scotch with a *shpritz* of soda."

"I hope it's more than a *shpritz.* Those are

sixteen-ounce glasses."

"Should last us a spell. Good for what ails you."

"Is Bobby doing his homework?"

"He is if his teacher assigned a website with cameras inside the cheerleaders' locker rooms."

"Great." Steve sat up and swung his feet over the edge of the hammock. "Ooh."

"You okay, son?"

"When I was running on adrenaline in court, I was fine. Now I'm just a little woozy."

Herbert handed him a drink. *"L'chaim."*

Steve tilted his glass toward his father. "Confusion to the enemy."

The men drank, and Herbert said: "So what do you hear from Victoria?"

"Jury went out at eleven this morning."

"You oughta be there."

Steve shook his head, and billiard balls bounced between his ears. "It's her case. Not mine."

"So?"

"When she gets a verdict, it should be her moment. She deserves her autonomy."

"What kind of word is that? 'Autonomy'?"

"Victoria's word."

"Thought so." The old man took a long

pull on the Scotch. "So we gonna talk, or what?"

"I dismissed the Bar suit, if that's what you're wondering."

"That ah already know."

"How?"

"Pinky Luber told me."

"You're still talking to him?"

"Talk? Hell, ah'm taking Pinky fishing next week."

"I still don't get it, Dad. It's like you forgot what he did to you."

"Ah haven't forgotten. Ah've forgiven."

"Is that some Zen thing, Dad? How do you get to a place where you just move on?"

"Comes with age and experience. And the knowledge that we're all damaged pieces of equipment."

Steve let himself smile. That was pretty much what he'd told Victoria. *"We're all flawed."* Could he hold his father to a higher standard than he held himself? "I shouldn't have poked around in your life, Dad. I had no right."

"Like ah said, the truth can be painful. You mad at me for what ah did all those years ago?"

"No, I guess not. Not anymore."

Herbert raised his glass in a salute. "You're a good kid. Ah should tell you that once in a while."

Steve let that soak in a moment and took another sip. The alcohol was already going to his head, and he'd barely made a dent in the drink. Then he blurted out: "I lied in court, Dad."

Feeling ten years old: *I'm the one who threw the baseball through the window, not Janice.*

"What are you talking about?"

"In Griffin's case. I lied under oath."

"Jesus."

"Willis Rask said if I told the truth, Griffin would get off. But the state could never pin anything on Robinson."

"Fowles didn't shoot Stubbs?"

"Robinson ordered him to. But Fowles didn't do it. Stubbs got shot when they struggled over the speargun."

"Holy shit."

"Can you believe it? Junior Griffin was right from day one. Stubbs pretty much shot himself and Hal Griffin fell down the ladder trying to go up and call for help."

"What about that magnetic slate? You write that confession?"

"No, I didn't lie about that. Fowles signed the slate because he accepted moral responsibility for the death. I took that as permission to say he shot Stubbs."

"A helluva rationalization. Welcome to the club, son."

"The liars' club?"

"The ends-justify-the-means club."

"Like you and Pinky?"

"Like a lot of people, son. It's not all black and white. There are a thousand shades of gray."

"So I guess I owe you an apology."

"For what? Lying in court? Or busting my balls?"

"Both."

"Forget it. It's over."

"You're letting me off that easy? Don't you want to hit me with at least one I-told-you-so?"

"Hell, no. Ah want you to finish your drink, then fix mah damn satellite dish."

FIFTY-FOUR: GO HENCE WITHOUT DAY

Victoria's heart was beating at a staccato pace, and she could feel her face heating up. Hal Griffin squeezed her hand so hard, she heard her knuckles crack.

As the clerk prepared to read the verdict, Victoria feared she wouldn't hear the words above the *ker-thump*ing in her chest.

"We, the jury, find the defendant Harold Griffin not guilty on the charge of murder in the second degree."

Yes! I did it. Okay, Steve helped. But I did it. A murder trial.

Griffin let out a long, whistling breath.

Waddle asked that the jurors be polled, and each affirmed the verdict, good and true. Judge Feathers thanked them for their service and told Griffin he was free to "go hence without day." Waddle gave Victoria a tight little "Congratulations" and said he'd be convening the Grand Jury to consider murder charges against Leicester Robinson.

Sheriff Rask winked at her and gave two thumbs-up.

Minutes later, on the courthouse lawn, she was surrounded by reporters, courthouse regulars, even a few curious tourists. She answered questions and posed for photos. An enormous bearded man in flowered shorts shoved a microphone in her face. Billy Wahoo, radio host, who now claimed he'd told his listeners Griffin was innocent and Victoria would prove it.

She broke away from the reporters, and Griffin hugged her once, twice, three times, then hurried off. The Queen was waiting at the airport, the Gulfstream's engines were already warming up. They'd planned a little celebration. Just the two of them, his place in Costa Rica.

Junior picked Victoria up and twirled her around, a Ferragamo pump flying off. He retrieved it from under the kapok tree, then knelt at her feet. Prince Charming to her Cinderella. She put a hand on his shoulder for balance and slipped her foot back into the shoe.

You're sweet, dear hunkalicious Junior, but you're not my prince.

Then she saw Steve across the street, standing in the doorway of the Green Parrot, a beer in his hand. Violating the open container law, a misdemeanant in nylon running shorts and T-shirt. She motioned Steve to come over, join the fun, but he shook his head. A moment later, she headed his way.

They walked along Duval Street, Victoria bouncing on her toes, swinging her purse.

Steve knew the feeling. Not so much joy as a lightness in being. First, the crushing weight is lifted, that über-gravity of responsibility a lawyer bears when defending a client charged with murder. Then a sense of personal redemption: The state with all its money and all its minions condemned your client, branded him a murderer, and you're the tough guy who stood in the alley, arms crossed, saying, *"You'll have to go through me, first."*

But no chest-thumping, no triumphant exultation. More a vicarious pleasure for this living, breathing person who depends on you the way a patient depends on a surgeon.

"I wish you'd heard my closing." Victoria's cheeks were still flushed with excitement.

"Willis said you were riveting. And ravishing."

"I came up with a theme and drilled it into the jurors, just like you taught me."

"The 'extra step.' Willis told me."

Victoria's voice fell into its courtroom cadence. *"In most cases, the defense is content to show there's reasonable doubt as to guilt. But here, we took the* extra step. *We've proved not just that Harold Griffin is innocent. We've proved who is guilty. Clive Fowles murdered Ben Stubbs."*

Steve chose not to disagree. It was, after all, his story.

"I kept drilling it in," Victoria continued. "We took *this* extra step. We took *that* extra step. Then I asked the jurors: *'So what did the state do? The state charged the most convenient person, the other man on the boat. The state* skipped a step. *They skipped over the real killer and hauled the wrong man into court.'"*

"Nicely phrased. Easy to remember. What'd you say about Robinson?"

" *'Leicester Robinson is a man of great intellect and ability. But utterly amoral and totally corrupt. Like rotten mackerel by moonlight, he shines and stinks at the same time.'"*

"Cute. But didn't I use that once?"

"Twice. But I changed snapper to mackerel for the alliteration."

"Nice work all around. Great job."

She beamed at him then skipped a step of her own. If her mood were any more airy,

Steve thought, she'd be floating. They passed an ice-cream parlor, the aroma of hot waffle cones wafting onto the sidewalk. Next, he knew from personal experience, would come her hunger pangs.

"I'm famished," Victoria said. "Want to grab lunch?"

Aha. Right on cue.

"I can always eat, Vic. You know that."

The cafés were jammed with the cruise-ship passengers, unleashed on the town for five hours before the horns blew and they rushed back to the harbor like rats heeding the pied piper.

"What about here, Steve? Your pal's place. We'll get that barbecued tuna you like so much."

Sure enough, they were in front of the Margaritaville Café, one of Jimmy Buffett's restaurants. The place was packed, with a line of starving patrons snaking out the door. Most had that pudgy, sunburned, tropical shirt right-off-the-hanger Midwestern look. Steve and Victoria moved to the end of the line.

"And how about some shrimp with andouille sauce?" she continued.

"Absolutely."

"But let's start with chowder with conch fritters and smoked fish spread."

"Anything you want. I'm buying."

"In that case, a couple of rum runners. And key lime pie for dessert."

More than she usually eats in a week.

He had planned to wait until she was on her second rum runner, but as they reached the end of the line, he just blurted it out: "Should we talk, Vic? About the future."

"Yes. I've wanted to."

"You really made a name for yourself with this one, so I'll understand if you still want to fly solo, but I'm thinking we shouldn't break up the firm."

"I'm thinking the same thing."

"Really?"

Could it be this easy?

"Handling Uncle Grif's trial was good for me," she said. "Really good. But we're better together than we are apart."

"Couldn't agree more."

"But you've got to give me room to grow."

"Lots of room. Lots of growing. No problem."

They inched forward but were still nowhere near the front door. "And we need to make some changes," Victoria said.

"Change is good."

"Those ads on the back of the Metro buses. Our faces right above the tailpipes. Let's get rid of them."

"They're good for business," Steve protested.

"They're tacky."

"They're gone. What else?"

"I want you to stop representing The Beav."

"Why? You know I don't mess around with the girls."

"It's unseemly."

"Jeez, Vic. You're starting to sound like your mother."

She shot him a look and he surrendered. "Okay, okay. Scratch The Beav."

That drew a look from the middle-aged woman in front of them, a tourist with eyeglasses on a faux pearl chain. Her husband wore madras Bermuda shorts with a long-sleeve white shirt.

"I wonder if your buddy's here." Victoria peeked around the people in front of them. The line wasn't moving. "He'd give us the VIP treatment for sure."

"I don't think Jimmy Buffett waits tables, Vic." Tangy smells drifted over them. Something was gnawing at Steve, something other than hunger pangs. "All we've talked about is Solomon and Lord. What about . . . ?"

"Steve and Victoria?"

"Yeah. Aren't we better together than apart in that department, too?"

"I guess so." She leaned over and kissed him. "But I need a little time, okay?"

"I've been thinking about everything that's happened since the day the *Force Majeure* crashed."

"Me, too. Starting with your wanting to have sex in the ocean."

The woman in front of them turned and gawked over the top of her eyeglasses.

"I'm going to be a better person," Steve said. "A better dad to Bobby. A better son. A better partner to you."

"Don't get too much better, Steve. I kind of like you the way you are."

"Really? You don't want me to change?"

"Just one thing. From now on, total honesty. Complete candor and openness. Not even a white lie."

"*No problema.* By the way, did you know I was Phi Beta Kappa?"

"I'm serious, Steve. The truth. The whole truth. And nothing but the truth."

Not exactly the phrase he wanted to hear. "The most beautiful words in the English language," he said.

There was a commotion in front of them. A buzz in the conversation. Then someone applauded. A balding, suntanned middle-aged man in shorts, sandals, and a flowered shirt came out of the restaurant. People in line stopped him and shook hands. Some whipped out tour maps and pens and seemed to be asking for autographs.

"Steve! Look, it's Jimmy Buffett."

Steve craned his sore neck to get a better look. "You sure? Looks like one of those impersonators to me. Maybe he's got one in every restaurant."

"No, it's him. C'mon, Steve, say hello to him."

"Why so excited? You're not even a fan."

"But you're a major parrothead. And you're his bud. Maybe you can plan a fishing trip."

In a moment, Buffett worked his way to their position.

"Jimmy!" She grabbed one of his hands with both of hers. "I'm Victoria Lord, and here's your buddy Steve." She looked around. "Steve?"

He had wedged himself between two tourists. Victoria grabbed him by an elbow and dragged him over. "Maybe you two can chase the wily wahoo, or whatever it is you like to do."

Appearing confused, the man extended a hand to Steve. "Hi, I'm Jimmy Buffett. Welcome to Margaritaville."

"Steve Solomon." They shook hands.

"Wait a second," Victoria said. "Don't you

two drink and fish together with Sheriff Rask?"

"You know Willis?" Jimmy said. "Helluva guy. Well, nice meeting you, Steve." He moved down the line and shook some more hands.

Victoria cocked her head and studied Steve, who seemed to be counting the eyelets on his Reeboks.

"You can't change, can you, Steve?"

"We are who we are."

"You're right." The line moved a few paces, and they stepped with it. The aroma of fresh-baked bread grew stronger. "My mother. Your father. You. Me."

"What are you saying, Vic?"

"You taught me more than how to cross-examine. Remember what you said about your father? *'Love means accepting the other person just the way he is. Because he has to do the same.'*"

"Yeah?"

She moved closer and nestled her head on his shoulder. "What's the ocean temperature today?"

"Warm. Eighty, eighty-one, maybe."

"Sounds wonderful. I know a secluded beach just off mile marker thirty-two."

"And . . . ?

"You have swim trunks in the car?"

611

He shook his head.

"That's all right, Steve." She slipped her arms around him and drew close. "You won't need them."

■ ■ ■ ■

SOLOMON'S LAWS

■ ■ ■ ■

1. If the facts don't fit the law . . . bend the facts.
2. Always assume your client is guilty. It saves time.
3. Beware of a sheriff who forgets to load his gun but remembers the words to "Margaritaville."
4. You can sell one improbable event to a jury. A second "improb" is strictly no sale, and a third sends your client straight to prison.
5. "Love" means taking a bullet for your

beloved. Anything short of that is just "like."

6. The client who lies to his lawyer is like a husband who cheats on his wife. It seldom happens just once.

7. When meeting an ex-girlfriend you dumped, always assume she's armed.

8. If a guy who's smart, handsome, and rich invites you and your girlfriend to a nudist club . . . chances are he's got a giant *shmeckel.*

9. The people we've known the longest are often the people we know the least.

10. Choose a juror the way you choose a lover. Someone who doesn't expect perfection and forgives your bullshit.

11. If you're afraid of taking a big lead, you'll never get picked off . . . but you'll never steal a base, either.

12. When a man and woman are in total sync — thinking each other's thoughts, making each other laugh, bringing each other joy — they've hit the sweet spot, and just being together is ~~better than~~ . . . almost as good as sex.

ABOUT THE AUTHOR

Paul Levine worked as a newspaper reporter and trial lawyer, practicing law for seventeen years, trying cases in state and federal courts and handling appeals at every level, including the Supreme Court, before becoming a full-time novelist and screenwriter. The winner of the John D. MacDonald fiction award, Levine is the author of the Jake Lassiter novels, which have been published in twenty-three countries. *To Speak for the Dead,* the first Lassiter novel, was a national bestseller and honored as one of the best mysteries of the year by the *Los Angeles Times.* He is also the author of *9 Scorpions,* a thriller set in the U.S. Supreme Court.

He was cocreator and coexecutive producer of the CBS television series *First Monday,* and has written extensively for *JAG.* He lives in California, where he is at work on the third Solomon vs. Lord novel, *Kill*

All The Lawyers. Visit his website at www
.paul-levine.com.

The employees of Thorndike Press hope you have enjoyed this Large Print book. All our Thorndike and Wheeler Large Print titles are designed for easy reading, and all our books are made to last. Other Thorndike Press Large Print books are available at your library, through selected bookstores, or directly from us.

For information about titles, please call:
  (800) 223-1244

or visit our Web site at:
  www.gale.com/thorndike
  www.gale.com/wheeler

To share your comments, please write:
  Publisher
  Thorndike Press
  295 Kennedy Memorial Drive
  Waterville, ME 04901